THE
CURTAIN
FALLS

CAROLE GURNETT

WARD
RIVER
PRESS

Published by
Ward River Press 2015
by Poolbeg Press Ltd.
123 Grange Hill, Baldoyle,
Dublin 13, Ireland
Email: poolbeg@poolbeg.com

1

A catalogue record for this book is available from the British Library.

ISBN 978-1-78199-922-6

Printed by
CPI Group (UK) Ltd, Croydon, CR0 4YY
www.wardriverpress.com

About the Author

Carole Gurnett was born in England in 1958 and moved with her family to Ireland at the age of sixteen, settling in County Clare and going to school in Limerick. She studied English and History in University College Cork. She now lives in Limerick with her husband George, and two daughters Julie and Tess.

She has had a wide variety of jobs in her life, ranging from working in a horticultural nursery to managing a credit union to caring for children in an after-school facility.

She loves Kerry for the scenery, the walking and swimming in the sea. She does some running – very slowly! – and, of course, she loves reading.

Chapter One

The 22nd of June, 1897, was a day spent wholly in celebration. Her Royal Highness Queen Victoria, Monarch of England, Ruler of the British Empire, Empress of India, had reigned for sixty glorious years. Today was her Diamond Jubilee.

In Mansfield, the town council had constructed a great wooden archway across the main street. It was decorated with yew and red ribbons and across the top of it was a banner – '*God Save The Queen*' – with Union Jacks on either side. Flags from every nation in the Empire were strung like washing from window to window, some familiar, others less so, from places like Sierra Leone, Gibraltar, the Cameroons, Jamaica, the Gold Coast. Later there would be a parade through the town but it was still early morning and the inhabitants had not yet stirred out. Today of all days, a good breakfast was needed.

At the Church of St. John the Baptist in Dublin three priests concelebrated first Mass. Special prayers were offered in honour of the Queen's anniversary. Afterwards, the congregation shifted to the field next door where there was a coconut shy, tombola, donkey races. Toffee apples were given out among the children and there was soup and freshly baked bread for the adults.

The villagers of Watley-Bascombe ate lunch outside in the street, seated at a 'T' of linen-covered tables. The scene was a study in tone, from the top table where the local squire and his family sat – all crisp, high notes of black riding boots and white parasols – through the middle shades of green, grey and tan down to the muted lower end with well-worn knickerbockers and gaiters and oversized jackets of indeterminate colour. Beneath the tablecloths, children played and dogs rooted for scraps.

In the back garden of a house in Ullapool some of the neighbourhood children were forming a tableau for the amusement of their parents. In the centre, a ten-year-old girl posed as Britannia. Her helmet and shield were made from papier mâché, her trident was a broom handle. The rest gathered around her as her loyal subjects, the girls with tartan sashes, the boys wearing kilts and on their breasts medals from ancient wars lent to them by fathers, grandfathers, great-grandfathers.

In Swansea, there was to be a great bonfire in the market place. The ten men who formed the Organizing Committee were having their photograph taken standing in front of the gigantic mountain of wood and rubbish that was soon to be lit. They inflated their chests, raised their heads and, for a full minute, kept perfectly still for the camera.

At Chelsea Barracks in the City of London, two thousand troops assembled. They were of every race and colour, from as far afield as Kingston, Jamaica and Canberra in New South Wales, all proud to serve the Queen and her Empire. Four carriages laden with dignitaries led the way, the rank and file following. They marched through the streets, six abreast, keeping step to the Guards' Fife and Drum Band. Well-wishers lined the route, waving miniature Union Jacks and cheering for their British soldiers, some of whom came from places they had never heard of. Ladies swung their skirts in time to the music. Gentlemen nodded, remembering past battles, lost and won.

There was a thunderous roar of approval as the procession of soldiers entered Trafalgar Square. The rejoicing crowds were everywhere: young men perched precariously on Nelson's Column, helping others up, or sitting astride the great bronze lions, arms around each other; on the steps men and women hugged.

Many were singing their hearts out:
"*Some talk of Alexander, and some of Hercules,*
Of Hector and Lysander, and such great names as these;
But of all the world's brave heroes, there's none that can compare
With a tow, row, row, row, row, row for the British Grenadiers!"

Outside the Colosseum Theatre the first carriage drew up, the others pulling in behind it. The foot soldiers were directed around to the side entrances.

Charles Gray, Business Manager, who had been watching from inside, stepped onto the red carpet to greet the four guests of honour who were alighting. His Highness, the Maharaja of Cooch Behar, was wearing his national dress which included a turban adorned with so many jewels that they appeared to be spilling out of the folds. King Lewanika of Somaliland, dressed in animal skins, was the tallest, darkest, straightest, thinnest man Charles had ever seen. The Right Honourable Richard Seddon, Premier of New Zealand, was spry and neat in a dark suit. Field Marshall Thompson was decked out in ceremonial red with a chest full of medals. His luxuriant moustache, waxed at the ends, was a wondrous sight even in the midst of all this foreign splendour.

Charles exchanged pleasantries with them and escorted them upstairs to the front row of the dress circle which gave them the best view in the house. There was much bustle and excitement as the ushers guided guests to their places and soldiers filed into the stalls below to take their seats. The play they were about to see was *Waterloo* by Arthur Conan Doyle, chosen especially to appeal to this audience which was predominantly made up of the military.

Charles checked once again to ensure that his charges were happy and comfortable and, as the houselights dropped, he withdrew to stand at the back on his own and watch.

The curtain opened.

On stage, a humble kitchen scene with a young woman, played by Marguerite Davenport, preparing breakfast. From the wings an aged voice calls out, "*Mary, Mary, I wants me rations!*". This, to prepare the way for Edmund's entrance. On he comes as an old man, shuffling, bent double, half mad, shaking his head and taking swipes at it with his fist like a dog with a fly in its ear. The gas footlights flare to lend incandescence to the star of the show. He hobbles to the fireplace, looks around, lowers himself into an armchair, every movement slow but full of character. Absolute silence in the theatre.

Remarkable how he can hold the stage with so little, thought Charles.

He had heard it said before that those who were addicted to opium or morphine could never experience again the intensity of their first encounter with the drug no matter how many times they tried. He was addicted too, except that every night from the back of the dress circle he relived to the full that first time he saw Edmund Jeffers on stage. He was never disappointed.

It had been in Dublin. Edmund was the guilt-ridden Mathias in *The Bells*, a foul murderer, the basest of characters. Edmund played him with ferocity, almost as a wild-eyed madman but then, at moments, with such pathos that the performance had drawn tears from Charles.

Charles left the theatre that night light-headed. This actor was an artist of the highest order, of that he had no doubt, a man with the ability to create beauty from torment, beauty from ugliness, hatred, greed. Or from nothing at all.

The next day, feeling compelled to meet this great man, he had called to the Shelbourne Hotel where the cast was staying. In the past Charles had done some theatrical criticism for a student publication and he used these credentials to effect an interview with Edmund Jeffers. They had a very pleasant conversation spread over several hours. Charles worked as an inspector in the Probate Office but his first love was the theatre and he had strong, well-informed views on it. In addition they discussed art, politics, cricket, music and seemed to have very similar tastes in all. They parted the best of friends.

That night Charles went to the Queen's Royal Theatre to watch *The Bells* again. He went every night for a week and with each viewing he was more impressed.

Six months later, a telegram arrived on his desk at work. It was an offer of employment from Edmund Jeffers. He said he had just leased the Colosseum Theatre in London and he wanted Charles Gray to join him there as business manager.

Charles was a sensible man and he forced himself to think seriously about such a change in his situation. Was it wise to abandon a promising and secure career in the Civil Service, even if it was dull? And for what? He barely knew Edmund Jeffers. The Colosseum Theatre could fold in a matter of weeks. And what exactly was meant by 'business manager'?

He let two days elapse to be sure of how he felt but his initial reaction won through. On the way home from work at the end of the second day, he stopped off at the Post Office and sent the following reply: '**Thank you. Arriving London tomorrow. Charles Gray.**'

Never once had he regretted the decision and these few stolen moments at the back of the theatre were nightly confirmation that his judgement was sound, that if he could not be a creator himself – and he could not – he had at least been creative with his life.

But for now he had to tear himself away and resume his duties. There was no room for error tonight. He walked the upper corridors and the ushers straightened at the sight of him. He checked their uniforms and nodded his approval – they were all too tense for the exchange of unnecessary words. Once the performance was over their work would begin, work that was every bit as vital to the success of the night as was the play itself. The audience had to be managed, guests pampered, the stage transformed for the reception to follow and all to be done with smooth efficiency and speed.

When he reached the foyer, the staff were waiting for him, lined up, facing each other across the marble floor. A discarded ticket stub caught his eye and he glared at it until Ned, who was nearest, picked it up and made it vanish into the pocket of his maroon livery trousers. Charles tut-tutted and shook his head, but this was no time for verbal admonishments. He knew anyway they were disappointed to be found wanting.

He continued his inspection in the downstairs saloon where they were polishing glasses and arranging them on tables in great tiered pyramids. The smell of whisky punch filled the air with its sweetness. He checked his timepiece. It was vital that everything should be in order before the final curtain call.

As soon as the actors had taken their last bow they were chased off to their changing rooms to keep them out of the way. The auditorium also was cleared. The bulk here were ordinary soldiers and these were duly marched back to Chelsea Barracks where supper awaited them with double rum rations. The dignitaries and guests that remained were directed to the downstairs saloon where they were plied with port, hot whisky punch or cups of tea.

At last, work could begin. Charles gave the order and the stage was cleared of all properties and scenes, the flies were raised, as was the curtain, and a carpet was rolled out to cover the floor. Then the huge double utility doors at the back of the theatre were opened and in with a rush of cold air came a procession of handcarts all laden with bolts of cloth. The sides of the stage were festooned with Turkey Red hangings and a ceiling was created with great lengths of billowing, white gauze which criss-crossed the stage and through which an electric chandelier was lowered like an apparition through the clouds. In came the property men with potted palms and aspidistras which they placed along the front of the stage to prevent people falling into the orchestra pit.

Up on ladders in the auditorium, a clutch of electricians was attaching to the front of the dress circle a gigantic Union Jack made out of red, white and blue light bulbs mounted on a frame.

Charles stood centre stage, the ringmaster, shouting instructions, indicating the correct positions for items and, ever mindful of the time, chivvying everyone along at a furious rate. He sent for scissors and began trimming the foliage of several plants which he considered too untidy, or likely to obscure the view from the stage of the soon-to-be-sparkling Union Jack.

They were ready now for the tables which were carried in, with cloths on them, by teams of men. Then came the florists, each with an armful of blooms with which to decorate every table. There were lilies and gardenias, bringing with them the smells of Christmas spice and expensive soaps and Charles' favourite, Bells of Ireland, which reminded him of his homeland. He loved their ancient, ascetic look against the luxuriance of the other flowers, and the way their prim, little lime-white tongues just peeped out.

Next came the food which was brought on silver dishes and placed on the pristine tablecloths. Vast arrays of cold meats; assorted fowl; lobster that had been removed from the shell and dressed; poached salmon with transparent cucumber fish scales; carrot salad, beetroot salad, vegetable salad, all in jelly; artichokes with a dipping sauce; spinach and eggs; savory rice; currant jelly; apple fritters; cheese; celery; tall glasses of sweets and nuts; candied and crystallized fruit; fancy biscuits; preserves.

In the orchestra pit a pianist was limbering up with finger exercises while the string players set about tuning their instruments.

The vast chandelier above the stage was switched on and every glass and piece of cutlery, every silver dish and bottle of champagne lit up too. From the darkness of the auditorium, the Union Jack blazed forth in electric light bulbs.

The musicians began to play the Allegro Vivace from Shubert's Trout Quintet with its strains of tinkling water.

Charles looked at his watch. He was pleased to see that the whole operation had been completed in slightly less time than the forty minutes allotted. He hurried off to the downstairs saloon.

There he found the room was packed with quite a mix of types: military men from all corners of the world, each more exotically attired than the next; a large number of colonial premiers; maharajas, princes and ranees from all over the Empire; statesmen; ecclesiastics; authors; artists; actors; ladies of fashion; men of science and commerce; members of the Press. But it was not difficult, even in this crowd, to locate Edmund, he being a good head and shoulders above most average-sized men.

His hair was damp, combed flat. His dark blue coat, as always, was immaculate. Edmund was heedless of dress himself but had a good tailor who understood his lanky frame. He was leaning forward the better to hear the lady at his side, his hands clasped behind him. That sight of him, the slope of his back, the tilt of his head, the cutaway style of his jacket, put Charles in mind of a raven – glossy, curious, quick. He knew Edmund was watching for him so it was easy to catch his eye.

Edmund took the signal. He raised his hand and called for hush.

"Ladies and gentlemen," he said. "Friends. We are ready now to receive you. Please, follow on."

He invited Marguerite Davenport, his leading lady, to take his arm and like some Shakespearean hero he led the company back to the stage where the sumptuous reception awaited.

Once supper was over, the tables were moved back to make room for a troupe of Indian entertainers. They were four men in baggy trousers, bare-chested, bare-footed, one with a drum strapped over his shoulder. They stood still in a row for a long time; even their eyes were fixed. Then one of them let out a sudden howl and from stasis came frenetic activity. The performers juggled balls and batons and glasses. Coloured silks streamed from unlikely places and all the while the musician beat out a loud, strange rhythm on the tom-tom.

Violet Jeffers found the noise and the movement overwhelming. She could feel a headache coming on and in order to stave it off she decided to slip away for half an hour to some place quiet.

All the exits were manned by detectives, a precautionary

measure to ensure the safety of all the jewels and gold on show amongst the guests. She didn't feel like explaining herself to them, so she chose to slip out past the Green Room and lose herself in the warren of wardrobe and dressing rooms that occupied most of that side of the theatre. She came to her husband's dressing room, switched on the light and went in.

She took a perverse pleasure in commandeering the only armchair in the room as usually, when she came to visit her husband backstage, this same armchair was occupied by Marguerite Davenport, the Colosseum's leading lady. Many was the time Violet had been forced to sit on the four-legged stool at the mirror while Marguerite and Edmund continued a conversation, he dressing behind the screens while she, Marguerite, languished upon the cushions here . . . and, all the while, Violet smiling and pretending she didn't mind.

Being in this room on her own always made Violet feel oddly excited. Edmund, of course, loved it here. There was more of Edmund Jeffers to be found in this twelve-foot by twelve-foot space than in any part of their home in Belgrave Square. Here one could trace his story, beginning with his early belief in himself, through the dedication, passion and hard work of the intermediate years and on to this, the culmination of his hopes and dreams: the Colosseum.

She moved from the armchair to the mirror and opened the top drawer where Edmund kept his most precious possessions. He often related the tale of how, at the age of nineteen, he had won £20 in a lottery which had enabled him to leave the bank where he was working at the time and fulfill his long-held ambition of joining a touring company of actors. He spent years in the provinces with Jennings' Stock Travelling Company, playing bit parts and creating business on stage to get himself noticed. Some of the articles from that original lottery purchase had survived and were here, namely a pair of white kid gloves, three wigs of different colours and styles, a pair of braces fit for a clown, a pipe and a silk cravat. She took them out of the drawer, lined them up on the dresser and looked at them. It seemed incredible that Edmund's reputation, his fame, his entire theatrical empire, had started with these few oddments.

Violet had aspirations of her own. She had been open from the very start about her desire to become an actress. Edmund had urged her to read Diderot, Coquelin, Scott and Archer and he had tried to discuss with her their opposing theories about the drama and acting. But Violet was no didact or debater and, while Edmund would argue for ever over any aspect of his beloved craft, she felt no such inclination herself. What did it matter to her whether a good performance originated in the head or the heart so long as it was good? So long as it brought recognition?

What she wanted, and needed, was practical training. She had explained that to Edmund and he had assigned to her some small parts in recent productions but nothing very challenging. And that she found disappointing.

She picked up the white kid gloves that had served Edmund well in so many parts over the years. She recalled he wore them quite recently when he played Digby Grant in James Albery's *Two Roses*. He used all his old props when they were appropriate even though he could have had spanking new ones. Perhaps, in doing so, he was reminded of how far he had come. The gloves were grey now and hardened to the shape of Edmund's hand. She slipped one on, her fingers curling to the contours of the leather. It felt so intimate that she removed the glove immediately and put it away in the drawer with its partner.

Around the mirror and tucked in behind it were numerous cards and letters which Violet scanned now. There were the usual greetings, including one from Edmund's mother wishing him good luck with *Waterloo*, and the 'revels' afterwards. There were lots of invitations to soirées and dinner parties, most of which he would be unable to attend because of his work commitments, and there was the announcement of a new exhibition at the National Portrait Gallery which Edmund evidently was planning to go to, as he had dog-eared it. And then, at the very top, was another, which she took down. A postcard featuring a photograph of a young woman wearing drawers and black stockings and nothing else. She was carrying a tea tray with cups and saucers on it that only partially covered her naked breasts. '*More tea, Vicar?*' was the caption underneath. On the back was written, in Marguerite's hand, '*Oops, wrong costume change!*', a reference to her own legendary – and extremely tiresome – mistakes with wardrobe.

Violet tore it up before she even had time to think. She slipped the pieces into her evening bag. This type of display she found intolerable. It was not that she feared the relationship between her husband and Marguerite was anything other than platonic. They were friends and always would be, welded together by their own histories. Marguerite was Leading Lady to Edmund's Leading Man and together they had reigned as King and Queen of the Colosseum for the last ten years. It was inevitable that from time to time she would be excluded from their tight working friendship. What she had not anticipated, however, was being made feel like an interloper. Edmund and Marguerite were closer in age, had so much in common, were so comfortable together, had such an empathy with one another that in their company Violet always felt inadequate.

Such thoughts she kept to herself but this card, given pride of place in Edmund's dressing room and no doubt taken down for everyone to see and snigger at, announced to the world that her husband was altogether too familiar and open with Marguerite.

She, Violet, felt displaced because of it. It was demeaning to be superseded in this way.

She was on the point of leaving the dressing room when she spotted Edmund's spectacles lying on the cover of a book he had been reading earlier – *The Way We Live Now* by Trollope. She picked them up and brought them with her.

By the time she got back to the stage, the Indian performers had finished their act. There was enthusiastic applause. The ladies fanned themselves and squealed with the excitement of it all, while the men tried to work out how the tricks were done. Violet melted into the crowd, hoping to drift around the stage unimpeded, but Mrs. Ashbourne, an awful woman who thought that being wife to the Chief Executive of Coutts' Bank meant she could waylay anyone, had other ideas. She was a large woman, breathless even when resting, and she now took hold of Violet's hand in both of hers and patted it with such vigour that her double chin wobbled.

"Oh, Mrs. Jeffers – Mrs. Jeffers, I beg of you," she said. "Tell me, please, about these Indians. Where are they from and don't say India. What I mean is, how can I get them?" She took a gulp of air. "It's Georgiana's Coming Out next month and really they would make a delightful addition to the party."

"I will get an address for you," Violet said and tried to pass on but Mrs. Ashbourne was not yet finished with her.

"That trick with the box and the knives, my dear, how is it done?" She gave Violet a look of such earnestness that it seemed she really expected her to know.

"I couldn't say," Violet said.

"What a fibber you are," Mrs. Ashbourne said. "I can tell just by looking at you that you know. But I won't pester. All I'll say is that it's horrific to watch, horrific but thoroughly engrossing." She had to take two breaths before continuing. "I was waiting,

13

actually waiting for the blood to start spurting out. I had my handkerchief at the ready in case it was needed." She dragged out from her bosom a tiny piece of lace.

"The Indian theme is perhaps a little overworked this year, don't you think? We only just got away with it tonight," Violet said. "Everyone, and I mean everyone, is doing it and I can't tell you how many enquiries I've had this evening about these same entertainers."

There was a modicum of satisfaction to be gained from the telling of this lie. The woman was at least wrong-footed.

"Oh goodness! In that case, my dear, I won't have them," Mrs. Ashbourne said. "I'm glad you told me. There is nothing worse than being à la mode. You know much better than I what's popular these days. Living in Hampstead is like being marooned on a desert island, you hear nothing there. I don't know how many times I've told Mr. Ashbourne we should move, if only for the girls' sakes. They're growing up quite uncivilized, you know."

"Then perhaps they are best contained where they are," Violet said, with such sharpness that Mrs. Ashbourne could not fail to feel it.

She let go of Violet's arm. Her breathing appeared to steady.

"Mr. Jeffers is keeping well, I hope." Her smile was pure poison. "What they say about actors is most unfair – your husband is so refined and charming – and I always mention that whenever the topic is raised in company. Why, no charity event is complete without there being at least half a dozen actors on the guest list. They bring such colour, don't you know? I won't keep you from your guests any longer, my dear . . . You must excuse me."

Violet could not say she was sorry to have offended Mrs. Ashbourne, except that her abrupt departure left her now standing on her own. There were several groups of foreign-looking men around her, all of them in deep conversation. And therefore, she could not help but be drawn to what was happening over on her right-hand side where Marguerite Davenport had surrounded herself with several of the military top brass. She was wearing a gown of blue-green satin that changed colour with the slightest movement, going from purple to blue to gold, just like a peacock's breast. The décolletage was wide and deep. Decent, but only just. A black feather fan allowed her to cover and uncover that famous cleavage with dance-like aplomb.

"It is indeed a Golden Age for the theatre, Colonel," Marguerite was saying. "Marvellous plays, marvellous roles, marvellous managers . . ."

"Marvellous actresses, if I may be so bold," a second man offered.

"My dear sir, you may be as bold as you like. If boldness brings with it compliments of that sort, then I shall surrender completely." And with this, she raised her hands in submission.

There was much laughter and the Colonel, in an aside to his neighbour, said, "Charming, utterly charming".

Some gruff old fellow asked Marguerite which playwright, currently writing, she most admired. She let them wait for the answer while she thought – as if she needed to – the black feather fan resting on her bosom like a bird with its wings spread.

"I see much to praise in Ibsen," she said, at last. Some of her circle nodded, some raised eyebrows. "But, for me, Arthur Wing Pinero is Life itself."

And with that the fan resumed its flutterings.

"*The Second Mrs. Tanqueray*, isn't that one of his?" the Colonel said, stroking his moustache. "Why, you must play her, Miss Davenport. It would be a mortal sin if you didn't."

"I'm afraid, Colonel, that one more mortal sin would make very little difference to my poor, blackened soul."

There followed a cacophony of guffaws and gallant protestations on Marguerite's behalf which died away the moment she began to speak again.

"However, I have, for a long time, yearned to play Paula Tanqueray. And who knows, perhaps one day I will."

"Hear, hear," said one young fellow who appeared quite overcome.

At that point Marguerite noticed Violet standing alongside, listening. She smiled and stretched out an arm to welcome her in.

"No, I'm looking for Edmund," Violet said. "Have you seen him anywhere?"

Marguerite suggested that she might find him over by the orchestra pit and she was right. He was in company with Lord Cromer, the British Pro-Consul from Cairo, and three of his Embassy staff, all of them dark-suited, dark-haired men.

She handed her husband his spectacles.

"Just what I needed, my dear," he said, putting them on. He reached into his waistcoat pocket for a piece of folded paper. "I believe you must be clairvoyant."

"No, I saw you struggling to read that note earlier and I thought it might be important."

"Clairvoyance and clear-sightedness, they are one and the same."

And then, in a reflex movement, Edmund and Violet ducked their heads because that is what everyone else around them did. There was the sense of something – a missile? – passing overhead.

Edmund recovered and, shielding his eyes from the light of the chandelier, gazed up towards the roof.

"It's a bird," he said, spotting it. "A swallow by the look of it. Must have got in when the doors were open. I don't like it – it's jolly bad luck."

The creature swooped down again through the canopied ceiling across the stage and up out of sight. The guests peered nervously up through the fabric, trying to anticipate where the bird would next appear.

Edmund dispatched Jim, one of the carpenter's lads, up the ladder to the bridge where he was instructed to wave a broom about in order to frighten the bird in the direction of the back doors of the theatre which were opened now to allow it escape. The great swathes of cloth billowed in the breeze that came in. The ladies pulled their shawls tighter about them. Up above, Jim did a little dance and several of the onlookers clapped and cheered. It was like another novelty act.

The bird took off again. It shot upwards seeking refuge in the darkness of the fly tower but as it flew overhead, Jim, raising his broom, unintentionally made contact with it. The bird dropped down, down, landing in the canopy just above Violet's head. Through the thin cloth, the bird could be seen flapping its wings and sliding down to the lowest point, its progress marked by a browny-red streak. There were horrified gasps.

"Sorry, Chief," Jim shouted down to Edmund. "Didn't mean to hurt it."

Charles appeared on the scene with another one of the carpenter's lads and a stepladder. The boy climbed up and managed to get his hands on the injured bird. He brought it down against his chest. Its black eye was turning milky, its breast was leaping, one wing hung down, the feathers all at awkward angles. A number of ladies looked away. Edmund got hold of a black cloth bag normally used for holding dress jewellery and the bird was slipped into it. He, Charles and the boy took it away.

The piano quintet had ceased playing while all this was going on and resumed now with a new piece. Violet thought it was Brahms, but it was, in any event, so brisk, so obvious an attempt to lift the mood that it had the opposite effect and deadened the atmosphere. People were still looking upwards, discussing what had happened and willing a different outcome. One got the feeling they would start leaving soon.

And then Edmund came back from the wings, his arms raised above his head, a look of beatific calm on his face. Everyone turned to him, expectant.

"Ladies and Gentlemen, all is sweetness and light," he said, from the middle of the stage. "It will gratify you all to learn that our feathered friend has recovered fully, thanks to the ministrations of Charles here. Take a bow, Charles . . ." (Some muted cheers) "As we speak, that little swallow is flying home to kith and kin with wondrous tales of the Colosseum. Tales of its magnificence and hospitality . . ." (delighted laughs and clapping) ". . . of the excellent plays and play-acting to be seen . . ." (even louder hoots of approval) ". . . of the grandeur and respectability of its very worthy patrons." Here he made a great show of curtseying and there was huge applause. He waited for silence. "A most perceptive visitor, he was. So, let us drink and make merry in his honour."

There was laughter, glasses were refreshed, conversations renewed. Disaster had been averted. Relief brought with it a giddy, thrilling edge so that the crowd seemed more furiously convivial than before.

Violet watched her husband. There was the slightest puckering between his eyebrows that told all. He came back to her side, the diplomats rejoined them and he continued a story he had already started about the time Marguerite played Joan of Arc. She had refused to adopt the traditional boyish, cropped hairstyle for the role as it was unflattering and insisted instead on a "simple bun and a few arranged curls". They had many arguments over it, but eventually Marguerite won out.

"The funny thing was," Edmund said, "that after a while audiences came to accept the new hairstyle and, by the end of the run, not only had it caught on as a new fashion, but it was deemed a more accurate representation of Joan of Arc's coiffure than the usual bob. Which I believe says a lot for Marguerite's powers of persuasion."

Violet could only think how willing people were to be deceived in this and more recent matters. She had seen the slow blink in the bird's eye, the broken wing. It was lying in a dustbin now, of that she was sure, with its neck wrung. But no one wanted to know that.

Edmund was laughing, savouring the joke of Marguerite's vanity, but she knew he was thinking about that bird. He was superstitious – there was no whistling allowed in the Colosseum, no real money or jewellery permitted during a performance, no peacock feathers. Always there was a ghost light left on. Blue was unlucky on stage, unless matched with silver. Yellow was the Devil's colour. She knew his head was full of bad things now, of omens, disaster, downfall. And, deep down, she felt a little glad.

Chapter Two

Neither Edmund nor Charles ever drank alcohol during Colosseum functions but afterwards, when all the guests had gone, they liked to have a few glasses together and discuss how the night went. To this purpose they were in the office they shared, down in the belly of the theatre, a circular room without windows containing two large desks that faced each other, a fireplace and two armchairs. It was untidy with books and files and letters everywhere but, thanks to Charles, not without organization.

Edmund took a large gulp of his brandy and let it do its work. He could not help letting out a deep sigh.

"How the hell did it get in?" he said.

"It was a blasted bird, Edmund," Charles said. "Nothing more. Unfortunate, given the occasion, but what can we do?"

"It makes me shudder to think of it."

"Then don't."

"You know how I hate the thought of bad luck. That bloody bird will haunt me now for weeks."

"Then you shouldn't let it. We make our own luck in this world, good or bad."

Edmund laughed. "That statement is quite simply preposterous," he said.

Charles tried, unsuccessfully, to hide his grin. Then, he said, "You gave a fine performance tonight, by the way. And a good showing from the press, eh?"

Edmund rested his head back in the winged armchair and focused on the evening's successes. He wanted to be coaxed out of his bad humour.

"We certainly gave them plenty to write about," he said. "What a spectacle, the Empire's finest – kings, princes, maharajas, generals. I have to say I found it all very moving, that sense of brotherhood among nations, of friendship that crosses boundaries of race and creed. I suppose we are seeing the very best of what an empire can do, the civilizing influences it can bring, the benefits for so many people."

Charles rose and poured them both another drink.

"I wish I had your generous spirit," he said. "But I think, in the end, it all comes down to clothes. Dress 'em up right and you can turn beggars into heroes."

"You're a lying dog, Charles. I know very well you were as proud as I was."

"Nothing stirs the spirit so much as sartorial elegance," Charles said, sitting down in the armchair opposite. "Our friends from overseas, of course, are experts at this but even our own military bigwigs were pretty impressive tonight, out in their colours and with all that metal pinned to their chests." He paused. "I'm sure if you looked closely at those medals you'd find that half of them are just foreign coins with holes put through and ribbons attached."

"I do believe there's more of the Fenian in you than you care to admit, my friend."

"Just keeping a healthy cynicism about my colonial masters." Charles bowed his head in mock servility.

"Well, you can say what you like about the English, they at least have names that are pronounceable. You can't go wrong with a Jones or even a Carruthers. The very worst one might encounter is a Ponsonby-Allingham. Whereas some of our brethren from overseas . . ."

"I don't know what happened to Harold," Charles said. "We rehearsed all those introductions at least four times, you know."

"One very fat, mustachioed Indian chap came up, and Harold bellowed out, 'The Maharaja Growlsinbed!' prompting the drunken retort from somewhere in the crowd, 'Does he, by Jove? And how the blazes would you know?'"

This, they both found very amusing.

When their laughter subsided, Charles said, "I will speak to him – it really isn't good enough."

"Leave him alone. I think it rather added to the festivities. As did a certain snippet of information that happened to come my way." Edmund took another sip of his drink and couldn't keep from smiling. "The Lord Chamberlain, it seems, has been casting a friendly eye in my direction, a very friendly eye."

Charles peered at him. "Gossip or fact?"

"Fact. Heard it from Lord Salisbury tonight."

Charles whistled through his teeth. "Sir Edmund Jeffers. Nice ring to it."

"They want another actor. Irving was two years ago and a very popular choice. Wouldn't be until the new year, of course, but I think I can wait . . ."

"Cheers," Charles said, raising his glass. "It would be premature to say anything else so I'll leave it at that, but cheers."

They sat in companionable silence, glad of the quiet after all the commotion of the evening. Certain ideas that had been fermenting in Edmund's mind over the last few days came to the fore and he decided it was time now to test them.

"All this pomp and ceremony," he said. "Well, it's given me a hankering . . . a hankering to do something on a grand scale. *Julius Caesar* springs to mind."

He was gratified to see the leap in Charles' eye as he leaned in closer to listen.

Edmund continued. "I see it in terms of colours: red and white. Red banners everywhere, red carpet for Caesar, red tents on the plains of Phillippi, Caesar's murdered corpse horribly hacked, blood oozing, a lot of blood –"

"Except not spilling over into the orchestra pit like in *Macbeth*," Charles said.

"And then, the white," Edmund went on. "White robes for everyone, of course, white pall for Caesar, white columns, doves, rocks. And anything else we can make white." He was looking at the wall behind Charles where he could see, in his mind's eye, everything he spoke of. "The first three acts, full of dazzling light – sunrise through the windows, slants of sunlight across interior floors." He used his hands to demonstrate the pattern and the impact of the shafts described. "The final two acts, the descent into chaos, a murky midnight blue. We will use sapphire mediums on the limelight, the blood will look black in it; the white, grey. The tents, when they are on fire – I want the smell of burning."

"We can try feathers," Charles said.

"Yes, good. But the key to it all is sound. We will need drums, trumpets, horns, war-like instruments. No music, only heralds and martial statements and all as loud as possible, deafening." He could hear it, feel it, smell it, see it. "The time is perfect for this kind of play, I'm sure of it."

"What about the set?" Charles said.

"Classical yet modern. Clean lines, dramatic, solid, monumental. When you look at it, it should seem unthinkable that a civilization like this could ever end." Edmund stroked his chin. "Alma-Tadema is the only man for this."

"Then you must have him."

They went on in this vein for some time, Edmund doing most of the talking with Charles offering practical suggestions and words of encouragement. Often these sessions went on all night and by morning Edmund would have a dozen sketches drawn up with notes in the margins and arrows pointing everywhere.

This evening, however, Edmund began to notice a certain restraint in Charles which inhibited the flow. He sat a little too much on the edge of his seat, his glass of brandy almost untouched.

"All right," Edmund said to him, finally. "Out with it."

"I don't wish to put a damper on things," Charles said. "But . . ."

"But you will."

"It's Mrs. Curran . . ."

Edmund sank lower in his armchair. He put his feet on the fender though there was no fire to warm them.

"I know you don't want to hear this, Edmund, but her solicitor has been in contact again. This time she is determined to sell, nothing will stop her."

Edmund took his time in answering.

"What about our offer to up the lease?" he said, eventually.

"I have told you this before, Edmund. 'Upping' is not what she wants. A large amount of cash is." He met Edmund's look and replied to it. "I know, I know, we could, at a stretch, gain another ten per cent but what would be the point? It would still be like fighting the enemy with a broken spear."

"Surely I have some money? I mean my own, private —"

"No, you don't."

"Don't I? You can be very blunt at times, Charles."

"You have mortgaged your house already. There is no more you can do." Charles hesitated. "Unless you wanted to approach your father-in-law for a loan."

Edmund looked away and stared into the empty fireplace.

"Just an idea," Charles said. "Not a good one. Stupid, in fact."

"Conflict of interest," Edmund said, as if that was the reason. "He can't own the Metropole and at the same time have a financial stake in the Colosseum."

"Can't he? I mean, yes, of course. Anyway, Mrs. Curran . . ."

Mrs. Curran was Edmund's bedrock. She owned ninety per cent of the Colosseum and had leased it to Edmund for the last decade for an embarrassingly small amount. Never once in all that time had she interfered on a practical or an artistic level. Total freedom was her gift to him and it had meant that Edmund, with complete honesty, could call the Colosseum 'his' theatre even though, legally, he possessed only a tenth of it, shares that had been given to him by Mrs. Curran. The arrangement had been so perfect that he could not countenance a future without it.

"Must she sell, Charles? Is there no alternative?"

"You know there is not. She is returning to America. It is not unreasonable of her to want to put settlements on each of her children before she leaves."

"Then I have no theatre," Edmund said, throwing up his hands. "I must talk to her, change her mind . . ."

"Charm will not work. She needs the money."

"I have neglected her. It is all my fault. She hasn't been to one of our functions for . . . well, for a long time. Probably, she does not realize how much we value her patronage. I should go to her, remind her of the work we –"

"Edmund, she needs the money."

"You know, when she and I were working together I always found her a very honest actress. She dealt in pure emotions only. Complexities did not suit her, not that I ever regarded that as a failing. She was very good to me, very good. I will go and see her. I haven't seen her for a long time."

Charles stood up, set his glass firmly on the mantelpiece and held on to it. "Listen to me, please." He tapped the glass twice on the marble shelf. "There is nothing to be gained from such a visit. The woman needs the money. It's as simple as that."

A silence fell and Charles sat down again. He took a deep breath and tried smiling but there was no disguising his exasperation.

"All is not lost, however," he said. "Mrs. Curran wishes to sell her shares in one lot to an individual who would be supportive of the current regime in the theatre. That is her preference. It is not, however, a guarantee."

"Ah." Edmund sat up straighter in his armchair. "Then we must campaign. Approach all those we know who hold the Colosseum in high esteem, people with money, people we can bamboozle or bully, preferably both. Maybe we could put a syndicate together. We need to establish terms."

"We are in no position to be talking about terms," Charles said. "And perhaps it's best to avoid the notion of a syndicate for now. We should be aiming for one compliant owner. What we do not want is a gaggle of geese, I mean investors, shooing about the place, this way and that, in a mad search for returns."

"And hissing when they don't get them, to take that dreadful analogy further still." Edmund got up, went to the sideboard. "Have another drink, old boy?"

Charles drained his glass and handed it over.

"Look," Edmund said. "Why don't we compile a list of likely purchasers and see if we can seduce them?"

Charles nodded, looking much happier.

Edmund poured out the brandies and returned to his armchair, pounding the cushion behind him to make it more comfortable.

"We will start work on the list tomorrow," he said. "That's settled."

He would have liked now to return to the subject of *Julius Caesar* but touching on one unpleasant topic had put him in mind of another. And one that he could not bury.

"Clive Potter," he said, eventually. "Clive Potter pours scorn over everything I do and, the awful thing is, people actually listen to him."

"Yes," Charles said. "But short of drowning him or shooting him, I don't know what we can do about Mr. Potter."

"I favour boiling him in oil."

Charles laughed, fell into a brief reverie. After a while, he said, "If we can't get rid of him then maybe we should think about using him in some way."

"I can't see how. The man is an out and out charlatan."

"The thing is, he is influential," said Charles. "After Archer and Shaw, he is the critic most read. And heeded. A bad review from him can be devastating, as we know. You cannot deny that his piece on your Lear had a terrible effect on audiences that time." He paused. "And we could do without that kind of publicity. Especially now when the Lord Chamberlain is looking over our shoulder and we need a new investor."

"To think he had the audacity to call my Lear a 'blithering idiot' who didn't know whether to 'whinge' or 'rage' at the elements. And then to say that I was so caught up with striking an elegant pose that I neglected the very heart of the role. I know how to take criticism, you have to in this profession. What I cannot abide is unfairness." Edmund wrapped his legs tightly one around the other. "In every role I have ever played, the character is everything to me. I plumb the depths and play with certainty. I'll admit I am not infallible. There are times when I get it spectacularly right and, equally, there are times when I get it spectacularly wrong. But I am never without conviction." He stopped himself there, rotated his head slowly to relieve the muscles of his neck. "I know you've heard that umpteen times before, Charles, but it still fires me up to think of the effrontery of it. He has cut up nearly every one of my performances. I cannot always be wrong. Other critics do not think so, audiences do not think so."

"No, they do not," Charles said. "His comments are unjust, unwarranted and very unwelcome. Particularly at the present time." His expression changed suddenly then, became almost playful. "But did you know that Mr. Potter has written a play?"

"Good God, what did any of us do to deserve that? I'll wager it's set in a dingy sitting room with characters even drabber than the curtains. Oh, and they all have socially significant problems."

"I have read it. It is . . . how shall I put it . . . a worthy affair."

Edmund studied his companion. "What are you cooking up, Charles?"

"I think we should option his play –"

"I have no intention of ever staging anything that scorpion has put his name to!"

"Of course not, out of the question," Charles said. His mouth twitched at the corners. "We are very busy here at the Colosseum. We wouldn't be in a position to start any new production until at least next autumn. And by then there'd be some other obstacle and it would have to be put off for another year, more's the pity, and so on and so on. In the meantime, having accepted his play and paid him a substantial amount of money for the honour of it, we would, in effect, be buying his good opinion. He won't criticize the Colosseum if he is shortly to join us in a venture."

"In other words, we bribe him?"

Charles shrugged his shoulders. "Better to say that we arrive at a mutually acceptable agreement."

"Except that we don't hold up our end of the bargain," Edmund said. "He never gets to see his play performed. Why don't we just offer him money to give us good reviews, leave the play out of it altogether?"

"I am quite sure that the promise of money means little to Clive Potter. He is at heart a vain man, who lives frugally, a man who would much rather have the opportunity to inflict on the public his dreary political opinions in the form of a play than receive any amount of riches. And can you imagine how much he would enjoy the supreme irony of being able to pontificate from the Colosseum stage, in this theatre that is the embodiment of the establishment? He would revel in it. As he would in seeing his name on the billboards and in the newspapers and hearing it on everyone's lips."

"What a brilliant piece of psychoanalysis, Charles. I do believe you've missed your calling."

"Besides, I would be very wary of being open with him, of letting him see our real intentions. He could be dangerous in that respect. Better to be obscure."

"I suppose you are right," Edmund said. "And by the time Potter realizes that play of his will never see the light of day, I'll have my knighthood in the bag and we'll have found the perfect owner for the Colosseum. We'll all be happy then, except for Mr. Potter, that is. But we will compensate him well, Charles. We will be generous."

"Of course."

"Then let's bring him in as soon as possible." Edmund filled his lungs with air as though bracing himself for a brisk walk. "Do you know, I'm suddenly very hungry."

Charles went off and returned with a tray of leftovers from the night's banquet. They feasted on quail and asparagus and macaroons and more brandy and were quite merry as the night wore on. By five in the morning they had tired of conversation. Edmund resigned himself to sleeping in his armchair which was large and soft and very comfortable. He finished his drink, allowed his eyes to close. Behind him he could hear Charles tidying up his desk as he always did before going home, no matter what the hour. Then, Edmund's feet were lifted gently, placed on a footstool. A rug, taken from the sideboard, was draped over him. Edmund mumbled his thanks but he was already drifting into slumber. His head was a welter of bright lights and champagne and Indian conjurors and laughter and gleaming Union Jacks. But dark thoughts crept in and he slept fitfully.

Chapter Three

Every morning, even if it was raining, Edmund stopped the hansom cab at Trafalgar Square and walked the rest of the way to the Colosseum. Invariably he chose the opposite side of the Strand to stroll along in order to maximize his view of the theatre all the way down. It was a sight he never tired of.

The exterior reminded him of a wedding cake with its columns and moulded plasterwork and stuccoed walls in cream and white. And then, by way of contrast, the steps led up to four sets of double doors – dark mahogany with brass handles – that set a very serious tone. During the day, the building made little impact on the street. Omnibus passengers drove by it, oblivious – likewise pedestrians and traders who flocked past constantly. But come night-time, when the façade was lit up and there were queues outside and the air was alive with the hum of expectation and the aroma of roasting chestnuts, it was different. Everyone loved the Colosseum then. Everyone was in awe of it.

Twelve years had passed since the day Edmund had first seen the Colosseum. Then it was a dowdy, third-rate establishment with a repertoire as uninspiring as the décor. Edmund was fresh from Jennings' Stock Travelling Company, with whom he had toured the provinces for eight years perfecting his craft. In London, however, he was unknown. He was twenty-five years of age, low on funds and determined to launch himself on the unsuspecting capital. To this end, he auditioned everywhere, including the Colosseum one rainswept Thursday afternoon.

The owners then were an American couple, William and Beatrice Curran, both actors who also managed the theatre between them. Edmund Jeffers was nervous that fateful day. He made some errors with the text and he lumbered about the stage with the awkwardness of a youth unaccustomed to the size of his own body. Neither was he handsome. And yet the Currans were impressed. They saw he had an instinctive ability to bring darkness to the sunniest of characters, levity to the most solemn, tenderness to the most cruel. They used him after that in several minor roles and were pleased. Very soon, and to the chagrin of those who had graced the stage of the Colosseum for many years and felt they had precedence, he was given more substantial parts, often supporting William Curran in the lead.

And then, William Curran contracted tuberculosis and had to spend a year at a sanatorium in Scotland. In his absence, Edmund was the natural choice to replace him as leading man and this he did. His leading lady, Mrs. Curran, was then twenty-four years his senior but the disparity in their ages deterred neither of them and they played lovers in countless sentimental melodramas that were the stock-in-trade of the Colosseum at that time.

When William Curran returned from Scotland, he was a weak man. He retired from acting but continued to direct the company in the same worthless plays that he – though not any more, the public – favoured. Edmund had pleaded with him to diversify and had been frustrated so often that he was contemplating a move to another theatre when, in 1887, William Curran died. With his death, Mrs. Curran lost her appetite for the stage and decided to give up acting altogether and retreat to a cottage in Epsom. Before leaving, however, she leased the Colosseum to Edmund for a nominal sum with her blessing to do with it as he pleased.

From the start, Edmund's attitude was proprietorial. He knew exactly what to do. He established his own permanent company of actors with Marguerite Davenport, a promising unknown, as his leading lady. The repertoire included a mix of Shakespeare, Boucicault, Victorien Sardou, Tennyson. Thus, unashamedly, Edmund indulged his passion for the romantic past and audiences seemed to like it. But it was his portrayal of Cardinal Wolsey in Shakespeare's *Henry VIII* that shook them. Six foot three and swathed in robes of vermilion silk, Edmund's Wolsey was a man of intellect, a diplomat, a politician. But with eyes of fire. He played the part for eighteen months and by the end of the run he was famous.

The Colosseum prospered. All Edmund's money and all profits made by the theatre were used for improvements to the building, in return for which Mrs. Curran gave him a ten-per-cent share. The gallery was removed and a dress circle put in. Electricity was installed front of house and in the dressing rooms, but not on the stage as Edmund did not like its flattening effect. He preferred gas and limelight which combination produced much softer, harmonious impressions. Beneath the stage, a sophisticated system of counterweighted elevators was installed which enabled ships to be sunk, homes to collapse, thunderstorms to devastate. Gradually, all the soft furnishings were renewed too, the upholstery and curtains in royal blue and the carpet in red. On the walls were prints of Burbage, Betterton, Garrick, Macready, Kean, the theatre greats, and every alcove housed a statue of a Greek or Roman scholar. In the ten years that had elapsed since Edmund took over, the Currans' shabby playhouse had been transformed into one of the most revered and influential theatres in the country.

This morning, Edmund dodged the traffic as he crossed the road and went up the steps to the Colosseum. He opened the doors and exulted in the smell of floor polish and lilies that greeted him, a curious blending of the wholesome with the exotic. They had decided to receive Clive Potter in the accounts office rather than in the comfort of their own domain downstairs and Edmund found Charles there, already waiting. Bernard, the clerk, had gone for an early lunch.

It was another twenty minutes before Clive Potter finally arrived and, when he did, he made no apology for being late. He stood square in the middle of the office. His Mackintosh was wet and exuded a dead-animal smell.

"Let me take your coat," Charles said and, to spare them all the stench, he consigned it to the cloakroom in the foyer.

Potter took his seat on the far side of the desk from them. He had attempted a beard since the last time Edmund had seen him, presumably to disguise what was a very prominent, thrusting chin, but the hair that had grown was so sparse and of such poor quality that, if anything, it accentuated the very flaw it was meant to conceal.

"Good to see you," Edmund said.

Potter made no response, only sat and waited. The colour of his suit came very close to yellow and he wore an oversized bowler hat which he only now removed with inordinate care and positioned on the desk in front of them as though establishing a talking point. One might have thought him ridiculous but for the suspicion that everything about him – the inferior clothes, the beard, the stinking raincoat, the clownish hat – was designed to offend.

34

Edmund had Potter's play on his lap. He riffled the pages with his forefinger over and over again. Terrible title, *Woman*. Terrible play. He had forced himself to read it and there was not an ounce of wit or style in it. Dull, dull, dull, nothing but a miserable rant on the social and economic privations suffered by an impoverished (and unprepossessing) mother of two, recently widowed. Granted, the 'problem' play was popular these days but this offering was more sermon than drama. It was dour, moralistic, and written without the least feeling or instinct for character, suspense or dramatic conflict. But what else could one expect from a cheap journalist and part-time theatre critic who believed a stage play was simply an elongated newspaper article with actors talking?

Edmund stroked the manuscript. "This is good work, Mr. Potter," he said. "New, challenging, it throws up issues that haven't been dealt with before, at least not in this way. It's subversive."

Potter nodded. "Subversive." He snatched at the word as though it was his property alone. "I like that."

Edmund pressed on. "We would like an opportunity to work on *Woman*, see what we could do with it . . ."

Clive Potter's eyes flared. He had a curious habit of stretching his eye muscles at intervals which gave him the look of a man habitually surprised.

"How exactly did you folks get your hands on my play?" he said. "I don't recall sending it to you."

Edmund sighed. "Mr. Potter, if we can't even get past the preliminaries without an argument . . ."

"Apparently you gave it to Mr. Beerbohm Tree at Her Majesty's," Charles said. "He wasn't in a position to take up on it himself so he passed it on to us. I don't see that there is anything to object to in the manner in which we –"

"All right," Potter said. "Continue."

Edmund took a deep breath. "As I was saying, we would like to option your play with a view to staging it at some time in the future."

"When in the future?"

"Ah, that is for Charles to say. As always, I am at his mercy. When, Charles?" He looked at his business manager and tried to keep the mischief out of his eyes.

Charles, with his best poker face, said, "You do appreciate, I am sure, Mr. Potter, that a theatre of this size has a large number of commitments. And, of course, if a play is doing well, we will extend the run, so it is difficult to say with certainty when —"

"Give me uncertainty then," Potter said.

Charles assumed a benign expression. "We have a tight, tight schedule and an American tour in the offing. However, I think we could see our way to beginning rehearsals for your play next year. November or December perhaps."

Potter gave a derisive laugh. "What's that? Eighteen months away?"

"Please remember, this is the Colosseum," Charles said. "We plan years in advance."

Potter stared at them both, looking first at Edmund and then at Charles. "What exactly do you want with me and my play?" he said. "I wouldn't have thought 'new and challenging' — your words, by the way — were exactly your cup of tea. Usually you prefer to exhume Shakespeare or Goldsmith. All you have to do then is throw in a few nice costumes and a lot of overacting and, hey presto, you have yet another success for the Colosseum on your hands. And all done with the minimal amount of effort."

"Shakespeare and Goldsmith are two stalwarts of the British theatre, Mr. Potter," Edmund said. "And we are very proud to have them in our canon. Without them there would be no British drama today — none to speak of, anyway."

Potter's eyes flared again. "Still, you must get tired of the same old repertoire. Surely you yearn for new territory, new worlds, new forms and style? If one does not explore, one only stagnates."

Edmund knew he should resist getting drawn into an argument but he couldn't let Potter away with that statement.

"There is no such thing as 'the same old repertoire'," he said. "And it surprises me to hear a man who proclaims himself an authority on the theatre say so. It does not matter when a play was written, whether four hundred years ago or yesterday, but it must be approached with a fresh eye." He lobbed Potter's play back onto the desk. "There are always new insights, new interpretations, new dimensions. My performance of King Lear is nothing like what an Elizabethan actor would have produced in his day. I bring the weight of my experience to the role, the influence of the changing world —"

"You end up shackled to the past. This place . . ." Potter's eyes swept the room, "this place is in danger of being fossilized."

"Why bother even meeting us then, if everything we stand for is anathema to you?"

They ended up locked in a stare. Potter's eyes were green with splinters of orange and he couldn't keep the hungry look out of them.

Charles' calm voice intervened. "Here at the Colosseum, Mr. Potter, we are very much indebted to the classical drama. That is where our roots lie. We do, however, have a strong interest in contemporary works. In the last year alone we've had Conan Doyle, Henry Arthur Jones, Gilbert. And, from time to time, we like to introduce new playwrights like yourself. We are not afraid, as the saying goes, to branch out occasionally."

"As long as you don't branch out so far that the tree topples over," Potter said.

"Unlikely, given the might of this particular tree," Edmund said gravely.

"We are most anxious to secure the option on your play, Mr. Potter," Charles said. "For a two-year period, if that is agreeable."

Potter looked at Charles sideways. "What are you offering?"

"Five hundred pounds," Charles said.

"Make it six hundred," Potter said. "And I want Marguerite Davenport to play Eleanor, and you, Mr. Jeffers, to play Edgar, the villainous Edgar."

"Marguerite and myself take all the leading roles," Edmund said. "Though I am surprised you want me in your play after all you've said about my inadequacies in the past."

"Yes," Potter said. "But you do have a certain slavish following that is useful."

Edmund leaned forward. He could feel his own face blanching. "Listen, Mr. Potter," he said. "If we are to collaborate, we need to understand each other. Here at the Colosseum we are like a family, bound together by loyalty to a common cause. We all keep the faith." He paused. "I will go further and say this, that with each full house at the Colosseum you are a heartbeat closer to getting *Woman* on our stage."

He had been too blatant. He knew it from the way Potter grinned, showing bottom teeth that were lopsided and stained near the gums.

"Why, Jeffers," Potter said, "for all your fine talk and fancy ways, you're a scoundrel underneath. But don't worry, that won't stop me doing business with you." He sat up in his chair, adjusted his collar. "How does this sound? 'Magnificent performance, stupendous production, a tour de force, superb artistic achievement'." He sniffed. "A thousand pounds will buy you those words."

"Eight hundred, not a penny more," Edmund said.

"And I'll see my play on the Colosseum stage?"

"That is the plan," Edmund said, looking down at the desk.

"We are offering to buy the option on your play, Mr. Potter," Charles said. "We are not bound in law to use it. You understand that?"

Potter retrieved his bowler hat and put it on. "I want my play on at this theatre," he said, sounding like a child demanding his favourite toy.

"We are offering you very generous terms," Charles said. "We could not and would not do so unless we planned to follow through on the project."

Edmund took the cheque book out of the top drawer of the desk and began to write. "Eight hundred seals the deal," he said.

Potter nodded. He knew he had done well.

Edmund handed the cheque over and they all shook hands. Potter folded the cheque three times, very precisely, and tucked it into his wallet.

Charles got his coat from the foyer and helped him into it.

"Roll on the rehearsals," Potter said, with a wicked smile.

He turned to go. Even his walk, which was somewhat flat-footed, was pugnacious. The glass door shook in its frame as he went out.

"That was costly," Charles said when they were alone.

"And most unpleasant too," Edmund said. "Having one's ulterior motives exposed like that. Still, I suppose at least now he fully understands us."

"Yes," Charles said. "Which leaves me feeling decidedly queasy."

Chapter Four

Violet Jeffers had no interest in the daily domestic round. She involved herself as little as possible with the planning of meals, the hiring of staff, the furnishing of rooms, the paying of accounts and trusted it all to Mrs. Philipps, the housekeeper. This formidable woman ran the house and servants in military style. However, being thus freed from household duties left Violet with very little in the way of distraction.

Edmund was hardly ever at home as he was busy with the preparations for *Julius Caesar* and was also performing as Svengali every night in *Trilby*. Marguerite was the artist's model Trilby, of course, but, sadly, no part had been found in the play for Violet. She could perhaps have whiled away the hours on her own doing embroidery or tapestry or tatting collars and cuffs but she had never seen the point to any of those activities and even reading became wearisome when there were so many hours spent on it. Neither had she close female friends to whom she could now turn. In the afternoons, society ladies called to see her and she, in her turn, visited those it would be churlish to ignore but she

40

derived no pleasure or satisfaction from social intercourse of this kind.

Being the daughter of Lord Leopold and Lady Constance Barrie, Violet had automatic status and, while she enjoyed her lofty position in society, she had inherited from her father's side of the family enough of their rebellious spirit to make her want recognition for an achievement that was greater than a mere accident of birth. And so she had decided to become an actress. In marrying Edmund she had believed that station in life was assured her. She had the necessary talent, of that she was certain, and reasonably good looks. She knew there was plenty to learn about acting and she had kept her patience for four whole years and learnt it. But still Edmund did not assign any of the good roles to her. Occasionally, she got some bit part but nothing substantial and she was becoming restless. A course of action had presented itself to her that night in Edmund's dressing room when she had come upon the indecent postcard from Marguerite. For therein lay the problem. She, Violet, would never get the chance to demonstrate her full potential with Marguerite in situ at the Colosseum. Marguerite Davenport was the obstacle. And one that had to be removed.

Violet awoke one morning full of determination. She breakfasted alone, then ordered a cab for eleven o'clock.

For a week it had been very hot with temperatures well up in the eighties and, while at first this had thrilled the inhabitants of London, now they were exhausted from it. The cab driver, wiping his brow on his sleeve, put down the hood of his vehicle so as to allow Violet the luxury of a gentle breeze as they trotted along. The streets were quiet; already it was sweltering. The few shoppers who were out remained in the shade of awnings where complete strangers exchanged anecdotes about the scorching heat that was afflicting the city. It was safe to assume the same conversations were happening in the park where Violet spied through the fence indolent mothers and nannies slumped on benches with fractious infants rolling around on the grass at their feet.

At her parents' house in Kensington, the morning room was on the first floor at the back. Even with the French windows thrown open onto the balcony, the atmosphere inside was muzzy, smelling of warm milk. A climbing rose had engulfed the balcony railings, the drooping flower heads shedding pink petals all over the metal latticed floor. The impression thus created was one of glorious abandon, not a concept Violet normally associated with her old home. Of the garden, only the treetops were visible from inside – great clouds of yellow-tinged foliage – beech, ash, lime.

Lady Constance Barrie was seated at the escritoire facing the wall. She was writing a letter but had placed her chair at such an angle that it allowed for conversation with her daughter while she wrote. From time to time she cooled herself by waving a lacquered Japanese fan. Violet poured them both a cup of tea then drank her own as she walked about the room, looking at pictures and ornaments she had known all her life.

"How is Edmund, dear?" After every one of her mother's utterances one expected to hear a sigh follow on.

"Suffering from birth pangs," Violet said. Her mother looked up. "I'm talking of the new play – he's in the throes of it."

"Oh, I see." Constance sealed an envelope. After a while, she said, "What is it again?"

"*Julius Caesar.*"

"I hope he's given you a decent part this time."

"There are no decent parts for women in *Julius Caesar.*"

"I'm sure there is for Marguerite Davenport," Constance said, laying aside the first letter and starting another. "We all know Edmund is not averse to embellishing Shakespeare when it pleases him. A few choice speeches inserted here and there are no bother to him. If he can do it for Miss Davenport, I'm sure he can do it for you, dear."

Violet stood looking at a picture of horses that she knew by heart.

"I play Calpurnia," she said. And to add some grandeur to the miserable few lines of prosaic dialogue that had been entrusted to her, she said, "That's Caesar's wife, you know."

Her mother's pen ceased scratching across the page. She turned around.

"Am I to take it then that your artistic career is blooming?"

Violet walked off to the other side of the room. She picked up a bronze statue that was new. It represented the fat twins, Romulus and Remus, dangling from the pendulous, swollen teats of the poor she-wolf.

"What a ghastly thing," she said, setting it down again.

"Really, Violet, if you insist on following this peculiar course in life then at least aim high. Be a grande dame of the theatre – there is something in that – but a soubrette?" She turned back towards the wall, resumed her work, then stopped. "You know, I don't understand you. What good is a husband if you refuse to make use of him? I am sure Edmund would oblige. He should. After all, you brought plenty to this marriage and I don't see why other people should get all the advantages. And you needn't pretend the thought has never entered your own head." She pulled herself in tighter to her task. The back of her neck was like a girl's, thin and long with unlined skin and downy hairs at the nape, rather shocking in its perfection. "Of course, she is a great beauty, Marguerite Davenport . . . which always helps." This said as though it were an idle thought.

43

The front door opened downstairs and there were voices below which indicated that Violet's father was home.

A minute or so later, Leopold came in with hugs and greetings for them both. Before sitting down, he stood at the French doors to gaze out over the balcony and take in the sights.

"Isn't the garden superb?" he said, presently.

"You should leave more detailed instructions, Leopold, for when we are away," Constance said. "That pond is choked. I'm sure the fish will die."

"Tom knows what to do," Leopold said, coming to sit down on the sofa beside his daughter who had just settled there. "After all, we don't want it all box hedges and straight lines like we have at Warrickstown. No, I like it like this, almost wild, and in the heart of the city too. Do you know, Violet, a heron came down – yesterday, wasn't it, Constance? I was sitting right here. A heron came down, swooped over the pond and fished out one of the carp, a big one at that, wriggling and flopping all over the place. I must have pelted a dozen cushions at it but, needless to say, I missed and it got its meal in the end."

"It took Louise half an hour to find all those cushions," Constance said, "and when she did, most of them were in such a state that I had to give them away to Tom. I thought he might be glad of them in the potting shed but all I got was a grunt from him. I don't know why I bothered."

"Funnily enough, there's more wildlife to be seen here than at Warrickstown," Leopold said. "Even the grouse seem to have deserted us there." His eye found the teapot. "Ah, tea, just what I need."

"Ring Louise for some more – that must be cold," Constance said.

"No, it'll do fine."

"I really don't know why we have servants then."

44

"Believe me when I say I'm not the least bit concerned with sparing Louise," he said. "I simply happen to prefer tea tepid. As you well know."

Constance shuddered her distaste.

Leopold poured out his tea, holding the pot up high so that it made a vulgar splashing sound in the cup, a move designed as much to annoy his wife as to amuse his daughter.

Constance gathered together her papers. There were two high spots of colour on her cheekbones.

"I'll finish these in my room," she said. "Where there's peace and quiet. Come and say goodbye before you leave, Violet."

When she was gone, Leopold said, "Was I very wicked?"

"No more than usual," Violet said, smiling.

Leopold relaxed, stretching his arms out along the back of the sofa, his cup and saucer balanced on his lap. He had all the confidence of a rich man and the daring of a happy one.

"Tell me about the celebrations last week," he said. "Though from the papers you'd think it was more the Colosseum's Jubilee than the Queen's. All those princes and maharajas – the *Illustrated London News* was crammed full of it. Quite put us, at the Metropole, in the shade. So, tell me, what was it like lording it over everyone, you and Edmund?"

Violet put down her tea.

"What's the matter?" he said.

"I think I was somewhat eclipsed on that occasion." Violet's heart beat a little faster. "Which is nothing out of the ordinary . . ."

"Are we talking here of the Old Enemy?"

"Yes, very old. Though no one seems to see that."

Leopold laughed. "The famous Barrie spite is alive and well in you, Violet, my love. Other great families embrace honour or courage, but we Barries stick with plain old jealousy." Then, seeing she was upset, he slipped an arm around her shoulders.

"Come on, Violet, I'm only joking. You are young and beautiful and clever and one day, very soon, you're going to have what you want. But it means hard work and a tough hide. You mustn't let that floozie annoy you so."

"If I had even one of the roles that she complains about, I'd be overjoyed. She moans non-stop about everything at the Colosseum. It's really very wearing. All she wants, all she talks about are Pinero and Ibsen."

Leopold snorted. "Not much likelihood of Edmund tackling either of those two, I should think."

"She is restless and it really is too bad of her – we all have to suffer because of it. She has no idea of how pampered she is at the Colosseum and she won't know it until finally she gets what she wants and . . . oh, would I ever live to see the day . . ." She looked down at her hands, waiting for her father's response.

"You think she is considering leaving the Colosseum?" he said.

"Oh, I doubt that," Violet said.

"But you think that perhaps she could be tempted away from it?"

Violet raised her eyes. "I suppose it is possible," she said. Then, "Actually, yes, I believe she could be."

"How long is she with Edmund – ten years? Well, we wouldn't want her getting stale, would we?" He smiled at her. He had very dark eyes, almost black. What made them extraordinary was a tiny explosion of browny-red in one iris which always reminded her of a firework in the night sky. "There is some discussion at present as to what play the Metropole should stage next. In the circumstances, I think it will have to be Pinero, don't you? Ibsen is a bit too avant garde, even for us."

"She has her heart set on *Mrs. Tanqueray*."

"Then *Mrs. Tanqueray* it is." He took on a formal tone as he addressed the imaginary board members. "It is our duty, gentlemen, to embrace the future, to encourage our own contemporary playwrights. Arthur Wing Pinero is a case in point, a man who understands the problems of our age. And, what's more, I have it on good authority that Miss Marguerite Davenport – yes, she of the Colosseum – seeks a change of employment, and wouldn't she make the perfect Pinero heroine? What an asset she would be to this theatre, what a prize, what a gift . . . et cetera, et cetera." He wound up the speech with a flourish of his hand. "I shouldn't think I'd have much difficulty in persuading them."

"Oh, but Papa, I couldn't ask you to do that."

He laid a hand on her arm to placate her. "You didn't ask me to," he said. "Let me see what I can do. Just get that husband of yours to take you seriously, do you hear? I want to see your name on the billboards along with his. Let that be your side of the bargain."

Violet was not a demonstrative person. She smiled, squeezed Leopold's arm and thanked him discreetly. For she knew another, better way to show her gratitude.

"I have some news," she said. "Mrs. Curran is selling her share of the Colosseum. That is, ninety per cent." She had his attention right away. Leopold was a man who liked to acquire. "Edmund cannot afford to buy her out but he and Charles are busy prospecting for the right type of investor, some poor fool with more money than sense. They want to handpick and Mrs. Curran will probably let them."

Leopold raised an eyebrow. He shared with his daughter an innate dislike of other people's cosy arrangements.

"They have made a list," Violet said. "And you are not on it."

Leopold thumped his chest with his fist. "That oversight cuts me to the quick," he said. "My own son-in-law." He watched her, knowing there was more to come.

"Mrs. Curran is a silly woman," Violet said. "Much influenced by charm and flattery and especially partial to gentlemen of a certain rank, in their middle years, with refined tastes."

"I'm warming to her," Leopold said.

"If you would like I could introduce you to her. She loves horse-racing, goes to all the meetings . . ."

"Do you know," Leopold said, "I haven't been to the races for years."

"The next big meet is Sandown, two weeks away."

"Is it, by Jove? Then, what do you say we take a couple of boxes, invite the Carringtons and the Penfolds to join us and make a right royal occasion of it?" He clapped his hands together, already intoxicated with the idea. "We'll have the best hamper in the ground – Cook will have to get good warning – and we can put on a few bets. Did I ever tell you about winning that double on the Oaks? Oh, way back – I was still at school. Gained a grand total of two shillings and sixpence which bought currant buns for everyone in my form. Haven't had a bet since."

"Then let's hope you're still lucky, Papa," Violet said.

Chapter Five

Number 10, Arlington Villas, was one in a long terrace of red-bricked houses situated in the outer reaches of Islington. Each was well-proportioned, with steps leading up to the front door and with a basement underneath. In their day, they had been fine residences but in recent years their dignity had been undermined by broken railings and dirty windows, by the junk that had accumulated on the steps, by the stench of rubbish everywhere and by the soot bags that piled up on the footpaths for weeks on end so that whenever it rained, inky black stains spread out from them. Once, artisans, schoolteachers and clerical workers would have lived here but most had moved on, leaving this a neighbourhood in decline. Another few years and it would be a slum.

Why Clive Potter had chosen to live in this seedy backwater, when he could well afford better, was a matter of some discussion amongst his journalistic colleagues. Potter was circumspect about his choice. He liked the district or, rather, he was comfortable in it. It sat well with his own anti-bourgeois sentiments while at the same time he felt superior there, for he was better educated, better paid and better known than any of his neighbours.

Something of the same reasoning might explain how he was attracted to Rosalind, his common-law wife who came from the roughest part of Rotherhithe and had hardly any schooling. She was, however, a beauty with flawless white skin and uncontrollable red hair that seemed fired by electricity. Unlike the majority of her class who were built for hard work, she was light-boned with narrow shoulders and hips, slim wrists, long fingers. In her dress she was modest, which was misleading as her speech was often coarse, her instincts entirely carnal.

In the study, a table large enough to seat eight served as Potter's desk. It was covered with mounds of books, newspapers, maps and jottings with only a small, clear space for the man himself to sit. There was a bookcase in the room, full to capacity, and there were books in piles upon the floor and on the mantelpiece.

Clive Potter was working on a new play about cotton-mill workers. He had spent the last four weekends in Blackburn talking to employees, getting their stories, and now he was trying to craft a play out of all that research, a play that would rock society, a play that would change laws and mark him out as a social reformer.

There was a knock and the door opened.

"What?" he said. Rosalind refused to answer until he raised his head. "What?"

"A gent to see you, with his boy."

Rosalind never took names. She resented answering the door and ushering in guests, said it made a servant of her, his servant. He found this ironic and rather amusing as she never objected to the gross liberties he took with her person nor paused to wonder what they made of her.

Before he could reply, she indicated to the visitors to enter, standing back to allow them in. She winked at the boy as he passed.

Potter threw down his pen – he did not welcome the interruption – and looked at the newcomers. They shared the same, slightly quizzical expression across the brow. The man stood there fingering a crumpled hat, unable, it seemed, to give an explanation for his presence. His moustache and sideburns were copious, sand-coloured and looked soft and shiny like head hair.

"Your name, sir?" Potter said.

"Godfrey Wilkins, and this 'ere's my son, Will."

Potter nodded to the boy, shook hands with the father.

"Sit down," he said.

They took seats on the other side of the table which necessitated Potter moving away some of the debris and paperwork on it in order to see them properly, a task he found bothersome.

"Well?" Potter said, when they were settled.

"I'm Godfrey Wilkins –"

"And this is your son, Will. Yes, yes, I know."

The man smoothed the back of his hair as though he had just been told it was sticking up.

"You write for the newspapers," he said. "Read some of your articles. Nah, I should say Will read them to me." His mouth sounded sticky. His accent, just a bit too soft for the East End, bore traces of a rural upbringing. "It's good what you write, good the things you say 'bout . . . Well, 'bout what's going on, 'specially 'bout workers and that." He looked down at the hat he was holding in both hands. "There's not many will do it."

Probably, the man was a saddler by trade. There was a smell of neatsfoot oil off him. His hands, pinkish at the joints and

51

stained orange round the cuticles, seemed to suggest years of soaping leather.

"The police don't do nothing," Wilkins said.

"The police?" Potter leant forward, planted his elbows on the table. "What exactly do you wish to tell me, Mr. Wilkins?"

The man took a deep breath. "There's an 'ouse down Bermondsey way where we live, where the tanneries are, and there's bad things going on. There's —" A glance at his boy made him clam up.

"What kind of things?"

"It's an 'ouse of ill repute. Children, if you get my drift."

"Do you mean a brothel?"

"I do, sir."

Potter sat back in his chair and assessed the man. He looked sensible, hardworking, awkward in this milieu, fiddling with his hat the whole time, not knowing what to say. It had not been easy for him to come, that was obvious, which lent strength to his words.

"What ages?" he said.

"Young." It seemed he had nothing more to add but then, "Six or seven years old, some of 'em," he spluttered out, shaking his head in disbelief at his own words. "It's not right, really it's not."

"You mentioned the police — they know about this?"

"They've raided it a few times, found nothing. It don't go on there, see. Deal gets done and kids are taken off for a spell. So I'm told, anyway."

"Who told you?"

"People."

"What people?"

"What does it matter? People, right? Everyone knows it. They're doing it to little kids, girls and boys, both." His breath whistled through his nostrils. "I'm sorry, Mr. Potter, makes me livid to think of it. Do you 'ave kids?

"No, I don't."

Wilkins nodded as though understanding now why there was no common ground between them.

"Details, Mr. Wilkins, give me details."

"A Mr. and Mrs. Taylor what owns the 'ouse. They run it as a Christian charity, get money from the church for what they're doing . . ."

"And the name of this Christian charity?"

"Bluebell something or other. They get kids from the streets, orphans and such like, and make a show of training 'em for service." He was still fiddling with his hat. He looked down at it now. "They never get to play outside, you know."

"Well, that's hardly a criminal offence, is it?"

Wilkins made to get up. "Look, if you're not interested in this, if you don't believe me, we'll be on our way."

"No, no." Potter motioned to him to remain seated. "Please continue."

Wilkins turned to the boy. "Tell 'im, Will. Tell 'im what you saw."

The lad had not been paying attention and was taken off guard.

"Remember, you was delivering fish . . . 'e does that on a Friday. Go on, Will."

"I rang the doorbell . . ." Will looked to his father who pointed at Potter to let the boy know where to direct his words. "I rang the doorbell and the missus come out." His voice had more edge to it than his father's. "She wanted some 'errings and I was just wrapping 'em up when I saw this door opening. It was a girl that done it, got 'er fingers round the bottom of the door, see. In a right state, she was – bloody nose, 'air all over the place.

She was lying across the floor and I reckon 'er leg was tied to something 'cos she couldn't go no further. 'Er lips moved though and I could read what she said. It was, "elp'." He whispered the last word like it was his own dying breath. "When the missus saw what I was looking at she slammed the door on 'er. 'That's one of my charges,' says she. 'A very naughty girl. All she 'ad to do was say she's sorry, but no, she's too stubborn. Now a little boy like you wouldn't be that stupid, would yer?' and she pays for the fish and gives me a thrupenny bit for meself."

"A thrupenny bit, mind," Wilkins said.

Potter digested what he had heard. "Perhaps it is simply a case of discipline. Have you never raised a hand to your own son, Mr. Wilkins?" he said.

"I've never battered 'im and tied 'im up, sir. And if I did, then I belong in gaol, just like they do." He spoke with such force that his moustache plumped up like the hackles on a dog's back. "There's something very wrong going on in that 'ouse. A blind man could see that. Little children, sufferin' . . . Think of it, man . . . Think of it . . . No, it doesn't bear thinking' about." There was no trace of nerves in the man now. He was fearsome. "And gentlemen callers at all hours. 'Benefactors' is what they've told the neighbours. Toffs, a lot of 'em. Think they can come down our way and do what they bloody well like – excuse my language."

One could not help but be influenced by Wilkins' air of probity. Potter waited for him to cool off.

"How do you think they find out about what's on offer at this establishment?" he said.

"There are types who make it their business to know all the foulest deeds that go on in a city like this and who don't mind taking a few shilling on the back of it."

That was true. Potter had used a good number of them

54

himself for various stories. He tore a sheet of paper from the back of a notebook.

"Now, Mr. Wilkins," he said. "Perhaps we could go over some of these particulars again."

He wrote down names, addresses and anything else that might be useful and, when he had enough, he said, "Thank you very much for your time and trouble, Mr. Wilkins. Now, I seem to have mislaid my cheque book . . ."

"No, I don't want money, Mr. Potter. I want you to take this on. Will yer?"

"Possibly," Potter said. "Very possibly."

"I'm glad to 'ear that," Wilkins said, still not leaving. "And if I can be of any further —"

"I have your address here, don't I?" Potter tapped the page in front of him with his pen. "I can contact you if necessary."

Not that he had any intention of doing so. There could only ever be one owner of a story like this. He shook hands with them both.

"Before you go," Potter said. "Might I just ask, why did you bring your son with you today when obviously it pained you to speak of these things in front of him? You yourself could easily have told me what he saw."

Wilkins looked at him as though he didn't quite believe the question.

"Because I want 'im to know that we can all stand up for what is right," he said. "Regardless of who we are or where we come from. I want 'im to know we all matter."

Potter nodded. "Do you mind seeing yourselves out?"

The two had got as far as the door when he called after them. "One more thing, Mr. Wilkins. What is your trade?"

"Saddler. Messrs Pelham and Co. We make all the 'arness for the 'ousehold Guard."

Potter smiled to himself. "Just so, just so," he said.

He waited to hear the front door close. An idea had already begun to form in his mind that appalled and thrilled him at the same time. There was nothing new about child prostitution, it had been reported in the newspapers umpteen times. Brothels were discovered, premises closed down, children whisked away, those responsible charged with the crime. Nothing too interesting in that. He, Clive Potter, could do better. To engage the public, a story like this needed to be personal. The writer must fade into the background and the child must come to the fore. What he needed was testimony from the children themselves – how they got to be in that situation, where they came from, the type of acts they had to perform – without being too explicit – and who with. What way were they treated by their 'employers'? Were they paid, were they fed enough, were they ever let go? These were the questions any reasonable person would ask. The answers, he was sure, would show that these were ordinary children, children with difficulties who had been preyed upon, children anyone could know. They were random victims, a realization that was bound to frighten the doting mothers who read about it in the newspaper. Likewise the trusting fathers, the jovial clergymen, the tireless schoolteachers. Frighten people and they listen.

It was all taking shape in Potter's head. But there was only one way to obtain the necessary information and that was to get inside the system, follow it through from beginning to end. It meant – and there was no avoiding this – posing as a client. The more he thought about it, the more he liked the idea.

The *Pall Mall Gazette* or the *Daily Mail* would appreciate this approach. It was revolutionary, exciting. He would gather enough material for a series of explosive articles which would reveal, in more detail than ever before, the plight of the child prostitutes, the type of men who used them, the criminals who ran them.

He must protect himself, of course – every step must be well documented, every detail discussed with the editor. But it was a bold plan that could have far-reaching effects. There would be weeks of controversial copy with his name attached, evidence to be passed on to the police, the culprits who ran this ugly trade sent to gaol, newspapers selling like hot cakes – and he, Clive Potter, hailed as a national hero.

Tomorrow morning, early, he would call on Bartholomew Crowe, the editor of the *Pall Mall Gazette* and outline his proposal. But for now, he was hungry, he needed his supper.

"Rosalind," he shouted.

After eating he would need to sit down, make notes, refine every aspect of his plan and prepare himself for tomorrow's interview. But he couldn't concentrate on an empty stomach.

"Rosalind! For God's sake, woman! Where are you?"

Chapter Six

Originally, the Barrie family were millers though this fact was rarely, if ever, alluded to. Leopold's great-great-grandfather was the man who sowed the seeds to a fortune by building a mill on the river Arun near Horsham. One mill became several and several became a chain. Success and wealth ensued and within two generations the Barries had severed all links with the milling trade in favour of business interests that were less visible and more lucrative. Leopold's grandfather bought a baronetcy which his only grandson duly inherited.

In marrying the Honourable Constance Cockcroft, the daughter of Viscount Monmouth, Leopold had succeeded in pushing his ancestors' lowly commercial beginnings even further back into the past.

Leopold was very rich already. He had substantial shares in diamond and gold mines in South Africa – Cecil Rhodes was a personal friend – had stocks and bonds in a range of banks and institutions, owned property in Paris, New York and London and had vast tracts of land in Texas. The union with Constance made him richer still but, more importantly, it made him respectable.

Like all respectable men, he was always busy. The sheer number and variety of his investments commanded much of his time. He sat, when necessary, in the House of Lords and also served on several boards and committees, some of them for charities. The Metropole was his city hobby and he involved himself in the running of the theatre whenever he felt like it. When in the country, he liked to hunt and shoot. He bought art and thought nothing of criss-crossing Europe for weeks on end in search of obscure paintings and sculptures to add to his private collection.

In dealing with people, he could be diplomatic when he chose, appearing to be diffident when he was not at all and listening to every opinion when really he heeded only his own. Quite willing to force decisions, he did prefer to guide them and always began proceedings by employing, in a tactical way, his considerable charm.

And so it was at the next monthly meeting of the board of management of the Metropole Theatre that the board members believed it was they who selected the next play, they who offered the part of Paula Tanqueray to Marguerite Davenport, and they who drew up the actress's extremely generous contract of employment.

Marguerite Davenport received Lord Leopold one afternoon at her apartment. He put to her the offer from the Metropole and, though at first she was unwilling to commit, the more they spoke the more she felt her resistance weaken. She admitted, yes, her acting had become jaded at the Colosseum, the roles being either too familiar to her or of a type that fell in so completely with her stage persona that she performed them by instinct. Yes, she wanted something else, something better. She felt on the verge of accepting the new position but held back, saying she needed time to think. She was given one week to make up her mind.

Almost as soon as Leopold departed, doubts set in. The ten most important years of her life had been spent at the Colosseum. The successes there, the failures, the friendships, the enmities – these had shaped her, transformed her from the promising ingénue she had been, to the stage star she was today.

And what of the greatest influence of them all? Edmund. The man who had taught her, believed in her, befriended her, protected her, cared for her with such intensity. She had not yet mentioned the proposition to him but the thought plagued her as she returned to her dressing room, having just played Trilby for the one-hundred-and-fifth time.

The door closed behind her. She stepped out of her dress and left it in the middle of the floor. The skirt collapsed but the bodice remained stiff and upright so that the garment had the look of a proud but scuppered sailing ship. Marie, her dresser, came and picked it up, put it away. Marguerite wrapped herself up in a silk dressing gown and sat down at the mirror. She pulled off the blonde wig under which her own auburn hair was tied back and clipped flat to her head. She started to remove her make-up which was chalk-white to suggest, in the closing scenes of the play, Trilby's fading health.

Marie bustled about behind her, tidying and humming. She broke off and pointed to three bouquets lying on the floor.

"Lord Holbrook, Sir William Forbes and Mr. Cardew," she said, assigning each one its donor.

Marguerite's eye picked out the bunch of orange gladioli, a flower she detested. The stiff stalks were spread in a way that resembled a Scottish bagpipe.

"Mr. Cardew, I see, has excelled himself tonight," she said.

The girl laughed. "He tries so hard, Miss," she said.

Marguerite wiped away the last of the paint from her face. Beneath it, her skin was pink and living. Trilby had departed.

"Marie, darling, please tell me you can do something with my hair," she said, peering at herself in the mirror. "I'm having supper with Lewis tonight and that wig has ruined me."

Marie smiled as she took the clips out of Marguerite's hair, sprayed it with water and brushed it. She then proceeded to tuck and tie and finally produced a loose chignon that was very flattering.

Marguerite dusted herself with powder.

"I don't know what I'd do without you, Marie," she said into the mirror.

There was a knock on the door and Edmund came in. He sank into the armchair beside her.

"No, it really was the worst insult of my life," he said, continuing a conversation they had been having earlier. "In the third row of the stalls and she was knitting. That's enough to bring us a hundred years of bad luck. I saw her, everyone saw her, I could even hear the needles." He imitated the woman's action with his fingers, hunching his shoulders and pinching his lips in a study of fanatical concentration. "I was acting my heart out and she was knitting."

Marie giggled.

"Roger was right," Marguerite said. "We should have confiscated it."

"So much for my Svengali . . ."

"They're all the same, audiences, after the first month or so," Marguerite said. "It's as though really they meant to go and see George Robey at the Tivoli but by some accident they find themselves with us instead. And they're not best pleased."

Edmund laughed outright and Marguerite took the opportunity to dismiss Marie.

61

The girl put on her hat and coat.

"And please, take the flowers," Marguerite said to her.

"What, all of them, Miss?"

Marguerite nodded. "Perhaps your mother can make something of Mr. Cardew's offering. I'm afraid it's quite beyond me."

"Oh, thank you, Miss Davenport."

Marie swept up the flowers, cradling them in her arms. She reached for her umbrella which was hanging on the costume rail.

"Now, now, Marie, you won't be needing that," Edmund said. "I know what you've been up to, walking home on your own at night, but I won't have it, young lady. You're to use a cab like everyone else."

"But, Chief, it's only round the corner."

"It's not safe," he said. "And what I mean by that is, it's not safe for me. Your mother would have my guts for garters if she knew. Either take the cab or I will escort you home myself, not an option I'd recommend. I promise I'll make a show of you by singing 'The Maid and the Magpie' outside your front door in my best soprano, wake up all the neighbors. They'll be saying what low company Marie Lucas is keeping since she joined up that Colosseum."

"Then I'll take the cab, Chief," the girl said, reddening.

"Wise choice."

When Marie had departed, Edmund said, "Do you know, I think we should go back over the opening scene tomorrow afternoon, shake ourselves up a bit. Nothing to do with you, darling, you're perfect, but Roger has slumped rather. If we changed the rhythms a bit, it might bring him to life. What do you think?"

"Fine by me," she said.

He picked up a Lyceum programme that was lying on the

dressing table and began to leaf through it while Marguerite finished her toilette.

A memory came to her unbidden. She had been in hospital for six weeks, having undergone surgery to her back during the course of which she had been advised never to have children as a pregnancy could cause irreparable damage to her spine. This news combined with the pain she had endured and the long period of inactivity had depressed her so much that, when it came time to return to work, she did not want to. That first day back turned out to be a drab afternoon in March and her spirits were so low that everything, even her movements and thoughts, seemed unfocused. The theatre was darker and danker than ever. She felt like running away except that she knew there was no escaping the terrible loss of never having children of her own.

But when she entered her dressing room what a sight awaited her. The room was awash with daffodils. The walls and the ceiling were carpeted with them and on the floor there were vases and glass bowls filled with them. Her mirror was framed with daffodils, her screens covered in them. They were all over her table, in cups and bottles and in amongst her face creams and make-up, her brushes and combs. It was like stepping into a golden shrine with light so strong it lit up every part of you, even the inside. She could not help but smile to be surrounded like this and the tears that came to her eyes had nothing to do with grief.

It was all Edmund's doing.

"A little sunshine to pierce the gloom," he had said, standing behind her.

She didn't want this memory now. Emotional ties should not be allowed to dictate the course of a career.

Edmund was studying the cast list in the Lyceum's programme with great intent. His hair was beginning to turn silver, just enough to gleam beneath the lights.

"Good God, they've taken Paul Lloyd back," he said, with a guffaw. "I would have thought he was finished after that drunken —"

"Edmund, I've had an offer from the Metropole," Marguerite said. "A contract for five years on very generous terms. They'll be opening the new season with *The Second Mrs. Tanqueray* and they want me for Paula."

Edmund looked at her, then back at the programme as though seeking confirmation from the written word that he had heard her right. Then he tossed it aside.

"I knew this would happen," he said, with a sigh. "Have you given them an answer?"

"Not yet."

"If it is a question of money, and I rather think it is not, the Colosseum can better anything the Metropole has proposed."

"You are right, it is not about money." She found it impossible to expand further or even to look at him so she distracted herself by tightening the lids on all the pots in front of her.

Edmund said, "You have wanted for a long time to do Pinero and I have ignored that fact. I should never have gone ahead with *Julius Caesar*. There is nothing in it for you, nothing to speak of. We cannot change it now but we could discuss the next . . . I am open to suggestions. I know sometimes I behave like a tin-pot tyrant but . . . dammit, Marguerite, I don't want you to go."

"And I don't know if I want to leave either but sometimes I feel so . . . empty . . . Having said that, when it comes to the crunch I don't seem able to make up my mind . . . I hate it, this indecision." She was close to tears.

They sat for a while in a deep silence until Marguerite spoke again.

"And then I start to think about all the plays we've done

together, you and I. Even that awful one of Buckstone's when, at great expense, Eleonora Duse made a special appearance as Mrs. Fosbroke and no one in the audience could understand her accent. Or that time in *The Corsican Brothers* when you fell through the trapdoor in the fight scene. And remember that dress, the one I wore for Lady Macbeth that had beetles' wings sewn into it. And the night you said, 'baboon's blood' instead of 'dragoon's blood'. . ." They both managed to raise a laugh at this. "I learned everything I know, from you."

"That kind of modesty doesn't suit you, Marguerite."

Edmund's mouth was a thin, tight line. Perhaps he was angry with her.

"You are a great actress and I think you know that. Certainly, I knew it the very first time I saw you on stage. Since then you have devoted yourself to the Colosseum utterly and completely. I couldn't have asked for more."

Marguerite sighed, got up, went to her wardrobe to select a gown for the evening then felt unequal to the task and sat down again.

"I have wanted this for so long," she said. "And now that it has come . . ."

Edmund was sitting with his hands clasped between his knees, shoulders hunched. His expression betrayed nothing.

"As you know, I hold rather old-fashioned views on the drama," he said, straightening. "I favour the Romantic Classical repertoire and that happens to suit the audiences here. This is a large theatre and we cannot afford to take risks. If the fare here no longer satisfies you then I think you should seriously consider the Metropole's offer. You have a duty to yourself as an actress not to regret what might have been." He rested one hand on his thigh like an old man with a bad back. "You will be sorely missed from this theatre both professionally and personally. It will be a dreadful loss to me not to have you by my side . . ." He took a deep breath to control the flow of emotion that was breaking through. He was giving her what she hadn't realized she wanted: her release. "You owe nothing to the Colosseum or to me, Marguerite. If ever there was a debt, it has been repaid umpteen times."

Marguerite got up. "Generous to a fault," she said, leaning down to put her arms around his neck. "I have never deserved you. Am I a fool to leave?"

"I would be a fool to stop you."

She rested her cheek on top of his head and he gripped her arms, wrapped himself up in them and they rocked back and forth together in a silent, loving farewell.

They were parted by a knock at the door and Lewis's entrance.

Evidently he had come straight from his bath, as his blond hair was still damp and a little unruly, his sallow skin tinged pink. Unusually, he was wearing a stiff, high collar. He was handsome without realizing it and Marguerite felt a surge of pride as much for his unaffectedness as for his good looks.

"Edmund, you remember Lewis, my baby brother," Marguerite said. "Just returned from Paris."

Edmund rose to shake hands.

"It must be five or six years since I had the pleasure," he said.

Marguerite slipped behind the screen to get dressed while the two men talked about the play. Once again, she was grateful to Edmund. This time for simply behaving normally with Lewis, as if the Fleming sodomy trial had never happened. The repercussions for Lewis of supporting his friend, Robbie Fleming, in court had been severe. He had lost his job, been shunned by many and, eventually, for fear of prosecution himself, had gone abroad. But that danger was past now and he was back in London where Marguerite intended to keep him.

She put on a sombre, charcoal-coloured silk and chose to wear only a pearl-encrusted brooch with it. Now that her mind was made up regarding the Metropole's offer, she was gripped by a kind of delirium. Hardly happiness, more like a backlog of emotion that she found disorientating. She saw from her reflection in the mirror that even the plain grey dress did not deaden her vitality. Her eyes glittered, her complexion was luminous. She took down a black cashmere shawl and, rather guiltily, covered herself with it.

"Where are you dining?" she heard Edmund ask Lewis.

"The Cecil."

"They have a new chef," Marguerite said, rejoining them now. "From Paris too. Used to be in that famous place just off the Champs Élysées, *très chic* . . . the name escapes me . . ."

"Fabien's," Lewis said.

Edmund raised his eyebrows. "You know it?"

"Know *of* it. I rarely dine in the best sort of restaurants," Lewis said. "Except when I'm with my famous sister, of course."

"The reason he doesn't eat in good restaurants is because he shuns society, Edmund. He'd much rather have a bowl of soup in a backstreet tavern than the most sumptuous dinner in a top-class hotel."

Lewis grinned. "Totally untrue. But I'll admit that the finest company and cuisine can be had in the lowliest of places. I refuse to be fooled into thinking I am eating well simply because a place has linen napkins and pompous waiters."

"Tonight, however, he is obliging me. There will be napkins and pompous waiters a-plenty," Marguerite said.

Perhaps she was being too effusive in her attempt to dispel the awful sadness that was welling up inside her. She patted Lewis on the chest.

"Very dapper," she said.

On cue, Lewis pulled at his collar and muttered in his good-humoured way something about how outdated it was to have a dress code.

"Perhaps you'd care to join us for supper, sir?" he said to Edmund.

Marguerite was taken by surprise as Lewis never issued invitations to people he hardly knew.

Edmund was gracious but declined, saying he had a prior engagement. But, before they left, he took Marguerite's hand in his, put it to his lips, kissed it. He did not say goodbye. If he had, it would have destroyed her.

Chapter Seven

It was in the National Portrait Gallery that Edmund and Violet first met. Edmund had been invited to deliver the inaugural address in a series of lectures. Each week, distinguished practitioners from a range of artistic disciplines were given the freedom to talk about whatever they desired.

Edmund's topic was one dear to his heart: 'Acting – Towards Respectability'. He had opened with a quotation from the Reverend Thomas Best, a clergyman who, at the beginning of the century, had raged against the theatre and the loose morals it encouraged.

"'*Contamination by the stage is worse than Cholera, for whereas the victim of that disease will go to Heaven, those who frequent the theatre will, most assuredly, go to Hell.*'"

A ripple of laughter went around the room as Edmund knew it would. He pointed out that today such comments were greeted with amusement and disbelief and that this was evidence of how far the profession had come since the Reverend's time. The drive to improve standards had been generated from within the acting fraternity, he said. He described the extravagantly ambitious productions of Edmund Kean and the lengths to which William Charles Macready went to rid his premises of the prostitution and drinking that had overtaken most other theatres. He spoke too of the role that royal patronage had played in encouraging serious drama and improving moral standards.

"Through the efforts of so many who have gone before," he said, "so many actors and actresses who suffered privation and abuse because of the way they made their living, this profession is now a truly honourable one. Long may it continue."

There was loud applause when Edmund finished and then he took questions from the floor. Most of these did not relate to his speech at all. The audience wanted to know what parts he most enjoyed playing, how he prepared for them, who were his own favourite actors and how he was able to play twins on stage at the same time, a feat he had performed fairly recently in *The Corsican Brothers*. One man stood up and said that he believed Edmund Jeffers, through his magnificent work at the Colosseum, had done more than any man in England to bring theatre and the drama "out of the Dark Ages" and every man, woman and child should be very proud of that fact. This resulted in a standing ovation.

Afterwards, champagne was served and Edmund mingled. He was congratulated at every turn and just to get a breather he separated himself from the main crowd and sauntered up to the first floor, glass in hand, to view the artwork.

Edmund was already acquainted with Lord Leopold Barrie and, when they ran into each other in front of a drawing by Constable, they stopped to exchange greetings. Leopold introduced his daughter, Violet. She had accompanied him to the lecture that night because Lady Barrie was indisposed. They discussed Edmund's speech, the drawings and paintings in their vicinity, the recent renovations to the building. Throughout all this, Violet remained detached. At first, Edmund took her silence for rudeness but her expression was pleasant and alert and it became plain to him that she was more entertained by her own thoughts, by her own assimilation of what was going on around her, to take much notice of direct conversation. She held her father's arm and stood a little bit back from him, demurring to his presence or perhaps using him as a shield. Edmund was so accustomed to fervid greetings from lady admirers that Violet's inattention intrigued him. He saw her indifference as a challenge.

"Such a pleasure to meet you, Miss Barrie," he said when Leopold was drawn away to one side by another acquaintance. "Especially given the dismal company that surrounds us." He pointed out one or two of the grimmer portraits glowering down at them from the walls.

"Well, I suppose, compared to them I have a somewhat pleasing countenance. Is that the way you compliment all your lady friends?"

Edmund, appalled by his own insensitivity, could not assess the extent of the damage done. Was Violet seriously offended by his careless remark? Or perhaps, as he suspected, she was amused.

"Forgive me, I honestly didn't mean that the way it sounded," he said. "Please accept my most humble apologies." He bowed to her.

"I've been warned about actors," Violet said. "Not to believe a word they say."

"Then I am damned from the outset," Edmund said. "Though I should like to know by whom."

"Didn't someone once state that acting and dissembling were one and the same thing? A famous philosopher. Yes, one of the Greeks, I'm sure," she said, with a playful look in her eye.

"Then your Greek philosopher was confused. To dissemble, one must conceal, while acting is all about revelation."

"I stand corrected," she said, her gaze floating away.

"Tell me, what other communications have you had recently from the Ancient Greeks?"

Her eyes shot back to him and she laughed.

They met each other for the next five weeks at the same event. He and Violet formed the habit of strolling around the gallery together after the lecture, commenting on the paintings, joking about this one's funny moustache or that one's haunted eyes and they would chat about things that had happened to them in the intervening days. It had been suggested to Edmund that at his age, thirty-three, he should be married and while he had supposed marriage to be quite possible it had remained a rather vague notion until Violet presented herself. As a prospective wife she was very attractive, having status – the daughter of a peer of the realm on one side and old nobility on the other – and wealth, as well as good looks. Her figure was slight, athletic, almost boyish but very delicate, and she had pale skin and full rounded lips of the deepest, natural red. She was much younger than he but, as the only child of attentive parents, she had grown up quickly and seemed older than her twenty-two years. Did she possess charm? Not the easy, platitudinous kind, certainly, but she was plucky and he admired that.

He began thinking of her one afternoon, anticipating their next meeting, and realized that not only did he enjoy her company but over the preceding weeks he had, in effect, been wooing her.

The lectures ended but the courtship progressed. Edmund became aware of an edginess to her nature. It was like knowing there were seething currents of water beneath pack ice. Moods would descend from nowhere and then just disappear. She seemed either satisfied with everything in her life or else wholly dissatisfied. Her dark brown eyes, soft one minute, harsh the next, held the key to her feelings, if only one could read them.

One day, in a moment of quiet confession while she was sitting on her childhood swing in the garden of her parents' London home, she told Edmund of an incident that took place while she was at finishing school in Vernier, not far from Geneva.

It happened one Sunday afternoon, she said. They were all supposed to be in the library writing letters home but she had slipped out to keep a rendezvous with Gustav Finkler, the local apothecary's son for whom she had a fancy. She sat side-saddle on the bar of his bicycle and they ventured out into the countryside for a picnic – unchaperoned, of course. When they returned, the school principal and Gustav's father were waiting for them in the town square. Gustav got a boxing from Mr. Finkler for canoodling with a lord's daughter and Violet was whisked back to school by Miss Wren, who was white-faced with fury. Miss Wren did her best to hush up the matter, more for the school's sake than to save her errant pupil's reputation, and wanted to send Violet back to England. It was only by Leopold's intercession and a very substantial donation to the school fund that his daughter's expulsion was averted.

Violet assured Edmund that no actual indiscretion occurred. It was puzzling though that, while she treated the whole episode rather like a joke, she seemed nervous in the telling of it. He began to suspect that the event had greater significance than she admitted. Perhaps she had really loved this young man? Perhaps the assignation was not quite as innocent as described? Many suitors would have shied away at the merest hint of injudicious behaviour on the part of the beloved one, but for Edmund this proof of venality in Violet's character – as opposed to wickedness – proved enchanting.

A matter of days after this conversation took place, Edmund asked Violet to marry him.

Lord Leopold and Lady Constance were keen that the

wedding of their only child should be celebrated in the church on their country estate at Warrickstown. Edmund was categorical that it should take place in London. For convenience, he said, but the real reason for his obstinacy was that he wanted to plant a marker early on. For, while there were many positives associated with this newly formed link to the Barrie family, Edmund felt it needed to be made clear from the very beginning that, despite their immense wealth and influence, he would never subjugate his own wishes to those of his in-laws.

In a move much appreciated by Edmund, Violet concurred with her fiancé's view that London was the better venue and, though she came under pressure from her parents, she did not waver. They were married at St. Martin-in-the-Fields in Trafalgar Square on the 4th of May, 1893.

At their house in Belgrave Square, Edmund and Violet were breakfasting in the dining room. With three tall windows facing east, the sun would have streamed in unchecked but for the blinds being half-lowered. Neither husband nor wife could bear brilliance first thing in the morning.

There was a pile of letters by Edmund's plate. He picked one up and opened it. Sitting sideways to the table, his legs took warmth from the sunshine while his upper body remained in the shade cast by the blinds. The letter was unimportant and he discarded it, returning to his plate of bloaters and grilled tomatoes. He ate because he knew he should. His appetite was always small.

Violet, opposite, took the top off her boiled egg, burned her finger, sucked it.

"Was it very late when you got home last night?" she asked.

"One-ish, I think," Edmund said. "Conan Doyle was in magnificent form, one story after another, no stopping the man."

He leaned back in his chair, buttered himself a piece of toast. "But then, what would you expect from a man in love?"

Violet looked up from her egg.

"Who is it now?"

"A Jean something – another singer, only this time one who can actually sing."

"No doubt she is beautiful too. Ugly men are always such sticklers in that department," Violet said. "Not that his infatuations ever last long. I expect this one will be over by lunch."

"No, no, this time it is Love. He has set her up in a flat in Chelsea. He stays there when he's up from the country."

"Is that all you men do at these dinners – gossip about each other's love affairs?"

"The whole world knows about this one," Edmund said, opening another letter. "Arthur makes no secret of it."

"I pity his poor wife. She's not well, Edmund, you know that, don't you?"

"Oh, Louisa doesn't have an inkling about any of this. Anyway there's never any impropriety in these little passions of his. He picks these goddesses and then he loves them from afar, so to speak. This one is no different, even if he is seriously in love. You know Arthur – his sense of honour is unfailing."

"How can you say so, Edmund? The man is in love with a woman not his wife." Violet was flushed. "What does he do about it? Does he try to forget her, does he distance himself from her? No. He pursues her, forms a relationship with her, even lives under the one roof with her whenever it suits him. And, what's worse, makes a public show of it. To vindicate himself he has chosen to broadcast certain details which suggest that, technically at least, he is not adulterous. But really, Edmund, anyone with any moral courage must see that, in essence, he is unfaithful. This is your honourable man?"

It had been Edmund's intention merely to inform his wife of a fact that she would hear soon enough from another source. He had not envisaged a wrangle. He wanted an end to the conversation.

"He believes he is doing the honourable thing and I have to admit that, on the whole, I think he is too. He is protecting his wife from –"

"Then he, and you, are wrong," Violet said. "In fact, Arthur is doubly dishonourable. He is misrepresenting himself to two women."

Edmund sought sanctuary in the letter he was holding. The silence that fell opened a disturbing space between them.

After a while, Violet poured herself another cup of tea, took a sip, then put it down. When she spoke, her voice was bright, like she had decided to begin the morning all over again.

"Have you decided yet who is to replace Marguerite?" she said.

He refrained from looking up. "You know we haven't. Charles and I must discuss the contract first."

The truth was that he didn't even want to think about Marguerite's successor. Marguerite was gone – there had been prolonged and emotional tributes to her – and yet he did not feel their partnership was truly dissolved. There was no one to match her. She was irreplaceable, of that he was sure. Her on-stage style so perfectly complemented his own that as a pair they were complete. While he gave physical expression to the inner torments of a character, she was mainly pictorial in her approach – all grand gestures and uncomplicated emotions delivered with such honesty that she could melt the hearts of any audience. They played well off each other. It was as though their bodies were linked by invisible threads so that a movement in one created a corresponding movement in the other. It was the kind of symbiotic union that he wanted to have again but knew he never would.

"You and Charles have discussed names, surely?" Violet said.

"Very briefly, hardly at all. It's something we must do."

"What are your thoughts on the matter?"

"Ellen Terry would, of course, be marvellous," he heard himself say. "But I doubt we can poach her from the Lyceum."

"Does it have to be someone of that stature?"

"Other possibles are Rose Saunders, Sarah Goody, Mary Nugent, I suppose." He scanned the last letter, rose from the table.

"The Squire and Marie Bancroft made a very successful team," Violet said, out of nowhere.

Edmund laughed. "As do Benson and Hedges, if it comes to that."

"What I mean is, they are husband and wife and have done very well together . . . I just wondered if my name had ever been mentioned during your discussions with Charles . . ."

It took him a moment to realize what she meant. He sat down again.

"My dear woman, I had no idea you were interested."

"I'm not looking for any favours," she said. Her manner was very correct as though she was dealing with a stranger. "I thought I might have been considered on my own merits. I have been with the company for four years and I have played countless minor roles and some secondary ones. I have never suffered a bad notice. In fact, the *Saturday Review* thought my Helena very good indeed −"

"Please, Violet, I am perfectly well aware of your considerable accomplishments." Violet was, and probably always would be, an adequate bit player but no more. Her acting, her approach to the work, her ideas surrounding it, were uninspired. "You must do comedy," he said. "It would suit you. Yes, I'm convinced it would. People think acting comes by instinct but it doesn't – it's a craft. There is nothing natural about acting. It takes time to learn that." He played with the cutlery on the table. He knew he had not succeeded in distracting her. "No," he said, finally. "I do not think you have yet fully served your apprenticeship."

She got up, went to the window and hoisted up the blind. She frowned as the sunshine hit her.

"You're disappointed, I know you are, and I'm sorry for that." He followed her, rested his hands on her shoulders, kissed the top of her head. Her body was rigid.

Violet said, "So when, in your estimation, will I be ready to take on the leading roles? I don't see why you can't give me a chance like you would anyone else. Perhaps it is a disadvantage to be your wife."

"You understand, I know you do, that I must do whatever is best for the theatre," Edmund said, removing his hands from her shoulders. "The staff and actors rely on me to make the right decisions. I cannot allow you to take on a role that is beyond your ability. You lack the experience to –"

"I lack the experience because you will not give it to me."

Edmund walked back to the table, sat down again.

"You have never yet demonstrated that you can inhabit a character in the way that you should or that you can cómmand the stage with your presence. We are not talking here of some tupenny ha'penny parish hall where everyone comes along to see brothers, sisters, uncles, aunts in action. This is the Colosseum. Massive amounts of money go into every production here. We cannot afford to fail. It's a huge responsibility taking a leading role in one of the Colosseum's plays. We cannot risk the fortunes of everyone involved in the theatre to satisfy one of your fancies!"

"When will I be ready then? How long does it take?"

"I cannot say."

The silence that followed almost suffocated them both. Edmund hadn't realized that Violet's aspirations ran so high or perhaps he would have steered her earlier onto another path. He had presumed that acting was to be a pastime for her, nothing more. Her father was a dilettante and he had taken it for granted that Violet would be happy to be one too.

He glanced at his fob watch.

"Lawrence will be waiting for me at the South Kensington. I must go."

Violet continued to stare out of the window.

"We could do *Our American Cousin* if you were interested," he said to her back. "Some fine comic moments in that. Or perhaps Wilde. You said you liked Wilde."

She turned around then. The sun lit her from behind, gilding the stray hairs around her head, igniting them. Her face remained in shadow.

"It was not by chance that Marguerite was offered another position," she said, her anger quite evident despite the measured words.

"What do you mean?"

"I mean these things don't happen by accident."

"I don't understand . . ." he said, though he was beginning to. "Are you saying that you had Marguerite removed?"

"Hardly removed. She was, by all accounts, very eager to accept the Metropole's offer."

"So your father had a hand in this?"

"More than a hand."

"Why? Why would you do it? So you can get better parts? Surely not." Edmund had seen his wife behave spitefully on occasion – a flash of temper over an ill-chosen gift or a moment of impatience with one of the servants – but nothing on this scale. It made him wonder if he had read the situation correctly. "Violet, please tell me that's not the reason."

Violet sighed heavily. She did not move or speak in her defence.

Edmund crumpled. This was more than selfishness, there was malice in it. Violet knew well that Marguerite's departure from the Colosseum would affect him deeply and permanently and yet she had engineered it for her own gain. He had to sit down.

"You would do this for a role in a play?"

"I would do this, and more, to win the respect that should be mine."

"Then you have failed utterly," Edmund said, straightening. "You are nothing but a spoilt child, Violet. That is all you will ever be."

"Thank you for that, Edmund," she said, with chilling intensity. "And while we are being brutally honest with each other, I should inform you . . . it is my duty to inform you, that Mrs. Curran has made a decision regarding the sale of her share of the theatre."

This was news to Edmund. "Really?"

"You will be pleased to hear that she is selling it to my father."

"*What?*" Edmund turned to stone.

"Yes, they met at the races in Sandown. The deal was done over dinner. We celebrated with pink champagne."

"You were there? Leopold is shortly to own ninety per cent of the Colosseum and I wasn't even told?"

She nodded. Another betrayal.

"Good God, Violet, what kind of a wife does this to her husband?" His left knee started jumping and he had a curious melting sensation in his stomach. "Let me get this straight. You told Leopold that Mrs. Curran was selling, you encouraged this, even though you knew your father was the last person on earth I would want to be involved with?"

"My father is as good an owner as any."

"No, he is not." Edmund stood up suddenly. "He is too rich, too influential and too damned opinionated to do business with ... this puts me in an impossible position. I cannot work with the likes of him."

"Perhaps you have had your own way for long enough."

"What is that supposed to mean?"

She dismissed his question with a shake of her head but her eyes were fearful as if she had not, until now, fully realized the extent of her transgressions.

He turned on her.

"You have behaved abominably, there is no other word for it. Acting against your own husband's interests. Have you no loyalty? I can't believe you have done this – taken Marguerite from me and now, yes, my theatre too – and all so that you can indulge some private whim of your own, some notion, some ridiculous plan that you, of all people, should become an actress."

Violet, who had been so controlled throughout, sparked at this. She flew from the window, leaned right across the table at him, her eyes horribly dark and staring.

"No," she said. "You are the one with the notions and plans. That is a luxury forbidden to me."

Chapter Eight

It was too late to try and change Mrs. Curran's mind. Papers had already been signed, the deposit paid. The sale was well on the way to being finalized. A financial settlement was to be made on Edmund in consideration of the renovations carried out at the theatre but he had as yet received no communication from Leopold or his solicitor regarding what arrangements, if any, would be put in place for future leasings of the Colosseum. Charles had written twice to open the discussion but there had been no response.

Despite the air of uncertainty, business carried on as usual. *Trilby* had been well received by critics and audiences alike though there had been a marked decline in attendances following Marguerite's departure from the company. Her understudy, Alice Hedderman, had replaced her in the role but the search was still on for a permanent leading lady. To play Trilby O'Ferrall at such short notice was a lot to ask of Alice and, though there were some nice touches to her performance, there was nothing unique in her handling of the character. Before leaving, Marguerite had coached her well and perhaps that was a mistake because what they now had was a Trilby similar to the original, but very much a paler, diluted version.

Alice was not easy to act with and Edmund did not enjoy the experience. It felt lonely being on stage with her. She lacked intuition, could not vary the pace to suit the audience and even though she was younger and slimmer by far than Marguerite, her movements were not as fluid. She was always bumping into furniture or sitting down too heavily, which was probably due to nerves, but these blunders seemed to knock everyone else off balance too.

Julius Caesar was due to open early in September and Edmund put all his energies into this. The play did not require a strong female lead, which was convenient, and with all the preparation and research that had been done he had high hopes for it. A successful run was vital. Good box office returns would hopefully strengthen Edmund's bargaining power with his father-in-law when it came to renegotiating the lease. For Leopold was a businessman before anything else and properly respectful of a healthy bank balance. Also, Edmund reasoned, if they were making a fat profit, Leopold was far less likely to interfere with the way the theatre was being run. And then there was the Lord Chamberlain to impress – Edmund wanted his name on that Honours List and what better way to achieve it than with an artistic and commercial success? *Julius Caesar*, then, was to be his showcase.

Edmund engaged Lawrence Alma-Tadema to design the set and costumes. For several weeks, the two of them haunted the Roman Gallery and the Graeco-Roman rooms at the British Museum, seeking out paintings, statuary, architecture, pottery, sarcophagi, reliefs, mosaics, anything that would help them towards an authentic recreation of Ancient Rome.

In the Reading Room, Edmund spent most of his time boning up on Roman history. Among other tomes, he consumed Plutarch's *The Lives of the Noble Grecians and Romans*, which was Shakespeare's own source material. His stack of notes grew by the day and when he didn't feel like writing he just read and let himself absorb the words, the ideas, the images. *Julius Caesar* was a difficult play to interpret. Were the assassins right to kill Caesar? Did they topple a tyrant or destroy a hero? Were they farseeing men or were they deluded? Were they honourable or dishonourable? To understand the setting, was to understand the play.

In Lawrence Alma-Tadema, Edmund found a man who shared his passion for authenticity. He was a gentle, quiet man, methodical in his ways but with the broadest and bravest artistic vision. Their collaboration was a happy one. This plundering of history and the flood of ideas it released Edmund likened to bathing in the ocean during a storm. It was thunderous, dizzying, exhilarating. And sometimes, exhausting.

Almost the whole afternoon had been spent 'dressing' the new play. For several hours, Edmund, Lawrence and Charles had sat in the darkened auditorium while Wardrobe arranged various swatches of cloth under limelight and gaslight for them to judge the effects.

There were always times like this leading up to a new production when one's energy flagged. The day's proceedings had tired Edmund disproportionately and, despite resting beforehand, his performance that night as Svengali, which he had to admit had been faltering of late, reached a new low. As soon as the curtain fell, he returned to his dressing room without speaking to anyone and locked the door behind him. Not even Charles could coax him out.

Despair had been dogging him for the last couple of days and now, with this last indignity, he let it close in. His head was full of problems. They had overrun the budget for *Julius Caesar* by several thousand pounds already, with still more to do. Then there was Marguerite's departure and his fruitless search for a replacement, and Leopold's purchase of the Colosseum and what it would mean for everyone who currently worked there. On top of that, relations between himself and Violet had been strained of late, and his own workload and the ever-watchful eye of the Lord Chamberlain just added to the stress.

He removed his make-up and got dressed, gripped by a sudden desire for anonymity. Even though the weather was mild for the time of year, he put on his great coat, turned up the collar and wrapped a scarf around his neck. He listened and when it was quiet slipped out of his room unseen, went down the corridor and out through the side door which led into a deserted alleyway.

Before emerging onto the Strand, Edmund took a moment to linger in the shadows and watch. Light spilled out from the entrance of the Colosseum. Several carriages were waiting for patrons presumably still ensconced in the downstairs saloon bar. There was a scattering of men and women in evening dress conversing on the steps. One lady was having trouble with her shoe and she was using the arm of a very handsome young man to balance herself while she tried to fix it. Both were laughing.

Edmund turned in the opposite direction and headed along the crowded street towards Waterloo Bridge. He pulled his collar in tighter. The atmosphere seemed somehow thick and there were smuts in the air. Sounds were muffled and the lighted street lamps bled into the darkness like watercolour, wet on wet.

He crossed the river and scuttled into the laneways beyond. His pace slackened to match the momentum of Southwark pedestrians who seemed to have significantly less sense of purpose than those on the other side of the Thames. The sweaty armpit smell of yeast and hops from Barclay & Perkins caught at the back of his throat until he got used to it. The area was not alien to Edmund. He wandered as far as St. George's Church in the Borough where a dead dog lay against the churchyard wall. The lane being too narrow for a vehicle of any kind, it was a mystery how the animal had met its end. Blood, no more than a thimbleful, had congealed on the ground beneath its nose. It was a miserable sight, made all the more so by the fact that the poor creature displayed no outward signs of injury. People passed by without a glance but Edmund was drawn to watch over it as though he expected it, any moment, to get up and walk. It was only when an old woman said, "That your dog?" that he said no, and turned away. Perhaps a drink would help relax him, lift his spirits. He knew of a public house nearby that he had been in once before and now he sought it out.

There was no light on in the porch of The Bricklayer's Arms but he could see that the china plates which decorated the walls in that tiny space were chipped. He stood looking at them for some time, listening to his own breathing before committing himself to the interior.

Inside was bright, with mirrors everywhere and brass taps and a brass foot rail that ran the length of the bar. Brass spittoons too. The room smelled of sour milk. Behind the bar, up high, there were porcelain barrels with pictures of stags on them and ornate lettering that declared the contents to be Jamaica Rum, Pale Brandy, Special Scotch. There was sawdust on the floor and the ceiling was baked brown from nicotine. A few men, still in their working clothes though it was late now, leaned on the bar, feeble from drink. In front of the darkened window, a group of young men, respectably dressed, were playing cards.

Edmund ordered a brandy and took it into the snug at the far end. He sat, took a gulp of his drink, leaned back so his head rested on the panel behind and closed his eyes. Possibly he fell asleep for a few minutes. Certainly he heard no one approach but became gradually aware of a presence. His eyelids flickered and he caught glimpses of cavalry twill pants, a brown plaid jacket, a pint pot on the table. When he opened his eyes fully he saw they belonged to a renegade from the poker party, a handsome fellow in his late twenties who sat sideways on his chair with one arm hanging over the back of it. He had a cigarette in the other hand. His head was tilted back as he blew smoke rings up at the ceiling.

"By all means, make yourself comfortable," Edmund said.

Detecting hostility, the young man shrugged and started to get up.

"Don't mind me," Edmund said, relenting. "I've a savage tongue when I'm tired. Please, join me."

"Promise you won't bite?" his new companion said, resuming his seat.

"Promise."

"Haven't seen you hereabouts before," the stranger said. His face, wide at the cheekbones, tapered down to an insignificant chin and gave the impression it was draining away, like sand through an egg-timer.

"Just out for a stroll, got thirsty."

"You came to the right place then." The man's mouth was so small that when he grinned it left the rest of his features unaffected.

"What's your name, my friend?" Edmund said.

"Gilbert."

"In that case," Edmund said, "I'm Sullivan. Which makes us a tuneful pair, at any rate."

Gilbert swallowed the last of his drink and Edmund went to

the bar to buy him another pint of bitter and for himself a double brandy. When he returned to the table, Gilbert was jacketless, his sleeves rolled up to reveal muscular arms. Beneath the taut cotton of his shirt it was evident that his shoulders and chest were well developed.

He worked as a clerk, he said. "In a posh counting house."

"That explains the physique then," Edmund said, with a smirk.

"Heavy ledgers and very high shelves," Gilbert said, demonstrating a movement akin to lifting weights. "What about you, Sullivan? In between waving your stick about, what do you do?"

"See these?" Edmund said, spreading his hands like fans in front of his face. "These are the tools of a Master Magician. In these here fingertips, there is magic."

Gilbert raised an eyebrow. "You should let me be the judge of that," he said.

Edmund's mouth was dry, his head fuzzy and aching with a familiar tension. It was not too late to disentangle himself. He could get up now and walk out, never come back here again. Instead he asked Gilbert for his hand, took it in his own, traced lines on the palm of it with his trembling forefinger.

"Can you feel it, the magic?" he said.

A seriousness had descended on them both.

"It's potent," Gilbert whispered, his fingers closing over Edmund's.

They walked to a house that was divided into flats, one upstairs, one down. Inside the front door, before a flight of bare, wooden steps, Edmund put his arm around Gilbert's waist, slipping his hand beneath the belt at the front.

"Take your time, mate," Gilbert said. "Let's get inside first."

Upstairs there was a small sitting room with a bedroom on

the left. As soon as they got in, they fell against the wall, bumping heads, devouring each other. Edmund could feel and hear the other man's rising breath. He pulled off Gilbert's jacket, yanked the shirt over his head but the buttons of his fly were too tight against what was inside so he left them to their owner to undo. Edmund, his lungs heaving, flung off his coat and his trousers and then, somehow, the two of them were on the floor, grappling with each other, slithering, striving for the bed. Gilbert bent over the side of it, his legs splayed. Edmund was on his knees behind, his hands working Gilbert's pelvis beneath him. The relief, the smell of this man's body, the vigour of the act finally drew forth a great bellow from Edmund as though he was proclaiming an oath from on high.

That night the bed was too warm and they were too lustful to rest properly. Edmund woke at first light, the sheets sweaty and twisted around his legs. He opened his eyes to find Gilbert beside him with his boots, vest and trousers on. He was propped up on pillows, smoking a cigarette.

"You've got to go soon," he said, without looking at Edmund. He plucked a speck of tobacco off his tongue with a finger, wiped it on the sheet. "My mate works nights. He'll be home soon."

Edmund took in the room. A bed and a chest of drawers were the only furniture. There was a large window with curtains made of such thin stuff that the sun shone right through them, showing up every thread. There was a smell of onions cooking in the downstairs flat. For some reason this made him wonder if Gilbert was a molly and he tried to remember on what terms they had left the pub the previous night but couldn't. He didn't want to insult the man by offering him money if it wasn't appropriate. He covered his eyes with his hand as much to block out thought as light.

"I'm a soldier," Gilbert said, as though Edmund had enquired.

"You've got a soldier's stamina, right enough," Edmund said, nudging Gilbert's upper arm with his knuckles.

Gilbert pulled away. "Royal Artillery. Woolwich. Ring any bells?"

Edmund's mouth was dry and sticky. He needed a glass of water but denied himself.

"Last year I was in a play," Gilbert went on. "*The Lady of Lyons*, it was. Right load of hokum. A hundred and fifty of us got taken on as Supers." His eyes were deeper set than Edmund remembered from the previous night and so small that it seemed the high cheekbones below and heavy brow above were closing in over them. "We had to march across the stage like we were a complete regiment. On one side, off the other, then round the back and start all over again. I think the way you described it was 'in an unbroken procession'."

Edmund kept his eyes covered. "Is this leading somewhere?" he said.

"Well, it's leading up to the fact that I know who you are, chum." His voice rasped, like a razor slicing through paper. "I'd like to say the pleasure has been all mine, but I think mostly it was yours, Mr. Jeffers."

"No, you are mistaken, my . . ."

Gilbert grinned and nodded to Edmund's great coat, still lying on the floor. "Your credentials have been checked, no use in denying it."

Edmund swung his legs out of the bed and sat on the side of it. He felt sick, very sick. He pulled his clothes over towards him, got dressed where he was, trying to keep his movements slow and deliberate, not wanting it to look as though he was running away.

"Your friend will be back soon," he said.

"Did I mention that my friend is having difficulty with the rent at present?" Gilbert said.

Edmund nodded. "I suspected he might." He stood up, took out his pocket book and emptied it on the bed – two sovereigns, a half sovereign and miscellaneous coin – about the equivalent of a month's pay for this man. "It's all I have," he said.

"That should cover it," Gilbert said. "But understand this. Rent has to be paid every month. Two and a half sovereigns, come hail or come shine."

"No," Edmund said. "It ends here."

Gilbert was ominously still. "It ends when I say it does."

"I will not be blackmailed. I've paid you more than decently." He put on his coat, checked that he was leaving nothing behind. "Look," he said. "Let's forget this little unpleasantness. We had a good time. Shake my hand."

Gilbert pinched out the burning tip of his cigarette between finger and thumb, put it behind his ear for later.

"You've missed the point, Edmund, old chum," he said. "It's not about whether I'm happy with your little gift – it's about how much value you put on your good name."

"I told you already, I won't be blackmailed."

A door opened somewhere, followed by a heavy tread on the stairs.

"Who do you think would most like to hear my story? The police, the newspapers or your wife?"

"I warn you not to set yourself up against me," Edmund said. "You are nothing beside me, your word is nothing beside mine. I will destroy you, if necessary."

"And to think you were whispering sweet nothings in my ear all night . . . But look what I have."

He opened his left hand which had been clenched all along, to reveal Edmund's fob watch, the one that Beatrice Curran had given him when she retired from the Colosseum.

"Give that back." Edmund grabbed his arm but Gilbert freed himself and was off the bed in one easy movement.

He swung the watch by its chain, like he was teasing a dog with a treat.

"Very conveniently, it is engraved with your name. Lends a bit of weight to my story when I come to tell it," he said.

A figure filled the doorframe, a young man in working clothes who didn't seem the least bit surprised by what confronted him.

"And here's my witness. Joe, meet Edmund Jeffers, the famous actor."

Joe squared himself up. He was big and solid, game for a fight. It was time to leave but, when Edmund tried to, Joe barred his way.

"Remember, rent falls due on the first of every month," Gilbert said, from behind. "If you can't find us, we know where to find you. Got it?"

Time seemed suspended. Nobody moved. And then Joe exploded with his fist. It felt like a boulder in Edmund's solar plexus and it knocked the wind out of him. He fell to the floor, gulping air as the pain swallowed him, rising up through his body to his heart and lungs. Just as he thought he would suffocate he managed a sharp intake of breath.

Gilbert was standing over him now too.

"I said, 'Got it?'" He kicked Edmund with his boot into the small of his back which set the nerves screeching up his spine, through his kidneys. "Any arrears and I'll be singing my head off. The whole world will know about your grubby little habits."

He felt himself dragged by the legs out onto the landing, then with a foot pushed down the stairs. He had sense enough to grab the bannisters and break his fall but he took a nasty blow to his head on the way down. The door closed upstairs and there were muffled voices. They had finished with him.

He pulled himself up and got out into the empty street where he was able to walk with the aid of walls and gates to cling to. He did not recognize where he was, had forgotten the route taken from The Bricklayer's Arms last night but he kept going until he saw the steeple of St. George's Church and aimed for that. The dead dog was still there. He sat on a bench beside it to rest for a while, to ease the aches in his body and let normality encroach. By the time he got to his feet again the streets were beginning to come alive. Labourers, huddled against the morning cold, made their way to work and from behind the high wall of the brewery came the growling of the draymen and the clink of metal as horses were harnessed for the day ahead.

They were all squalid encounters and he always felt guilty afterwards but this time he was desolate. He had allowed himself be seriously compromised and now he was being blackmailed. How long would that last? For the rest of his life? And could he ever be really confident that this man would keep his silence? Even a hint of that kind of scandal would be ruinous for Edmund Jeffers. And what about the future? Where were these needs of his going to lead him? Because they could not be contained, he could not deny his own being. These lapses, he reasoned, merely satisfied a biological imperative that had more to do with reaffirming himself than with actual pleasure. For that reason, he never felt that he had betrayed Violet in the truest sense. He would never bestow upon another the feelings he had for her. She was his wife and he loved her, in every way but one.

Going back across the river, the water was still and black with a veil of mist rolling off it. A gust of wind sent vapour scudding under the bridge like a whipped dog. The closer he got to his usual haunts, the more he felt afraid of what he had done.

The Colosseum was empty so early in the morning and would be for another couple of hours at least. He let himself in through the side door, made his way to the upstairs bathroom where he threw off his clothes and got into a hot bath – there was still enough water left in the tank from the night before. He lay there for a long time until the water cooled and he began to shiver. Then he got out and stood in front of the mirror, wiping it with a towel so he could see himself. His reflection was blurry as though seen through tears. He examined his torso and back which had blotchy red marks, beginning to bruise. He moved nearer to study his face. Luckily, it bore no cuts or discolouration that he would have to explain. He hardly dared look into his own eyes but, at the last moment, he did. And saw in them a future he did not want. There would be other nights, other men, other sordid couplings that gratified and disgusted in equal measure. He looked away. He had the eyes of a predator. But he felt like the quarry.

Chapter Nine

The editor of the *Pall Mall Gazette*, one Bartholomew Crowe, was a man not averse to risk-taking. As soon as he heard Clive Potter's ideas about infiltrating the world of child prostitution, he was enthusiastic. He liked Potter's plan to pose as a client, thought it the best and most direct route into the story and was certain that the public would love this approach too, as long as the resulting reports kept just within the boundaries of good taste. His only worry was that there might be legal repercussions.

In the event, solicitors were consulted and affidavits were signed in order to protect all participants from prosecution. After that, Clive Potter was let loose.

He was a man on a mission, putting aside all other work to concentrate on this. His journalistic career had provided him with books full of contacts, many of whom were familiar with the murkier seams of London life. This resource, coupled with a generous expense account from the newspaper, made it possible for Potter to buy all the information he required.

With the connivance of two associates, he constructed for

himself a family history and an identity that would stand up to vigorous enquiry. He was Donald McGregor, an ex-army man who now worked as a railway clerk. His adopted name, McGregor, could be found in the appropriate military records and on the payroll of the Great Northern Railway Company. Under this alias, he tracked down various elusive members of the criminal underclass and managed to secure an interview for himself with Mr. and Mrs. Taylor at their premises in Bermondsey.

The building was red-bricked, tall and narrow, with derelict neighbours on either side, the rest of the street being taken up by warehouses. All around were factories and tanneries and the air reeked of glue and grease and putrid animal skins. A polished plaque on the wall announced '*The Bluebell Charity School for the Training of Children to Service*'.

Inside, the parlour was small and dark and was dominated by a large white marble fireplace which seemed to be the only bright thing in the room. Bert Taylor, in dirty working clothes, rested his elbow on the mantelpiece, his foot on the dented fender. He remained aloof, presumably the better to observe proceedings while his wife did the talking.

"The children who come here are destitute," Mrs. Taylor said. "Either cast off by their parents or else without any." She paused and it took him a few moments to realize that it was expected he should be pleased by this.

"I can see you are very careful," he said, belatedly.

"We school them in all aspects of service. Obedience and hygiene are top of our list of priorities – and an eagerness to please, which is essential in this line of work."

She spoke in a slow, deliberate way without the least trace of irony and could have passed for any respectable woman with philanthropic tendencies except that her eyes were too searching.

She was too alert to his every nuance.

"McGregor is a Scottish name, I believe," she said.

"Yes, my great-grandfather came from Dundee to London – oh, I suppose a hundred years ago, and the family has been here ever since. Can't be much Scottish blood left in our veins at this stage . . . though I do have a fondness for Scotch whisky," Potter laughed, "which I choose to blame on my heritage."

Mrs. Taylor frowned. She was barely touching middle age and was fine-featured, handsome even, but solemn in her dress and manner.

"We do not approve of intoxicating liquor in this house," she said, as though there could be no worse depravity.

Potter had got the tone wrong. He was trying too hard to be jovial, friendly.

"No, and nor should you," he said, suitably humbled.

A girl of about ten entered, carrying a tray with a pot of tea and some cups on it which she placed on the table between Potter and Mrs. Taylor.

She was a slight, pale thing with mousy hair and had on a white apron that seemed too bright and clean for the rest of her. She stared right at him, her eyes all-knowing, dark circles underneath them like smudged thumbprints. Across the bridge of her nose, a smattering of freckles which should have given her a childish look were, on her, more like an affront to innocence.

Potter eyed her up and down as he thought he should.

"You may pour," Mrs. Taylor said to the girl. "This is Mary, Mr. McGregor, a very able girl and willing."

Again, nothing suggestive in her inflexion, nothing overtly stated. It was disconcerting the way the whole conversation was conducted at a remove like this.

"She is very pleasing," Potter said.

"And stronger than she looks. You may leave now, Mary."

Mary turned around and curtsied to Potter before going. Part of the drill, no doubt.

"Who told you about us?" Bert Taylor this time, in a voice low and rumbling like an old dog growling.

"An individual named Robert Ford suggested I might find what I was looking for here."

"Ford don't put himself about much," Taylor said. "Not the sociable sort. How d'you meet 'im?"

"I was taken to him by an acquaintance of mine."

"Name?"

"Colin Westhrop."

"Never 'eard of 'im."

"Aren't you lucky," Potter said. "He's a bad egg if ever there was one. We shared a dorm in the army and while overseas we discovered we both had the same, rather unusual, needs. You're spoiled for choice in India, you know. They're much more sensible and relaxed about this kind of thing abroad. Better attitude altogether."

"Don't give a tosser for attitudes," Taylor said. His skin was dark and grimy with black pores as though he had spent his entire life in a coalmine. "You 'ave a want that I can fulfill. You pay, I provide. That don't mean I think it's normal." He paused to see if Potter dared counter this view. Then, when he did not: "What regiment you serve in?"

"Gloucesters, First Battalion."

"Stationed at?"

"Kabul. And afterwards, Kandahar. Then, Cawnpore."

"Your Commanding Officer?"

"Colonel James Fitzroy."

"Where d'you work in the Railway?"

"Booking Office at King's Cross."

"When did that station open?"

"1852."

"How many stops on the line between there and Edgeware?"

Potter paused, tried to count. "Thirteen," he said. "No, twelve." He could feel the sweat breaking out on his back.

Taylor walked around, circling the chair so he could get a better view of Potter.

"That old ferret, Ford, how d'you track 'im down?" he said.

"My friend Westhrop knows a Mr. Brevis. Mr. Brevis of Chancery Lane?" He waited until he saw recognition in Taylor's eyes. "Well, Mr. Brevis brought us to meet the charming Mr. Ford."

"'Ow come Westhrop ain't 'ere 'imself if 'e 'as the same dirty 'abits you 'ave?"

Potter smiled.

"He's back home in the bosom of his family again. More convenient to keep it all under your own roof, if you know what I mean."

Taylor studied him. "Ford says you're all right. But that other stuff I asked you, it better check out." He gave a loud snort to clear his nose. "You can go through the details with my wife," he said and left them to it.

Throughout her husband's contribution Mrs. Taylor had remained still, her head bowed, her eyes cast down, but now she reasserted herself. She invited Potter to take the brass bell on the table beside the tea tray.

"We do have girls younger than Mary if you would care to see, and some boys. Please, just ring the bell," she said.

"No, I think Mary will be perfect for what I have in mind." The girl looked intelligent enough and lucid, well able to give him the information he required.

"A wise choice, Mr. McGregor. She is very skilled. For what duration do you require her?"

"I think two days would be sufficient. Monday and Tuesday of next week." Then, maintaining the pretence, "My usual help will be returning on Wednesday. Gone to the funeral of a parent."

Mrs. Taylor smiled for the first time, pleased with his collusion.

"Cash in advance, you understand," she said.

"Yes, yes, of course."

Potter handed over the agreed sum. Mrs. Taylor reached into the chimney alcove for a cane and, using it, rose with difficulty. As she was already seated when he had come in, Potter had not noticed before that she was lame. She went to the desk, unlocked a large maple box and put the money into it.

"Until next Monday, then, Mr. McGregor."

They shook hands. Her grip was strong first, then limp. She rang the bell again.

He had his story, the story of the decade. It was all he could do not to let out a celebratory roar as he followed Mary along the gloomy hall. When the front door opened, the sun, high in the sky, pierced the dark interior and warmed the spot where they stood.

"Well, Mary, I'll be seeing you again soon enough," he said. He could not help but look at her as at a prize.

The girl stared back at him with dead eyes.

Chapter Ten

The whole summer had been hot and dry, perfect for ice-cream sellers and the owners of seaside hotels, but not to the liking of theatre companies. The heat kept people away and attendances were poor not just in London but countrywide. At the Colosseum, in an attempt to entice punters in, the use of gas jets was kept to a minimum and chilled lemonade was served during the interval, free of charge. But despite these measures, audiences dwindled.

And so, when August came and with it the annual holiday, it was with a great sense of relief that the Colosseum's doors were closed to the public for three whole weeks. Edmund took off for Rome and Naples to sample the everyday flavours of Italian life in final preparation for *Julius Caesar*, due to open the second week in September. Violet accompanied him on the trip.

Charles Gray spent the first five days of the vacation in Dublin, visiting family and friends. He returned to London afterwards and resolved not to stir again for the duration. He visited the office frequently to catch up with outstanding paperwork despite Edmund's entreaties that he must rest. But holidays really were for people who disliked their occupations, who spent fifty weeks of the year anticipating the delights of a fortnight's respite from drudgery. With Charles the opposite held true. He found this yearly spell of freedom tedious and yearned for the ordinary working routine which provided him with so much enjoyment and satisfaction.

Avoiding the sun, he had spent much of the day indoors with a novel, which was unlike him. Apart from reading plays that Edmund asked him to, he avoided fiction. It seemed somehow self-indulgent, given that he worked in a theatre, to immerse himself in yet more make-believe. Therefore, usually he felt obliged to choose current affairs or biography but this book by Disraeli, which he had owned for several years and not read, had presented itself the previous night and he had fallen under its spell.

He lunched alone and dined alone, speaking only to Mrs. Wilson, his housekeeper, on domestic matters. The day passed and not unpleasantly either, the evening turning cloudy and very humid. Flies butted against the window panes as though driven demented by the torpid atmosphere. He began to feel restless from his long spell of inertia and annoyed that he had spent the greater portion of the day on a book that was amusing but hardly enlightening and would serve no more useful purpose in the future than to provide him with some trivial party conversation.

He decided that physical exercise would stimulate him. To this aim, he put on his jacket and top hat and headed out, southwards down Great Cumberland Place and into Hyde Park.

The air lacked oxygen. It was as though every lungful had only half its usual revitalizing power. Cyclists, walkers, even children seemed listless. Whole families were gathered at benches having abandoned their apartments and city gardens in favour of green open space. They were reading, playing cards, fanning themselves, eating sandwiches. All sounds were muffled. There must be a storm coming, thought Charles as he made his way across the grass towards the Serpentine in the hope that there at least conditions would be fresher. He arrived at the water to find a group of men in swimming togs lined up on the bank. They were waiting for a signal. A green flag was hoisted on a pole and the swimmers leapt and dived into the river amid whoops and yells, the water boiling with their antics. Each one of them was pale and lean but all the arms, faces and necks were tanned and Charles guessed they were labourers of some sort, letting loose after a day's hard grind.

Three in particular took his notice. They stood apart from the rest of their comrades, waist deep in water, intent upon some trick. Two of them bent down in the water while the third, a curly-headed youth, balanced himself on the submerged bridge his friends had made of their hands. On a given count, he jumped and at the same time was catapulted into the air like a human cannonball. The flying youngster hugged his knees and attempted to turn somersault but failed and landed flat on his back, which must have hurt though he didn't let on. He rolled over, fell into a lazy breaststroke. His muscular shoulders broke through the surface of the water, then slid back under. Ripples trailed out behind him like streamers in the wind.

A voice called out, "Come on in! Cool yourself down!" It belonged to one of the swimmers and the invitation was directed at him, Charles. He hadn't realized he had been staring so. He doffed his hat and declined as any gentleman would.

The three were laughing and slapping the water with their hands, jeering and cajoling him to join them. They turned him into a spectacle. Strollers stopped to watch.

"Not for me, I think," Charles said and walked on with apparent nonchalance.

The curly-haired fellow would not let him go. He had a good backstroke and kept pace with Charles as he moved along the bank, his friends encouraging the chase. Charles kept his eyes fixed straight ahead. At last they came to the bridge which allowed Charles to cross over and branch away from the water.

A shout overtook him. "See you tomorrow!"

The incident left him feeling feverish. The embarrassment of it and the necessary quickening of his step had caused him to sweat. When he had gone a safe distance he found a vacant bench and sat down to recover. His mind emptied and he remained there until it began to get dark and it was time to go home. He decided to take a different route back and headed away across the park, keeping well away from the river. On his way he halted at the statue of Achilles where quite a few other people were milling about, and one or two were sitting on the pedestal steps. This monument to the prowess of the Duke of Wellington, by its sheer size alone, had to impress. One was forced to look up at the vast, naked figure and marvel at brute strength made beautiful. Given its provenance – cast from twelve French cannons – and the fact that its purpose was to celebrate a staid, military figure, there was something rather strange about the choice of Achilles for this statue, the boy who once hid himself in a harem disguised as a girl and who had one fatally vulnerable flaw.

He must have spent a long time regarding Achilles for when next he looked around he noticed dusk was turning to night and the park was almost empty of its daytime visitors. Two men on a seat nearby took his attention. They were both wearing panama hats. One was in his fifties, the other much younger and they mirrored each other's poses – legs crossed, knees touching, heads inclined.

A horrid fascination settled on Charles. His eyes were drawn to them at every opportunity. Their conversation was deep and intense and they seemed oblivious to all else. Charles recalled that he had heard rumours about this great statue and the type of individuals who congregated here at night. He walked around the plinth to gain a better view of the two men and then it became plain that this couple were holding hands. The younger leaned over and whispered in his companion's ear, something that caused them both to laugh, then he lifted his friend's hand to his lips and kissed it.

Charles looked back up at Achilles, at the muscle and tilt of his thighs, the thrust of his pelvis, at the sword he was brandishing, and there seemed to be very little of the Duke of Wellington about the statue now. His enjoyment of it was corrupted by the presence of these persons. While he bore no ill will to any of their kind he had to admit that their proximity had a sullying effect, causing him to avert his eyes from the monument.

He left the park in rather a hurry, turned onto Park Avenue and bumped against someone evidently on his way in. Far from being discommoded by the collision, this man appeared pleased. He raised his hat and apologized, though it was not his fault at all, and then made further comments about the weather and how the drought had dried up the greens where he played golf and, all in all, he delayed in a very unseemly fashion. He was wearing a red carnation in his buttonhole and Charles remembered someone once telling him that this was a sign. Charles detached himself without a word.

It was nearly midnight when he got home, having walked the streets for some time. Mrs. Wilson had left a supper of cold pork, bread and butter in the dining room. He ate though he wasn't hungry and allowed himself two glasses of port, no more, before retiring.

Upstairs, as he lay in bed, it occurred to him that despite his busy life he was lonely. He had plenty of company in the normal course of his day at work but not of the intimate kind. If he had a wife and family he would not get the restless feeling he had now that always ended in a headache and a rather sordid act. It was the result of his unnatural bachelor status. He lay stretched out on his back. For a brief while he savoured the pure, sensual beauty of his own body. Recent sights and preoccupations flashed in and out of his brain like light bulbs exploding – the bathers tussling with one another; the young man's lips against his lover's ear; Achilles, heroic in his nakedness, declaring himself a man first, a warrior second.

And afterwards, sleep.

Chapter Eleven

Mary sat on a chair at the kitchen table, hands tucked under her thighs. She was swinging her legs backwards and forwards. Clive Potter took his time explaining to her that he did not require the usual services, that he just wanted to talk to her. She looked at him with pity.

"I'm a newspaper man," he said. "I'm going to do a story on you."

He had said as much to Rosalind though he had omitted any mention of the Taylors or their establishment in Bermondsey and had been vague about the true nature of Mary's circumstances. The less she knew, the better it was. He had been surprised by how well she took the news that they were to have a guest for a couple of nights. Despite the extra work involved – and she was always complaining about that – she had been quite excited at the prospect. She spent several days preparing the room upstairs for the child – mending, cleaning and tidying obsessively and even went so far as to borrow an old doll's pram, a cloth rabbit, a draught board and some picture books from her sister-in-law which she thought Mary would like.

Rosalind came into the kitchen now with her box of rags and polish and put them in the cupboard over the stove.

"Well, luvvy," she said, turning to the girl, "what about elevenses? You 'ungry?"

Mary nodded.

"Some 'ost 'e is, eh?" Rosalind threw a glance at Potter. "'E'd starve to death if it meant saving 'iself the bother of moving."

She went to the pantry and returned with last evening's mutton joint which she set on the table and began carving. She served the meat on a plate with some bread and butter and a glass of milk.

"Eat up," she said. "You could do with a couple of roses in them cheeks of yours." Then, to Potter, "Want some?"

"We have work to do," he said.

"I'll take that then as a 'No, thank you kindly'."

She retreated to the scullery where she clanked around the place, humming to herself, and he was sure, despite the noise, that she had an ear to their conversation.

"What I want is a bit of privacy," he yelled over his shoulder. "Any of that to be had around here?"

Rosalind emerged. She snatched at the jug on the table and poured out another glass of milk for Mary.

"Never let them grind you down, luvvy," she said. "Men, that is. Always know you're better than them."

With that, she grabbed the sweeping brush from the corner and took it with her upstairs.

Potter turned his attention back to Mary.

"Now," he said. "What I need from you is an account of how you came to be living with the Taylors, the types of things they get you to do, how you are treated, the quality of provisions, accommodation, that sort of thing."

Mary stopped chewing her food and stared at him. Even her feet were still.

"Perhaps we should take it one step at a time," he said.

"I don't want to get in trouble," she said.

"You won't. No one will know you've told me. Your name will not appear in the article. I'll bet lots of the clients have asked you the very same things I'm going to and you had no problem answering them." He waited. "Am I right?"

He took the cap off his pen, wrote the date at the top of the page.

Mary resumed the swinging of her legs. The toe of one shoe caught on the stone floor and dragged across it.

"Don't do that," he said.

"What?"

"That thing with your legs."

She stopped but she lifted her head and gave him an eye like a horse fighting the bit.

"The Taylors," he said. "Are they really man and wife?" Their unlikely union had baffled him from the start.

Mary shrugged. She ate another piece of meat from her plate.

"How old are you, Mary?"

"Eleven," she said. "I think."

"How old were you when you first went to live with Mr. and Mrs. Taylor?"

"Seven, eight maybe. No, seven."

"We need to be precise."

"Seven then," she said, to appease him.

Potter dropped his pen. "Mary, listen," he said. "I am writing a series of articles for the newspaper about the Taylors and the kind of business they run. We need to tell everyone about the hateful things they make you and the other girls and boys do. These men pay Mr. and Mrs. Taylor for the privilege."

"What's 'the privilege'?"

"The things they do," Potter said.

"Did you 'ave to pay for me?"

Potter frowned. "Yes, but that's different. Anyway, you can see how important it is for me to get the facts right. Hopefully, when people read this they will close down Mr. and Mrs. Taylor's so-called school and you and all the other children will go to live in a nice house with a kind person to look after you."

"Where is this nice 'ouse?"

"What I write must be accurate, otherwise there is no point. So please, think things through before you answer." He poised himself, pen at the ready. "How long are you with the Taylors?" He met with a blank. "What age were you when you first went to live with the Taylors?"

"Eight. I was eight," she said.

Potter sighed. "You're sure of that, are you?"

"I forgot Susan 'as a Bible with lots of names written in the front of it and the dates when each was born. She always says, 'That's my family in there and I can carry them round with me wherever I go.'"

"And what has this to do with your being eight?"

"Susan is one of the names. 'Er birthday is the twenty-ninth of March, eighteen eighty-seven, so mine must be as well. We're the same size, see, and we both landed at Bluebell's round the same time."

Potter added question marks on his page beside the numbers eight and eleven.

"How did you end up with the Taylors, Mary?"

"Me ma died and there was only me."

"What about your father?"

"Dead too."

"Oh dear." He wondered should he commiserate.

"Got this though," she said. There was a leather thong around her neck which she tugged at now to bring something up from inside her clothes. Attached to the end was a wedding ring which she showed him. He reached for it, wanting to check if there was any engraving inside the band but she grabbed it back before he could and stuffed it down the neck of her dress. "That's all I 'ave of 'er, of them," she said.

"And you had no one else, no relatives?"

"Nah. I went to live next door."

"So, the neighbours who looked after you, tell me about them."

"They 'ad a little girl same age as me, Cathy, and three boys, older. Mrs. Roberts, she was nice but always tired and then there was another baby on the way and next thing was Mrs. Taylor come to visit."

"Did Mrs. Roberts explain to you who this visitor was?"

"Just said that Mrs. Taylor ran a school for girls to train as servants for the big 'ouses and the good thing was that you didn't even 'ave to pay."

"And what did you think of Mrs. Taylor the first time you saw her?"

"I thought she was a very grand lady. That day she 'ad on a lovely white lace collar and cuffs and I never in my life saw anything as clean and bright as them. Even Mrs. Roberts was looking at them and she dusted off the chair before Mrs. Taylor sat down in case any bit of 'er got dirty. She smelled pretty too. Mrs. Roberts said afterwards it was Parma Violets, all the way from Italy, but I thought she smelled like sweeties."

This girl was good, Potter thought. She knew how to tell a story.

"And then you went with Mrs. Taylor to Watling Street."

"Not straight away – a few days later. Or weeks maybe, I don't remember. When will I be going to that other 'ouse, the nice one you was talking about?"

"Just leave the questions to me," Potter said.

"Why can't I go there now?"

Potter looked at her. "Do you like blancmange?" he said, remembering Rosalind had made some as a treat for later on, when Mary had eaten her dinner. "Well, do you?"

Mary smiled, showing two front teeth at odds with each other and a big gap between them, attractive in a child perhaps but they would make her ugly as a woman.

"Well, I'll get you some from the pantry but only after you've talked to me, understand? Now, what are the Taylors like to live with? Are they kind to you?"

"The missus ain't too bad, most of the time, except if you forget to polish the front doorstep or sweep in the corners and once I spilt some soup for 'er supper on the dining-room table. If you upset 'er like that she screams and shouts to beat the band, whacks you with that stick of 'ers but it don't 'urt none. She's got a lame leg, see, can't balance properly."

"How did she hurt her leg?"

"Dunno." Then, as an afterthought, "Master, I'd say."

"Yes, tell me about Mr. Taylor."

"You said I could have some blancmange."

"Tell me something about Mr. Taylor."

"What about the blancmange? You promised."

Her gaze was cold. She had learned the kind of stubbornness that could never be overcome, not even by physical force.

"All right," he said.

He got up, fetched two bowls of blancmange, one for Mary, one for himself. They ate in silence. When they had finished he gave Mary a second helping and another glass of milk to stave off further interruptions.

"Now, let's get back to Mr. Taylor, shall we?"

"'E's bad," she said. "All bad."

"Explain what you mean by bad," Potter said.

She bit her lip and her eyes flitted from his face to the page and back again. She delayed and then, with sudden deliberation, she pulled up her sleeve and turned over her forearm to reveal an old wound that stretched from her wrist right up to her elbow – a mass of red, puckered skin, raised and thick and angry-looking.

"'E done that with a flat iron."

"Why?" Potter said, recoiling.

"Teach me a lesson," she said. "I cried the first time a man, well . . . you know . . . 'cos it 'urts. And 'e complained me to Mr. Taylor." She sniffed, pulled down her sleeve. "I never cried again."

"Why didn't you ever try to run away, Mary?"

"'E'd find you, no matter where you were, take you back and then it'd be worse than anything you ever 'ad done to you before."

It occurred to Potter it might be a good idea to photograph the injury. "Let me see that arm again," he said.

She displayed the scar in a way that was most disturbing, as though she could read his intent – even held the limb up to the light.

"That all right for you?" she said.

Potter dropped his gaze.

"The customers," he said. "What manner of men are they?"

"Some are nice – I don't mind going to their 'ouses. They give you good things to eat. It's all right except for that other thing you 'ave to do, I never got used to that. They weren't always nice then."

"No, what I meant was, what station in life are these men? Are their houses big or small?"

"Some are proper 'igh-class gentlemen with 'ouses like palaces, others not so rich. None of them are poor though."

"What about names, Mary? Names are very important."

"All of them are 'sir' to me."

"You don't know any of their names then?"

She looked away, devastated. Life had taught her that her only value lay in possessing that which others wanted.

"No names, no addresses?" he said.

She swallowed hard.

Potter tossed his pen into the middle of the table.

"Then we can't go any further with this," he said.

He got up, walked to the kitchen window. Some waste paper had entwined itself in the railings above at pavement level and was flapping in the wind like a bird trying to beat its way free. No, he would not be satisfied with this girl's anonymous experiences. He wasn't going to all this trouble to simply trot out yet another tirade against the wickedness of the brothel keepers. He was after the clients. He wanted details, names that would lead to prosecutions, to reputations toppling. He wanted his own name to be forever linked with the stamping out of this hideous trade. He would be a champion, like Wilberforce, Kingsley or Edwin Chadwick . . .

He turned back into the room.

"Mary," he said. "I am going to ask you to do something for me, something vital. It will help you and children everywhere in your situation." He sat down again, decided against taking her hand in case it frightened her. "When I write this story, your story, Mary, I want it to be complete. Then you won't have to live this life any more. But to make it complete I need the names and addresses of those men you visit. And you have to help me get them. You are lucky, Mary, that you have been chosen to do this."

Mary shook her head and kept shaking it.

"No, no, sir, can't do that. 'E'd kill me, I mean 'e really would kill me."

114

"Then, dammit, we have no story." Potter pushed aside his notes as though they were all worthless now. He rubbed his face, ran his fingers through his hair, tried again. "Do you want to get away from there, Mary, lead an ordinary life, play in the park, have someone to care for you?" Even a child like this must have some hopes though she showed no sign of yielding. "Because you never will unless you help me get those names. Other children are depending on you." A faint flicker of the eyelids suggested this angle was working. "You could save your friends, get them a better life, get yourself a better life if you help me. It just means finding a letter," he said. "An envelope, anything that's addressed to the man in question. You hide it in your shoe or your stocking and keep it until I fetch you again."

"Mr. Taylor, if 'e found out, 'e'd slit my throat, honest 'e would."

Potter sat back in his chair.

"Mary, who is the oldest child at Watling Street?"

"Nancy, but she's gone now."

"Ah." He suppressed a smile at this piece of luck. "What age was she — twelve, thirteen?"

"Thirteen." She stared at him.

"Not a child any longer then," Potter said. "No more use for her at Watling Street. Shouldn't think Mr. Taylor has any qualms around disposing of what he does not need."

"You think Mr. Taylor done 'er in?"

Potter gathered up his papers. "Anyone see her lately?" he said.

Mary looked about her as though searching for the lost Nancy there in the kitchen. She swung her legs harder than ever.

"All right," she said, at last. "I'll do it. But you got to promise you'll come back for me soon or else I'll be —"

"I promise," Potter said.

115

Chapter Twelve

When the curtain fell on the opening night of *Julius Caesar*, there was a standing ovation. With so many friends and relations in the audience and the good will they generated being almost tangible, it would be foolish to read too much into this response, but Edmund, on the whole, was satisfied with the evening's performance. As usual, the coming weeks would be spent reassessing the piece and adjusting it where necessary. For to Edmund, a first night was never the culmination of the company's efforts. It was, rather, an indicator of work yet to be done.

However, to celebrate the beginning of the new run, a party was arranged. A light buffet had been set up in the downstairs saloon for the cast and a hundred guests. At one end of the room a table was laid out with cold cuts of meat and fowl and jellied tongue, with savoury rice and salads. And, for sweet, lemon mousse and almond tarts. At the opposite end, punch and champagne and other intoxicants were being served so there was a constant flow of people moving up and down between food and drink which added to the air of gaiety.

Friends and acquaintances shook Edmund's hand. Violet kissed him on the cheek and congratulated him. They were reconciled to the point where they engaged in polite conversation but steered well clear of anything deeper. He was relieved when she said she must go and attend to Lady Rumsfeld, who needed to be seated because of an ulcer on her leg.

Edmund looked for Marguerite. Since she had left the Colosseum he had only seen her on stage as Mrs. Tanqueray, in which role she had astounded not only him but the whole of London. When he saw her that night at the Metropole, he could not help but be proud of his part in her success, but while he was sitting there in the darkened auditorium an awful presentiment had come to him. He saw himself in the future, a much older man, frantically working the Colosseum stage opposite yet another unpromising ingénue and looking ridiculous in the process.

He found Marguerite in Roger Yates' company. She was wearing a lilac gown of some thin stuff that seemed to wind itself about her body in the most becoming way. The sleeves shone under the lights like dew-dropped cobwebs. Edmund kissed the back of her neck and he caught the familiar scent of her as she turned around. Beautiful as ever, her face was a little thinner than previously but with a new quickness to her expression that hinted at, perhaps, inner joy.

"Edmund," she said, "the play is wonderful. You were so right to play Cassius – you brought out his complexities beautifully."

"Hear, hear," Roger said.

"The murder is quite magnificent, so terrifying. The noise and the subdued light and all those men, full of hate . . . it was inspired." She smiled at him, a sublime smile that was all about her own happiness and the fact that she couldn't keep it in.

"The Metropole suits you," he said, experiencing a renewed pang of how much he missed her.

117

"Yes, I think it does," she said.

"It seems to suit Mr. Cardew too," he said. "It really is too bad of you, Marguerite, to take our most loyal patron with you. He's released his box here and deserted us entirely, you know, in favour of the Metropole, him and his gladioli."

"I have to admit it was rather comforting to see him in the audience the night we opened. His presence made me feel quite . . . well, quite at home really."

"He is besotted in the most pathetic way I've ever seen," Roger said.

"I give him no encouragement whatsoever," Marguerite said.

Edmund guffawed. "You blow kisses to him from the stage in front of the whole audience. That is his sustenance. He is like a camel. He can live off one of those moments for a year."

"One has to be kind," she said, smiling.

"Well, throw a little kindness this way," Roger said. "Because I want you to settle a wager between myself and William. It concerns a certain gentleman you are currently treading the boards with . . . and it is a matter of grave importance. Handsome, handsome Martin Harvey. Tell me, does he or does he not wear a corset on stage?"

"Why, Roger, I couldn't possibly divulge the private, the very private, not to say, embarrassing, vanities of my new —"

"There you have it, as good as a five-pound note to me," Roger said, clapping his hands together. "And I'll bet that's a wig he has too. Ha, he is fat and bald just like the rest of us." Then, addressing his own protruding belly, "Perhaps a corset would suit you too, my friend."

"Why stop at that," Edmund said, "when silk stockings and bloomers would be the making of you, Roger?"

"*Ooh la la!*" Roger kicked up his heel and fluttered his eyelashes.

When their laughter died down, Edmund called for another tray of champagne.

"Lewis is here somewhere," Marguerite said, searching the crowd. "I don't like to leave him too long. He says actors are only interested in talking to other actors, which is perfectly true, of course. Left to his own devices he'll probably strike up a conversation with one of the kitchen staff and end up out in the alley smoking cigarettes and playing skittles."

"I'll find him," Edmund said, giving in to what he knew was her purpose from the start. "Rescue your lost lamb."

He found Lewis at the buffet table. While others were daintily picking at the delicacies on offer, Lewis had attacked them full on. He was working his way through a generous plateful of food and seemed perfectly happy to be on his own.

"Lewis, good to see you again," Edmund said.

Lewis swapped his plate to his left hand and wiped his fingers on a napkin before shaking hands.

"Please, don't let me interrupt your meal," Edmund said.

Lewis quickly swallowed the last of his mouthful. "Have I been terribly greedy?" he said, looking down at a selection of bones, picked clean, on his plate. "Rather hungry, I'm afraid. Haven't eaten since breakfast."

"Well, it's good to know those quail didn't die in vain."

Lewis snorted. "Yes, I see what you mean." Then, searching for another topic, "Marguerite says it was very brave of you to play Cassius. Apparently most actors in your position would have taken the safe option and been Mark Antony or Brutus."

"It's very kind of your sister to say so but it was pure selfishness really that led me to choose the part. It is, I think, the best role in the play. Mark Antony is all fine speeches and nothing else and as for the honourable Brutus, well, he's tiresome to be honest, a man who does not know himself. Cassius, at least, understands who he is and can see the evil in his own heart. Which is refreshing."

Lewis was stumped. He had nothing to say except, "Well, good luck with the run anyway."

Surprising to find a man of his age who still had not mastered the art of bluffing, thought Edmund.

"I do go on, don't I?" he said, realizing he had embarrassed Lewis. "It's the actor's disease. Tell me, how are you getting on in London? Do you miss Paris terribly?"

They talked for some time about that city, Edmund having visited frequently. Lewis ate while they chatted and he became quite relaxed. There was no denying he was very handsome and well dressed – that was probably down to Marguerite – and mannerly, but for some reason one stopped short of calling him refined. He seemed to have none of the polish – or perhaps it was archness – that gentlemen usually acquire when they socialize in the best circles. His tanned face and hands suggested that this was the wrong milieu in which to judge him . . . he should be outdoors. Perhaps that was why he reminded Edmund of a lyrical past. He was like a character transported from Hardy, belonging to another era, another England, another landscape, one that was mucky and harsh, but honest; one where decency was more important than style.

Edmund was trying to remember the name of a bar in Montmartre in which he had whiled away many a pleasant hour over a glass of pastis.

"Cats everywhere," he said. "And the proprietress, a startling lady in her sixties with black hair and a back as straight as a rule. Serves the customers herself . . ."

"La Petite Horloge, I know it well," Lewis said. "And that lady, in her youth, was an artists' model. She sat for Ingres. He was very taken with her."

"There are a great many beauties in Paris and, amazingly, every one of them claims to have been an artists' muse."

"But this is true. Madame Chabrol told me so herself. Ingres made numerous studies of her and two finished paintings. She featured in *The Turkish Bath* though he did not use her face. He thought her too sophisticated for a brothel."

Edmund laughed. "Of course he did. And these other paintings of her? You have seen them?"

"Their whereabouts are not known."

"I think this Madame Chabrol is a good businesswoman. She knows how to draw a crowd."

"She told us many, many stories about those times she spent with Ingres."

"I'm sure she has quite a store."

Lewis set aside his finished plate.

"I will make a point of seeking out those lost works," he said. "I will find them in a book and – and – prove it to you that she is genuine."

"You mean, rub my nose in it," Edmund said. "Which I thoroughly deserve. I was born cynical – it's an awful burden. Do you have a strong interest in art? You paint?"

"I like to draw."

"Ah, that explains your career choice. Architecture, I believe."

Lewis gave a dismissive grunt. "If I can ever finish my apprenticeship," he said. "These London firms seem very unwilling to take me on. It's a very staid, closed world – architecture – and they certainly don't want anyone who was within an ass's roar of a notorious sodomy case."

"Quite," Edmund said, finding Lewis's candour alarming. He steered away from the topic. "Perhaps you'd try your hand at painting sets here at the Colosseum. The designers need assistants from time to time. Of course, we won't be doing a new production

121

for quite some time but if you were interested I could –"

"That's kind of you," Lewis said.

Marguerite came from behind and linked both their arms in hers.

"Edmund, I must go," she said.

"Why? What has happened to you?" said Edmund. "You haven't reformed, have you, since leaving us? Early to bed, early to rise, all that rot?"

"Yes, at the first stroke of midnight I turn into a pumpkin."

"That's the carriage surely, not you," Edmund said.

"Truth be told, I have a rendezvous with someone rather special tonight and I'm all a-dither."

"Anyone I know?" Edmund said.

Lewis scowled and released himself from his sister's grip to wander off into the crowd. Marguerite turned to Edmund with a wan smile.

"I know you'll say he's unsuitable. And I'm only going to tell you now because you'll hear of it sooner or later from someone else – but I don't think you're going to like it."

"For God's sake, tell me, put me out of my misery. How bad can it be? It's not Mr. Gladstone, is it, or Jack the Ripper?"

Marguerite did not laugh. She looked as though she might change her mind about telling him. Then, she said, "It's Leopold Barrie."

Edmund whistled through his teeth. "Oh, much worse than Mr. Gladstone, worse even than Jack the Ripper," he said. "Oh Lord, does that make you my common law mother-in-law?" She looked at him with searching eyes. "Good God, Marguerite. Are you mad? If you were young –"

"Oh, so I'm old, am I?"

"Younger. If you were younger, I'd say good luck to you, you're welcome to the old goat. He'd be at your mercy. You'd have your fun with him then drop him at the first indication of a lapse in your devotion or his. But you've changed. You mightn't realize it but you have, and it's only natural at your age to have an appetite for something more permanent, which you won't get with him. He's a philanderer, that's his nature."

"You have always hated him. Irrationally, if I may say so."

"You know his history as well as I do, the whole of London society knows it. He's hardly discreet, is he?" Edmund held himself back from condemning the man further. He calmed himself, said, "This much I guarantee you, he will never leave his wife."

"Oh, goodness, how you talk," Marguerite said, her face flushed, her bottom lip quivering. "I've had supper with the man a few times, that's all."

"He collects women —"

"That's not fair." Then, mellowing, she said. "Look, I must go. Please, don't let's argue."

She kissed him on the cheek.

He gripped her arm. "Be warned, Marguerite. No good will come of it."

The rest of the evening was a swirl of handshakes, congratulations, anecdotes and champagne though Edmund was no longer in the mood.

He didn't see Lewis again until much later, up in the foyer when everyone was going home. It had started to rain heavily and Charles was running in and out escorting people to their carriages, holding umbrellas over them. Edmund and Violet were bidding the guests farewell. Lewis came up the stairs on his own. He was inebriated but not incapable. He thanked Edmund for a lovely evening and walked out coatless and hatless into the downpour. Edmund watched him saunter along the pavement as if it was a sunny afternoon. He passed out all the cabs lined up at the kerbside and headed towards Piccadilly Circus. He was, evidently, drunker than he looked.

Edmund took an umbrella from the stand inside the door and followed. He called out after him.

"Lewis, old chap, take a cab, why don't you? You'll meet your death like this."

Lewis turned around. The rain had saturated him already. He blinked as water ran from his hair down his forehead.

"No, the walk will do me good." His speech was slurred. "Too much champagne." He grabbed onto the lamppost to steady himself.

"It's Knightsbridge you're going to, you know," Edmund said, catching up. "You'll get there via Australia in that direction."

Lewis grinned but didn't move from the lamppost.

"Come on." Edmund took him by the arm, brought him under the umbrella with him and they retraced their steps back towards the Colosseum.

An orange seller was coming towards them on her way home from Covent Garden, a miserable figure huddled inside a gabardine with the hood up. The wooden tray slung around her neck was full of fruit. It had not been a successful night for her.

"Stop, stop," Lewis shouted.

The old woman halted.

"No, it's all right," Edmund said to her. "We won't be requiring anything."

"I need oranges, half a dozen," Lewis said, swaying as he felt in his pockets for money. "Hell, no, a dozen."

"Take your pick, sir." The seller nodded her head and a rivulet of water flowed from the top of her hood into the tray.

"That's nice fruit," Lewis said, taking his time.

"You'd think he was picking diamonds for his girl," Edmund said, the backs of his legs getting a sudden cold lashing.

"I mustn't delay you," Lewis said. "No, I mustn't. You're soaking already, poor lady."

He selected the oranges he wanted and stuffed them into his pockets. He gave some to Edmund, held the rest in the crook of his arm, paid for them. The old woman chose another, held it out to him in her filthy, mittened hand like a jewel.

"You're my last customer of the night," she said. "And the most charming. You made it worth my while coming out."

Lewis took the orange from her, all smiles. He tried to say something, then couldn't.

"I'm too drunk," he said, sorrowfully.

Edmund guided Lewis back to the shelter of the Colosseum's portico. The cabs had all gone but one was passing on the other side of the road and he hailed it.

The cab driver pulled around. Edmund gave him Marguerite's address.

"Put the fare on my bill," he said.

Then he helped Lewis get in. The young man's eyes were half closed, sleep already taking him. Two of the oranges fell into the gutter and Edmund retrieved them – put them on the seat with the others beside Lewis.

"They'll do for your hangover in the morning," he said. "Best thing for it."

"Nah, can't abide oranges," Lewis said, his eyes fully closed now. "And neither can Marguerite."

Edmund laughed. "Goodnight, Lewis." He collapsed the umbrella, shook the drops off it and placed it in the cab with him. "You might need that later." To the driver, he said, "You'll have to get him out at the other end." He reached up and gave the man a shilling. "Look after him, won't you?"

"Don't you worry, Mr. Jeffers," the cabman said. "Will do."

Chapter Thirteen

A threatening telephone call from Gilbert – real name, Daniel Fraser – had resulted in Edmund putting money every month into an envelope and posting it to the man's address in Southwark. He didn't like succumbing to blackmail but what else could he do? He didn't have large amounts of money at his disposal – it was all tied up in the theatre – and so was not in a position to offer Gilbert and his accomplice a tempting, final settlement. It did occur to him to just call their bluff, let them say what they liked. After all, what proof had they of his involvement with them? His watch they could have found anywhere. But then, against this argument, he had to remember there was a knighthood in the offing and any adverse publicity at all would be detrimental to that outcome. Once or twice he wondered if it was possible to 'get rid' of people like this, but he didn't allow himself to dwell on that thought. The whole situation made him feel very insecure. Every month when he was sending the money off, he swore that before the next installment was due he would have resolved the problem. How, he still did not know. He told no one of his predicament.

One day, Edmund received a letter from the Lord Chamberlain inviting him to come and meet with him.

Sir Andrew Brereton's office was very familiar to Edmund. At one end of it were two gothic windows of a size and majesty to rival any cathedral and on the floor was a silk Persian rug of such intricate design and subtle colour that it seemed a shame to step on it. Edmund put aside such scruples, however, and walked straight across. Over the preceding ten years he had been in this room on many occasions and none of them pleasant. There had been countless wrangles over manuscripts submitted for licence and disagreements about what should be left in and what taken out of a piece and, at their last meeting, the Lord Chamberlain had prevented him from staging *The Inishowen Lad* on the grounds that it was 'too political'.

Brereton came out from behind his desk to shake hands, a thin, tall but undistinguished man. Physically, a poor example of his aristocratic line, he was, however, endowed with extraordinary political acuity and this had served him well in his career to date. It also made him a man to be wary of.

He invited Edmund to join him by the large stone fireplace where a chesterfield and a couple of dining chairs were informally arranged. Usually, they sat at his desk.

Edmund sank down into the chesterfield while Brereton settled himself opposite on a balloon-back chair.

"Would you care for a sherry, Mr. Jeffers?" Griffith, the undersecretary, said.

"That's very hospitable," Edmund said. "I don't mind if I do."

Griffith handed out two glasses, one for Edmund and one for Brereton then left the room without making a sound.

Edmund raised his glass to the Lord Chamberlain.

"Not my birthday, is it?" he said.

Brereton gave a token laugh.

"Yours perhaps?" Edmund said.

"Her Majesty, Queen Victoria, would like to thank you for your services," Brereton said, "not only to her gracious self, but to the theatre in general and to the theatre-going public. She recognizes the vast contribution you have made over the years to the creation of a modern British drama, which today is the envy of the world. The Colosseum is, in effect, our National Theatre."

Edmund sat perfectly still.

Brereton said, "Her Majesty and her advisors have decided to reward you with a formal recognition. A knighthood, to be exact."

Edmund thumped the arm of the chesterfield.

"By Jove, I like the sound of that!" He looked up at the vaulted ceiling and burst out laughing. "I'm bloody well delighted!"

Brereton waited for Edmund's rejoicing to subside and then, with a totally dispassionate look, said, "I must caution, however, that the Honours List will not be made public until the New Year, which means you must keep this private. Our meeting today is but a preliminary. I need first to relay your answer before the offer becomes official. But I take it you are of a mind to accept."

"There is nothing, nothing, that would give me greater pleasure."

"Then, I think, Mr. Jeffers, congratulations are in order. We have come a long way, have we not, from the disreputable penny gaffs of fifty years ago to the respectable West End theatres that are the mainstay of British culture today?" This, evidently, was a speech he had prepared. "There have been greats along the way, the likes of Kean and Phelps, Macready." He paused. "And now, of course, your good self."

Edmund hunched his shoulders and 'became' Uriah Heap.

"My part in it being but 'ever so 'umble'," he said.

The impression was lost on Brereton. He missed a few beats but continued, "As I was saying, theatres like the Colosseum are hubs of artistic excellence and that is praiseworthy. But equally important, in my view – in society's view – is that certain standards of morality and decency are upheld both on and off the stage. What I mean to say is this: we cannot and will not have the Honours List dragged into disrepute."

"Contrary to popular belief, we actors are not naturally licentious people," Edmund said.

"It was never my intention to imply that," Brereton said, drawing himself up slowly and with a patient smile, proclaiming himself a man of pedigree, every inch the second son of an earl. "But it is not unreasonable to expect certain standards from the recipients of an award like this which carries the Royal imprimatur. I have said nothing to you that is not said to every candidate at the outset."

"At the Colosseum, we work and work and work," Edmund said, striving to keep his tone civil. "Our heavy schedule imposes rectitude, no matter how much we might wish otherwise."

Brereton smiled. "I am sure you are beyond reproach, Mr. Jeffers," he said. "Unlike the rest of us."

Chapter Fourteen

On 21st September, one week after the opening night of *Julius Caesar,* the play was slated in the *Saturday Review.* The author of the piece was Clive Potter. In it, he called the Colosseum's production "**a strange concoction and a costly one**". And wrote, "**I have seen it staged with more success in my local parish hall by amateurs with little or no resources to draw on.**" Which was damaging enough. But he went on to launch a vitriolic attack on Edmund too. "**Has no one ever told Mr. Jeffers that Shakespeare should be played on the line and to the line with utterance and acting simultaneous?**" Edmund's performance he described as "**woeful**" and "**bizarre**" and suggested it could only be explained by the fact that "**Mr. Jeffers was intoxicated by more than the heady atmosphere in the theatre that night**".

Edmund, when he read this at breakfast, spilt tea in his lap. He jumped up, grabbed his coat in the hall and it didn't even occur to him that he should change his trousers before going out.

★ ★ ★

Rosalind Doyle was determined to have a maid and though Clive Potter had already refused this request several times over, the campaign continued. Getting a maid-of-all-works was but the first step of many in a plan that included marriage, the recruitment of further staff and moving house. Each little success would light the way to Rosalind's ultimate goal which was to establish herself as a respectable married woman and mistress of her own well-appointed home. For despite the pale skin, the copper hair, that look of heightened sensitivity and abandon she cultivated, Rosalind Doyle was no romantic. She had grown up in an all-male household with her father and five older brothers and that experience, in addition to honing her natural cunning, had taught her that without status and money – and sometimes even with it – all women were slaves.

On this particular morning, Potter was at home writing in his study and Rosalind was keen to prove that she was overworked. She swept the front steps and washed the study window inside and out until it screamed cleanliness. She shined the brasses and polished the handle on the study door to such an extent that Potter shouted at her to leave it alone. Outside in the hall, she rattled the metal pail and slapped it off the tiles when she was mopping up. Downstairs, she dropped the preserving pan on the stone floor, several times.

The scullery window was open and the click of metal taps on the pavement outside caused her to look up. Through the railings above she could make out a lanky figure in black hurrying past and was surprised to see him turn and leap up their own steps. There was a rap on the front door, repeated seconds later when there was no response.

Rosalind took off her apron and, using a scrap of mirror nailed to the inside of the pantry door, she rearranged her hair and dabbed her forehead and chest to remove any trace of perspiration. The knocking was getting louder and more insistent but Rosalind rushed for no one.

As she got nearer, she could hear the caller pacing back and forth on the step outside in an agitated state and when she opened the door there was a gentleman – oddly familiar – facing her. He carried in one hand a rolled-up newspaper with which he was slapping his other hand. The man's face was long and bony and grim-set, the eyes hooded, furious.

"Where is he?" he said.

"Where's who?"

"Potter."

She stared at him but wouldn't budge.

"My card, madam," the man said, calming himself.

Rosalind took it, motioned him into the hallway.

"I'll see if he's free, then," she said.

Potter looked up from his work when she went in.

"You got a visitor," she said. "Proper gent, only 'e's after your blood, I can tell." She read from the card. "Ed-mund Jeff . . . ers. Lord save us, not the actor, eh? What you done to 'im then?"

Potter winced. "Tell him I'm not –"

But at that moment the visitor burst into the room.

"I have business with this – this cretin!" Jeffers said, pointing at Potter with his newspaper. "You must excuse us, madam. I will not be stopped."

There was no disobeying this man. She backed out but left the door ajar as she went and leaned against the jamb outside to listen. After all, it wasn't every day you came across a famous actor, one you'd only ever seen before on posters or in cartoons in the newspaper.

"What is the meaning of this scurrilous attack?" Jeffers' voice thundered out.

She could see neither man but there was a thud and she guessed it was the newspaper being thrown down in front of Potter.

A heated argument ensued about a review of one of Jeffers' plays. Potter said that he was entitled to express an honest opinion on what he saw and if people didn't like it, that was their look-out. Jeffers replied that there wasn't an honest bone in Potter's body and that they had 'an understanding' and well he knew it.

"If that's the case," Potter said, "where's my play?"

"We've just started a new run, for God's sake. This was explained to you before. But getting back to that blasted article of yours, how dare you – how dare you make accusations of drunkenness against me? Lies, all lies, just to satisfy your own hatred. What are you trying to do, ruin me? That won't help your play one little bit."

"Oh, stop whimpering like a baby. I don't hate you," Potter said. "Only who you pretend to be. You and your lavish parties and your high-up friends and the way you think you can dictate to the rest of us plebs what art is. Oh, and by the way, I'm not interested in helping the Colosseum prosper so get that out of your head straight away."

There was a menacing lull. Rosalind imagined Jeffers working himself up into a lather while Potter remained dead still behind his desk.

Then Potter said, "I have been hearing some very nasty rumours about you . . ."

That smugness in his tone meant he was ready to pounce, that all exits were blocked and something in Rosalind identified with Edmund Jeffers then. She hoped he was clever, that he could find a way of deflecting the mortal blow she knew was imminent.

"I meet all kinds, you know," Potter continued. "Been doing

some research of a private nature that has taken me into some of the less salubrious parts of town. Spending a lot of time in pubs. Came up against a nice young chap who knows you, knows you well, by all accounts. He was inebriated, couldn't resist boasting to me about his latest conquest, a famous person. Had a watch belonging to the – er, gentleman to prove it."

A deathly silence followed until Potter spoke again.

"I can remember the inscription: *For Edmund Jeffers with Respect and Gratitude from Beatrice Curran.*"

"Yes, yes," Jeffers said, his voice small as if his throat was constricted. "I mislaid it some time ago – may even have been stolen. Where did you say you met this man?"

"In the course of our conversation, he gave certain details about a meeting between the two of you, certain intimate details that made even me blush."

"This is slanderous," Jeffers said, in a voice that lacked vigour.

"None of us are without sin," Potter said. "Why, my own domestic arrangement can hardly be said to conform to society's standard. Except that what I have is what every full-blooded male desires: all the pleasures a woman can bestow without any of the responsibility. People may whisper behind my back but generally they leave me alone to my good fortune. You, on the other hand, are what every full-blooded male fears and despises. And what does he do when he meets with the contemptible, this full-blooded male? He destroys it."

"What is it you want, Potter?"

"You know what I want, damn you."

"Money?"

"You'd like it to be that simple, wouldn't you? But no, what I want is my play on your stupid, self-satisfied, pretentious, middle-class stage. And I don't care if it brings your theatre down around your ears."

"It isn't even a play, it has no heart. You have no heart."

"I want it on by Christmas."

"Don't be ridiculous, *Julius Caesar* has only just started. No, I will not do it. I will not besmirch the name of my theatre with your –"

"A few words from me and your theatre will be well besmirched," Potter said. "Though you've got to get used to the fact that it's not your theatre any more. Perhaps Lord Barrie would be interested . . ."

"You have no proof of any misconduct on my behalf – only one vagabond's word against mine."

"Oh, I wouldn't go down that road of trying to prove anything; I don't need to. With time the faintest whiff becomes a stench. These things always begin insidiously. I have only to refer in my articles to 'your extremely private nature', 'your enthusiasm for Greek sculpture,' 'your passion for exotic plants', 'your close male friends', and people would get the picture soon enough."

A chair fell and there were scuffling sounds and what sounded like books tumbled to the floor. Various bumps and thumps followed that made Rosalind think Potter had been dragged from his seat and the two men were tussling with each other. Jeffers was breathless when next he spoke.

"Don't ever threaten me, do you hear?"

"Then live with the consequences."

Potter sounded as if he had been buried under a pile of cushions. Rosalind sensed that the altercation was over and only just had time to hide herself in a recess further down the hallway before Jeffers came out.

He shouted back over his shoulder to Potter, "Leave me alone and I'll leave you alone. Or else, do you hear? Or else." He turned on his heel and was gone.

Not that clever after all, Rosalind decided. All temperament and character but no brains. Potter would never leave him alone, surely he knew that. Never. It was the terrier instinct in him.

She went in and found Potter picking up scattered papers and books.

"I take it the gent's not staying for tea and muffin then?" She righted Potter's chair, sat in it, pushed everything on the table out of her way in order to put her feet up.

"I suppose you heard everything?" he said.

"I make it my business."

"Well, keep your mouth shut." He stood up, his arms full of papers and books – he dumped them on the table. When he saw her feet there, he reached out and caressed the inside of her ankle, pressed himself into her calf. He was fired up from what had gone before.

"What's all this talk then," she said, pulling away, crossing one ankle over the other. "This talk about 'all pleasure and no responsibility'?"

"Poetic licence," Potter said. He lifted her skirts, worked his way up the fullness of her leg.

"Entitles you to this, does it?" she said, sinking lower in the chair. "That poetic licence of yours?"

"This is only the start." He knelt on the floor beside her, kissed her. His breath was mustardy but not unpleasant.

She let her head fall back and he devoured her throat. Then, making to get up, she said, "Ain't got time for this. Too much work to –"

His fingers caught in the tangle of her hair and he held her fast.

"Get the ruddy maid, if that's what you want," he said. His eyes were glazed, his mouth fierce. "Just get her."

Chapter Fifteen

It may have seemed to many of Edmund's friends and acquaintances that he, Edmund Jeffers, had sprung from the womb fully formed at age nineteen. That was when he joined Jennings' Stock Travelling Company and he frequently told anecdotes of those days on the road. He was less forthcoming about his life before that. His modest beginnings and the monotony of living in a small town provided him with little in the way of amusing stories to tell. Therefore, it was hardly known at all that Edmund was born in Yeovil, the oldest of three boys, or that his father, Frederick Hewlitt, a strict Presbyterian, worked in the bank there and disapproved of his son taking up acting as a career. Neither was it known that Edmund's mother took the opposite view. She came from Trowbridge, which to the people of Yeovil represented the height of sophistication and worldliness. Anna lived up to their expectations. She was beautiful and intelligent, played the piano remarkably well and had a fine singing voice. From very early on in her marriage she was in demand as a guest at musical evenings and while her husband went to church meetings or retreated to his study, Anna hosted soirées of her own at home. Of the three boys, Edmund was the only one who attended these, the other two preferring to withdraw to the garden or an upstairs bedroom to play.

Frederick Hewlitt, given his Presbyterian background, was somewhat narrow in his view of what constituted appropriate entertainment. But though he had reservations about these musical events taking place under his own roof, he was not so mean-spirited as to forbid them altogether, especially when he knew how much they meant to his wife. However, he made it clear that he favoured a Baroque programme as there was nothing to fear in the restraint and discipline of Bach and Handel and Haydn. Any inclination to indulge in the Romantic repertoire, he discouraged.

Despite all the music and diversion, Anna could not be termed a gay soul. There was always a tinge of private sadness about her that, even though she was invited everywhere, kept others at bay. Edmund thought it was due to a sense of loss in her . . . after all, she was a talented musician who never got to play anywhere beyond the dowdy front parlours of suburbia. But if she had higher hopes they were never articulated and neither did they seem to detract from her devotion to her sons, husband and home.

While the qualities he had inherited from his mother were obvious to Edmund, what, he wondered, had he taken from his father? Doggedness perhaps. While Anna had all along encouraged his artistic development, his father had denied it every step of the way. He did not like actors, he said, or the world they inhabited, which was morally lost.

Edmund did badly at school and when he left at age fourteen, Frederick secured a job for him in the same bank as himself. Edmund stamped and filed and punched and counted for five years. The highlight of his week came every Thursday evening in the Town Hall when he rehearsed with an amateur drama group. Over the years, Anna, and sometimes his brothers, came to see him in productions of *The Countess Cathleen* and *The May Queen* and *Slave Life*. To test his talent, he arranged to travel to London and paid – as was the custom in those early days – to appear in a 'once off' with a professional cast. He played Hamlet and received some praise for it, returning home that same night. He got up early next morning for work as usual and, though everything seemed the same, it was not. Now he was certain where his future lay.

Around this time, he and his father stopped speaking about his involvement with the theatre as they always ended up arguing over it. Though they tried to avoid contention, it was as if the core conflict, even when not spoken about, infected all other areas of their lives and as time went on they could not agree on politics or sport or whether the window should be open or shut or if there was too much salt in the soup.

Freedom came when Edmund joined Jennings' Stock Travelling Company. They played fields and market places all around the countryside, steering clear of large towns so that Edmund came to associate acting with the smell of cow dung and the bleating of sheep.

Edmund spent eight years with Jennings and his travelling Company. When he had learned enough, he left and went to London. There, he felt it necessary to separate from his past so he changed his name from Hewlitt to Jeffers, took elocution classes to rid himself of his Somerset burr and in order to build up his physique – at twenty-seven he was barrel-chested and as gawky as an adolescent – he took daily swims in the Thames where he encountered water rats and dead dogs and the fishy seepage from Billingsgate. Edmund always maintained he owed his iron constitution to the resistance he built up in those early days of immersing himself in the city's filth.

Anna Hewlitt, on a visit to her son and daughter-in-law, disembarked from the train at Waterloo where she was collected by a hansom cab and taken to Belgrave Square. She had only just entered the hall when the telephone rang. It was Edmund. He was detained at the theatre but he wanted to make sure she had arrived safely. After taking off her hat and coat, she was brought into the morning room where Violet was waiting and there she was given tea and cake.

It was disappointing to find Violet thinner than before when what she most wanted to see was a thickening of the waist, a plumping of the breast. Those hopes having been dashed, Anna's interest in Violet waned. She and her daughter-in-law were from different worlds, different classes, had different attitudes, were, in fact, so markedly different as to have nothing whatsoever in common. Violet was not a chatterer, neither was Anna, and she suspected that Violet, as much as she did, yearned for Edmund to join them and ease the frequent longueurs.

With tea over, Anna went to her room to lie down for an hour before dinner. She was looking forward to seeing *Julius Caesar*, had read it three times in preparation for tonight's performance and when they dined, she ate little, her stomach churning, as though it was she who was to appear on stage.

Violet left soon afterwards to ready herself for her part in the play and, as was usual, Charles Gray came later on in a carriage to accompany Anna to the theatre. He presented her with a corsage of violets which were perfect against her dusty-pink damask gown. She joked about how Charles always managed to choose the right flower to compliment whatever she was wearing and he replied that the colours were the easy part to get right. Much more difficult was to find blooms that were sufficiently fresh and vibrant to match the vitality of her own fair countenance. They both laughed over that.

"I do so enjoy flattery, Charles," she said.

Once at the theatre, Charles never left her side. With every action and word he gave the impression that escorting her was the greatest pleasure of his life. They waited together in the foyer before the performance, admiring the fashion which always fascinated Anna as she was so seldom in London. Charles leaned close and in a voice of almost puritan decorum, poured into her ear the juiciest gossip on various ladies and gentlemen present.

When it came to the play, Anna watched her son with the same throbbing excitement and sweet sadness that she always did. Afterwards, Edmund joined them and Charles bowed out.

Edmund had put in a very fine performance and was energized by it. He whisked her off to Kettner's where he had booked a table for the two of them. Walking across the dining room, they had to stop several times for handshakes and greetings and she was introduced to everyone but was glad at last to be seated at a nice, private table over by the window.

Edmund breathed deeply. Now that his face was in repose, he looked tired.

"Champagne and oysters?" he said.

She nodded. The only time she had champagne and oysters was when she came to London. It felt decadent. She looked around. Midnight and the place was alive, every table occupied, imperious-looking waiters darting about, more dutiful than polite. At home, the extent of Anna's socializing was taking tea and sandwiches at someone's house after a musical evening. And so, in this atmosphere she felt exhilarated even before she touched the champagne. Above them, the ceiling was oval and domed, painted like a summer sky, bright blue with billowing clouds which, given the wintry night outside, added to her sense of unreality. The carpet beneath them was rich red, with swirls of golden rose-buds, a design that was echoed in tapestry on the backs of the chairs.

Edmund poured out the champagne. She drank the first glass quickly and felt the heat rise to her cheeks. She took delight in wondering what Frederick would make of it all or John or Robert who could be dour as their father when they chose. They would be mystified by the lateness of the hour, by the extravagance of having supper when dinner had been consumed already, by the cost of it all, by the vulgarity of a certain party at the far end of the room who were exuberant bordering on unruly.

"It was wonderful, the play," Anna said. "I can't think why that Potter man was so mean about it."

"Only for him, we'd have had full houses every night. But no, I'm not going to think of him . . . not when I have you here."

Anna smiled though she sensed he was troubled by this business with Potter, troubled perhaps in other areas of his life too.

"Violet is looking well," she said. "She is healthy, Edmund, isn't she?"

"Fit as a fiddle," Edmund said. He frowned. "Though a little bored of late. I promised to give her a good, meaty role in the next production."

"There are other, more natural ways, to keep a woman occupied," Anna said.

But Edmund left this hanging in the air.

"None of my business, I know . . ." She would like him to confide in her, lay certain fears to rest. She reached out and touched her son's hand where it lay on the linen tablecloth. She would never have done that with either of her other two boys. "A change of scene, a holiday, might . . . build her up."

Edmund covered her hand with his own.

"It's so good to see you," he said.

They talked of the play, of the outbreak of plague in Vienna, of the details that had recently emerged concerning the conditions in which Captain Dreyfus was being incarcerated on Devil's Island and of the freakish hurricane that had struck Camberwell the previous week.

She sat back and studied him. It had been six months since last she saw him and she was pleased that he looked in good physical condition. Always, he had been such a puny child and then, of a shot, his skeleton had seemed to grow, but without his skin keeping pace so it looked as though his bones were fighting to get out through it. As a man, he wasn't quite so angular. What weight he had gained was more muscle than fat, but the extra poundage never affected his face which was always gaunt but particularly so tonight.

"You seem a little anxious, Edmund. Is everything all right?"

"Yes, of course." And then, she felt, to ward her off, he said, "All this business with Leopold is rather unsettling. He is willing to lease the theatre to me but at a much higher price than Mrs. Curran and only on condition that he can have a hand in the running of things. He wants to appoint a Board of Management. I don't like it, I might as well tell you, but it looks like we'll have to settle for it." He ran a hand through his hair, massaged the back of his neck. She noticed the deep, dark circles beneath his eyes.

"You have invested so much in that theatre," she said. "You cannot let it go. Surely Charles has some devious plan up his sleeve."

"Even he is stumped." He took up the last oyster. "How are father and the rest of the family?" he said, before swallowing it.

"Mr. Crabtree retired from the bank and your father is now manager."

"You must congratulate him for me."

"John has opened a new shop in Garter Lane and Robert is still with your father in the bank. Lottie had her leg surgically straightened, I wrote to you about that, and now she's going around with a brace on her leg, asking everyone, including the coalman, to give her a piggy-back." It was all the news she could think of. "They send you warm regards."

Edmund raised his eyebrows.

"They are busy men, just like you. It would be nice if you came down to see us all." She said this even though she could not be sure what kind of a reception he would get if he took up the invitation.

"You're right, I could," he said. "Except that I'm not about to recant my life's work in order to do so."

He slugged back what was left in his glass and tried to make it look carefree.

"Your father is not as intransigent as he once was," Anna said. She was weary of always being the peacemaker between these two stubborn men and yet she persisted. "He can see now that there is no disgrace to being an actor."

"Well, that's very gracious of him."

"You think he is hard-hearted," Anna said. "Well, I can assure you, he is not."

Nothing from Edmund.

"For instance, he allows me to come and visit you. He could forbid it, you know."

"He lets you come because he knows you will anyway, no matter what he says or does."

"Yes, you're right," Anna said, smiling. "Bad example." She stared across the room to a party of gentlemen who were being served ice-cream sundaes in tall glasses topped with bunches of cherries.

"Your father keeps a book," she said, coming back to Edmund. "I found it in the bottom drawer of his tallboy. Beneath the lining paper, if you please."

"Whatever took you under there, Mother?"

"It may interest you to know that in this book your father has copied out, in his own hand, reviews of all your plays. He has been selective, only the good ones are in there."

Edmund kept unusually still. He said, "Why doesn't he just take clippings out of the newspapers and paste them in? Save himself a lot of trouble that way."

"Yes, I was wondering about that too," Anna said. "I have never mentioned my find to your father – you know how he is – so I can only surmise. In transcribing the words, he gets inside them, he claims you for his own."

Edmund drank off what was left in his glass, looked around for the waiter and ordered more champagne.

"All guesswork," he said. "I can see you're on another one of your crusades, Mother."

"For all the good it does," she said.

"He takes an interest anyway," Edmund said, and seemed glad when the champagne came. He poured it out, filled each glass to the brim. "He was a good father when I was young. Remember, he used to do that trick with the penny? He'd rub his hands together and make it disappear and we'd have to hunt for it. Could be anywhere, under a vase, on top of a picture. Once it was outside in the rockery."

"He still does that with his grandchildren," she said. Then, giving voice to the thought that constantly plagued her now, "We are getting old, Edmund."

He held her eyes for a moment, then avoided them.

"He took me to the public library one day – I was about twelve," he said. "He wasn't interested in taking me inside – he

145

had not brought me there for the books. We viewed the building from the outside, sitting on a wall across the road. He gave me a lecture on the architectural features. It was a fine building – still there, I presume – a nice square block with Romanesque arches, rather like a Roman bath house. He gave me the history of the building and the techniques used in the construction of it. Not once did he mention that it was beautiful – or even ugly, for that matter – those words were too emotive for him. But I remember sitting there in the sunshine and being happy. It was so simple."

Anna waited for more.

"That's why I remember it," he said, answering her look. "Nothing happened except we had a pleasant afternoon. We returned home, had supper and I played with my brothers. I think that was the last time Father and I co-existed in each other's company. After that something always ruined our interactions: a chance word, a look, a sharpness in the tone, on his side or mine."

There was a longish silence after that. A fresh batch of oysters arrived.

"Eat up, or they'll go cold," Edmund said. It was a joke they had, a reference to Anna's Aunt Edith, a domineering woman who fancied herself very 'grand' and who one day at the local hotel sent back her oysters complaining that they were 'underdone'.

Anna laughed. It was nice to know that the old life was still there, still a part of him.

"You needn't spread this around," he said, after a while, "but I have been informed by the Lord Chamberlain that my name will be appearing on the Honours List."

She could only stare at him and this he took for incomprehension.

"It means a knighthood, the second only actor in the history of this profession to be given one."

"Well, that's wonderful," she said, expressing delight when what she really felt was that he was drifting further and further away from her and Frederick and Aunt Edith and all the rest of their world. "Truly wonderful."

"I'm not allowed to broadcast it just yet . . . it's all very hush, hush. But it just shows how far acting as a profession has come."

"No," Anna said. "It shows what a fine actor you are and how much the profession of acting owes you in terms of its own respectability. I'm really glad for you, Edmund," she said. She stroked the back of his hand. "Yes, I am."

They ate supper and when they returned to Belgrave Square Violet had already retired for the night. Anna and Edmund were both nocturnal animals and though it was late they sat up playing piquet.

It was three o'clock when they went to bed.

When Edmund kissed her goodnight on the cheek, she held him.

"Just remember," she said. "Knighthoods aside and no matter what, you will always be my dear, dear son."

Edmund hovered. His face against hers, she could hear him swallow, feel him considering what words to say. And then the moment passed and they went to their rooms.

Chapter Sixteen

Two weeks had passed since the altercation with Clive Potter and still Edmund remained undecided as to what he should do. He had been surprised by his own capacity for violence, could remember clearly grabbing Potter by the throat with the full intention of strangling him before, thankfully, reason had intervened. He described the scene to Charles who, also incensed by Potter's unfair review, took a degree of pleasure in the details.

Of course it was an edited version of events that he offered Charles. He told him that Potter had attempted to blackmail him into putting on *Woman* by threatening to write other, more damaging articles about him. Naturally, he omitted any reference to his own homosexual activities or what Potter knew of them. He was sure that Charles had no inkling of this side of his personality and he could not now, after all these years, tell him of it. To reveal the truth – and in such sordid detail – at this stage would surely seem like betrayal to a friend. It was the thought of Charles' disappointment though that was the greatest barrier to openness. Charles loved, admired and respected a construct:

Edmund Jeffers, the actor, celebrity, respectable married man. It would be cruel now to inform him that this creature did not exist.

There was still the problem of how to silence Gilbert and his partner forever but this business with Potter was more pressing and had to be dealt with quickly. If Edmund chose to take off *Julius Caesar*, which was doing reasonably well and put on Potter's play, a certain flop, the consequences could be disastrous. The Colosseum would lose money, his own credibility would be called into question and Leopold Barrie would want to make changes, perhaps drastic ones. On the other hand if he refused Potter's demand he would be disgraced in public. His family, his friends, society would shun him.

Charles was surely the only man to find a way out of this quagmire and yet Edmund could only tell him half the story.

"Let him do his damnedest," Charles said. He was sitting at his desk surrounded by papers. On a plate beside him he had a scone, buttered and cut into cubes, which he popped into his mouth at intervals while he worked. "He's already suggested that you were drunk on stage which is about as low as anyone can go. I mean, what more can he say?"

Edmund was too jittery to sit down. He turned his back and poked at the empty fire grate with his foot.

"Really, it doesn't do to have the Lord Chamberlain bombarded with negatives about me . . ."

"Oh, tosh," Charles said. "There are so many others singing your praises that the danger is he'll get sick of the tune. You know that as well as I do."

"Still, I am a little concerned."

"I say, let Potter go to Hell . . ."

But Edmund kept wracking his brain for some way to resolve his situation. Both options seemed ruinous to his life and career and, as it was not in his nature to precipitate his own downfall, he kept postponing the decision. Perhaps if he postponed long enough, he would at least get his knighthood before the vultures had a chance to descend.

He was preoccupied with thoughts such as these when one day he ran into Lewis Davenport on the steps leading up to the Colosseum. There was no avoiding him. Had Edmund emerged from the theatre a second or two earlier, he could have skipped across the street and pretended not to have seen him. For though he felt himself drawn to Lewis, it was wiser by far to stay away from him. He could never contemplate an alliance with a man who was part of his own social circle. It would be far too dangerous. As it happened, they almost bumped into one another.

"I came to return your umbrella," Lewis said, holding it out. "I'm sorry it took so long."

"Really, there was no need," Edmund said, taking it from him. "We have an endless supply of umbrellas here at the Colosseum. I truly believe they breed with each other under cover of darkness."

Lewis nodded as if confirming the theory and put his hands in his pockets. He remained planted on the spot so Edmund could not move either.

"Actually, what I really wanted to do was apologize," Lewis said. "Apologize for my conduct of the other evening. It was disgraceful."

"It was?"

"Yes, I have no tolerance at all for alcohol."

"Oh, that!"

"I should stick to milk – it's the only drink that agrees with me."

Edmund laughed. "Then next time we have the pleasure of your company we'll make sure to have a Jersey on standby. Now, tell me, how is Marguerite keeping? Please let her know it is proving impossible to fill her shoes."

Lewis's face dropped.

"She's fine," he said. "Well, not fine, no, she's not fine. Her voice is a little better, but it is still weak . . . and, in other ways, she's not quite . . . Gosh, that sun is very bright," he said, shielding his eyes. "It's made me quite dizzy."

"Have you had lunch yet?" Edmund said, aware that he was breaking his own unwritten rule but he needed to question Lewis further about his sister.

"What?"

"Lunch. It's a meal eaten sometime between breakfast and supper. Care to join me? And maybe by the end of it we'll have got some sense out of you."

They went to Simpsons in the Strand where there was the usual crush of theatre people, civil servants, bankers and politicians. Edmund was greeted by several tables. They were swiftly seated in a booth near the window and their orders taken.

"Now," Edmund said, leaning forward, elbows on the table, "tell me what is going on with Marguerite. You make it sound so mysterious."

"Do I?"

The soup arrived. Lewis tore open a bread roll, took a mouthful of soup, pronounced it good and then lost himself in the eating of it. He seemed to have forgotten the thrust of their conversation.

"I have been a friend of Marguerite's for many years," Edmund said. "If there is something wrong, I would like to know. I may be able to help."

Lewis finished his soup then sat back in his chair. "I'm sorry but I really needed that," he said. "Forgot about breakfast this morning."

"Starvation seems to be quite a habit of yours," Edmund said. "How wonderful it must be to live with no set regimen."

"It's not wonderful to get too hungry," Lewis said. "When I met you on the steps earlier, I almost fainted."

"I frequently have that effect on people. Nothing to do with my charm, I'm afraid, just mothballs in my pockets."

Lewis's smile was easily prompted but it was equally quick to fade. He was anxious and unsure, that much was obvious. It was easy to read him, not because he was unintelligent or lacked depth but because he was totally without guile.

"Whatever you tell me is in the strictest confidence, of course," Edmund said.

"Well, it's probably not as serious as all that," Lewis said. "I don't want to give the impression that –"

"My dear chap, give me whatever impression you like but for the love of God, tell me what is going on. And begin at the beginning: Marguerite as Mrs. Tanqueray, wonderful reviews, good box office, things couldn't be better. Now, continue."

The waiter laid two plates of roast beef in front of them.

Lewis said, "As you know, *The Second Mrs. Tanqueray* is still running but, unfortunately, without Marguerite in the lead role. First of all, she lost her voice."

"Clergyman's sore throat," Edmund said. "Common enough amongst actors though I've never known Marguerite to be afflicted."

"The doctor said there was nothing wrong with her, at least nothing physical wrong with her. He said it was in her mind."

"In her mind?"

"I have suspected it for some time," Lewis said. "We have a family history, you know. I have seen it before."

"I am sorry to hear that," Edmund said. "But perhaps you are mistaken. She seemed so well at our opening night. Really, she seemed so well."

Lewis put down his knife and fork. His stare was fierce.

"I know my sister," he said.

"Of course you do."

"It's been gradual but lately it's as if a great sadness, like a cloak, settles over her sometimes. She can sit by the window for an hour at a stretch. There is no distracting her and yet she sees nothing, only the inside of her own head, I suppose. Last night I played Nellie Melba on the gramophone, a great favorite of hers, as you know, and she didn't even notice. Once, she would have danced around the room with joy at hearing her sing."

He took up his knife and fork again, began to eat.

"Is she lucid?" Edmund said.

"Yes, but so subdued. She shows no desire to converse . . . And then she has spells when she seems almost normal."

Edmund said, "And yet the Metropole offers her all she has ever wanted. She should be so happy. Do you think there is a root cause to this melancholy or is it all the fault of genetics?"

Lewis sighed. "It is not all the fault of genetics. May I be frank, sir?"

"I've a funny feeling you're going to be, regardless."

"It's your father-in-law. I never approved of that liaison. I think it has been damaging to her, very damaging."

"Don't tell me she's fallen for the old reprobate?"

Lewis nodded, mournfully.

"Well, he must be one of the worse people anyone could choose to fall in love with," Edmund said. "He is too restless, too selfish, too much in awe of himself to make anyone else happy. If she's looking for cosy nights in by the fire, cracking chestnuts, she's going to be disappointed."

"She already is."

"Even if he fell madly in love with Marguerite, I know he would never leave Constance. It is his connection with her that distinguishes him from all the other outrageously rich men in this country. He won't give that up."

"We went to a function at the Metropole not so long ago," Lewis said. "Leopold was there with his wife, fussing over her and being oh so gracious to everyone else. I could tell it was an awful strain on Marguerite – everyone at the Metropole knows of their arrangement. While Lady Barrie was chatting with some members of the cast, Leopold came over to where Marguerite and I were standing. He took her by the hand and, in my hearing, said, 'Your acting, at all times, my dear, does you credit. And never more so than now.' His attitude was so thoroughly cavalier that I turned around to rebuke him, only Marguerite acted first. She swiped him across the face with her clenched fist, just as he deserved."

Edmund guffawed. "Bravo, Marguerite."

"She made quite a dramatic exit and the whole episode caused an awful stir. It was very embarrassing, especially for Lord Barrie. His poor wife kept smiling throughout but she must have guessed what was going on."

"I'm sure it wasn't news to her."

Lewis winced. "But don't you understand?" he said. "It doesn't do to be so public about things. The fact that everybody knows already, including Lady Barrie, is not the point. It's the breach in etiquette that matters. Marguerite will suffer for it. Look, I know what I'm talking about . . . the effects of the Fleming case . . . well, I'm still feeling them."

Lewis's openness, the casual way in which he referred to his own sexuality seemed – albeit unintentionally – to demand some form of reciprocation from Edmund, a similarly personal response of which he was incapable. He turned away, signalled to the waiter to bring them coffee, then returned to the conversation from a fresh angle.

"Surely she can be persuaded to give him up," Edmund said. "She must see that no good can come of it."

"Do you think that I haven't tried that already?" He spoke with such vehemence that a hush fell at the adjacent tables for a few seconds. He leaned forward. "I'm sorry," he said. "I shouldn't take it out on you."

To Edmund it didn't feel as if he had.

"But you have no idea what it does to me to see my sister so – so reduced by that man," Lewis went on. "She will never give him up, I know it. She has no enthusiasm for anything other than him, not even for her work. I fear for her."

"Then she must see a doctor, the sort who specializes in this kind of emotional disorder."

Lewis's expression froze. "I won't have her . . . shut away," he said.

There was something so poignant about this statement and the way it was said that Edmund, who had been about to speak, found himself taking a gulp of air instead.

"Look," he said, recovering. "I know a good man. Philbert is his name. He's a psychotherapist, very modern, studied in Austria. I think only in very extreme cases would there be any question of committing the patient. I'm sure it won't come to that with Marguerite. But you do agree she needs to see a specialist?"

Lewis tapped the side of his cup with the teaspoon. He had a lost look about him. He nodded without lifting his eyes.

"I could, with your permission, make an appointment with Philbert," Edmund said. "I know him personally. He will see her quickly."

"We'd just be getting an opinion, then?"

"Yes. He will suggest treatment, I am sure, but that can be taken one step at –"

"Our mother spent time in an asylum," Lewis said. His eyes were blurry. "I don't want that for Marguerite."

155

Edmund took his time in replying.

"I know you don't," he said, at last. "But Marguerite is unwell. Let her see this man and take advice from him. Believe me, from what I've seen he is very much in the business of keeping people out of asylums, even lost causes."

Lewis roused himself. "So, we would be in charge, we would have control?"

"He is a private doctor, yes."

Lewis allowed himself a few moments to think about it, then said, "You are right, it must be done. If you wouldn't mind making the necessary arrangements, and as quickly as possible, that would be most kind. Oh, and what about the fee?"

"I charge nothing for my pearls of wisdom," Edmund said, raising his hand in a royal salute. He had already decided to foot the bill himself as Lewis had no employment and possibly no access to Marguerite's accounts either. "I am told his fee is moderate," he said. "But let's get her there first."

Lewis smiled. His skin was smooth, with a sheen, and for the first time since they had sat down to eat he looked untroubled.

"Lucky I met you today," he said.

The next day, a Saturday, Edmund called around to Marguerite's apartment with the news that he had secured an appointment for her at Dr. Philbert's rooms in Bedford Square for the coming Thursday.

"I'm pleased about that," Lewis said. "Now that I've thought about it."

They went to find Marguerite. She was dozing on a chaise longue in the drawing room. It was in this very room that Marguerite always entertained. Edmund had been to so many wonderful parties here – bright affairs with Marguerite ministering to everyone, telling stories and even singing – that it was shocking, both to see her prostrate and the room so dismal. The curtains were closed when they went in and Lewis drew them back, saying that she had a visitor.

She turned her head slowly to see him and a smile flickered on her lips. The change in her was terrible.. Her face was pale and pinched, and because she had lost so much weight, her eyes seemed to bulge. She resembled one of those wretched individuals one saw in engravings of workhouse inmates from fifty years before.

Betty, Marguerite's maid appeared, looking nearly as wretched as her mistress, and asked Edmund if she could get him something.

"And I'm going to bring you some soup," she said to Marguerite, her voice soft and quavery. "No ifs or buts."

Edmund pulled over a chair and sat beside Marguerite. He had planned to be jovial, to cheer her up but now, faced with the reality of her condition, words failed him. He took her hand in his and fought to remain in command of his emotions while Lewis explained to her that she needed to see a doctor and it was all arranged.

"You're going to be well again," Edmund said, stroking her forearm.

"I hope so," she said.

Lewis left them alone.

There was no real conversation.

"I should never have released you," he said. "You should never have left the Colosseum."

"I feel so sad," she said, "that it frightens me." And she laid her head back on the pillow as though that utterance alone had drained her.

He found a copy of *The Moonstone* on her bookshelf and read to her for an hour, managing to raise a smile from her on a couple of occasions.

* * *

Dr. Philbert had built up quite a reputation for himself in the area of mental illness. He was a disciple of Sigmund Freud's and one of the few progressive souls in London who believed in the power of the subconscious to influence conscious behaviour. His methods had been very successful in a number of high-profile cases.

Lewis took Marguerite to see him on the allotted day and Dr. Philbert diagnosed an acute form of depression, advising first daily and then weekly sessions of psychotherapy in order to unlock whatever buried emotions were causing her current malaise. In addition, plenty of rest, a little gentle exercise and pleasant company in short snatches would help, he said. He foretold a favorable outcome.

The doctor's optimism was borne out over the following weeks. Edmund called as often as he could and each time he found Marguerite a little stronger and more alert. Betty always provided plenty of tasty morsels for tea which they took in the drawing room, seated in the large recessed window that overlooked the street. They chatted and Marguerite seemed to find comfort in remembering the old times at the Colosseum.

Lewis had found himself a job as a clerk with a wine merchant in New Bond Street which at least satisfied his need to be financially independent. When he came home in the evening, he would sit with Marguerite and Edmund and they would fall in and out of conversation, watching the street below from the window and reading snippets to one another from the newspaper in a way that Edmund found very pleasant.

A very close bond existed between Marguerite and Lewis and, though Edmund was aware of their family history, he became better acquainted with it during these interludes when brother and sister together recalled the past. They had been born into a theatrical family – the only two surviving children of ten and Marguerite the elder by six years. The Davenports were a family act. They sang and danced and toured the country constantly, not because they were so much in demand, but because they went wherever there was hope of work. They had no permanent home. The mother, Iris, was subject to bouts of depression which necessitated her going away to the asylum for long stretches. She was the first to die. Worn out from losing children, living in poverty and battling her own demons, she succumbed to a chill that turned into bronchitis and ended up as rheumatic fever. After her death, Marguerite and Lewis and their father, Maurice, continued to tour. Six months later, Maurice killed himself by cutting his wrists in the bathroom of a cheap hotel in Hartlepool. The manager, on top of the usual room rate, charged the children an extra pound to pay for the cleaning up. Marguerite was sixteen and Lewis ten. They had no relations that they knew of.

Lewis had always hated the stage and showed no flair for it and so Marguerite launched herself on a solo career as a singer of comic songs. She got enough work to support the two of them and send Lewis to school but what she really wanted to do was become an actress. She got small parts in several West End productions. Marie Bancroft at the Haymarket liked her and used her frequently. Eventually, she landed herself a plum role as Olivia Primrose in *Olivia* and that was when Edmund discovered her, picking her from all the talent in London to grace the Colosseum stage alongside himself.

Success followed on success and they became one of the most famous on-stage couples in the country. After that, Marguerite's career and finances were secure. When Lewis was eighteen,

Marguerite paid for him to be apprenticed to a firm of architects, Lincoln and Bennett's, in Grosvenor Square. But, before his training was complete, the Fleming sodomy trial took place and Lewis offered himself as a character witness. He stated, in open court, that he was a friend of Reginald Fleming's not a lover, that he had known the man for years, and that he respected and admired him. Reginald was convicted. It was inferred, correctly, that Lewis was of the same persuasion as the defendant, though the prosecution team were unable to find any corroborating evidence. His reputation, however, was ruined. The senior partners at Lincoln and Bennett's terminated his employment with them. He went to Paris. As an alien, he was barred from resuming his studies there and had to settle instead for a draughtsman's position in a tiny office just off the Place de Clichy where he remained for five years. He had recently returned to England in the hope that all would be forgotten and he would be able to finish his apprenticeship. However, he found all doors closed to him.

Any man, having set his sights on an architectural career and who found himself at thirty years of age in a lowly clerk's job was, in Edmund's view, perfectly justified in feeling bitter about it. Yet Lewis showed no signs of this. He worked every day at the wine merchant's without complaint and in the evenings tended to his sister with a patience and loyalty that was inspiring to watch.

For Edmund had made a study of Lewis and was impressed by him. Here was a man who did not seek anyone's good opinion. He could enter a room without saying a word, sit on the sofa, fold his hands, let the conversation glide over him and only when he felt inclined make some comment or other. Sometimes, without any preamble he would produce a sketchpad and make pencil drawings of the fireplace or the lamp or the bookcase.

One day he did a sketch of Edmund but was not pleased with it, saying that he had given him a monstrous nose that he didn't deserve. Edmund stopped Lewis from throwing it away – it was a good likeness, if something of a caricature – and asked him if he could keep it. It would come in useful, he said, if he ever needed reminding that he was not a handsome fellow because one look at it would dispel that notion. When he got back to the Colosseum, for safekeeping, he slipped the drawing between the pages of Talma's *Essay on the Actor's Art*, a book he referred to often.

It was an enclosed world at Marguerite's apartment and while he was there Edmund put aside his own problems. He never once suggested that there was anything amiss.

One Saturday afternoon, Edmund arrived as usual and, instead of being led straight to Marguerite in the drawing room, Betty the maid, red-eyed, said, "Mr. Jeffers, oh I'm so glad you're here. Something terrible has . . ." Overcome by emotion, she guided Edmund to the study where Lewis was waiting for him, sitting on a chair by the window.

The room was warm and Lewis had closed his eyes against the slanting sunlight. His hair was tossed as though he had come straight from his bed. He jumped to his feet, a letter in his hand.

"Thank God you've come," he said. "It's bad news, very bad news, I'm afraid."

"But she was doing so well . . ."

"It's this letter – it's from the Metropole, from Leopold Barrie in effect. They've cut her off . . ." Lewis scanned the page for the exact words. "'. . . *due to your protracted illness, the Board of Management has reached the regrettable decision to terminate your contract with the Metropole Theatre, effective immediately. One month's salary is to be paid in lieu of notice plus statutory holidays . . .*' and so on . . . Can they do this?"

Edmund could not hide his relief. "I thought for a moment her condition was worse. May I?" He reached out for the letter, read down through it. "I would say it seems they are within their rights to do so, but why a theatre would cast off its most valuable asset in this way makes no sense to me."

"It suits him to get rid of her. He doesn't want her any longer," Lewis said. "So he just tosses her aside."

"Even Leopold Barrie is not that crass," Edmund said.

"It is all his doing, I'm convinced of it." Lewis walked across the room, arched his back to stretch it. "I cannot show her this, I simply cannot. It will break her."

Edmund delayed. He was about to launch himself on a course of action he did not want to take, but there seemed to be no alternative. At length, he said, "I will go and see Leopold myself. I will try and change his mind. I can promise nothing, I am not close to my father-in-law, but I will do my best."

Lewis turned around.

"Then I will go with you," he said.

"No, I think it would be best if –"

"Why? Because I might say the wrong thing?"

"No," Edmund said. "Probably you would say too much of the right thing which is much harder to take."

Lewis smiled. He folded the letter up and put it away in his pocket.

"Thank you for doing this. I know you would rather not." He extended a hand and they shook. "You're a true friend."

Edmund released his grip early. He felt the room unbearably warm.

"Let us go to Marguerite," he said.

Chapter Seventeen

Leopold Barrie was a man of exquisite taste and this was, in Edmund's view, his only commendable feature. Lord Barrie's private art collection was world famous, the envy of friends and enemies alike. Mostly housed at his country estate, Edmund had been stunned on first seeing it. There were paintings by Delacroix, Ingres, Turner, Degas, Caillebotte, Sisley and Morisot as well as older works such as a bust of Costanza Buonarelli by Bernini and an engraving of the Nativity by Dürer that dated back as far as 1504.

Leopold was known too for his generous commissions. G.F. Watts' huge portrait of Lady Constance, which graced the dining room at Warwickstown, had commanded a record sum and was appreciated as much for its cost as for its accomplishment. Burne-Jones had spent an entire year there too completing a fresco on the end wall of the first-floor gallery. Entitled *The Four Seasons*, it was a sequence of pastoral scenes executed with such breathtaking delicacy that Edmund, on beholding it, was speechless for several minutes.

Latterly, Leopold had begun to collect theatres, or rather, substantial portions of them. And this, to Edmund's mind, was the definition of the man. He loved theatres but cared little for drama. Oh yes, he could discuss at length all that was currently on show in the West End. He was intelligent, articulate, a sound logician, but the play did not exist that could move him. He had never cried for Beauty.

Family obligations dictated that Edmund and Leopold must spend time together and this they could do, and civilly, provided the occasion did not last too long. But, on a deeper level – and they both were aware of this – they were antipathetic towards one another.

It was, therefore, with a certain amount of dread that Edmund set off one morning after breakfast to meet Leopold at his club, the Whitehall in Parliament Street. They had made the appointment for eleven o'clock but Edmund left home early and took the route along the Embankment to allow himself time to gather his thoughts for what promised to be an unpleasant interview.

A stiff breeze blew but the air was warm and unwholesome like stale breath in a sick room. The river was sluggish, the water having a viscous quality to it and an orange hue that made it look like molten chocolate. The walking, even though it was not strenuous, brought him out in a sweat and he slackened his pace. It was then that he noticed up ahead, on one of the slipways, that a knot of people had gathered. He could discern a bargeman in blackened clothes, a female servant with a shopping basket over one arm and a young woman of more refined appearance who stood a little apart from the others covering her mouth with a handkerchief. The presence of a policeman confirmed the suspicion that something was wrong.

When Edmund reached the slipway, the full horror of what had happened became evident. Someone had been pulled from the river. The bargeman was wet up to his waist, the policeman had his notebook out. At Edmund's approach, the group fell back as though only too willing to hand over to him this grisly scene. And then he saw that it was a girl who lay on the stone, obviously dead. Not in the water long enough to be swollen but her skin was blue-white like old china and her lips were purple. She had black stockings on, but no shoes. One of her legs was caught up under her, the knee bent at a curious angle. The bargeman, an old, slow, heavy fellow, cupped his hand under her tiny foot and straightened her leg, gently placing it down again beside the other. The refined young woman sobbed.

"Is there anything I can do, Officer?" Edmund said.

The policeman shook his head. "Nothing anyone can do for her now."

"She was tangled up in my rope," the bargeman said, owning responsibility. "Poor little mite. Must have been playing down here last night and fell in. I don't know how many times I've told them not to play round the boats, but do they listen?"

Edmund could not take his eyes off the little body. Ever so slight with thin, matted hair and eyes so black he could see his own reflection there. He wanted to close them but feared the hard, cold touch of her.

The bargeman shook his head. "I'm always telling them . . . always . . ." There were tears in his throat.

The servant, a housekeeper type, clicked her tongue in a disapproving way. Whether she was critical of the bargeman or the heedless child or just the sheer unfairness of the world, it was impossible to say.

The policeman got down on his haunches to have a closer look. He lifted the child's chin and pulled away the collar of her dress to reveal a thin, whip-like mark across her windpipe and some slight bruising.

"Strangled by the look of it," he said.

The two women gasped at this. The bargeman walked away to the water's edge and stared out.

Edmund looked at the little girl who lay dead at his feet and said, "Who would do a thing like this? Who would kill a child?" The question was unanswerable, he knew that. It was nonsense even to ask it but this demand for an explanation somehow deflected from the awfulness of the scene in front of them. "Who?" he said, almost pleading.

"Killed upriver, I shouldn't wonder and dumped in," the policeman said. "Putney, I'd say." As if it was well known that that was the way they treated their young up there. "More bodies than fish in this stretch some days."

The refined lady removed the handkerchief from her mouth just long enough to say, "There's something round her neck, Officer."

The policeman pulled aside the child's wet hair and discovered a leather thong. "Could be we've found the murder weapon," he said.

He hooked it with a finger and fished it out over the top of her dress. There was a ring attached to it. He checked the inside of it for engraving but there was none so he laid it down on the child's breast. He stood up, wiped his hand on his trousers and shook his head.

"Another nobody," he said. "City's full of 'em."

When Edmund arrived at The Whitehall Club, fifteen minutes late, and asked for Leopold at the front desk, his voice seemed too loud, his movements too rushed, in the still, dark interior. Stuffed animal heads looked down at him from the walls as he climbed the stairs. All around him one clock after another chimed the quarter hour.

He found Leopold in the reading room on his own, thumbing through a newspaper. He sank into the buttoned-leather armchair opposite his father-in-law. A waiter appeared.

"I'll have a large brandy," Edmund said.

"Earl Grey for me." Leopold put aside the newspaper. "This business with Parr's Bank is a bit dubious, isn't it?" he said. "Sixty thousand gone, just like that? There's talk that one of the cashiers had 'problems'. Sixty thousand is a hell of a lot of problems, if you ask me."

The waiter returned. Edmund downed half of his drink in one go. It was like swallowing a firebrand. His gullet and stomach flared up as the liquid went down. The sensation, unpleasant as it was, at least distracted from the terrible images that were swamping his brain in the wake of what he had just witnessed. The respite did not last long, however.

Leopold was staring at him.

"Bit early for that, isn't it?"

"I came upon something really horrible on the way over here. A child was taken from the river near Westminster Bridge. She had been murdered."

"In that case, have another one," Leopold said. "I knew something was up the minute you came in."

Edmund refused the offer with a wave of his hand. "She was about ten," he said.

"Were the police there?"

"Yes, it was all being dealt with in the proper manner. Strangled, by the looks of it. Killed and then thrown into the river." There was a dip in the seat of Edmund's armchair and it required some considerable effort to sit forwards successfully. "The truth is I feel quite peculiar about it. Obviously, it's a terrible thing for the poor girl and her family, a dreadful crime, but it seems to have destabilized me . . . in a more personal way.

I can't get it out of my head . . ."

"Have another drink," Leopold said.

"It was all so – so casual, I suppose. And here am I going about the place putting on plays, eating dinners, going for walks and thinking that is normal. Then I discover there's another normality I know nothing about."

"Don't you read the papers? This kind of thing happens all the time."

"It's different when you stumble upon it." Edmund put down his glass. "Don't mind me, it's the brandy talking. Probably all be forgotten by tomorrow."

There was a respectable delay while Leopold poured out his tea. He took several sips, then pushed his cup away as if he'd had enough already.

"You wanted to see me about something?" he said.

"Ah, yes." Edmund took a moment to adjust his thinking. "It's a delicate matter and not one I bring up lightly. But, as you are aware, Marguerite Davenport is a very dear friend of mine and has been for ten years or more. She is unwell."

"Yes, the larynx can be temperamental."

"She is suffering from melancholia."

Leopold pursed his lips. "Then I am sorry to hear that."

"Is it true that the Metropole has terminated her contract?"

"Yes. And don't look at me like that, as if I'm the Wicked Stepmother. It wasn't my doing, it was a board decision. She has missed something like thirty performances which is not acceptable. We have taken legal advice on it."

"You have the best actress in London in your employ, one of the greatest artists of our time, and you cannot exercise a little patience?"

"We cannot wait indefinitely."

"Marguerite Davenport is the best asset a theatre could have.

Any board of management in its right mind should see that. They are not stupid, are they, these board members? And surely, even they must have a sprinkling of human kindness in them. Marguerite, I promise you, will soon recover her health. I appeal to you, Leopold, to do what you can to change their minds."

"That is out of the question."

"Why?"

"Because the decision is made."

"But it can be overturned."

"It won't be."

Edmund stopped, looked at his father-in-law. Leopold returned his gaze, unblinking.

"You mean," Edmund said, "you will make sure it won't be, is that it?"

"I don't take kindly to accusations," Leopold said.

"Look, I know what is going on between you two."

"There is nothing 'going on'."

"Don't play me for a fool, Leopold – the bloody birds in the trees know there is. She is not a woman to be trifled with. When she gives her heart to someone she expects the same in return."

"As do we all," Leopold said.

"You cannot keep her hanging on like some sort of jackanapes, hiding her in the closet whenever you hear footsteps coming. Either marry her or drop her." The air prickled between them. "I'm sorry. I'm a little churned up today. What I am trying to say is that Marguerite is the type of woman who wants all or nothing. This in-between state does not suit her at all and neither is it good for her reputation." He paused, breathed deeply. "I believe it is unfair of you, Leopold, to protract the affair in this way when you have no intention of doing . . . well, of doing the decent thing."

Leopold gave a dry laugh. "Unfairness is the way of the

world, old chap. You have just spent the last half hour telling me about a murdered child pulled from the river."

"Can you not see what this is doing to her? The doctor has diagnosed a form of melancholia."

"So you keep telling me. Surely I am not to be held responsible for tipping the precarious balance of Marguerite Davenport's mind? She does a pretty good job of that herself. And I resent your impertinence. Only the fact that you are my son-in-law is preventing me from having you thrown out."

Edmund got up, walked to the window and looked out at the unkempt backs of the houses opposite. Below him were the higgledy-piggledy yards with their washing lines and coalhouses and sheds half falling down. It was another world to the street out front from which Edmund had entered the club, where the terraces on either side were uniform and immaculate, like false teeth.

"Look, I can do no right by the woman," Leopold said, calmer. "If I stay away she pines to an unnatural degree so that I worry and, when I see her, it is never enough."

"Do you have feelings for her?" Edmund continued to stare out of the window. He did not want to see Leopold's expression.

"Of course I have feelings for her. What do you think I am? Why do you think I put up with this – this mess?"

Edmund turned around. "This mess, as you call it, is entirely of your own making. I urge you to resolve it."

"There is no resolution. I am married and always will be. Marguerite knows that."

"But she cannot accept it. If you cannot marry her then I believe, as a gentleman, you should end the thing."

"I refuse to take instruction from you, Edmund, regarding my duty as a gentleman."

There was another long, tense silence.

Then Leopold said, "Listen, I have a wife, a very tolerant wife who makes few demands on me. She does, however, expect to be treated with respect, which is no more than she deserves. There was an incident recently at the Metropole when Marguerite behaved monstrously. Constance's position was seriously undermined and I won't have it. I won't have her publicly humiliated. I'm afraid Marguerite has become something of an embarrassment lately."

"An embarrassment? The woman is in love with you!"

Leopold seemed to look in upon himself. "Then God help her," he said.

"So this is the real reason the contract has been torn up – you want her out of the way. Lewis said as much but I would not believe him, could not believe you capable of so cynical a move."

"People need to realize that Love is no different from anything else in life," Leopold said. "There are consequences if you break the rules – it's as simple as that."

"You have taken away her heart, her reputation, her career. You have ruined the woman and you do not even have the decency to care."

"You are wrong, I do care. But there is nothing to be done about it."

"Then I will take her back at the Colosseum myself."

"I am afraid that is not possible," Leopold said. "It is not possible because I, as majority shareholder, will not allow it." His expression was flat and there was no emotion in what he said, only centuries of certitude.

"Then I bid you good day, sir," Edmund said, and left without another word.

On his way back to the Strand he passed the slipway where the dead child had lain. There was no trace of what had happened. Even the barge laden with coal had departed and pedestrians were passing by, oblivious. Sunshine had pierced through the canopy of cloud and brightened everything. The leaves in the trees overhead cast a dappled shadow where he walked, and created a pattern across the pavement that with every wafting breeze, slid over and back like the ebb and flow of a luminous tide.

Two children ran by, laughing, one chasing the other and it felt, to Edmund, as though he was part of some great conspiracy.

Chapter Eighteen

Rosalind Doyle was only four years old when her mother died of scarlet fever leaving her in the care of her father and five older brothers. The Doyle males were a volatile lot, easily riled and prone to bouts of drunkenness but they were also fiercely loyal, generous and loving. One by one, they left school and followed their father into St. Katherine's Dockyard where they were known as 'The Regulars', not one of them having missed a day's work since he began.

The running of the household fell to Rosalind as soon as she was old enough to manage and, though the work was hard for a child, she was loved and minded and sometimes even pandered to in that family of men . . . but rarely understood. To Rosalind, it was like living amongst people who spoke English but with a strange and difficult dialect where the most important words, the ones that made sense of everything, were unintelligible.

The only female who had any impact on Rosalind's life was a formidable aunt, of whom she was very fond, a sister of her father's who visited often. This lady, Ellen Doyle, despite a deprived childhood and barely any schooling had fought her way up by a circuitous route to qualify as a midwife at St. Thomas's Hospital. She owned a house in Lambeth and lived in the downstairs rooms while she let the upstairs to a student doctor who was afraid of her. Even her own family was a little scared of her – a woman with property, a career and a towering personality. She was, in her youth, attractive but Ellen Doyle never married. Perhaps it was the large number of bad husbands and fathers she met in the course of her employment that scared her off the matrimonial state. Their exploits provided her with excellent source material and she regaled the young Rosalind with endless true accounts of deserters, philanderers and wife-beaters. She covered every example of cold-hearted behaviour that men display towards the bearers of their children. Mothers and infants were always the sufferers and, invariably, in these stories, one or the other – sometimes both – ended up dead. Thus Rosalind grew up with the impression that men, if tightly managed, could be protectors of the women they loved. Left to their own devices, however, they were more likely to be scoundrels. The trick was to know that and take control.

It was, therefore, in a spirit of helpfulness that she sat down to write the letter. At no point did she sense that she might be destroying dreams or happiness or even love with her words. She believed it was more the case that she was providing the information and means with which to achieve these ideals.

The process was slow as she had received little instruction in forming her letters correctly though she could read tolerably well. It took several attempts to get the phrasing right and to produce a clean, legible copy but when it was finished she put on her shawl and took an omnibus to Trafalgar Square. There she hailed a delivery boy with a satchel on his back and gave him a penny to take the letter for her. She followed at a little distance and watched him as he entered the Colosseum Theatre.

Violet Jeffers hated Calpurnia. It was bad enough having to perform as Caesar's wife nightly without having to rehearse her during the day as well. There was nothing in the twenty-seven lines of dialogue, nothing in the two hundred and three words that Calpurnia spoke, to inspire any fresh approach to the character. Violet had Calpurnia's dullness to perfection. And yet today Edmund had insisted on going over her part. In Act One, Scene Two, she had only to say '*Here, my Lord,*' in answer to Caesar's call and she had been made to repeat it at least eight times.

Edmund was sitting halfway back in the auditorium, with Charles by his side. He stood up and, from the shadows, said the line himself the way he wanted it. She copied him. Apparently, unsatisfactorily. He tried again. Still she did not grasp it. He walked down to the front of the stage. He rarely got cross at rehearsals but she could detect in his voice a note of irritation that she, his wife, should be so obtuse. He wanted more urgency, he said. He wanted a wildness in her look to suggest that the City of Rome herself was on the brink of anarchy and destruction.

She tried again.

"Too much," he said, shaking his head.

Violet could not understand why he was putting so much emphasis on a throwaway line and told him so.

To which he replied, clearly affronted, "Throwaway lines are just that. I have disposed of them before we even begin."

It was five o'clock when they finished up.

Violet went straight to her dressing room, collected her belongings and put on her coat. But before leaving the theatre she went to the office in the lobby and checked her pigeonhole for mail. She found two pieces. One was a letter, possibly from a

175

fan, which she stuffed into her bag to read later. It put her in mind of the bundles of letters from admirers that used to arrive for Marguerite, so many, in fact, that a pigeonhole was deemed inadequate and a laundry hamper was installed to accommodate them.

The second item left for her was a note from Edmund to say he would be detained at the theatre that evening as he and Charles needed to go over the budget for the coming quarter and they might as well have supper brought in for them while they did it.

For the third time that week, Violet would dine at home, alone.

It would have been easier and more pleasant to eat in the drawing room where she could have sat in her favourite armchair and taken her meal at the card table in front of the fire but Violet thought to do so might make her appear disconsolate to the staff and so she opted for the dining room instead. The huge table was set for one and there was a little glass vase by her plate containing a sprig of winter jasmine. Violet ate without enthusiasm.

Afterwards, upstairs in her bedroom, there was a good hour to pass before she had to leave for the theatre and perhaps this freedom made her rather aimless in her preparations. She washed her face and dried it, rearranged her hair, applied some eau de cologne to her wrists and temples and when that was done she sat on the bed to think about what she should do next. It was only then that she remembered the letter in her bag and took it out. She opened it.

'*Mrs. Jeffers,*' it said, '*I am writing to you as a friend. I feel obliged to inform you . . .*'

The hand was childish. There was no signature at the end or any indication as to who had sent it.

'*I feel obliged to inform you, before it comes to be known by all and sundry, as it will, that your husband is engaging in abnormal acts with other men. At least, I know of one such act and with an individual of lowly rank. Just ask him where his watch is.*'

Violet threw down the letter as if it had stung her but her eyes never strayed from where it lay on the bed. Minutes went by then, steeling herself, she picked it up again and resumed reading.

'*Your husband's sin is not your sin and yet, if this ever gets out, your name will be as mud beneath the feet of decent folk. I tell you this not that I might gain but that you might take some action to save yourself (and him, if you should choose) from the awful fate that awaits. I know this must be unwelcome news but I hope the knowledge of it will help spare you plenty of heartache in the future. For this reason, though I cannot sign my name to this letter, I consider myself (and hope you will too) a true well-wisher.*'

A terrible stillness came over Violet. She sat on the edge of the bed, the letter in her hand, examining the objects on her dressing stand: the brush and mirror with the mother-of-pearl backs to them that she never used, the cloisonné pot in which she kept her rings, the ebony tea caddy inlaid with ivory, the lavender-scented pomander that she had taken out of the drawer that morning and forgotten to put back.

She returned to the letter, read it through three more times. The information contained therein about Edmund, while it was horrible, upsetting, offensive, was not altogether shocking to her and for that reason she had little doubt that it was true. There had been from the very beginning of their marriage and even before that a certain lack of ardour in their physical relations. Edmund was a vigorous, strong, healthy man and surely subject to the same natural urges as any. Yet it often felt, during the act of love, that they were less intimate in the marital bed than they were sitting across the dining table from each other at breakfast next morning. Neither had she expected the frequency of their couplings to taper off quite so early in the marriage, a development she accepted without complaint. It was, in fact, a relief to her.

For Violet had not been totally honest with Edmund – or with her father, for that matter. The incident in Switzerland with the apothecary's son was rather more serious than the harmless schoolgirl dalliance she had described to them all. She had almost come to believe that version of events herself but in her most private moments the truth would not be denied. She could still see the twilit forest and hear the rooks circling above with their raucous, jeering cries. The earth was damp beneath her, his breath moist against her face. The words, gentle at first, then insistent. His hand heavy on her throat, the ripping of her underclothes. Then he was on top of her, pressing down so she could barely breathe let alone move. And afterwards, while he buttoned himself up, he told her to stop snivelling, that what she had lost wasn't so very precious after all – he could vouch for that.

But she was practical as ever. They were miles from anywhere and so she rode on the bicycle behind him all the way back to Vernier, her arms around his waist as though still in the thrall of Love's Sweet Dream. She played the besotted young woman because if she spoke out against Gustav, revealed that she was no longer a virgin – her maidenhood lost to a man of lowly status – the shame for her and for her father would have been too much to bear. She married without telling anyone about it and then she feared being 'found out' in the marriage bed as much as she feared the sexual act itself. Edmund, however, never discovered her secret though he must have sensed her innate distaste for the physical expression of their love and this, she had supposed, explained to some degree the gradual decrease in sexual activity.

When she analyzed how she felt now, 'betrayed' did not seem an apt description. She was angry that her husband had taken such risks with his own and therefore with her, reputation – and disappointed that for all his artistic high-mindedness Edmund, like the basest of men, was a slave to his own bodily impulses. There was even a tinge of regret, now that she had confirmation she could never be the object of his desire. The thought that he had committed adulterous acts with men rather than women she did not find especially repugnant. Sexuality of whatever kind she found unpleasant. If this ever became public, it was the words she would dread more than anything else – 'pederast', 'invert', 'sodomite', 'onanist' – words that would keep resonating forever. What people said was far more important than what they thought.

And where was Love in all this? Every day she prayed that no harm would befall her husband. She enjoyed his company, admired his talent, worshipped his status, thought him handsome and witty, and was proud to be seen in his company. Was not that Love? They did not have the kind of passion one read about in silly novels but who would want it anyway? Surely theirs was a dependable kind of love, the type that was the bedrock of most marriages, the kind of love that could survive a setback like this, if only it could be kept secret?

Violet sat for a long time. She did not cry. After a while, she got up and pulled on her gloves. She folded the letter in half, then in quarters and stuffed it down inside her corset beneath her breasts. The hard edges of the paper stuck into her but she kept it there all night, even when she was on stage playing Calpurnia.

Chapter Nineteen

Violet considered how best to deal with the anonymous letter and its contents. She did not have any friends to confide in and she was reluctant to approach her father just yet as it was still possible that no one need ever know about it. As for confronting Edmund, one anonymous letter seemed too little evidence to go on. What she did not want was to be faced with a welter of denials from him or, if he confessed, apologies and vague promises to do better. She would keep closer counsel. Firstly, she needed to ascertain the veracity of the allegations – after all, there was a slim possibility that they were false. Once Edmund's transgressions were confirmed, she needed to know the details and the extent of them before she tackled him. The more she could find out at this stage, the stronger was her position.

With this in mind, an advertisement in the *London Times* caught her eye. It was a large one, with a double border all around.

'**Mr. Alfred J. Hutton,**' it said. '**Private Investigator. Metropolitan Police background. Discretion and confidentiality guaranteed.**'

Violet telephoned to make an appointment. She went to his rooms in Chelsea, feeling very nervous but determined not to reveal the purpose of her visit until she was sure of him.

Alfred J. Hutton met her at the front door and escorted her to his office. He was tall but rotund, his torso egg-shaped, his movements surprisingly nimble given his size. He wore round black spectacles that sat high on his nose very close to his eyes and gave him the look of an eager schoolboy.

When they were seated, Mr. Hutton summoned his housekeeper for some tea and they sat in silence while the old lady brought it in on a tray and poured it out for them. He told her he wanted no further interruptions and she withdrew from the room.

Mr. Hutton slurped his tea, then without any prompting he launched into a summary of his experience, his working methods and plenty other extraneous detail. He told Violet that he had worked in the Metropolitan Police Force for forty years, rising to the rank of Chief Inspector from which he had retired two years previously. He was married to Elsie. They lived in Greenwich. His two sons were grown up and a great source of pride to him, his eldest having just qualified as a doctor, the younger an engineer. In his spare time he grew roses and entered them in competition at the local shows. He dealt, in the main, with missing persons and divorce cases and with solicitors trying to trace the beneficiaries of wills but he could turn his hand to anything. After all these years, he said, nothing surprised or shocked him.

"Anything said within these four walls is kept here, I can assure you of that, Mrs. Jeffers." He looked at her with a steadfast gaze, assessing her as much as she was assessing him.

"Do you grow the rose Albertine in your garden, Mr. Hutton?"

He pushed his chair away from the desk and folded his hands in his lap.

"I do, I do indeed," he said, as if they were discussing a mutual friend. "I like the old ramblers but I have other favourites too. 'Belle de Crecy' for instance." This said with absolutely no trace of a French accent. "For scent you cannot beat 'Conrad Ferdinand Meyer'. Exquisite. You are an enthusiast?"

"No, but I am familiar with Albertine. It grows in my parents' garden."

"She is beautiful, very beautiful."

He sat, seemingly lost in thought. He was a patient man. It was the fact that he had not yet asked her why she had come to see him, that made her speak. She told all.

He listened without interrupting. When she had finished, he looked at the anonymous letter through an eyeglass and felt the paper between his thumb and forefinger. He pouted slightly when he was concentrating.

"Cheap paper, poor schooling. You did not see who delivered this letter to the theatre?"

"No, it was waiting for me in the office."

"Did anyone in the office see who delivered it?"

"I have not asked."

Mr. Hutton nodded. "Do you have any suspicion as to who this letter could be from?"

"None."

The meeting concluded with Violet engaging Mr. Hutton to keep Edmund under surveillance for one month, after which time they would meet again to discuss his findings, if any.

A month later, the morning of their second interview, Violet woke with a start. Edmund was already up eating his breakfast when she came downstairs to the dining room. She took the lid off a tureen and helped herself to some grapefruit segments which she dredged with sugar.

Edmund looked up from his newspaper.

"You're pale," he said, studying her face so closely that she blushed. It was as if he could see straight into her, as if he knew of her meeting with the private investigator, as if he knew all about Mr. Alfred J. Hutton and how he had been occupying himself for the last four weeks.

"I didn't sleep well," she said.

He put down the newspaper, poured out tea for her and refreshed his own cup.

"Everything all right?" he said.

"What do you mean?"

"What I say. Is everything all right?"

"Of course it is," she said, reaching for some toast. She buttered it, heaped on the marmalade though she had no intention of eating it. "Isn't it always?"

Edmund, diplomatically, took up his newspaper again. A few minutes later, he gave a derisory laugh.

"Listen to this. Something from the archives," he said, and read out loud. "*At the battle of Majuba Hill, the first of the wounded was a little bugler of the Dublin Fusiliers. He'd received three wounds to the chest and one in the right arm that had shattered the limb completely beyond saving. He managed to drag himself to the rear to seek medical assistance. The chaplain said: "How old are you?" "Fourteen years and seven months," was the reply. Asked respecting his wounds, the little bugler said, "It is nothing, only a slight stinging in my right hand." What stamina, what bravery we take for granted in our nation's soldiery!*" Edmund deposited the newspaper on the table. "What exactly would the *Times* have us believe? That we should have an army of children who are either too stupid or too young to understand the seriousness of their situation? Why, it's absolute nonsense. I'm surprised at the *Times*."

"The report came direct from the battle site, did it not? I

presume the journalist must have witnessed this scene," Violet said.

"Presume all you like, but a fourteen-year-old boy with a mangled chest and his arm hanging off does not complain of a 'slight stinging in my left hand'. It is a complete fiction."

Violet stared at him.

"And you," she said. "You are always so meticulous in separating truth from fiction?"

He caught the sharpness in her tone but reflected for a moment before speaking.

"You know, I think sometimes, truth and lies are the same thing."

"You frighten me, Edmund, when you talk like that."

"No, take this case in point," he said. "A man came up to me in the street one day. He knew who I was. He was ragged in appearance and had a cast in his eye and I thought he was going to beg money from me. Instead, he asked me for a job. He said he had a wife and four children, that they were homeless due to the fact that his house had been burnt down the previous week. He was a carpenter, decent and hard-working, he said. To me, he looked shifty."

"Most unsavory," Violet said.

"It's very hard to trust a man with a squint. You always think while one eye is proclaiming the truth, the other one is declaring it all lies. Anyway, for whatever reason – his poor eyesight perhaps – I took him on. I found out afterwards that there was no wife, no children, no fire and he had never worked as a carpenter."

"A born liar then."

"No, not at all. He needed to say those things to convince me of the truth because he was a decent and a hardworking man. He is still. Been with me for ten years now. It's Tom Harper I'm talking about. Now, you wouldn't call him a blackguard, would you?"

Violet said nothing, nervous of where this premise might lead.

Edmund said, "I think what I'm saying is that a person may feel they have been lied to, when, in essence, they have not."

"A lie is still a lie, Edmund. No matter how much you wish it was not."

Edmund stood up and kissed her on the top of the head.

"I'm off. Join me for lunch?" he said. "We haven't talked properly for a long time."

Violet focused on the toast she had been unable to eat, began to cut it into even smaller pieces. "I promised my mother I'd nip round with some of that perry that Mrs. Phillips made. She wants to try it out for her next dinner party."

"Another time then," he said, lingering behind her.

She did not look round. "Yes, another time."

At a quarter to eleven, Violet took a hackney cab to Sloane Square then got out and walked. It was a chilly morning and she went briskly. In a perverse way she hoped Mr. Alfred J. Hutton would have plenty of information about her husband's sexual relations with other men. At least then there would be no uncertainty, because that was what she disliked most about her current situation.

"Would you care for some refreshment, Mrs. Jeffers?" Mr. Hutton said, when they were seated either side of his desk. The glare from the window reflected on his spectacles so she could not see his eyes.

"Not on this occasion, Mr. Hutton, thank you," Violet said. She wanted to transact her business as quickly as possible and with the least amount of humiliation. On the desk between them there was a brown, manila folder and nothing else.

"I have here the results of my surveillance on your husband,"

Mr. Hutton said, sliding it across the polished wood to her as if he was playing a game of chess and this was his opening move. His hand rested on it, like a paperweight. "I have listed his movements beginning on the twenty-first of last month and finishing on yesterday's date. I observed only one assignation of the type that has concerned you, the details of which are contained herein." He removed his hand from the file. "You may prefer to take it away with you, look at it in private."

"No," Violet said. "I will read it here, if you don't mind."

"Then I will leave you alone to –"

"Please stay."

"Very well," he said, and to spare her what embarrassment he could, he got up from his desk and crossed the room to the bookcase.

"Please take your time, Mrs. Jeffers."

She could hear him behind her pulling out a book to read.

"Ask me anything you like, anything at all."

Violet left on her navy, pigskin gloves though they made it difficult to turn the pages. Here before her was her husband's life, catalogued as though somehow she had had him reduced to mere words on paper.

Mr. Hutton had a tidy, even hand that was easy to read.

'*10.15 a.m. – Visits barber shop, Messrs. Barnes and Sons at Bedford Street.*

'*10.45 a.m. – Takes coffee at Gatti's Café on the Strand. Exchanges greetings with several other patrons. Leaves alone.*

'*11 a.m. – Returns to Colosseum Theatre.*'

Every minute was accounted for. She scanned through the report, noted that there were several visits to Marguerite's apartment, of which she knew nothing, but she did not stop until her eye settled on an entry halfway down the third page.

"This is the assignation to which you referred," she said.

"Edmund went to a pub in Drummond Road and left with another man. You say they went together to Southwark Park."

"That is correct, Mrs. Jeffers." Mr. Hutton remained at the bookcase behind her.

"They climbed over the fence?"

"Yes, the park is normally closed at that hour."

"I see."

"This must be very difficult for you," Mr. Hutton said.

"It is. But please tell me the truth. No shadows on the cave wall. I am able to face reality, you know."

Mr. Hutton snapped shut his book, replaced it on the shelf and returned to his desk. He sat down.

"Yes," he said. "I believe you can."

"There seem to be certain omissions in the text here," Violet said, indicating the handwritten pages.

"I thought it wise," he said. "In case this information should fall into the wrong hands. And, I have to confess, I wanted to protect you from some of the more disturbing details."

"If I was afraid of what you might find, I wouldn't have hired you, Mr. Hutton."

He bowed his head to accept her point.

"Was this man known to Edmund, do you think?"

"It is unlikely that they knew each other – their backgrounds are too dissimilar," he said. "Subsequent enquiries have shown that your husband's companion was one Wilfred Oliver, a baker from Lambeth."

"Is this man a prostitute in his spare time?"

Mr. Hutton took a handkerchief from his pocket and blew his nose with force.

"You are very direct, Mrs. Jeffers," he said.

"I am," Violet said, waiting for the answer.

"I did not witness any money changing hands. This individual

187

has his own shop and in my experience men of his station do not usually take a professional interest in sexual matters."

"When they were in the park together . . . could you see what they were doing?"

"I could." He shifted his gaze.

"Please tell me, Mr. Hutton."

"Then prepare yourself, my dear," he said. "You are very young . . . but I can see that you are determined. I witnessed sexual activity between the two."

"Exactly what did you see, Mr. Hutton?"

He looked towards the ceiling, searching for a way to describe the scene with sensitivity.

"After some preliminaries, a certain act was performed," he said. "An act that between men is considered a consummation."

Violet felt suddenly as if she was there, crouching in the bushes, watching. She could hear the grunts, the slap of flesh off flesh, get the yeasty, salty smell. Their strength frightened her, the anonymity, the gut-churning lust of it nearly overcame her. She had to shake her head to dislodge the thoughts, a little gasp escaping her.

"A glass of water perhaps?" Mr. Hutton said.

"No." Violet brushed a hand across her forehead. "I mean, no thank you, Mr. Hutton. How long did it take, the whole episode in the park?"

The question seemed to confuse him and she had to repeat it.

"I think if you look just here," he said, pointing to the relevant entry. "Nine forty. And they left the park at . . ." He strained to read his own handwriting upside down. "Ten o'clock."

She willed him to go on, not trusting herself to do the sum.

"So that makes a total of twenty minutes," Mr. Hutton said.

She held him with her eyes and would not let him go.

He said, "The intimacy, I should think, lasted less than five minutes."

"Thank you, Mr. Hutton, for being so frank," she said.

There was nothing further to say. She needed to get away from that stifling office and Mr. Hutton's intense gaze. She tried to push the pages of the report back into the folder but her hands were shaking and they would not go in.

Mr. Hutton relieved her of them.

"When you have finished with these," he said, upending the paper and tapping it into a neat pile which he inserted into the file. "You should destroy them. There is no point in taking risks." He fastened the brown covers in a double bow which he tied with the same care one might lavish on a bundle of love letters. "I am sorry, truly sorry, to be the bringer of such bad news."

Violet settled her account with him, even managed a few comments about the weather.

They shook hands at the door before she left. Mr. Hutton held on to her hand and looked at her intently.

"You are young, Mrs. Jeffers, and I am not," he said. "And, let me tell you, the only benefit to getting older is that I know when to say a thing, even if it means overstepping the boundaries of politeness. So please do not think me rude when I tell you that I have studied the world and the people in it long enough to recognize a woman of fortitude." He let her hand drop, tilted his head back to peer at her obliquely. "You are disheartened by what you have learned here today, as any woman would be, but you will not let it get the better of you, I can see that. You have, Mrs. Jeffers, more character than you think you have and much more than you know what to do with. You must be resolute in circumstances such as these."

She watched him as he opened the door for her – an aging, overweight, ex-policeman – and wondered how he, better than anyone, could know her so well.

Chapter Twenty

Clive Potter read about Mary's fate in the newspaper, a couple of column inches on page five of the *Evening Standard*. He had known straight away that it was Mary even before he read the bit about the wedding ring tied on the leather thong around her neck. He shouldn't have left her so long with the Taylors but in the end he had no alternative. The child was unable to read and at first this had not seemed to be a problem but when he had 'hired' Mary for the second time, expecting her to bring evidence of the identities of her abusers, the difficulty became apparent.

They were sitting in the kitchen of Arlington Villas when Mary, evidently pleased with herself, had presented him with the stub of a used theatre ticket, a shopping list covered in food stains and the score sheet from a game of Gin Rummy that assigned each player an animal name He had taken them from her and, without a word, thrown them all straight into the kitchen stove. He looked at her astonished face.

"Useless," he said. "I've told you this before: I need names, addresses, not this rubbish."

"I ain't doing it no more," she said. "If 'e catches me robbing, I'm done for."

"But it's vital you do this, Mary."

"Why? So's you can get in the newspaper, make a few bob off my back? Like all the rest, you are."

Her lips were pressed so tightly together they looked white. She seemed tougher than the last time they met, as though she had found out since then that the whole world was against her.

"Now, listen to me, young lady," Potter said. "You made a promise and —"

"Nah, you made the promise," she said. "You promised that I'd see the back of Watling Street but I'm still there, ain't I? You promised to get me out."

"How many times do I have to say this? You need to bring me names and addresses and then I can get you out. Bring me a letter or a document of some kind that will identify one of these men. That's all you have to do."

Her head fell forward, lank hair covering her face. She gave a hard, dry laugh.

"That's all, is it? Easy for you to say. They watch you like an 'awk in them 'ouses in case you pocket the silver. Get someone else, someone who can read, someone who ain't as scared as I am."

She looked up then and he saw she was crying.

"Tears won't work with me," he said. "Do you know how much time and effort I've invested in you? Do you think I'm about to throw all that away?"

"I ain't doin' it," she said.

He stood up, felt in his pocket for coin.

"I'll give you two shillings," he said. "Think what that'll buy you."

"Is that 'ow much my life's worth to you? You can keep your

two shillings. You can keep your five shillings and your pound, I don't want 'em. I ain't doing it, I'm telling you."

"In that case, I'll have to speak to Mr. Taylor." He didn't need to look at her to see she was frightened now. He could feel it in her silence. "Yes, I'll have to explain how you've been unobliging, how you have left me feeling unsatisfied. I'll tell him you are obstinate and willful, all of which is true."

"You wouldn't."

"I would. Because I know Mr. Taylor has ways of making you compliant."

He saw her stroke the damaged flesh on the inside of her arm where the iron had burnt her. Her eyes were reddened and swollen but she had stopped crying.

"You ain't no gent," she said, finally. "You think you are but you ain't."

He sent her back with instructions to steal from clients' desks, wastepaper baskets, coat pockets, bedside lockers. He told her to search Mrs. Taylor's office too. He told her again to search for letters and opened addressed envelopes and this time showed her some of his own so she would recognize exactly what he wanted. If she didn't get names and addresses this time, he said, the whole scheme would have to be abandoned and she would be left with the Taylors until she was too old to be of any use to them. And God knows what would happen to her then.

Obviously she had done as she was told. And been caught.

To be sure the girl in the newspapers was definitely Mary, Potter telephoned the Bluebell Charity School looking to 'hire' her again but was told by Mrs. Taylor that she would be unavailable for the foreseeable future. He asked no further questions but presented himself to the police instead.

A Detective Inspector Findlay was in charge of the investigation, a man with a square jaw and tight skin and eyes that were small and black, like a mouse's. Potter explained to him about his current project, how he was gathering information about child prostitution in the city and how he suspected that the dead child might be Mary, his informant. Findlay checked the veracity of his story by telephoning Bartholomew Crowe at the *Pall Mall Gazette*. That done, he took Potter with him to Charing Cross Hospital to identify the body.

The nurse who met them at Reception knew the inspector and the type of business he was usually on so she must have thought that Potter was a relation of the deceased because she shook his hand and commiserated with him then led the way to the mortuary in silence.

Down in the bowels of the hospital it was cold and smelt of formaldehyde. Potter felt sick. The mortuary was an oblong room with a stone floor and white tiled walls. The two short walls had shelves on which there were countless demijohns and mysterious brown bottles. Ranged along the length of the long wall opposite the door was a row of trolleys, each covered with a white sheet, but with a pair of feet exposed and facing outwards.

A man came out from an unseen room and greeted them. He was wearing a white overall, unbuttoned, and there were crumbs on his waistcoat. He sauntered over to the corpses, checked the labels attached to their toes and called them over when he had located the correct one. They approached and he whipped off the sheet as though he was performing a magic trick.

There she was, still the same pallor to her skin but with purple bruising round her neck that made her look dirty. Thankfully, her eyes were closed but he couldn't say she looked restful. No, she had the appearance of someone shut off from suffering for the briefest of spells but who was expecting to be thrust back into the midst of it at any moment. Potter cleared his throat.

"That is definitely her," he said. "Unfortunate."

Back at the police station, they drank tea together in the detective's office and chatted about Potter's work. Detective Inspector Findlay was well acquainted with it. He enjoyed Potter's theatrical reviews, liked the way he stuck a pin in the pomposity of some of those involved with drama at the highest level. But what he really admired were Potter's articles for the *Pall Mall Gazette* or the *Graphic* or the *Illustrated London News*.

"That's proper journalism," he said.

He had read one of Potter's pieces recently about the women employed as matchmakers at Bryant and May's.

"A down-to-earth story about down-to-earth people," he said. "Times are changing, perspectives are shifting. We need more writers like you who are prepared to say what needs to be said and not what the stuffy upper classes want us to hear." He stabbed the air with his forefinger as he spoke.

They talked about rugby football and a recent game between London Scottish and Richmond at which they were both present. They discussed Mr. Kruger and the worsening relations between the Transvaal and England and then they swapped opinions regarding the efficacy of Beecham's Pills in combating bilious disorders.

Eventually they returned to the matter in hand. Findlay had the teacups removed and took out his pen, uncapped it. His expression was imbued with a new gravity.

"Now, Mr. Potter," he said. "Please tell me everything. Take your time and leave nothing out. Even if you think it is unimportant, it may not be."

Potter spared no detail. He outlined how he had posed as a client in order to get inside the Taylors' business with a view to putting them and the men who availed of their services behind bars.

"I should think so," Findlay said.

Potter referred to the injury on Mary's arm which they had both looked at earlier and which was proof that Taylor was a man of violent temper. He suggested that Taylor was the killer and gave a thorough description of the man from the grubbiness of his skin to the thick, clumsy hands, to the lumbering walk of him. He could see that Findlay was impressed by his powers of observation.

The inspector had brought the post mortem report with him from the hospital and he read through it now, out loud. The victim had been subjected to extreme violence prior to strangulation, it said. There was extensive internal bruising of the abdomen and two fingers of her left hand were broken.

"So you see," Findlay said. "Information may have been extracted from her before she died, information that could put you in danger. We are dealing here with hardened criminals. I take it she did not know your real name?"

"No."

"Do the Taylors have an address for you?"

"Not one that exists."

"That was wise. And the child, did she know where you live?"

"She was in my house a couple of times . . . but I'm fairly sure she didn't know the address . . . or how to get there."

"Hmm . . ." Findlay looked concerned. "I suggest that you have no further dealings with these people. It might be some time before we have Taylor safely in custody. If he's guilty, and it looks as if he is, he could have done a disappearing act."

"You don't seriously think that Taylor is going to come after me, do you?" Potter said.

"It is possible," Findlay said. "Likely, I'm afraid, now that the corpse has been identified. But hopefully we'll catch him very soon."

"And what am I supposed to do in the meantime – just keep looking over my shoulder?"

"Write your articles, make it all public. That way there is no point to his hurting you."

"Hurting me? Can't you give me protection or –"

"You do your job, Mr. Potter. And I'll do mine."

The next day, Potter returned and handed over all the notes he had gathered on the case. The suspect had gone missing. A week later, however, Taylor was spotted back in town and it was known that he would be spending the night in Watling Street. Findlay invited Potter, in his capacity as a journalist, to accompany the police operation to capture him. They raided the house at four o'clock in the morning, Potter in tow. Mrs. Taylor and her cook were arrested, and all the children taken into care. Taylor himself managed to scramble out of an upstairs window, down a drainpipe, across the shed roofs onto a patch of waste ground and had proved elusive ever since. If Potter had stopped to think about it, he would have been worried.

He was too busy, however, writing a series of articles for *The Pall Mall Gazette*. The latest one, entitled "**The Web of Woe at Watling Street**", lit the imagination of the entire population of London.

'**It is a misty, spring morning and early, very early. London is sleeping the Sleep of the Damned. Out of the haze, soundlessly, there emerges a crack force of twelve police officers under the command of the redoubtable Detective Inspector Findlay. They enter Watling Street, a quiet, nondescript, semi-industrial quarter and steal along the footpath like natives in the jungle. Closer and closer they come to number twenty-four, the House of Shame . . .**'

It was talked about everywhere. Potter was sought out by the *Daily Telegraph*, the *Morning Post*, the *Standard*. He was interviewed by the *Times* about his part in the whole affair and invited to give his views on what should be done to stamp out this despicable trade. Editorials in all the newspapers paid tribute to him. The *Illustrated London News* and the *Graphic*, with input from Potter, carried artists' impressions of Mary on their front pages. They made her pretty, which was only right.

Rosalind was the only one who did not praise him. She had cried when he had told her of Mary's fate – there was no way, given the publicity, that he could keep it secret. She would not listen to what he said about the 'greater good' but kept remembering how the child had sat on the bed upstairs, cradling the cloth rabbit in her lap, a book held open in front of her. Rosalind said she had watched, spellbound, from the landing as Mary pretended to read, concocting a story as she went along about elves living in the roots of a tree. The moment she saw Rosalind, she had flung the book away.

"No need to be ashamed, girl," Rosalind had said. "Take your pleasure where you can find it. It's yours and yours alone. Remember that."

The way Rosalind told the story, Potter got the impression it was meant as a warning to him of some kind though he didn't quite understand how.

After that Rosalind did not speak to him for a week or more. The recently appointed maid-of-all-work, Eleanor – a plain, stupid girl – bore the brunt of her temper. From his study he could hear Rosalind downstairs in the kitchen constantly berating her over real and imagined misdemeanors.

Time, however, softened her mood and with less for her to do in the domestic sphere, Rosalind made a habit of taking a walk every afternoon. She returned always with a fresh flush on her cheek and a gleam to her eye that made her seem ferociously alive. And he noticed her in quiet moments too, how she gathered herself in to feed upon some private contentment that made her smile when she thought herself unobserved. One supper time she began to chat affably and flirt with him a little. Normal relations were resumed. He should have suspected something.

Eleanor had finished clearing away the supper things from the back parlour, leaving the two of them together. They had eaten well; whatever her other shortcomings, Eleanor was a good cook. Rosalind looked radiant that night. Her eyes were alight, her skin glowing, and there was a slightly reckless quality to the way she laughed and tossed her head. Her dress was trimmed with lace, through which he could see the swell of her breasts, smooth and white. Round her neck she wore a chain choker with a droplet of purple glass hanging from it, some cheap thing he did not recognize. But the pendant rested in the cleft of her collar bone and quivered with every beat of her heart in such a way that he felt compelled to reach across the table and lift it away from her skin. It felt warm in his palm. He went around the table to her then, leant down to kiss her but she stood up and walked away, smoothing her dress as if it was ruffled.

"Can't 'ave the servants coming in on top of us," she said.

"What servants?" Potter said. "You don't mean Eleanor?"

"It ain't proper."

"Since when did you worry about proper?"

"Since . . ." Something outside distracted her though it was dark and she went to the window.

Thwarted, Potter threw himself down on the sofa.

"Left my umbrella on the omnibus this morning," he said, with a sigh.

"Not the only thing you've left behind recently." She came

and sat beside him. "Very careless with your belongings, you are."

Her tentative smile, so uncharacteristic, made him sit up.

"What are you talking about?" he said.

"I mean, I'm up the Swanee, that's all." She saw he was blank. "In the family way. Bun in the oven."

"What?"

"With child, to folks like you."

"I don't believe it," he said.

"Why not?" Rosalind said. "What do you think 'appens when people carry on the way we do?"

He looked down at the floor beneath his feet and wished all this away.

"How long have you known?" he said.

"Four months."

"Four months? Jesus, Rosalind!"

"I 'ad to be sure," she said.

"You've left it very late to do anything about it," he said.

She gave him a hard look but made no reply.

"Because you've got to get rid of it, you know that."

The nearness of her, the sound of her breathing, the smell of her hair, repulsed him now and he got up, went to the decanter on the table and poured himself a glass of port. He gulped it down and felt calmer.

"It shouldn't be too difficult to find the right person to do the job. You know, get rid of it."

"No," Rosalind said. "That's against my faith."

"Your faith? You weren't in a church since the day you were baptized." He went for the port again, drained the glass in one go.

She was looking at him mercilessly. "I won't do it," she said.

"You won't?" he almost shouted. "Well, go on, just for the laugh, tell me how you propose to deal with this situation then?"

"The proposing," she said, trying to be coquettish, which did not suit her, "I'll leave to you."

"Never," he said, shaking his head, pouring out another drink. "No, no, that will never happen."

She jumped up from the sofa, came to him, took his arm. "I want to 'ave this child, our child. It feels good." She tried to force his hand onto her stomach but he shook her off. She followed him. "I think we could 'ave a good life together. As man and wife."

"Forget it," he said. "Forget it now. We either get rid of this – this thing or, when it's born, farm it out."

"No," Rosalind said, her temper rising. "I won't allow that."

"Then count me out, I want nothing to do with this."

"Well, that's ugly, ain't it?" she said, abandoning her coaxing tone, hands on hips now, like a fishwife. "You're all talk about your workers' rights and exploitation and all that lark. Fancy talk, all of it. Don't cost you a thought to leave me in the lurch like this. You just 'ave your way and –"

"Nobody has ever 'had their way' with you, Rosalind. Nothing happens except according to your plan."

"I'll tell the world this bastard is yours, see if I don't. One bastard begets another!"

"Can I even be sure it's mine?" He saw her flinch. "Your breed are all the same – you've got an itch, it doesn't matter who in the wide earthly world does the scratching. Now think about it, how could I have you for a wife?"

She had moved away, was standing with her back to him and though she was angry, he knew her well enough to realize she was reassessing her position. As was he. Potter liked the arrangement he had with Rosalind. He didn't expect it to last many years – he could not bring himself to envisage a middle-aged Rosalind – but it suited him currently and he did not want the bother of having to recreate with someone else what he already had.

"Look, let's sit down," he said.

She sat beside him on the sofa, calm but with no softness in her at all.

"Perhaps we can reach an agreement."

She looked at him, then away again. Her body was stiff but her eyes were alert and he could tell she was receptive.

"What about this?" he said, thinking quickly. "You may live here and keep the child, if you must, but it won't bear my name. I will support you both as long as you stay here but not if you leave, no matter what the circumstances surrounding your departure. What do you say to that?"

"The child will be a bastard."

"A very comfortable, well-looked-after bastard."

He could see Rosalind calculating the advantages and disadvantages of his offer.

"Come on, Rosalind. We were made for each other, you and I."

"I want an allowance of my own," she said. "'Undred pounds a year."

He laughed. "I couldn't possibly afford –"

"I know what you earn and you can."

He shook his head, knew there was no point trying to negotiate with her. She had reached the limit of her compromise.

"All right," he said. "If you accept my terms."

She gave him a bitter smile.

"As you say yourself, it's in my breed. I got an itch, it don't matter to me who does the scratching, not even if it's you."

That didn't mean Rosalind gave up trying to get him to wed her though. She argued, she pleaded, persuaded, threatened and even flattered but Potter did not relent. Rosalind was a convenience, a very pleasing one at times, but not the kind of woman he would ever marry.

Several tumultuous weeks passed, followed by a gradual return to equilibrium. As Rosalind put on weight and her condition became more obvious it seemed they needed to talk about it less. Her silence on the subject he took to mean that she accepted the status quo.

One evening, when Rosalind had been feeling unwell and gone to bed early, Potter remained downstairs, working. His study was too cold so he set himself up at the table in the kitchen where it was warmer

Eleanor had gone home for the night so he brought a plate of cold roast beef and pickled onions from the pantry, opened the stove door to let out more heat and sat at the table to continue with his work. He was writing yet another piece for the *Pall Mall Gazette* about his friend, Mary, the child prostitute who, through her courage and determination, had battled against her oppressors and won − metaphorically speaking, that is. Who would have thought that his two encounters with her would have produced so much material already and more to come?

The coals in the stove had plenty of life left in them but, even so, a momentary chill ran over him as he was reminded of the last time he sat here with Mary. He was sorry about what had happened to her but he couldn't help thinking that the story wouldn't have had the same impact on the general public, and consequently on the authorities, if Mary had lived.

He heard it, and didn't, at the same time − the scullery door grinding on the uneven flags, a sound so familiar that it hardly registered. By the time it struck him that Rosalind had already locked up and gone to bed and that the scullery door should have been bolted like all the rest, it was too late. There were two men in the room with him.

202

He swivelled and just caught sight of them — one tall and broad, the other slighter, with the smooth jaw of a youth — before the overhead bulb was smashed and they were plunged into semidarkness. The moon shone through the window and cast a square of silver light on the floor.

Potter jumped up.

"What's going on, what's the meaning of this?" he said.

The larger of the two men grabbed him by his tie and pulled him close. By virtue of sheer size, he was strong but his face was blubbery and loose.

"I'm Tom Doyle," he said. "That's my brother, Vincent. Come to 'ave a little chat, we 'ave. But before we start, a warning. No need to mention any of this to the Peelers as there's three more at home who'll give us an alibi."

So they were Rosalind's brothers. The relief that this was not a punishment from the Taylors elicited a smile from Potter.

"Think it's funny, getting my sister knocked up?" Tom said, shaking him by the neck.

"No, of course not — I —"

"We're here to make sure you get her out of that bit of trouble."

"I tried already," Potter said, clawing at his assailant's hand which was almost choking him. "I wanted her to get rid . . . Look, let's sit down, discuss this sensibly."

"Nothing to discuss, mate," Tom Doyle said, holding him firm. "You marry 'er, no one gets 'urt. Understood?"

Vincent, the younger man, lunged forward, his mouth drawn in and twitching.

"You do the right thing by 'er, you 'ear?" he said.

It was then that a movement caught everyone's eye and they turned to see Rosalind standing at the bottom of the stairs in her long white nightgown, her stomach protruding like it was about to explode. The grossness of it embarrassed him.

"Rose!" Vincent was so startled that he took a few steps towards her before checking himself.

"Go on back to bed, Rose," Tom said. Potter had no idea they called her 'Rose' at home. "We'll look after this. Go on, upstairs."

"All right," she said. Her eyes were round. She looked frightened, but not for herself. She held onto the bannisters and used it to pull herself back up the stairs.

"Rosalind!" Potter shouted after her. "Ring the police! Your brothers mean me harm. Quickly, go, for God's sake, hurry!"

The door at the top of the stairs was open. She stood for a moment there, the orange light of the hallway reclaiming her from behind. She was looking down.

"Don't be too 'ard on him, will yer?" she said, to her brothers. "I want 'im breathing."

He saw now that she had planned this with them, left the back door unlocked . . . Had she even described the type of 'roughing up' she wanted him subjected to?

"Bitch!" he shouted after her and would have shouted worse but Tom smacked him hard across the mouth.

"Call 'er that again and I'll kill you," he said.

Potter could taste blood on his lips. "Let's be rational," he said, but it was difficult for him to talk because his face was numb. "Perhaps we can reach a financial settlement that would suit all parties, yourselves included."

"'E thinks this is about money," Vincent said, twitching all over now. He walked away then came back again. "Jesus, 'e thinks this is about money."

"You trying to insult us?" Tom said, yanking Potter's tie, almost lifting him off his feet with it. "You marry my sister, right, make an honest woman of 'er. Our people, we've always lived decent and your little worm ain't going to change that, you 'ear?"

Vincent went behind Potter, kicked him in the back of his knees so his legs buckled and he collapsed on the floor, landing on the point of his shoulder blade. The pain shrieked along his collar bone, into the base of his throat. He rolled over onto his back, the broken light bulb crackling beneath him. His arm was limp, as if it did not belong to him any more. Tom was standing astride him with a club in his hand. He swung it, burying its head in his ribs, then knelt beside him on one knee, like a Father Confessor.

"You going to marry 'er or not?"

Potter was gasping from the blow. "I'll marry the cunt, if that's what you want," he said.

He got a kick in the side from Vincent for that. And another. They had steel-toed boots on; these lads were dockers.

"That's for thinking she's not good enough," Vincent said. He drew back his leg to repeat the punishment but Tom prevented him.

"Stop," he said. "I don't like the look of him."

Vincent's face, upside down, loomed above Potter's. "You'd ruin 'er life, you would, and it wouldn't cost you a thought. We're like cattle to you." He went on and on, spitting as he spoke.

Potter looked up through the spray of sparkles, magical in the moonlight. There was blood in his mouth which he swallowed but more came up. It started to trickle out through the corner of his mouth. It felt like a spider creeping across his cheek and down his neck.

"'E needs a doctor," Tom said.

But neither he nor his brother moved.

Chapter Twenty-one

Edmund's mother died. Acute double lobar pneumonia leading to pericarditis, is what the doctor said, caused by a micro-organism too small to be seen by the naked eye. She became ill on a Tuesday. On Saturday, his father telegraphed him to come urgently and Edmund got to Yoevil just in time to see Anna. She did not have the strength to open her eyes but when he took her hand in his, he heard on her breath, on a sigh, the words, "My son, my son." It was as though she had been waiting for him. Two hours later, she was dead.

Violet came down on the train and she and Edmund, given the strained family relations, put up at the White Hart Inn close by for the duration of the funeral. Edmund could not help but feel sorry for the father who had once antagonized him so. Now an old man and crippled by grief, he seemed to get greyer and more stooped by the day. His expression emptied as though the only way out of this pain was to disengage entirely from the world.

There was a rapprochement of sorts between Edmund, his

brothers and his father that ended in handshakes and vague undertakings to see more of each other. But as he left the house in Orchard Grove, he was haunted by the awful realization that the connection with his family, weak as it had been for the last two decades, ceased altogether with his mother's death. For Anna was the channel, always had been, even when he lived at home.

Edmund returned to London and threw himself back into his work. He had never before felt as lonely as he did now. It had been lonely when he had first left home to join Jennings' Stock Travelling Company and also in those early days in London when he knew no one. But what had sustained him then and ever since was the comfort of knowing, at all times, that he had his mother's belief. She was the only human being who could love him, who could understand and accept him fully, win or fail. She was the only person he could have trusted with the whole truth about himself and known that it would not change her feelings for him in any way. Now she was gone.

To Violet and to most people he appeared to be coping well with his loss. He worked and socialized in the normal manner but he missed her every minute of every day. They had had a connection that was stronger than place or time. He would like to think it was stronger than death too, but he doubted it.

Charles, in his usual restrained style, was very kind. He said one day, "I did not see your mother above three times a year and yet I feel her loss terribly. All along I thought of her as a gentle person. Now I realize she had, in her own way, tremendous force. I think that is the mark of someone rare, that they impact upon you without you even realizing it." He went back to tidying his already tidy desk. "I've wanted to say that for a while."

Edmund was so moved that he could not speak and Charles, after a while, went on to the next order of business.

Despite his grief, Edmund had two pressing problems to deal

with. Regarding the first, he had managed to get Gilbert to promise that he would not divulge any information about their night together for as long as the rental on his flat – and now an extra monthly stipend – continued to be paid.

"One hint of scandal and the payments stop," Edmund said. "So it's in your own interest to safeguard what has become a very substantial income for you."

As regards Clive Potter and his damnable play, Edmund felt he had no choice but to succumb. He agreed to stage *Woman* but, unbeknownst to Potter, he had commissioned Henry Arthur Jones to make changes to it so that it was at least playable. Potter would be furious when he found out but Edmund would deal with that particular onslaught when it came. And so his life was, just about, under control.

Charles, ill informed about Potter's blackmail threat, was mystified by Edmund's decision to put on *Woman*, but he did not argue against it. He was not a man to take financial risks, not even small ones, but though he must have had plenty of objections to this production, he chose not to air them. Instead, he stressed the positives. He said the play would be inexpensive to put on, that they would in all probability break even and there was always the advantage that it might draw a different clientele to the Colosseum who might become regular patrons. Edmund knew when he was being humoured. Charles was just doing his best to help him through his mourning.

Marguerite had responded well to Dr. Philbert's sessions and Edmund went often to visit her. He found her so much improved that he took the liberty of approaching Tree at Her Majesty's and, describing Marguerite's recent illness as 'exhaustion', he secured for her an invitation to play Hedda Gabler later on in the year, as part of that theatre's Millennium celebrations. Marguerite received the news at first with trepidation but, as time went on, with growing delight.

Edmund and Marguerite spent whole afternoons together dissecting old productions and laughing themselves silly. As Marguerite gained in strength, they went out on excursions, often for a walk around the pond in Kensington Gardens and once to Grosvenor House for an exhibition of miniatures which they both found enthralling. Then back to Marguerite's apartment where Betty had tea and Victoria Sponge with cream and strawberries awaiting them. When Lewis returned in the evenings after work, he seemed genuinely pleased to see Edmund. He said his sister was always in such good heart when she spent an afternoon with him.

But even in this quiet household, sinister rumblings could be heard.

"It is a question of honour," Lewis said, one evening. "We cannot abandon our fellow countrymen to a life of servitude in the mines of Johannesburg. They have no vote, no say in the running of their lives and yet it is their labour that is making the Transvaal rich. Kruger is exploiting them. Can that be right?"

"No, it is not right, but it does not justify war," Edmund said. "The plight of those 'uitlanders' is being used by Lord Salisbury as a smokescreen and we shouldn't fall for it. Our government is far more interested in getting its hands on as many diamonds and as much gold as it possibly can while at the same time doing its damnedest to stop Mr. Kruger being lovey-dovey with the Germans. Is that worth fighting for?" Edmund felt these were much more Charles' words than his own but he needed somehow to dampen Lewis's fervour. "And who are these Boers anyway? Only ordinary farming folk."

"I grant you, the Boers are tough, plain, God-fearing people," Lewis said, "but that does not make their dealings fair."

"There it is again, this British obsession with fair play,"

Edmund said. "All very fine when you're talking about cricket and rugby football but, believe me, when there are pockets to be lined, even our most respected countrymen discard it without a thought. Ask Dr. Jameson and Mr. Rhodes about that."

But flags, economies, foreign policies meant nothing to Lewis. He only ever saw things in terms of human beings, their sufferings, their dilemmas. Lewis was an idealist who would never accept that the world had a way of muddying even the most noble objectives.

Of course, Edmund left what he really wanted to say to Marguerite.

"People die in wars," she told her brother. "And suffer terribly. That is the reality. There is no glory in it. Please remember that, Lewis, before you do anything daft."

To which Lewis replied, "There won't be a war. Kruger will back down. But the important thing is to make a stand."

And then Clive Potter was murdered. It came as a terrible shock to the whole of London. Straight away, Edmund told Henry Arthur Jones to stop working on *Woman*. He had come around to the opinion, he said, that Potter's work belonged in the dustbin and not on the West End stage and the wonder was how he had not seen it before. The play was ditched and one threat to Edmund's private life was removed, leading him to feel quite buoyant if a little guilty that this peace of mind had been achieved through the cold-blooded murder of a man.

A few days after Potter's death, Edmund returned after lunch to the Colosseum to find Charles in the office with two policemen. He was not, at first, unduly alarmed.

One was a Detective Inspector Findlay, a man of solid bearing with a jaw so square that it rendered the rest of his face irrelevant. The other man was younger and in uniform with pale eyes, pale hair, pale skin, which taken altogether gave the impression he was translucent.

"We have a few questions to put to you, Mr. Jeffers," Findlay said. Then, casting a furtive look at Charles, "You may prefer to do this in private."

With a sudden horrible premonition, Edmund said, "It's quite all right, Charles. You should go."

Charles went out and, as he did so, removed the wedge from beneath the door to let it close.

The younger officer mooched about the office, remaining just outside Edmund's field of vision.

"This sounds serious, Inspector," Edmund said. "What's it all about?"

Inspector Findlay patted the sides of the armchair he was sitting in.

"Comfortable, this," he said.

He looked up at two pictures that adorned the alcove by the fireplace, one an engraving of the Colosseum dated 1803, the other a painted portrait of Sarah Siddons. He spent a long time gazing at both while at the same time demonstrating by his expression that he had no interest in them whatsoever.

"I take it you are acquainted with the theatre critic, Clive Potter," he said at last. He had an edge to his voice that ill suited his West Country accent.

"I am. Dreadful business."

"When was the last time you saw him, sir?"

"I think it must have been when he came here to discuss the optioning of a play he had written. We decided subsequently not to go ahead with it."

"And you haven't seen him since then?"

"I believe not."

Inspector Findlay seemed to lose himself in the study of his nails. He picked at some loose skin.

"Because we have it on good authority that you visited Mr. Potter at his home on . . . Help me out here, Sergeant Greene."

Sergeant Greene stepped forward with his notebook open.

"The first of October," the sergeant said.

"A Miss Rosalind Doyle will vouch for that," Findlay said. "She remembers you calling on that date."

"Of course," Edmund said. What had possessed him to lie like that when there was no need? He tried to appear nonchalant. "Quite forgot about that."

"Odd it should slip your mind, sir," Inspector Findlay said. "Because you and your behaviour made quite an impact on Miss Doyle that day."

"Would you care for tea or perhaps a drink, Inspector?" Edmund said.

Findlay ignored him. "Perhaps you could recount for us the gist of your conversation with Mr. Potter on that date," he said.

"It was business. We discussed this play of his and . . . What exactly is this all about, Inspector?"

"A violent row ensued, I am told."

"It was a row, yes, and it got out of hand but there was no damage done."

"Violence was used though?"

"Well, yes, if you —"

"And what instigated this violent outburst?"

"He had pretty much cut me up in the paper that day. I thought it disgraceful and unwarranted and I told him so."

Sergeant Greene, evidently tired of snooping, came and leant against Charles' desk. He folded his arms as though preparing to watch a side show.

"You nearly strangled Mr. Potter, did you not?" Findlay said.

212

"Don't be absurd. I grabbed him by the neck, true enough and I shouldn't have. I did a lot of ranting and raving and in the end I just stormed out. It really amounted to nothing."

Findlay's eyes narrowed to slits. "Then why did you lie about having been with him on that date?"

"I didn't lie. I simply did not recollect."

"Mr. Jeffers," Findlay said, "are you a gentleman of . . . how shall I put this? A gentleman of eclectic tastes?" He looked to his cohort. "You see, Sergeant Greene, I can be tactful when I try." A ripple of amusement passed between the two men. "In other words, Mr. Jeffers, sir, is your bias towards the male? Are you a homosexual, an invert, a pederast?"

Edmund stood up. "If you came here to make ludicrous accusations I must ask you to leave, gentlemen. I have important matters to see to."

"Miss Rosalind Doyle overheard your entire conversation with Clive Potter that day, including certain references to a 'friend' of yours and what you got up to together. All confirmed by him, of course, when we tracked him down. Please sit," Findlay said. His lip curled. "Personally, I don't give a tinker's curse who you bugger, so long as it isn't me." At this, a hoot of laughter came from Sergeant Greene. "However, Section 11 of the Criminal Law Amendment Act of 1885 is not so tolerant."

"It is hardly ever invoked, you know that," Edmund said.

"If I had my way —"

"I won't be bullied, Inspector. In fact, your conduct here today has been appalling. I will be reporting you to the appropriate body."

"You see that, Sergeant Greene? Plenty of fight left in the old dog yet, isn't there?" Then, turning to Edmund with a tepid smile, Findlay said, "Naturally, you cherish your wife, your theatre, your reputation, your good name. Copulating with members of the Queen's Armed Forces is . . . well, it's not what people expect to hear about a character such as you, is it? Just a whiff of a whiff of a scandal like that would be enough to ruin you. Now what interests me is how far you would be prepared to go to stop that information getting out."

"Are you suggesting that I killed Clive Potter? You must be mad, it's preposterous."

"You were physical. You had him by the throat."

"If I wanted to kill him, I could have done so there and then."

"Whatever else I think, I know you are not stupid," Findlay said. "Rosalind Doyle let you in, remember?"

"What can I say? I did not murder him. Why, the idea of it is just –"

"This man was blackmailing you," Findlay said. "On the first of October, you use violence against him, you make threats . . . Sergeant Greene, the exact words, if you please."

Sergeant Greene held his notebook out in front of him. "*Ahem*," he said, and adopted the stance of a comic hero. "'*Just leave me alone and I'll leave you alone. Or else, you hear? Or else, I'll get you, see if I don't!*'"

"Nicely done, Sergeant," Findlay said.

"I don't remember saying 'I'll get you'."

"We have a witness who is very sure of what she heard. Anyway, threats were issued on the first of October. On the fifth of February, he is murdered."

"Exactly," Edmund said. "Why in God's name would I wait so long?"

"I really couldn't say. But this much I know: real life has a dreary habit of being predictable. I wish it wasn't, I wish it was more like one of your dime-a-dozen plays where nothing adds up, because then at least we'd have more fun. But no, nine times out of ten, especially in cases of murder, the most obvious solution is the correct one in the end."

"I ask you, Inspector, do I look like the kind of man who would beat a fellow to death?"

Findlay leaned forward in his armchair, suddenly animated. "And what kind of man would that be, Mr. Jeffers? Some drunken, depraved thug, I suppose, and not the high-class gentleman you would have us all believe you are, eh? Well, let me remind you, murderers come from all walks of life." He sat back, hands clamped to the arms of his chair. "Mr. Jeffers, I'm from Yeovil too. Not very far from your own home sweet home – though your accent and mine, well, there's nothing like about them, is there? I held on to mine and was proud to do so, whereas you ditched yours right off, ashamed of your lowly roots. You'd prefer to lick the drips off some toff's privy floor than speak the dialect of your own people. Well, you've conned your posh pals into thinking you're one of them . . . but you're not." He relaxed, stretched the fingers on each hand, like a cat putting out its claws. "So I would say, yes, you are the kind of man who could beat a fellow to death. Anyone can do it, if they stand to lose enough."

Edmund stayed quiet. He knew now this man was his enemy.

"Where were you on the night of the fifth of February and the morning of the sixth between twelve midnight and two?"

"Probably here, at my theatre."

"Until that hour?"

"Sometimes I sleep here. I don't remember that particular night. Was it a Saturday?"

"Yes."

"Then I slept here."

"Did you have company?"

"I was alone. Charles would have been here until about midnight but after that, no, Inspector, I have no alibi."

An expression akin to joy settled on the Inspector's face. "I should caution you, sir, against leaving town – we will need to question you further," he said.

"I will make sure to have my solicitor present."

"As you wish."

"I trust that until such time as I am charged with a crime, the details of my private life will remain so."

"That, I cannot guarantee, Mr. Jeffers. Unfortunately, information of this nature has an uncanny way of getting out. Police stations are notoriously leaky vessels."

"Then perhaps there is a way to caulk them."

"Are you bribing me? Because the last thing you need now is another felony against you."

"I think this interview is over," Edmund said.

Greene gathered himself. Findlay rose to go.

"I am not in the business of saving people from themselves," Findlay said. "Whatever happens now, you are unmasked."

There was no arguing with a man who hated you.

Edmund did not leave his armchair. He indicated the door.

"Good day to you, gentlemen," he said.

Chapter Twenty-two

Later on that afternoon, Edmund consulted his solicitor, Peter Matthews, and gave him a version of the truth that outlined the difficulties he was facing, even the accusations that had been made about his private life, but still shied away from complete openness. Matthews handled the matter with absolute professionalism, asking only the questions that were necessary and eschewing any personal comment. He told Edmund that while it was possible he would be charged with Potter's murder, it was unlikely. The police investigation was only in its early stages and he felt sure that as it progressed the true culprit would be found. However, this was a high-profile case and there would be a lot in the newspapers about it. And that, he said, was the most worrying aspect. The allegations made by Potter against Edmund would come out – there was no way of preventing this. To deny them would mean taking a libel case which was dangerous and could lead the plaintiff into even more perilous waters.

"What you need to avoid at all costs is a sodomy trial," he

said. "You could end up getting a custodial sentence. But innocent or guilty, the trial itself will put paid to your reputation."

"It looks like that is going to be the outcome anyway," Edmund said.

"It is bleak, I have to admit," Matthews said. He gave a sympathetic smile.

They shook hands.

Edmund had kept secrets for so long that he began to doubt his own reality. By his life and actions he had proclaimed himself to be that which he was not, even to his closest friends like Marguerite and Charles. He had offered his whole self to no one. And now that his duplicity in one area was about to be exposed, would it be assumed by all who knew him that the rest of his life was duplicitous too? This was how he thought in his darkest moments when it seemed even his success had been gained through stealth and dishonesty. And if it was possible for him to fall into this way of thinking, then surely everyone else would too. He felt his physical and mental energy sapped by these doubts. If there had been a battle to fight and win he might have rallied but no such opportunity presented itself. He was left waiting.

In the meantime, he had duties, the first of which was to inform Violet of what was to come. With this confession his life would start to unravel, he knew that, but it was kinder to give his wife fair warning of it and more dignified for both of them if they could begin the unpicking of their lives in private rather than wait until outside forces tore them asunder.

That evening, he sat in the morning room downstairs with the door ajar, listening for Violet to return from a visit to Lady Balfour. She came back at six thirty. Unseen, Edmund watched her as she removed her hat and coat in the hall and gave them to Hilda to put away. She studied herself in the mirror, unaware of his presence just inside the morning-room door. Her skin was so luminous, so white and immaculate, that the arrangement of Canna lilies on the table beneath the mirror seemed sullied by comparison. Her heavy eyebrows, dark eyes, the full, red mouth brought passion to the extreme purity of her look. How could his needs not be met by this exquisite creature? Before his marriage he believed they would be and ever since he had chastised himself that they were not.

She leaned through the flowers and pinched her cheeks for colour.

"Violet," he said, from where he sat. "May I speak with you?"

She swung around.

"Goodness, Edmund. You gave me a fright." Her complexion reddened of its own accord. She turned back to the mirror to adjust her hair. "Nothing wrong, is there?" Her hands stopped moving while she waited for his answer.

"No, no," Edmund said, watching Hilda's back as she struggled with hangers in the cloakroom.

Reassured, Violet came into the morning room.

"Lady Balfour sends you her regards, Edmund, in between taking swipes at the rest of the world, that is. She really is a most unpleasant woman. She and that horrid pug dog of hers are well matched. You'll never guess what the pest did today – only launched himself into Cecil Skeffington's lap and upset tea all over Lady Balfour's precious yellow chesterfield. She gave him – Cecil, that is – an awful dressing down over it. He took it well. Shall I ring Hilda to bring us some tea?"

"No tea," he said. "Actually, I think we should go upstairs where it is more private."

She knew then it was serious and questioned him no further

but turned and led the way to their bedroom.

Before midday the sun poured in through the window here, burnishing the furniture, the picture frames and vases with a golden hue, even in winter. But by this time of the day the sun was working its charm on the back of the house and their bedroom was drab and chill. Edmund remained standing. Violet sat on the little chair by the desk.

"I had a visit yesterday," Edmund said. "At the theatre. From the police." He focused on the hem of Violet's skirt, noted her booted foot which was just visible beneath. "They were asking questions about Clive Potter's murder."

"About Clive Potter's murder?" Her eyes were wide and staring, her mouth dropped open.

"Yes."

"But why were they asking you about it?"

"It seems I am a suspect."

"*What?*"

"It's ridiculous, I know. But I saw the man, oh, way back in October. We rowed, the scene turned very ugly. I made some stupid remarks which have been misinterpreted and it was all witnessed by some woman he lived with. It'll be sorted out in the end, you needn't worry about that. But there's something else I need to tell you." He paused, aware that he was on a threshold of sorts. "I've been very silly, Violet. I ask only that you can forgive me."

"What is it that you have done?" Violet said, in a voice so calm it forced him to look up. Her features were like carved ivory, her expression so cool it bordered on cruelty. "You did not kill Clive Potter, I take it."

"No, no." Edmund shook his head.

"Then tell me what you have done," she said. "And what Clive Potter has to do with it."

Edmund delayed. He rested his eyes on the hem of her skirt again.

"There is no easy way to say this, Violet, but sometimes, not often, I . . . I go across the river and meet other men . . ." Violet's toe slid away under her skirt. "With a view to becoming intimate. There have been quite a few . . ."

He found the courage to look at her. She was very still, her chin lifted high as she gazed away from him, out of the window at the dull, grey sky. Edmund knelt down before her, took both her hands in his and kissed her fingers though they were dead to him. He had not envisaged this passivity. He had hoped for rage and a painful raking out of each other's souls to be followed by a joint resolve for the future. It struck him that he was losing her. He kissed the palm of her hand.

"I love you, Violet," he said. "Though you must think I've an odd way of showing it. You are my wife, I love you, and want you by my side always. This other part of me is not important – it has nothing to do with love. You must believe me. I know I've been totally selfish. You are entitled to a full life, with children, and I have trapped you. I didn't think it would be like this but I will try, I promise you. I'm sorry, so terribly, terribly sorry." He rested his forehead on her hand. "I never wanted to hurt you. These lapses of mine, they mean nothing beyond the physical. And that need is part of my nature, much as I would have it otherwise. But there has never, in any of those relations, been a betrayal of my love for you or my respect or affection. I wish things were different, that I could be a proper husband to you."

His words dropped into silence. There was nothing more he could say without knowing what her feelings were. The sounds of outside floated in to them – children's voices, a barrow on the footpath, people going about their ordinary business – while he and Violet remained frozen in this tableau of misery.

At last, Violet spoke.

"You say these physical desires mean nothing to you and yet you risk all for them." Her breast was heaving. It was the only sign of emotion. "Have you ever consulted a doctor about your – your condition?"

"No," he said. "But then I do not regard the feelings that I have as an illness. They are unwelcome and inconvenient, yes, but they are inborn, instinctual. The impulse is beyond my control, though my actions are not and I must learn to restrain myself. I cannot change what God and Nature have pre-ordained, though, believe me, I have tried. I should never have inflicted myself upon you. In another time or place I would not have."

Her eyes were like mirrors reflecting back at him a cold, deep well of resentment. No sign of the burning anger and sense of rejection he had been expecting.

"But what use can God or Nature have for two creatures who abandon themselves to pleasure but can never procreate? Answer me that," she said.

"I do not know, Violet. But the fact that it is so, that good men have these leanings and indulge them, must surely indicate some kind of natural justice in the act."

"One might as well say murder is all right because it happens." She disentangled her fingers from his and sought out a perfumed handkerchief which she put to her nose. She inhaled the scent as though it had healing powers. "Why do you tell me these things now? We have been married for four years and you have never seen fit to do it before."

"I do not think I will be charged with Clive Potter's murder – the whole idea is absurd and there is no hard evidence against me except for the fact that we rowed." He stood up, ran his hand through his hair, felt incredibly tired. "But I'm afraid Clive Potter got to hear about a certain indiscretion of mine. He threatened

222

to make it public unless I put on his wretched play, hence the argument I had with him. Unfortunately, the police now have this information and it could land me in court yet. Either way, it's going to be in the newspapers. I am undone."

"So we both stand to be disgraced." Her eyes flashed. She leapt up and went to the window, her back to him. "I could live with it better if you had killed the man, do you know that? Have you no regard for me, for our life together, for our position in this city, that you would toss it all aside to go chasing around Southwark Park like a wild animal?"

"I'm ashamed of it," Edmund said. "Truly ashamed."

"So you should be. How can I face people when they know of this? I cannot face them. Were you repulsed by me, Edmund?" Her voice cracked and he resisted the urge to wrap his arms around her.

"No, Violet. Please, don't think that. It is I who failed you, not the other way round." A thought struck him. "I made no mention of Southwark Park. Why did you say that?"

She nodded. "I have known for quite some time about what has been going on," she said, strengthening. "And, despite the heartache it has caused me, I have been prepared to live with it, for the sake of our marriage, for the sake of propriety, but I am not prepared under any circumstances to be publicly made a fool of. I will not be pitied by all who know me."

How did she know? But the fact she did at least explained her subdued and rather frosty response to his admission and Edmund took comfort from that.

"We will safeguard your reputation, our reputations," he said. "We will face this together – Charles is a wizard with publicity –"

"Don't be stupid, Edmund. It is beyond even Charles to fix this."

He bowed his head, silenced.

"How did you find out?" he said at last. "And what do you know of Southwark Park?"

"I received an anonymous letter about your activities. To confirm the allegations, I employed a private investigator. I needed to know for sure."

It was unfair, given his own misdeeds, to feel aggrieved about Violet's consulting a professional about him, but he did on some level.

"You said nothing."

"That is correct."

"You gave no indication that you knew. There was no difference in you. I find that odd," he said. "And frightening. That you feel so little."

"Feel so little pain, is that what you mean?" she said, with a pitiless smile.

"I love you, Violet," he said. "I want you always to be my wife. Please, let us put this behind us, continue together. If we show solidarity, we can salvage our lives."

Violet frowned. Her eyes were blurry as if she'd been studying books in poor light.

"Continue?" she said. "But everything is changed."

"You knew already what was going on and you said nothing. If I promise —"

"No, not now, not now that everyone will know."

He could find no suitable reply but looked down at the rug beneath his feet, in a daze.

"You have lost it all," she said, standing up and moving towards the door. "You do realize that, don't you?"

Chapter Twenty-three

Edmund went to see Marguerite. Betty met him at the front door.

"Oh, Mr. Jeffers, just wait 'til you see her," she said, shaking with excitement. "You'll be rightly pleased, I know you will."

Betty escorted him to the drawing room where Marguerite was relaxing on the chaise longue by the window. Even in the harsh noonday light there was a hint of colour in her cheeks and a spirited lift to her head that was very encouraging. It was a holiday and Lewis was at home too. He sat a little apart from them, at a small mahogany table on which he was building a house of cards.

Edmund sat with Marguerite, enquired about her health and when the rehearsals for *Hedda Gabler* were due to start, then he came to the real reason for his visit.

"I have a confession to make," he said. "To both of you."

Lewis stopped what he was doing but remained seated. Marguerite's eyes widened.

"There will be certain stories circulating about me in the

near future and I would prefer to tell you this myself rather than let you read it in the newspapers."

Lewis stood up, came nearer.

"I have been unfaithful to my wife," Edmund said. "With other men." The secret he had kept for years was surprisingly easy to divulge, now that he had no alternative. He directed his words at Marguerite, keeping Lewis a blur in the corner of his eye.

But Lewis did not wait for any further explanation. He went back to the table where he had been sitting and, with a swipe of his clenched fist, he scattered the playing cards all over the floor. Then, grabbing his jacket from the back of the sofa, he said, "I'm going for a walk," and went out.

Marguerite reached for Edmund's hand.

"You silly boy," she said. "Why didn't you tell us before?"

"I've wanted to . . . No, that's not true, I haven't wanted to. I wanted everything to remain as it was. There is no end to my deceit really. I'm only telling you now because I'm forced to, which is not what you'd expect from a friend, is it?"

"That's why Lewis is cross. He has come to depend on you and he is very exacting of those he likes," she said. "But you and I are mere mortals." She patted his hand. "You are a dear, dear friend. And always will be. Though why you didn't say anything is hard to understand —"

"It's going to be quite unfashionable to know me. I'm sure at least three quarters of my acquaintance will suffer from collective amnesia and cut me dead in the street when they pass me."

"Well, boo to fashion," she said.

"And as for my knighthood . . . I'm sure the Lord Chamberlain will erase all trace of me. I shall be a ghost. It's so embarrassing. I wish I could hibernate, venture out when it's all over."

"Nonsense," Marguerite said. "Just remember, they can destroy the man but never the artist."

"Hardly reassuring," Edmund said, with a smile.

"Do you know," Marguerite said, "I think I suspected it all along. It may explain why recently I took such delight in seeing you and Lewis together."

"Oh no," Edmund said. "That can never happen. I am a married man."

"Gosh, how priggish you sound."

Edmund avoided her eye for fear she would be encouraged to continue in this vein. It was a subject best avoided.

"As for my father," he said. "When I think of him . . . God, the shock will be . . . No, I cannot think of him. It is too dreadful . . ."

A pair of swans appeared over the roofs opposite and Edmund leant forward and opened the window to hear the moan of their wings as they flew over. He closed it again when they had passed.

"Do you think he will forgive me?" he said. "Lewis, I mean."

"He may not," she said. "He cannot abide falseness in a person." She rested her chin on her hand and seemed lost in thought. Then, "I think he's going to join the army, you know, go to South Africa, only I'm too afraid to ask."

"But that would be ridiculous and foolhardy. What has possessed him to think of such a thing? You must talk him out of it."

"I have tried already. He might have listened to you. But I don't think so now." Marguerite's eyes filled up with tears. "My poor boy. If he goes, I will not be able to bear it."

Telling Charles was problematic.

They were in the office at the theatre, Charles at his desk, Edmund in his armchair.

After a period of quietness, Edmund said, "Charles, I have been foolish and very selfish and most undeserving of my friends."

Charles was concentrating more on the sheaf of papers he was sifting through.

"Foolish and selfish," he said, idly. "That sounds bad, very bad."

"Listen to me, Charles." He waited until Charles looked up. "It's going to be in the newspapers and all because of what happened to Potter. Even in death, the wretch continues to kick up a ruckus."

"What's going to be in the newspapers?"

"Potter alleged that I committed an indiscretion . . . with another man. And now, unfortunately, the newspapers have it . . ."

Charles remained incredibly still, hunched over his work.

"Then we should take a libel action against the offenders," he said. "They can't be let away with damaging a man's reputation like this."

"Yes, they can," Edmund said, "if I don't want to out-Wilde Oscar. I do not intend to spend my last years in jail."

Charles gazed at him with an eerily blank expression.

"It's going to be ugly, Charles. I am sure they will find individuals willing to speak out against –"

"Please." Charles lifted his hand to the side of his head as though to shield himself from a blow. "I do not want to hear this, do you understand? I have work to do, a lot of work."

He took down his hand, resumed his paperwork. His face was flushed.

Edmund left him alone. Silence was easier. Instead of badgering Charles, he focused his attention on writing a letter to his father in which he said he loved him and his brothers and was sorry for causing them this hurt. He made no reference to the precise nature of the scandal that was soon to emerge.

The day after he sent that letter home, the story surfaced in the newspapers. The general public was voracious. All editions reported that Edmund Jeffers had argued with Clive Potter shortly before his death and that he had been questioned by the police in connection with it. Sexual deviancy was implied; blackmail was mentioned. The reading public was hooked. Edmund tried to continue as normal, acting, dining out, attending functions. He had enough respect for himself to believe that others should and would treat him with dignity if he showed himself undefeated.

Charles refused to look at the newspapers at all and referred to the subject as "our little difficulty", as though it would all blow over in a week or two. At first it seemed he might be right.

In the immediate aftermath of the newspaper reports, box-office receipts at the Colosseum rose as punters, driven by curiosity to see the 'degenerate' at work, flocked to the theatre. It was short-lived, however, and very soon audiences fell away leaving cast and crew demoralized and the play mortally wounded. Callers to the house in Belgrave Square dwindled, invitations to various functions dropped off. He sensed a caution in his dealings with friends and acquaintances where before there had been only warmth. He went to a talk at the National Gallery and found himself, at the end of it, standing at the back on his own although he knew most people there. In the foyer of the Bank of England he overheard Lady Hazelmere, a relative of Violet's, say to her female companion, "We will acknowledge him if we have to, Elizabeth, but I warn you, the barest nod will do." And one night, during a performance of *Julius Caesar*, in the famous fight scene between Cassius and Brutus, Edmund was urged from the gallery to "kiss and make up, for goodness' sake," which remark was greeted by cheers and laughter from many among the audience, and not just in the stalls.

Downfall, he saw now, came not in one devastating blow but piecemeal, where every little erosion feels like total loss. Edmund began to withdraw. He felt disinclined to entertain and the Colosseum, once so famous for its lavish parties and enviable guest list, became a dull place.

At home, Violet had taken to eating breakfast in her bedroom now and invariably went to her parents' for dinner so they saw little of each other in private. When they did meet, she maintained a cool exterior and gave the impression that she had distanced herself so far from her husband and his sordid activities as to be little affected by them. She was unmoved by his entreaties for forgiveness and unwilling to resolve their situation. There was no mention of divorce, however, nor of establishing separate households.

If Edmund saw less of Violet at home, he was more in her company at the theatre than ever before. She had taken to coming into the office on a daily basis and, such had been his lethargy of late, he welcomed her help with the mountains of correspondence that had accumulated. She was methodical and reasoned in her approach and not at all put off by the hostile content of some of the letters. She took it upon herself, one morning, to read a manuscript that had been lying on his desk untouched for weeks and when he asked her opinion of it, he was impressed by her insight. It was all business between them though. He missed the gentle moments with her – the jokes, the idle conversation, the shared anxieties over domestic matters, their joint hopes for the future. But perhaps he had been without those for longer than he had realized.

Charles was his constant companion. He alone seemed to remain unchanged by everything that happened. He still maintained that even bad publicity had a value, was as attentive as he always was to Edmund's needs and never once put a direct question to him about the events that had led up to all this upset. He went about theatre business with his usual cheeriness. He discussed the weather, the likelihood of war, *Mrs. Dane's Defence* at the Lyric, the latest gadgetry in lighting and the controversy surrounding ladies playing tennis with skirts hitched in the public park. He created normality where there was none.

Chapter Twenty-four

Leopold Barrie came into the office at the Colosseum. He was stern.

"We have business to conduct," he said, and took a seat before it was offered. He removed his gloves, laid them out on his thigh, one on top of the other, before smoothing them out.

"I want Charles to stay," Edmund said.

"Very well."

Edmund and Charles sat in their usual armchairs either side of the hearth. Leopold sat at a point between them facing the fireplace.

"I have come here to inform you, Edmund, of a board decision taken late last night."

"Confound the board," Charles said, anticipating what was to come. "We managed perfectly well for ten years without any board."

Leopold would not engage with him. He said. "The board, Edmund, consider the recent revelations surrounding your private life to be detrimental to the reputation of the theatre here. As a result, you are to be offered the choice of either taking a sabbatical from your post here as actor-manager or resigning with a generous gratuity. The details pertaining to each proposal you will find herein." He rose to his feet, reaching to his inside pocket for an envelope which he placed on the mantelpiece.

"This is outrageous," Charles said, standing up, but Edmund waved him back to his seat.

"The sabbatical will last for a minimum of one year," Leopold said. "Whichever option you choose, it will be effective one month from today's date. That should give you time. There is no room for negotiation."

"The Colosseum doesn't exist without Edmund, can't you see that?" said Charles.

"You are wrong there, Charles. There is a very fine permanent company here to draw upon."

"All thanks to Edmund who has made it too easy for you leeches to come in and –"

"After one year of sabbatical, if that is the road you take, the board of management will consider an application for your reinstatement. It is possible by then that people may not care so much about all that has come out."

There was a lull. Charles was biting his lip, his fingers doing a dance on the arm of his chair. Leopold sat still. He had the calm of a man who knows he possesses all the power.

Edmund had to rouse himself. He stood up, walked towards Charles' desk.

"Well, I've been expecting this news," he said. "Though it disappoints me. Does the board of management really think that I can just walk away from the Colosseum, from the empire I have created, with nothing more than a backward glance over one shoulder?"

"Must I keep reminding you, Edmund, that the Colosseum

233

now belongs to me?"

Edmund spun around. "It will never belong to you."

"Look," Leopold said. "You can set up a new theatre somewhere else, away from London, away from all this publicity. We – I – will help you do so."

"Like where? The Outer Hebrides? Don't be ridiculous. London is the whole point. I am not interested in obscurity." He began to pace up and down as if he could outstrip the insults being heaped upon him. "I am a highly respected actor, for God's sake. I have worked long and hard, devoted my whole life to my craft and succeeded in elevating not only myself but my whole profession in the process. I won't be treated in this fashion, turned out of my own theatre. I have connections. My name means something in this town."

"Something unrepeatable."

"How dare you? My name is every bit as good as yours – better, in fact, for I earned mine while you had yours handed down to you."

"Well said!" Charles slapped the arm of his chair.

"At least I had the wit to keep my good name intact, unlike you," Leopold said. The lower lid of one eye twitched. "Let me tell you this, you are hanging on to your former status by your fingernails but you may as well let go. There isn't one of your erstwhile aristocratic friends who would invite you now into the bosom of their families. Not Lord Hazelmere, not Lord Balfour – I have it from their own mouths. I could go on but I am a merciful man . . ."

"This is getting us nowhere," Charles said, standing up.

"I wasn't going to make this personal," Leopold said, "but I find I cannot let it go. What galls me most is that because of your appalling misconduct, my daughter is suffering." He stood up now too. His leather gloves fell to the floor but he didn't retrieve them. "I never wanted her to marry you in the first place but she would have her way. If I ever thought for a moment that such a move would lead to this, to her being publicly embarrassed and ostracized from society, I would —"

"Do you think I am the kind of man who doesn't regret that?"

"All I know is you are the kind of man who propositions low-class thugs and commits acts of gross indecency with them."

Charles lunged at Leopold, grabbed him by the lapels of his jacket.

"You will retract what you have just said." His mouth was a thin, pale line and he was trembling. "Retract it, I say."

Edmund pushed between them, placed a hand on Charles' chest to ease him back.

"It's all right, Charles. It's all right," he said.

Charles relinquished his hold on Leopold and turned away abruptly.

Leopold straightened his cravat, settled his jacket. He gave a derisory laugh.

"Oh come on, Charles, even you must have taken your head out of the sand by now."

"Leave him alone," Edmund said.

"As for you, you have treated my daughter despicably —"

"I have never been wantonly cruel to my wife — you cannot accuse me of that. I have tried to protect her at every turn."

"Then why do you not keep your vile nature in check or, at the very least, be discreet? That is what we all do. I warn you that I shall have to consider what is best for Violet in this situation and I will act accordingly, even if that means damaging you further."

Leopold stooped to pick up his gloves.

There was no shaking of hands.

When he left, there was a vacuum. Charles remained at the sideboard, staring at the wall, his back to the room.

Edmund said, "I'm sorry, old boy, that you heard all that."

Charles lifted his head slightly but didn't turn around. His hands were joined behind his back, one set of fingers hooked around the other, gently squeezing.

"I feel a little unwell," he said at last. "If you don't mind, I think I'll go home for the rest of the day."

"Of course," Edmund said. "Go."

Charles tidied his desk in silence. He did not raise his eyes. When he went, five minutes later, he left behind him his coat and a bundle of files that earlier he had said he would work on at home.

Chapter Twenty-five

Leopold Barrie compartmentalized his life. He met with other men of commerce whenever the need arose, at the theatre he mixed with actors and playwrights, at the National Gallery artists. He was careful to spend enough time with family and friends to keep them happy. His mistresses, though they were never a secret, he liked to keep private. When he tired of the city he retreated to his country seat where he walked, rode and fished all day and socialized in the evenings with neighbouring families of similar rank, his wife by his side. His life was neat; he did not tolerate overlaps. This was the only way he could enjoy himself.

Constance had her moods, of course, but he could put up with them. His wife's air of jaded misery was always easier to bear at Warrickstown where there were eight hundred acres of parkland to escape into but even in London he found her manageable. At least Constance's ill humour was consistent and low key whereas he was finding Marguerite's unpredictability cause for concern.

Leopold had become better acquainted with Marguerite

during the rehearsals for *The Second Mrs. Tanqueray* at the Metropole and had been struck straight away by her poise and her sense of humour. On stage with six other actors, it was she who held his attention, held everyone's attention and without any effort on her part. Off stage, she adopted a slightly flippant attitude which seemed to suggest that while she was aware of her own innate abilities, she did not take them too seriously.

On being formally introduced to Leopold by someone who did not realize they were already acquainted, she had said, with reverence, "Well, well, it isn't often one meets with royalty." And then turned the tables on him by proffering her own bejeweled hand for *him* to kiss.

That was when he fell for her. Accustomed as she was to having her pick of suitors, Marguerite treated him with playful contempt. She was haughty and tempestuous and he craved her company, not like a man possessed but like a man who was considering being possessed. It was heady, joyous, sensual stuff and exhilarating to a degree he had not known before. He found it necessary to subdue his new-found exuberance for fear that those close to him – Constance in particular – would notice he was simply too happy and wonder why.

The change in Marguerite seemed to happen suddenly but reason dictated that it must have been a gradual process that went unnoticed by him. Until one evening when they had dined together at Prince's and returned to Marguerite's apartment. They were lying in bed. She was half asleep; he was contemplating leaving shortly in order to be home relatively early. Constance appreciated that. It was their way of pretending that he hadn't been out philandering all evening and thus made it possible for them to be civil to one another. It was important to Leopold to have peace on the domestic front.

Marguerite was on her side with her back towards him. He

ran his finger up and down the furrow of her spine, stroked her hip, sweeping down into the dip of her waist where the flesh was soft and deep and yielding.

"I'm going to miss this," he whispered into her neck.

"Miss what?" she said, tilting herself back so her head rested on his shoulder.

"I'll rephrase that," he said. "It's you I'll miss, when I go to Warrickstown."

There was tension in the pause that followed.

"When are you going?" she said, her voice dead.

"This weekend. For six weeks."

She sat up then, pulling the sheet off him to cover herself.

"With Constance?"

"Of course, with Constance."

"When were you going to tell me?"

"I just did."

"You left it until now? I won't see you again before . . ."

"You know I go to Warrickstown every summer." He got out of bed to look for his clothes. "You know that."

"Yes, but I thought . . ."

"It will be good for us," he said, for in truth he was rather looking forward to immersing himself in the sweet agony of separation. "It can only strengthen the bond between us."

But there followed a long and bitter argument that ended with Marguerite in a paroxysm of tears and he rampaging out, shouting that he wanted no more of it.

The next day, he felt sorry and went to her apartment where they reconciled but the whole episode had unnerved him, left him feeling tired and vaguely unhappy. As planned, he went to Warrickstown with Constance, but Marguerite had extracted a promise from him that he would return several times over the course of the summer to see her, which he did. These London interludes were not happy occasions. Leopold was resentful at having been dragged up from the country and Marguerite was over-anxious to please. At the end of the holiday, when he returned to the city from Warrickstown, they tried to continue on as before, but it was different. With each argument Marguerite seemed to drift further and further away from the person he first knew. The qualities he had so admired in her – her beauty, her independence, her carefree attitude, her vivacity – were disappearing fast like water down a drain and sometimes he wondered if they only stayed together because of a shared, forlorn hope that they could recapture the first flush of their love. Perhaps the best was behind them.

Then there was that awful incident at the Metropole. Marguerite had attended, looking dishevelled with her hair coming down at the back and her eyes opened wide as if in fright. He knew that she was stressed by the presence of his wife on the same night and he had whispered what he considered to be words of encouragement to her, his intention being to bolster her but she had turned on him, hitting him so hard across the face – and in front of everyone – that his eye swelled up immediately from the blow. She left in a hurry with her brother but not before that young man had given Leopold such a look of reproach that it embarrassed him to think anyone else saw it.

Ice was applied to the injury and Leopold, deciding that to leave would be a defeat of sorts, spent the rest of the evening circulating the room with a closed-up eye and a ringing in his ear.

When they got home, Constance was adamant, as he knew she would be.

"That woman must go," she said.

Marguerite's deteriorating mental health was apparent to all who knew her. Just over a year before, Leopold had had little difficulty in convincing the board of management at the Metropole that the theatre urgently needed Marguerite Davenport. Now he had no difficulty at all in convincing them that she was too unwell to continue and that it was in the theatre's best interests that they dispense with her services.

He went to see Marguerite afterwards when he knew Lewis would not be there but she was too lethargic to talk to him and he was reluctant to go again. So, even before Edmund had stuck his nose in, Leopold was beginning to distance himself from her.

But if Marguerite was incapable of speech, she wrote interminable letters which he received from her on a regular basis, sometimes twice in the one day. In these she beseeched him not to end their affair though he had never mentioned such a thing. Time went on and the tone of the letters improved, which Leopold took to be an indication that she was getting better. This meant he wasn't in the least prepared for what happened one night in late October.

He and Constance were playing dominoes in the upstairs drawing room. Leopold was bored by the game but he endured it in the knowledge that the hansom cab he had ordered would arrive soon and whisk him away to the Cavour, where he was dining that evening with some business associates.

Constance looked pale tonight, her skin dry and papery. She sighed, even when she won.

"Leopold, we should make a donation to Reverend Timmins' fund for the home," she said, gathering up the pieces for another game.

"Which home is this, my dear?"

"The one for destitute sailors. Or is it soldiers? One or the other. You've heard him talk about it on numerous occasions. Now that we're at war again, people will expect us to support it. Reverend Timmins will expect it. It's quite the fashion at the moment to look after veterans."

He held up a hand to stop her. "Consider it done," he said. "The sailors and soldiers of Kentish Town will be thanking their lucky stars they lost limbs in the Crimea when they see what your bounty brings them."

There was a knock on the door and the maid, Lucy, came in.

"That's my cab," Leopold said. "Always early when you don't want it to be."

"No, sir." Lucy's glance fell on Constance and leapt away again. "It's a lady to see you, sir. Says she won't come in though it's pelting rain outside and won't give her name either."

"Probably someone from the theatre with a message," Leopold said, sensing a need for caution.

He went downstairs where the front door was open and a figure stood huddled on the step, facing away. A squall rattled the letterbox and lifted the rug in the hall. The woman turned. It was Marguerite.

"That'll be all, Lucy," Leopold said, not looking at the girl. "I'll deal with this."

He waited until he heard the door at the end of the hall closing. Marguerite was wearing a light dress and evening slippers but no coat and she was soaked to the skin as though she had been walking out in the rain for hours.

"What the hell are you doing here?" he said. "My wife is upstairs. How dare you come to my home like this?"

But she was lost in some pain of her own and did not hear him.

"Lewis has gone," she said. "Lewis has gone."

"What – dead?"

The mention of death elicited a wail from her like a mourner in some far-flung land. He took her by the shoulders and shook her.

"I said: is he dead?"

"He's gone away," she said, quietening.

Thankfully, at that moment the cab he had ordered arrived so he bundled her into it while he went back inside for his top hat and cloak and to leave word that he was off.

He told the hansom to go to Knightsbridge and sat in beside her. The rain had got in under his collar, his hair was wet.

"This behaviour is unacceptable," he said to Marguerite. "Totally unacceptable."

But his anger bounced off her. She nestled close to him, put her head on his chest. He could feel the wet of her hair and her dress through his clothes.

"He's gone to South Africa," she said.

"I know, you told me that already."

"I'm so worried about him."

"Well, this roaming around in the rain achieves nothing, Marguerite." But he could see it was useless to remonstrate with her and so he fell silent. They rode on and he stroked her hair to calm her. Some time later, he said, "Let's get you home, safe and warm."

Leopold had heard such good reports of Marguerite's improved condition that he was astonished to find her like this. The setback, he supposed, must be due to panic. The shadow of war, the mobilization of troops and most of all, her dear brother's departure from these shores, must have tormented her to such an extent that her mind was overturned.

She fell into a death-like slumber which lasted the rest of the journey so he had to wake her up when they arrived and help her into the apartment, which was cold and dark and empty. Evidently, Betty the maid was on her night off. Obediently, Marguerite went to bed and he brought her in a mix of gin and water which he thought might put her back to sleep. She lay quietly enough but when he signalled it was time for him to leave she started to cry and held on to him. He could not relent.

"I must go," he said, prising her fingers off his cloak.

By the time Leopold got to the Cavour, his party was still waiting for him, though they were all several drinks the merrier. His reputation with women was legendary and so there were a few ribald comments on the reasons behind his lack of punctuality which he met well, given that the night's events had lowered his spirits considerably.

Marguerite's condition alarmed Leopold. Her lack of self-control was a danger to all who associated with her but especially to him. He consulted with doctors, took her to see more than one. Now that Lewis was away and Edmund was preoccupied with his own public humiliation, Leopold took it upon himself to make the decision that she should be sent away to 'convalesce'.

He informed Edmund of this fact one afternoon at the Colosseum.

"But why can she not convalesce at home?" Edmund asked. "Betty looks after her very well."

"Surely you do not begrudge her specialist care, Edmund? Don't worry – I will foot the bill."

"You know very well that's not what I meant."

He had noted how hollow-eyed Edmund was, how hollow-cheeked.

"She will not be allowed visitors at Jordanswood," Leopold said. "No newspapers either. They have a policy of isolationism there, the idea being that guests are cut off from the anxieties and everyday nuisances of the world while, at the same time, they are exposed to all that is good in it: fresh air, excellent food, beautiful, natural surroundings."

"I wish I could go too," Edmund said, almost smiling. "And where is this haven exactly? I should write to her."

"In Surrey," Leopold said. "But they don't allow letters either. As I say, they don't want the real world to impinge."

"Oh," Edmund said.

"If there is anything urgent you need to communicate you can do so through me," Leopold said.

Shortly after that interview, Leopold and Marguerite went by rail to Surrey, getting out at Hamley Station. Within minutes of the train's departure, the crowd had cleared and they were left alone on the platform. The station master glared at them through the window of his office and then forgot about them entirely.

Marguerite had been quiet all the way down and she stood now, silent, incurious, her hands tucked into the sleeves of her coat. A damp mist fell and the day was cold. Leopold stamped his feet to warm them and kept a look out for the driver from Jordanswood.

Then, from behind them, a voice said, "Lord Barrie?"

Leopold whirled round.

"Good God, man. Why did you sneak up like that?"

He almost regretted the sharpness of his tongue when he saw the sorry specimen before him, an ancient-looking creature, bent double, more fit for the sickbed than for work.

"Follow me, sir, madam," he mumbled.

The man lifted Marguerite's luggage with amazing ease for one so decrepit and led the way out to the waiting vehicle. This happened to be a landau with the hoods up, drawn by two handsome Shires in full harness, the splendour of the carriage and horses being in such marked contrast to the shabby driver that the effect was comical. He swung the bags into the boot without any apparent difficulty, then opened the door for Marguerite and Leopold to get in.

"I won't stay too long," Leopold said, as they set off through the Surrey countryside.

It was only four in the afternoon and the light was fading already. The carriage wheels hissed on a carpet of wet leaves. The branches of the trees were stark and black with drips hanging from them. There were drips on the undersides of gates and fences, drips on the arching branches of hazel that crowded the ditches.

"I'll see you settled," Leopold said. "And then return to London."

Marguerite looked away through the window, head bobbing with the horses' motion. Her auburn hair was beaded with moisture and strands of it spilled out from under a neat little hat. When she bent her head to remove her gloves, he glimpsed beneath her collar the pale perfection of the nape of her neck and remembered it warm and perfumed. He wanted to bury his fingers in that mass of hair, turn her face to his, and lose himself in her kisses. He reached for her hand which was resting on the seat between them. She turned around — beautiful as ever but vacant — and the stirring in him subsided.

"Lewis would be proud of me," she said. "He was always telling me to get away from London, to get away from you." She allowed herself a weak smile.

"Lewis will be fine, you know. The war will be over before we know it. These Boers don't seem to realize they're taking on the greatest fighting force in the world." But it felt as though he was talking to himself. "The rest here will do you good."

They arrived at the entrance to Jordanswood which was very grand with two huge, wrought-iron gates. A woman scurried out of the lodge to open them and curtsied as they passed in. The drive meandered, with woodland on one side and, on the other, open meadows dotted with elm and horse-chestnut trees.

"Dr. Asgard is expecting us," Leopold said.

At last, the house came into view, an impressive Georgian manor, four storeys high, with steps leading up to a double-columned portico. It was solid and impressive, rather than elegant. Some way back from the house and behind a belt of alders with bare branches, a series of other buildings could be seen, low and functional and running away from the eye. A gang of workmen were offloading bricks from the back of a wagon and stacking timber. Other than that there was no activity about the place.

They were shown into Dr. Asgard's office which was at the front of the house and had two vast windows that overlooked the pastures they had just driven by. In the middle of the floor stood a desk with a comfortable leather chair on one side of it and, amusingly, two straight-backed chairs on the other. There was a sideboard, several large vases of Chinese origin, some forbidding portraits on the walls, and brass statuettes just about everywhere.

Dr. Asgard arrived. He was a small, quick man with a grey beard that came to a point and curled beneath his chin like the dried-up tail of a smoked herring. He sat at his desk and opened a large ledger.

"I am sure you will find your sojourn here most beneficial, Miss Davenport. As I explained in my letter, we believe here in a regime of regular rest, moderate exercise and wholesome meals. Healthy body, healthy mind." Dr. Asgard peered over his spectacles to see how Marguerite was receiving this information. "We advocate here a 'Gospel of Fatness'," he said. "Which has nothing to do with cream cakes and pudding five times a day, oh no." He smiled at his own little joke. "No, it is about nourishing the self."

There was a knock at the door and a nurse of middle age came in. She wore a navy dress and a long white apron. A bunch of keys dangled from her waist. Marguerite's eyes were drawn to them. The woman stooped and whispered into the doctor's ear. Her hair was scraped back under her cap, all except for a row of neat, black curls at the crown, which were so girlish-looking that they made a mockery of the puffy, fallen face beneath them.

She left the room and Dr. Asgard said, "We should move along. I will be needed elsewhere shortly." He studied Marguerite for a long time. "I have heard such splendid reports about your acting, Miss Davenport," he said. "Though I have not as yet been lucky enough to see you perform. This place . . ." he threw his eyes around the room to denote the whole of Jordanswood, "this place takes up all of my time. But when next in London, it will be my pleasure to see you in a play."

Marguerite looked down at her hands where they lay in her lap, palms uppermost, fingers closing in, like curled-up autumn leaves.

Dr. Asgard turned his attention to Leopold. "Now," he said, "the letter from Miss Davenport's doctor, if you please."

Dr. Asgard read it and transferred some of the particulars into the ledger in front of him. He paused in his writing. "Your doctor has diagnosed melancholia, Miss Davenport. You will be pleased to hear that we have a very high success rate in treating melancholia."

Marguerite fidgeted in her chair.

"I have a train to catch," Leopold said. "Could we do this swiftly?"

Dr. Asgard, undeterred by Leopold's hurry, said, "A few weeks here is quite possibly all you will need, Miss Davenport. Now, Lord Barrie, you have the Reception Order?"

Leopold handed over the document and Dr. Asgard checked it.

"Signed by a magistrate, I see, and the parish clerk and by

your good self, Lord Barrie." He put it down. "There is no next of kin, then?"

"Lewis," Marguerite said as though she was calling her brother in a dream.

"Lewis?" Dr. Asgard queried.

"Lewis is Miss Davenport's brother," Leopold said. "He is in the army, gone to South Africa and therefore unavailable."

"And you, Lord Barrie, you are a relation?"

"In the absence of any close family, I am a friend acting in Miss Davenport's favour."

Dr. Asgard scrutinized him with eyes that could see beyond physiognomy, eyes that could root out thoughts, emotions, motives.

"I own the Metropole Theatre," Leopold said, with some ceremony, "where Miss Davenport has worked. I, or rather we, owe her a duty of care."

Dr. Asgard released Leopold from his gaze and resumed writing in the big ledger.

"What is this order?" Marguerite said.

Leopold willed her question to die, but it wouldn't.

"Leopold, look at me. What is this order?"

"Formalities, my dear. That is all," he said.

Dr. Asgard put down his pen, thrust his chin forward.

"I hope and trust that Miss Davenport has been fully informed about the type of institution this is and what admission here means." He removed his spectacles and rubbed the inner corners of his eyes, waiting for a reply. In the absence of which, he continued, "I distinctly remember, Lord Barrie, impressing upon you in the course of our correspondence how important it was that the patient be fully aware of proceedings, even if he or she is not in agreement with them. Deception at this stage can lead to enormous stress, which in turn can adversely affect the treatment we offer. I take a very poor view of it, Lord Barrie."

Leopold bowed his head and bore the reprimand. He had told Marguerite that he was taking her to a convalescent home, had concealed the true nature of their destination in case she refused to go or, even if she complied, that she would involve him in prolonged, tortured discussions about their relationship. It was cleaner this way.

"Please tell me what is going on." It was Marguerite, like a swimmer surfacing from the depths, with water in her eyes.

"Miss Davenport, this is Jordanswood Asylum," Dr. Asgard said. "It has been decided for your own safety that you need institutional care. I am just sorry that you had to find out this way. You have nothing to fear, Miss Davenport – please trust me. We operate a policy of non-restraint here so you will be free to go wherever you please – within the grounds, of course – and you may wear your own clothes. The public patients work in the laundry or make mats in the workshop but you will not be required to do so."

"I think I would like to leave now," Marguerite said, standing and waiting for Leopold to do likewise, which he did not. "I don't belong here, Doctor." She swallowed hard. "Whatever else I am, I am not mad."

"Miss Davenport, you are a very unwell young woman," Dr. Asgard said. "You are suffering from a severe depressive illness which will become progressively worse if left untreated."

"I wish to go now. I will see my own doctor, in my own time."

"Then I must inform you that you have been committed to Jordanswood Asylum under the 1845 Act." Dr. Asgard placed his hand on the Reception Order. "That is what this document is. I am afraid you do not have a choice in the matter."

"Is this your doing, Leopold?" Marguerite said, weakly and with such hurt in her voice that he could not look at her.

"It's for the best," he said.

The strength went from Marguerite's legs and she fell back into her chair. He put out a hand to steady her but she shrugged it away.

"How could you do this to me? After all we've – we've meant to each other?" Her words caught in her throat and she covered her face with her hands as she rocked back and forth, crying. It was a pitiful sight.

"Please, Doctor," Leopold said, "can we get this over?"

Dr. Asgard rang a bell and the severe nurse with the black curls reappeared.

"I think Miss Davenport could do with some water, Sister Barnes," he said, a significant look passing between them.

Sister Barnes went away and returned within a minute.

"Here you are, dearie," she said, pressing the glass to Marguerite's lips. "Drink it all up, it'll do you good." Her voice was surprisingly soft, as sweet as rose petals. Marguerite obeyed.

When she had finished the last drop, Sister Barnes helped her to her feet.

"You come along with me now," she said, and when Marguerite stumbled, "It's gone to your head a bit, that's all. Right as rain you'll be, in no time."

Sister Barnes guided her away but as Marguerite passed Leopold her eyes locked with his and he struggled to find the words with which to vindicate himself. He was about to ask for her forgiveness when he realized her look was not accusatory or angry or injured, merely blank.

When they were left alone, Dr. Asgard said, "A mixture of bromide of potassium and chloral hydrate can be useful in such circumstances. We don't like to use it, of course, but you made it necessary. It does no harm at all to the patient, wears off in a couple of hours."

"She will be well cared for, won't she?"

"Of course she will. We are professionals here and this is an establishment of the highest order."

"I hope I have made the right —"

"There is nothing to be gained, Lord Barrie, from wondering whether or not you have made the right decision in committing Miss Davenport. Right or wrong are immaterial at this juncture. The rule of law has taken over."

"Then, let me settle my account with you," Leopold said, taking out his cheque book.

"I believe you are familiar with the terms."

"I noticed on my way in that there is work going on to the rear of the house."

Dr. Asgard softened his tone. "Ah, yes," he said. "We are constructing a modest concert hall. It is good for the patients to put on shows and entertainments, good for the staff too. We all like to have a little diversion. It is ten miles to the nearest town, you know."

"Quite so," Leopold said, smiling. "In that case, I take it there is a building fund?"

Dr. Asgard smiled now too.

"There is," he said.

Leopold found his pen. "This will cover six months' treatment for Miss Davenport. She will need at least that. The extra is to help with your improvements here." He pushed the cheque across the desk.

Dr. Asgard looked at the amount. One eyebrow twitched. "That is very generous of you, Lord Barrie," he said, folding it up and locking it into his drawer. "Perhaps you would let me show you around Jordanswood. This is a thriving community — there is much to see."

Out in the hall, Dr. Asgard stopped an attendant and sent him to tell Sister Barnes that he was delayed and to postpone the hydrotherapy session until later.

Then he turned to Leopold.

"Upstairs first, I think. Please, be careful here." He took hold of the handrail on the magnificent, mahogany bannisters and shook it. The whole construction leaned dangerously.

"Very grand to look at," he said. "But riddled with woodworm underneath." He led the way upstairs. "When we are finished here, I will take you to see the foundry and the sewing rooms and the carpentry workshop so you can see at first hand what work we do here and the difference we can make to people's lives. We rely very heavily on donations and subscriptions such as yours, which, I am afraid, fall far short of how much it actually costs to run a place of this sort. At least, to run it as we would see fit. It is our aim," he said, "to make this the largest and best institution of its type in the south of England."

"Indeed," Leopold said, glad to have found the measure of his man.

Chapter Twenty-six

Marguerite went with Sister Barnes up several flights of stairs and along endless corridors. The nurse's voice, like a hum, was reassuring, as was the stroke and pat of her hand on Marguerite's. Marguerite obeyed all her commands, had no will to do otherwise. It felt as though she was inside her own head, looking out at a strange world where objects shimmered and moved so that even the pictures on the walls seemed alive. She turned her head, and tables, chairs, lamps left trails of themselves like shooting stars across the sky.

They came to a bedroom and she recognized her own trunks lying open on the floor while two female attendants, both young and plump and wearing grey uniforms, unpacked them. Sister Barnes guided Marguerite to the bed and told her to sit on it. She said she would be well looked after but that it would be to her own advantage to accept her circumstances and concentrate on getting better. Then she left her in the care of the attendants.

Afterwards, Marguerite realized that she had been drugged in Dr.

Asgard's office and when the effects of the medication wore off and the full impact of her 'prisoner' status descended on her, she lay down and cried for hours on end, refusing all food and consolation, until she fell asleep from mental exhaustion.

In the days that followed she raged – in so far as her depressive state admitted of rage – against her poor dead mother from whom she had inherited a faulty disposition, against the institution, against the doctors and nurses, against the other inmates and most of all against Leopold. The first time he came to visit her, she turned her chair around to face the wall and ignored him. No amount of pleading would get her to relent but still he left gifts and returned the following week and the week after that until his patience and desire for forgiveness impressed her more than the passing cruelty he had shown in committing her to the asylum.

The regime at Jordanswood helped to mollify her too. It was benign and, though she resisted at first, in time it won her over. They rose at eight, took gentle exercise at regular intervals, ate well, amused themselves with books and music and art and went early to bed. She found herself almost enjoying the routine.

Some of the inmates were, of course, wretched creatures and shocking to behold at first. There was one man who persisted in tearing the clothes off his own back so that, although he was issued daily with a regulation uniform, he went about in rags all the time without a care even for his own modesty. Others scratched non-stop or twitched or nodded their heads to such extremes that the defect overcame the personality and they were known to her simply as The Twitcher or The Scratcher or The Nodder.

Jordanswood was divided into two: the East House or private wing and the West House which was public. The public patients made up two thirds of the whole and were accommodated in four dormitories at the back of the house which were segregated according to gender. These inmates were expected to spend every afternoon in the workshops adjacent, the women sewing mats or laundering and the men doing some light carpentry. Apart from when exercising, the two houses did everything separately.

At mealtimes, Marguerite sometimes sought the company of Mr. Roberts, a law student who was very polite but who hadn't a reasonable thought in his head. An ex-governess, Eliza Morely, was another that Marguerite liked to sit with but this lady was subject to such lapses of memory and flashes of temper that often conversation with her was impossible. And what Marguerite wanted more than anything else now was peace. The lure of her old life faded. The theatre, parties, lovers, friends no longer appealed to her but seemed more like unnecessary complications.

The Jordanswood demesne extended to one hundred and fifty acres, much of it parkland but with some wooded areas and a lake walk of rare beauty. Twice a day there were exercise parties when the attendants escorted all the patients on a one-hour stroll around the park. But in the afternoons when the majority of the West House were busy at their labours, Marguerite could walk alone uninterrupted. She spent many pleasant hours wandering about or sitting on the bench by the boathouse which was her favourite spot.

Dr. Asgard occupied a suite of rooms on the floor below Marguerite's. He was a bachelor and it seemed that, apart from the necessities of washing, sleeping and eating, he devoted himself entirely to his work and was to be seen about the place sometimes at the oddest hours. He was always keen to converse with his patients wherever he met them and it was a matter of pride with him that he personally knew, and could give a potted history of, each and every inmate at Jordanswood.

And so one day, about a month after her arrival, Marguerite, well wrapped against the cold, was sitting on the wrought-iron bench at the back of the house when Dr. Asgard approached. She enjoyed these little chats of theirs as she had grown quite fond of the doctor and was amused at the way, small though he was, the sleeves of his jacket and the legs of his trousers managed still to be a shade too short.

He sat down beside her.

"You are looking remarkably well today, my dear," he said.

It was more a diagnosis than a compliment and it led Marguerite into asking him if she was well enough to go home, a question that she had not thought would have sprung to her lips.

He stiffened. "Evidently not, Miss Davenport," he said. His cold, black eyes bored into her and she was left in no doubt that she had, in some way, transgressed by asking this. "You are the best judge of your own psychological well-being and the fact that you ask me indicates uncertainty on your part. In other words, you do not trust yourself and therefore I do not trust you either." It didn't seem to Marguerite that their conversation was over but the doctor's gaze suddenly veered away to some place over her shoulder and he said, "If you'll excuse me, Miss Davenport, I have matters to attend to."

When Marguerite turned to see where he was going she saw Leopold had emerged from the drawing-room doors onto the terrace and the doctor was going to meet him. The two men shook hands with great gusto, exchanging pleasantries that she was too far away to hear. Dr. Asgard stood with his back to her thereby blocking a clear view of the exchange but it seemed, at one stage, as though he took something from Leopold – an envelope? – and slipped it into his pocket. The two men then

walked along the terrace away from Marguerite to the far corner
of the house from which height they could look out over the
construction site. The doctor spoke at length, waving his arms
about and pointing in various directions, presumably to explain
the layout of the proposed building. When they parted there was
another hearty handshake and she thought, from Dr. Asgard, a
slight forward tilt of the body almost suggestive of a bow.

Leopold saw her then, and waved. He came over and kissed
her. His cheek was smooth and cool and smelled of cologne. He
presented her with a bundle of letters from her apartment,
assuring her before she even looked that there was one from
Lewis. She found it, studied the envelope with its foreign stamps,
but decided to delay opening it. In the meantime, Leopold was
waiting. She could tell by the way he was trying not to smile that
he was hiding something behind his back. Now that he had her
attention, he brought it out. Chocolates from Bell's in
Farringdon Street, Marguerite's favourite shop. The box itself
was a delight, tied up in blue ribbon with white paper roses on
the lid. But most wondrous of all, little blue glass butterflies
hovered over the flowers, supported on wires that came up from
beneath. How Leopold must have guarded the package all the
way down on the train to prevent it getting crushed!

"Beautiful, so beautiful," Marguerite said. "Thank you, my
darling." She had not called him that for a long time.

He noticed, coughed nervously and it felt as though they had
been hurtled back to the very start, when they were but eager
acquaintances on the verge of knowing each other.

"Come," he said, taking her hand. "Let us stroll. I have much
to tell you."

The chocolates and the letters were dispatched to her room
with an attendant while they descended the stone steps that led
to the lawn. They took the right-hand path along by the lake.

Leopold tucked her arm beneath his elbow and covered her gloved hand with his free one. Despite the cold weather Marguerite felt warm and cheered inside.

"Paul Lloyd took a fall on stage at the Lyceum the night before last," Leopold said. "Broke his leg, but carried on until the bitter end regardless, so pickled in alcohol he didn't feel a thing."

"I do not think I have ever seen that man sober," Marguerite said. She took a deep breath, looked up through the naked branches of the trees where the crows were flapping and jostling with each other. She closed her eyes and smiled.

Later, alone in her room, Marguerite eagerly opened Lewis's letter.

Sunday, 28th November, 1899

My dear, dear sister,

I hope you are continuing well and getting stronger by the day. When I enlisted I did not foresee that I would be called up so soon and I am sorry that I could not wait until you were at the peak of health before I departed but I was certain you were very nearly fully recovered and Edmund, I trust, will look after you. I'm afraid I left in rather a huff with him, which serves him right for all his hypocrisy but I do hope the world is not being too unkind to him.

How are the rehearsals for 'Hedda Gabler' going? I am sure you are astounding them all at Her Majesty's. What is Tree like to work with? I hear he is a maniac, that he doesn't sleep at all and expects everyone else to keep the same hours he does. What with the new play and Christmas coming and the Millennium too, you and the whole city of London must be in a welter of excitement. By the way, any snow yet? How I long for snow!

We are stationed for the moment in Southern Natal near a place that I'm not allowed to give you the name of. Here they call it a town though in reality it is but a railway station out in the middle of the veldt with a collection of huts around it. The veldt, in case you don't know, is like a vast, flat desert but with great clumps of coarse, dry grass on it. We are part of Buller's force but all we have done so far is wait. We have been here for twenty-one days with nothing happening.

Today is Sunday so we get an extra hour in bed and a reprieve from drill. Even so, we all roll out of our tents at five thirty because with the sun up it's just too hot to stay in them. Not that there's any shade to be had outside but at least there is air. Most of us have sick bellies and the sunburn is something terrible. I'm not too bad, but the worst of them have great watery blisters on their faces and necks that burst and become infected. We're known to the Boers as 'Rooineks' which means, literally, 'red necks'!

Though there are plenty who are sick, thank God none of us has died in this camp but it is terrible to see how the poor horses are suffering in the mounted divisions. They have been shipped from the lush, green fields of England to this hellish terrain and they're not able for it. The least exertion causes them to lather up on their flanks and necks and no matter how much salt they get, their tongues are swollen and hang out from their mouths. Every day a few more have to be shot and we haven't even started marching yet.

Hopefully, we will see some action soon. There are rumours that we will be part of an offensive on a range of hills currently occupied by the enemy. If we succeed, it will be a great, logistical victory as it will leave the way clear for our army to follow through unimpeded.

We have not yet seen any Boers. We are told that they are

tough opponents but undisciplined; excellent marksmen but poor strategists. That remains to be seen. I would be lying if I said I wasn't scared but at least if the waiting was over we could get on with what we came out to South Africa to do.

Please write. A letter will find me eventually, I promise you, no matter where we end up. I could read it and feel I was back in the drawing room again, looking out over the street, chatting and idling.

Pray for me.

Your ever loving brother,

Lewis

Marguerite read the letter three times before putting it away in the top drawer of the tallboy in her room. She felt frightened for him and wanted to write back straight away, but didn't. She would wait until she was out of the asylum before doing that.

Chapter Twenty-seven

Black Week. Stormberg, Magersfontein, Colenso. Three major British defeats all within the space of five days. The war against the Boers was but two months old.

The newspapers were full of it: the incompetence of various generals; brigades being led astray by guides who had no English; the awful conditions being endured by soldiers; men often left stranded lying out on the veldt, defeated by the sun and the ants before even sighting a Boer.

Charles Gray wearied of reading about it. He leafed through the *Times* in search of more agreeable news and came upon another article that held his attention.

'**The murder of Clive Potter, theatre critic, newspaperman, social reformer and playwright, who was found beaten to death in his home on the fifth of February last, has remained unsolved. However, Chief Inspector Findlay, who is leading the investigation into Mr. Potter's death, has informed this newspaper**

that the police are now following a definite line of enquiry. Mr. Potter, a noted philanthropist, had lately, in an effort to expose the perpetrators of child prostitution, made contact with members of that criminal underclass. The police now believe that he was killed as punishment for the work he had done in this area. An arrest is imminent.'

The rest of the article was a tribute to the dead man and though Charles was reluctant to proceed any further, he did skim through it, a few choice phrases catching his eye. Clive Potter was, according to the *Times,* '**passionate and fearless**' in his writing about the theatre and displayed an '**abiding empathy with the plight of the working classes**'. And in addition to all that, he was being credited with single-handedly stamping out '**the evil practice of child prostitution**' for which '**he had paid dearly with his own life**'.

Charles sighed, folded up the newspaper and dropped it on his desk. He felt an actual physical urge to run out into the street and disavow every passerby of the belief that this person, Clive Potter, was a good man. Charles was well acquainted with the power of the written word, indeed had used it himself often enough in the service of the Colosseum, but to see it here, applied thus, sickened him. He knew nothing of Potter's effectiveness as a social reformer but, from his own experience of the man, he doubted that he empathized with the working classes at all or that he was motivated by any but the most egotistical considerations. In his own dealings with Potter, he had found him to be a self-serving philistine who praised everything modern simply because it was the fashion to do so. He liked to shock and be shocked and he based all judgments on these criteria, too stupid to know that art cannot be measured in this way.

The fireplace was still full of ashes from the previous night when he and Edmund had sat there drinking brandy into the early hours. They had discussed Leopold's ultimatum and reached no definite conclusion as to which was the better course of action. Charles favoured the sabbatical option as there was always the possibility that Edmund would be reinstated. Edmund, guided by pride, seemed more inclined to cut his ties with the theatre altogether and remove himself from his father-in-law's influence. Charles might have encouraged him in this had he sensed in his friend any of the enthusiasm and drive necessary for starting afresh.

The wood they had burned on the fire came from an old apple tree in Edmund's garden that had split its trunk and was felled the previous summer. The timber hissed and snapped and released into the room its sweet orchard fragrance. Now, in the morning, the air had turned cold and acrid and it caught at the back of Charles' throat, drying it.

"Good morning, Charles."

He was surprised to see Violet. She had been in the office much more of late but never in her husband's absence. She went to Edmund's desk and sat in his chair, positioning it to her satisfaction. Ever since the terrible rumours about Edmund had surfaced, Charles had noticed a new boldness in Violet's manner. Many women in her situation would have chosen to remain safely in the shadows, but she, on the contrary, seemed bent on defining herself in some way that had not yet become clear.

She picked up the silver paper knife in front of her and slit open one of Edmund's letters.

"Edmund has a particular system for dealing with his mail," Charles said.

"Does he?"

"Yes. He is meticulous."

She opened another envelope, read briefly through the letter, placed it to one side, picked up the next one.

"They must be stamped," Charles said. "It is important. If you continue to open letters, you need to retrieve the date stamp from Mr. Hayes – he borrowed it earlier."

She put down the paper knife with some force and Charles returned to the file marked '*Receipts*'.

There was silence for a long while and, when eventually Violet spoke, she opted for a carefree tone.

"Ah, I see you have been reading the *Times*," she said, eyeing it at his elbow. "It appears Clive Potter is our latest national hero. At least, according to all the newspapers this morning."

"Yes," Charles said, without looking up. "There are none so blind as those that will not see."

"He never struck me as heroic," Violet said. "In fact, he always reminded me of a down-at-heel stall-holder, the kind who pushes rotten fruit on his customers and swears it's best quality."

The aptness of her description brought a grudging smile to Charles' lips and he allowed himself to be drawn in.

"It gives me no pleasure to speak ill of the dead," he said, "but I will not lie either. I disliked everything about Clive Potter: his personality, his professional attitudes, his artistic pretensions. His prejudice against Edmund and this theatre cost us dear over the years. I can remember at least two productions that we were forced to take off after bad reviews of his, and thoroughly good plays they were too, but Potter ruined the audience for us."

Violet sat very still in her chair. She had been listening with an intentness that surprised him.

"He did make some valid points though," she said. "After all, how can the theatre move forward, expand, if it doesn't cast off the chains of orthodoxy? Surely that is liberating?"

"Cutting ourselves off from the experience and wisdom of centuries, from the eternal pursuit of true artistic achievement, from the great thinkers of the past like Aristotle, Samuel Johnson and Diderot cannot, in my opinion, serve us well."

"Every era has its share of great minds," Violet said. "And art, as I understand it, is not necessarily born out of experience and wisdom. Vision has something to do with it, has it not? I disliked Mr. Potter too, but not so much that I cannot concede he had some decent ideas regarding the theatre. He was not all bad."

"Just as none of us is all bad," Charles said. "But I, for one, will not be his apologist." He tried to immerse himself once again in his work but could not. "My dislike of the man does not in any way influence how I regard his views," he said, nailing her with a stare. "They are contemptible. And I am perfectly entitled to think so."

"Of course you are. But there are many others in the theatre world who consider that Mr. Potter was both erudite and prescient."

"Perhaps – your connection with the Colosseum having been relatively brief – you are not fully aware of the trials we have suffered at the hands of this despicable man. Otherwise you would not be defending him like this."

"I am not defending him. I am merely stating what I believe to be true."

She continued to peruse the letters and open drawers in Edmund's desk while Charles set about paying the outstanding bills of the month. He did not expect further conversation and neither was there any, but the silence between them was antagonistic and he was relieved when eventually she announced her departure.

At the door she stopped.

"I will return this afternoon," she said.

Chapter Twenty-eight

Lewis Davenport had enlisted as a private soldier with the Royal Fusiliers, City of London Regiment, and spent several weeks in training at Winchester before being sent out to South Africa in early October just before the official declaration of war. Along with the rest of his unit and other troops from all over England, he had travelled aboard the *Mauritius*, a merchant ship that was equipped to carry any type of cargo, except men. Fourteen hundred soldiers were crammed into the vessel which had only twenty toilets and five wash-hand basins, an inconvenience that became unbearable when large numbers of men were struck down by seasickness and diarrhoea. Luckily, Lewis was not affected by either.

Despite the diabolical conditions, spirits were high among the healthy. There were plenty of veterans on board, men who had served elsewhere in the Empire and quite a few who had fought in South Africa previously against the Boers and the Zulus during the seventies. These fellows held everyone's interest as they described to the uninitiated what awaited them – the harsh landscape, the climate, the wild animals, which were all just as much enemies of the British as were the Boers. Stories were told about previous campaigns in South Africa, stories so full of magic and adventure that they fired up the imaginations of the new recruits and it became a running joke to pray every night for war to be declared and once that was achieved they would pray even harder that it would not be all over by Christmas, as predicted.

Lewis was proud to serve his country and was committed to doing so. He believed he was in the right place at the right time doing the right thing and it occurred to him that perhaps he had never felt so complete before. But he wasn't so foolish as to be excited by the prospect of war. He still hoped, even expected, that Kruger would capitulate before any lives were lost.

Immediately on disembarkation at Durban, the Royal Fusiliers marched to the railway station from whence they were transported by train to the holding camp at Chievely.

The wait at Chievely seemed interminable but, at last, war was declared. Hostilities began. At Chievely, they polished boots, carried out fatigues, had kit inspections. Kimberley, Mafeking and Ladysmith were besieged by the Boers. At Chievely, the men hoisted a log between two wagons and had pillow fights sitting astride it. They drilled endlessly; there were parade services; a choir was formed. Then came the crushing news of the British defeats at Stormberg and next day, Magersfontein, and four days after that, Colenso. And still they waited. They had been waiting for two months.

Amongst the men the mood was restless. Many expressed exasperation, contempt even, of a military command that kept fighting men idle, impotent, while the war was being lost on so many fronts.

Finally, in January, they were on the move, forming part of Sir

Redvers Buller's column. The mission: to knock through the Rangeworthy Hills and liberate Ladysmith on the other side.

They set off at half past four that first morning but progress was slow. There were wagons and guns and oxen and mules to bring. They marched, struck camp that night, ate, slept, repacked, marched again. Day after day the same, sometimes covering as little as four miles before nightfall depending on how difficult the terrain, how many spruits there were to be crossed, how many cartwheels splintered and had to be replaced.

On the seventh day, from the slopes of Mount Alice, they looked down on the Tugela river three miles away, writhing over the open plain like a gigantic silver eel. Under Lieutenant-General Sir Charles Warren, they took a full day to reach the ford at Trikhardt's Drift, still another to build the pontoon and it would likely take two more to complete the crossing. With eleven thousand infantry, two thousand two hundred cavalry, thirty-six field guns and provisions, it was a major operation. All equipment, ammunition and supplies had to be unloaded on one side of the river, transported across the pontoon by hand, then loaded up again. The animals were swum over, the vehicles dragged by ropes. The big guns posed quite a challenge. Twelve-pounders and Howitzers were dismantled on one side, carried across, then reassembled on the far shore. The work was exacting and tedious, parts went astray, tempers flared.

It was midday and the sun was merciless. They had been on the go since dawn. Lewis Davenport was one of a chain of men on the pontoon spanning the river. A rhythm had developed along the line as they swung items from one set of hands to the next, finally depositing them on dry land at the end. Lewis's arms felt like they had been pulled from their sockets. The small of his back, his neck, his shoulders, everything ached. The wooden boards beneath their feet dipped as heavy weights passed over them. The water was clear and golden like China tea with smooth, round stones on the riverbed in shades of russet, blue and white. Some were speckled. Like eggs, Lewis thought.

Just then, he and his comrades were distracted by whistling and cheering. A little downstream a soldier had stripped naked and thrown himself into the river for a swim. Work ceased as they all looked at him to see if he would be hauled out and punished. It was forbidden to go in the water unless absolutely necessary for fear of catching enteric fever. The man did a frenzied front crawl out into the middle, then rolled over onto his back, rotating both arms simultaneously, kicking with all his might. He wasn't ordered out. There were whoops from the onlookers. Then one or two others dared to join him. Within seconds, scores of men had taken to the water. Beside Lewis, Georgie Carr grinned and threw off his clothes so Lewis did the same and the pair of them dived into the melée of swimmers. The water was so cold that it scalded Lewis's skin and stopped his breath, causing him to gasp for air and laugh at the same time.

The senior officers were standing around in affable form, laughing at the swimmers and chatting. Even Sergeant Ridley had his usual bad temper in abeyance and was standing on the pontoon, surveying the scene with something approaching amusement. Then, after ten minutes or so of fun, the order to get out of the water came and was relayed all along the bank from one NCO to the next.

Sergeant Ridley nearly herniated himself yelling at them, threatening all kinds of punishment if they didn't comply instantly. Lewis stole another few strokes, then like the rest hauled himself back onto the makeshift bridge to let the sun dry his skin before dressing. The swim had revitalized them, reminded them of who they were – vigorous young men on their way to battle.

The rest of the day was uneventful. Once the crossing was

complete and the bridge taken down, the convoy moved onward for another hour to Three Tree Hill where they struck camp for the night.

Corporal Drake, nicknamed Duckie, was in charge of the field kitchen for Lewis's section. The man had come to believe his own spurious claim that he had once been Head Chef at the Ritz Hotel and to prove it he had, in abundance, the rotten temper that is obligatory in that line of work. He was foul-mouthed and cantankerous but never vicious and for that reason the men enjoyed him and his tantrums. That night he served them up a dish he called 'Royal Chevril' and, though they all knew it was a stew of horsemeat and beans and little else, the grand title tickled them and made the thin broth almost palatable. Lewis pulled a blanket over his head to keep the bugs off his food while he ate but he could still hear Duckie in the distance whacking pots with the metal spoon that never left his hand and shouting, 'farking' this and 'farking' that, like it was ordinary conversation.

His belly full, Lewis strolled away from the main body of men and stood alone on a rocky outcrop. The Tugela was below him. Beyond it, westerly, the open plain ran off to the mighty Drakensbergs with their basalt summits. Resting on them was the sun, a great orange ball with bloody smears across it. It looked as though it might start rolling towards him at any moment, destroying all in its path. It was huge, like everything else in this country, huge and beautiful and cruel.

Two days later, under the command of Major General Woodgate, the eleventh brigade – which comprised the Second Royal Fusiliers along with three other Lancashire regiments and three batteries of the Royal Field Artillery – set out to capture Spion Kop, an occupied hill six miles away to the south-east.

It was a nighttime operation. With burnt sticks they blackened their faces and each man checked that he had a water bottle, one day's field rations, a rifle and a hundred and fifty rounds. Sergeant Ridley went through the hand signals one last time. There was nervous laughter and swearing until the order was given – no talking, no smoking – and silence fell. They marched to the foot of Spion Kop. Darkness fell in a matter of minutes and the full moon that was supposed to light their way up the kopje was smothered in thick cloud.

It was midnight before they began to climb the hill. They were like blind men, grabbing handfuls of vegetation to pull themselves up the steep slope. There were muffled curses as men came upon thorns in the scrub. After two hours of climbing, a damp mist made visibility even worse and soaked them to the skin. Lewis felt clammy beneath his uniform and, despite his exertion, he was chilled to the bone. His arms and legs were weak too from the strenuous climb. He pressed himself into the side of the hill. They were not far from the top. All around he could hear men eating biscuit or gulping rum to set themselves up for what lay ahead. Lewis took a swig of water from his canteen and retched. The moon peeked from behind a cloud, the mist blew off momentarily and revealed the summit one hundred yards or so above. The order came and they loaded their rifles, fixed bayonets. Lewis dropped his blade and couldn't find it in the dark. In a panic he ran his hands through the undergrowth and along the ground and when he came upon it he nearly cried with relief.

They waited until the scouts returned with word of the exact position of the enemy. They were to hold their fire until they hit flat ground, then it was a case of run like the blazes towards the target. They crept nearer and could hear the enemy talking. Then silence, followed by a challenge.

"*Wiede?*"

In response some joker from amongst the British shouted, "Waterloo!" and they all threw themselves flat on the hillside as the enemy replied with zig-zagging rifle fire. When they heard the rattle of empty magazines, the command was given to charge. A bullet whistled past Lewis's ear as he raced with the others onwards. The Boer encampment began to emerge from the mist, a circular structure made from mud. As they approached at full pelt, the occupants – at the very most, ten – scrambled out of the rear and scattered off in various directions. Nobody even bothered to fire after them.

Inside the fort they found bedrolls, tins of food, books, candles and several pairs of boots which the Boers had left behind when they fled. A billycan of water bubbled away on a little fire.

"Blow me, if they didn't boil the kettle for us," Sergeant Ridley said. He kicked the pot off its perch, killed the flame with dust.

When General Woodgate caught up with them he made a short speech commending the Corps for the bravery shown and the success they had achieved at a cost of only four men wounded. He led them in a round of three cheers which was the signal to those below that they had taken the hill. At that moment Lewis wouldn't have wished himself anywhere else in the world.

It was four in the morning when the sappers arrived with their shovels and began taping out the positioning of the trenches. Lewis and his mates took the opportunity to rest, lying on the ground in a bunch, each man's body a pillow for the next. He rested his head on Georgie Carr's stomach and within seconds was asleep.

It was the sound of metal scraping on stone that woke him some time later. He opened his eyes to a brightening sky with white wreaths of mist trailing upwards into the clear blue, like kites. Carr's stomach whined and gurgled under Lewis's ear. The atmosphere should have been tranquil but it wasn't. He sat up. Men were running about, yelling; a group of officers were conferring.

Lewis nudged Georgie Carr awake. And then he saw what all the commotion was about. The morning light and the thinning mist revealed that they had not achieved the summit of Spion Kop at all but were at least two hundred yards short of it. And, more worrying still, they were surrounded on all sides by neighbouring peaks higher than their own which, if not already occupied by the enemy, very soon would be.

Sergeant Ridley was going around, shouting and kicking sleepers awake.

"Ruddy scouts – wouldn't trust them to go to the shop for milk! We're for it now, lads, I'm telling you! On your toes!"

Lewis and Georgie Carr gathered their gear and scrambled into the nearest trench which was not nearly deep enough to give them proper cover but there was no alternative. All they could do was lie in it and wait.

During the night the Boers, probably alerted by the refugees from the mud fort, had managed to climb the northern face of the kopje and now they came streaming over the forward crest above the British position, taking cover behind rocks and boulders. Under fire, the sappers higher up the hill were forced to abandon their attempt to entrench in the correct place and they fell back behind the line. A party of forty or so under Thorneycroft moved up the ridge to try and beat the enemy back down the escarpment but they were felled with terrible rapidity.

Back in the trench, bullets were raining down everywhere. The soldiers, while firing at the enemy, were all the time afraid that they might hit one of their own. Lewis, who had thought he could get through this war without killing anyone, fired at men, watched them fall. In the back of his head was the dreadful realization that if they couldn't stop the Boers coming over the crest, they would soon be overrun and then it would be hand-to-hand combat.

But even worse than that was to happen. The enemy had managed to scale the neighboring hills with their guns and the artillery bombardment began. It was deafening and in between shells the ground rumbled beneath them like a mucousy chest. The British had not managed to get artillery up Spion Kop and so could not retaliate. While the Boer gunners were finding their mark, Lewis and his comrades could only wait. Georgie Carr vomited when a shell struck ten yards away, showering them all with earth and rock. Carruthers caught some shrapnel in his side. He was beyond help, that was obvious to even the most inexperienced, thrashing about on his back, a great metal shard pinning him to the ground. Each one of them wished him dead, as much to end their own agony as his. When his flailing subsided to a quiver, they all turned away, some to pray, others to forget. Lewis wept.

Strings of scudding 'pom-poms' snapped like firecrackers. The right side of the trench was enfiladed by Boer snipers from vantage points on the neighbouring hillside. With every sweep of rifle fire, more lives were lost. In their hurry to escape this latest threat, Lewis and his colleagues clambered over corpses like ants over leaves, seeking refuge in the curve of the trench. Lewis lay there panting, Georgie Carr beside him. Hours passed. The Boers managed to dig in not twenty yards away and had the advantage of higher ground. There was no water, no sign of reinforcements.

Panic spread when news came that General Woodgate had been hit in the head and Thorneycroft, a mere colonel, was now in charge. Their situation looked hopeless.

Eventually, a lull came. The big guns stopped, the rifle fire petered out.

Then Lewis saw white handkerchiefs and vests being waved. Several of the British were standing, giving themselves up.

A Boer leader stepped forward. He stood with one foot resting on a rock, a tall, thin man with a greying beard and a cartridge belt across his chest.

"Cease fire! You have three minutes to turn yourselves in – with your weapons!" he shouted in that strange, angular accent. He planted a stick in the ground to show them where to lay down their arms.

Georgie Carr got up.

"Fucking lambs we are," he said, "to the fucking slaughter."

Lewis grabbed his arm. "Don't do it, Georgie. For Christ's sake, don't."

Georgie wrenched his arm free.

"Don't dishonour those who've died already," Lewis said.

Georgie's mouth was set firm against him. The sinews in his neck were standing out, his head was shaking. A splutter escaped him and it looked as though he might break down but he held himself in. His anger had gone. It was fear and shame that gripped him now.

"Jesus, Georgie."

There was nothing more to say. They all knew what the right thing to do was but who could blame a man if he wasn't able to do it?

Georgie climbed out of the trench like someone in a trance. And then, out of nowhere, in the silence of the ceasefire, Colonel Thorneycroft came thundering along. From the lip of the trench he gazed down at them, a hulk of a man, covered in mud, the whites of his eyes flashing through the dirt on his face as he yelled at them just as the cannons had done all day long.

"No surrender! Get back in the line, men! Get back to Hell and fight like the rest of us!" He limped along the length of the trench, defying any to leave it, fixing individuals with a ferocious eye. "Stay and we have a chance. Leave and you're leaving behind dead men, you hear me, dead men!" He shouted so loud that he was left breathless. "Fight for God and Country!"

And they did. Georgie Carr slunk back into the trench and curled himself up into a ball. Lewis lashed out at him with his feet, kicking him, yelling at him until he realized it wasn't Carr that had enraged him but the impossibility of their situation and the unfair demands that Honour was making on them. He stopped then, turned his face into the mud.

Thirty seconds later, the barrage resumed. Reinforcements came but made no difference. Soon, in the trench, they were outnumbered by the dead. In the absence of sandbags, the bodies proved effective for stopping bullets but were bloody and fly-ridden.

Twelve hours they had of it altogether. Only when the light began to fail did the artillery and gunfire cease. Then came the cries and moans of the wounded, the dreadful aftermath of a day's butchery.

Georgie Carr and any others able to walk left the trench.

Lewis hadn't the strength to stand. Somewhere in the tangle of bodies around him, he felt movement. He pulled at the arms and legs of dead men and uncovered Greely, who was dying. There was dried blood on the inside of his lips and he wanted water but there was none to be got. Lewis leant down closer to catch the words the poor man was struggling to say but he couldn't make them out. Probably it was something about Love.

He saw the urgent look in Greely's eye and said, "Don't

worry, I'll tell her."

The beginnings of a smile appeared on Greely's face and then he died. Lewis sat by the corpse, staring at it, unable to move away even though there were plenty more who needed help and still no sign of the stretcher-bearers.

Sergeant Ridley came along.

"Come on, Private," he said. "Party's over, let's get out of 'ere."

Lewis did not move.

"We've lost it, son," he said then. "It's all theirs now, bad cess to them. They can 'ave every bloody inch." He took Lewis by the hand and yanked him to his feet. "Come on, lad," he said. "Let's leave 'em to it."

Chapter Twenty-nine

It felt like treachery to be alive, treachery to be walking, treachery to be deserting the dead. In the trench it had seemed like they were the only ones under siege but, as Lewis stumbled back behind the front line, he was horrified by the scene of devastation that seemed to stretch on forever. The ground churned, bodies strewn about, covered in wet, black earth as though oil had been spilled not blood. Medics and orderlies, just arrived, were poking around looking for survivors. Everywhere, crying men, horrendous injuries, soldiers dazed and swaying from exhaustion, some walking, some crawling, some falling asleep even as they moved. There was no organized descent of the hill; units had disintegrated. They were all stragglers. This was not a retreat, it was a rout.

Georgie Carr came from behind and threw his arm around Lewis's shoulders. They did not speak. Lewis had no words or thoughts in his head to share. They descended through the scrub, springy under their feet, not caring if they fell.

Back at camp, Lewis threw himself onto his blanket in the tent and stared at the tarpaulin above his head. He revisited all the familiar marks on it with a deep sense of gratitude: the spattered mud, the mould from previous campaigns, the stains and bleached-out spots that with some imagination transformed themselves into animals or trees. He allowed no other thoughts than these.

When he slept, it was fitful. He dreamt, not of the carnage he had witnessed but of repeatedly taking aim with his rifle, firing off ten rounds then changing the magazine. It was the sheer monotony of it that kept waking him. That and the burning of his cheek which was red and swollen from being pressed against the hot barrel of his gun all day.

Next morning they were treated to a special breakfast consisting of two slices of bully beef with biscuit and a goodly portion of jam, followed by lashings of coffee – not the real thing, of course, made from rye, but welcome all the same.

Duckie doled out the food without any swearing.

"Good to see you," he said to each man as he filled his mess tin.

Lewis sat on the ground to eat his. He leant against a rock. Men were standing or sitting or staring at their plates but there was hardly any talking. The accursed sun beat down on Lewis's sore cheek, setting it on fire, but he had neither the energy nor the will to move into the shade. Georgie Carr came over and squatted beside him. He was drinking coffee. There was a shake in his hand. He answered the question that Lewis couldn't ask.

"Two hundred and fifty dead, at least. Most of them in our trench. And about fifteen hundred wounded."

Lewis tried to eat. It was necessary to eat, he must eat. He shivered. He didn't know if he was hot or cold, sick or hungry, angry or sad.

"Farraday, Whittaker, Jones, Moran, Smith, Leavis, all dead. Moore and Rogers expected to die." Georgie drained the last of his coffee, turned the cup upside down to shake the drips out of it. "Ruddy shambles from beginning to end," he said. "Some bunch of farmers, eh?"

"Yeah, who'd have thought . . ." Lewis said, and his throat was hoarse. He must have been shouting and didn't remember it. His biscuit was so hard and dry he had to soften it with his saliva before taking a bite.

Georgie Carr stood up and then just as quickly hunkered down again.

"Look," he said, leaning in. "You saw what I did up there." He stared at Lewis. He had a cut on his forehead, a crescent of black blood, which made it seem as though he had an extra eyebrow. "I was a wreck, of no use to anyone, a stupid, bloody . . . Oh, Jesus, I just wanted it to end, that's all." He couldn't hold Lewis's gaze any longer, looked down at the ground. "I admit I'm a coward. When I was a child, I was always scared. There −"

"You don't have to explain," Lewis said. "I don't blame you for what you did."

"No, listen − there was a farm down the road from where we lived and they had a very cross gander that used to run out and attack whenever you passed. I always went the long way to school just to avoid meeting him − twice as far, it was. It wasn't that I was afraid of him pecking me. It was the noise he made, a kind of empty, windy sound like a bellows but it reminded me of the insides of a dead body." He bowed his head further, rolled the tin mug between his palms. "Still have nightmares . . . daft, isn't it? But I'm not a child any more . . ."

"This time you had good reason to be afraid."

"But not to turn my back −"

"You didn't," Lewis said.

"But if Thorneycroft hadn't come along that time . . ."

"Stop," Lewis said. "Stop torturing yourself. Yours was a normal reaction to what was happening."

"You didn't do it."

"Which would you rather be: a coward or a sodomite?"

"Jesus."

Lewis grinned. "I knew that would rock you. The thing is, we are what we are." He rooted in his pocket for a tin of clove drops and tossed it unopened to Georgie. "Yep, a coward and a sodomite, we're just what the British Army needs right now, aren't we?"

Georgie was shaking his head and laughing. "Well, no one can say you're not direct, Lewis, that's for sure." He prised the lid off the tin of sweets with a coin. "Right . . . OK . . . so that's the preliminaries out of the way . . ."

Chapter Thirty

In January 1900, an article appeared in the *London Times* bemoaning the disastrous course that the war had so far taken. There were, however, according to the article's author, two developments that augured well. One was the appointment and rapid dispatch to Cape Town of Lord Roberts as the new Commander-in-Chief of Her Majesty's Forces in South Africa. The other was the announcement by the War Office that it intended to constitute an Imperial Yeomanry.

'As part of this Imperial Yeomanry, the City of London is appealing to companies, educational institutes and private benefactors for funds to aid with the raising of a local volunteer force to be named the City Imperial Volunteers. To those among you who are able-bodied and sound of mind, who can sit on a horse or fire a gun, the call has gone out for you to join up. Have no doubt but that these Volunteer-Soldiers are the most public-

spirited and courageous of men who will represent our capital city with honour and dignity. Already the response has been overwhelming. The government has not to call this country to arms; this country has sprung to arms spontaneously.'

Charles was late but that did not stop him reading the article to the very end. He was in no hurry. There was little joy to be had from his work now. Edmund had, in the end, accepted the sabbatical offered by Lord Barrie with a view to applying for reinstatement when a year had elapsed. But for the immediate future, by the end of the coming week, Edmund would no longer be actor-manager of the Colosseum. It is one thing to be plagued by scandal, quite another to find oneself stripped of one's reason for living. Edmund went about the place like a man insensible. Charles tried to cheer him though this took some effort on his part because, while trying to be optimistic for his friend's benefit, in his own mind he harboured the suspicion that Edmund would never again be allowed return to the Colosseum.

He finished the scrambled eggs and rissole that Mrs. Wilson had cooked for his breakfast and eyed the bundle of files at the other end of the table that he had meant to peruse the previous evening but hadn't.

He got up, left instructions regarding his dinner that evening, gathered together the neglected files and walked to work.

The morning was bitterly cold and squally, with sudden gusts so strong that Charles felt himself being pushed from behind along the pavement as though by a tangible force. He got to the theatre some time after eleven, went downstairs and found Edmund in the office in his armchair, unshaven and still half asleep. A crumpled newspaper was lying across his lap.

"You look awful," Charles said.

"Thank you," Edmund said, flexing his shoulders and neck.

Charles dumped the files on his desk. "Cup of tea," he said. "Only thing for it."

He filled the kettle from the bathroom tap next door and lit the spirit lamp on the sideboard to boil it. There was never any chatter between them until at least halfway through the first cup of the day so the quiet was nothing unusual. He put four spoons of tea into the large pot, filled it with boiling water, found two cups, dropped a slice of lemon into the bottom of each and poured out the tea. He handed one to Edmund and sipped his own while sitting at his desk, poking at papers, half reading them. He needed to prioritize his work for the day but found himself unable to concentrate.

He could not help thinking about all the conversations, all the jokes, all the silences that had happened between himself and Edmund in this room; all the meetings they had had with actors, actresses, playwrights, publicists; all the cups of tea he and Edmund had drunk together here; all those summers spent sweltering down here, the door wedged open to capture the least breath of air; all the plays that were planned here, all the roles that were cast; the depressions when things went wrong; the bottles of champagne when things went right. Ten glorious years of it. And now, all about to end.

"A burst water main just outside the Savoy," Charles said. "Causing chaos. Omnibuses are backed up in both directions, ladies screaming, children bawling . . . two inches of water and we're all afraid of drowning."

"Listen, Charles, I've decided to join the C.I.V.," Edmund said.

Charles zoned in on the inkstand in front of him as though he had never seen it before. It was glass, blue-tinted with a dainty gold lip to it.

"That's the City Imperial Volunteers," Edmund said.

"Yes, yes, I know what it is," Charles said. "But you are raving, my friend. That's what comes of sitting up all night. Drink your tea and relax."

"No, I have decided."

Charles took his own tea and sat in the other armchair, face to face with Edmund. "You are an actor, for God's sake," he said.

"I am an actor who is prevented from acting."

"Oh, come now, don't tell me there aren't dozens of theatres out there who would jump at the opportunity to have Edmund Jeffers work with them."

"Yes, as some kind of spectacle for audiences to gawk at . . . I won't farm myself out that way."

"I wouldn't suggest that you should, but I think there are genuine —"

"I cannot work anywhere but here, at the Colosseum. Don't ask me to."

Charles nodded.

Edmund said, "It would be better for my wife, my family, my co-workers, if I just disappeared. That is what everyone wants though they're too polite to say so."

"Well, I don't want you to disappear," Charles said. "I think you're only feeling sorry for yourself, saying daft things like that."

"I cannot ever, ever face my father again . . ."

"He may come round . . . eventually," Charles said.

There was a lapse before Edmund raised his eyes and Charles saw in them the full extent of his desperation.

"Perhaps going to war might enhance my reputation in some way," Edmund said.

"Have you lost your mind? We're not talking here about fake swords and disappearing through trapdoors. This is real, a real war. Why would you go unless you had to? Good God, you were trying to dissuade young Lewis Davenport from enlisting not so long ago. What has happened to change your mind?"

"The prospect of coming home with a chest full of medals?"

"A chest with a ruddy great hole in it, you mean. I don't know why you're thinking this way. You're not a soldier, you know nothing of soldiering."

Edmund picked up the newspaper from his lap and waved it at Charles. "They are looking for volunteers, ordinary people, anyone in fact who can sign on the dotted line. I should be able to manage that."

Charles got up and paced over to the sideboard, then back again. He fought against a strong desire for a glass of brandy.

"Not ordinary people, no," he said. "What they want is hunting folk, shooting folk. For God's sake, Edmund, have you ever even sat on a horse or held a gun in your hand? The whole idea is preposterous."

"Calm down, old chap," Edmund said. "If they don't want me, they won't take me, though I can't see for the life of me why they wouldn't. I'm able-bodied and strong."

"Not exactly in the first flush of youth though, are you?" Charles said.

Edmund laughed with the ease of a man who has made up his mind and is not for turning. "And neither am I confined to a bath chair, I'll have you know," he said. "Conan Doyle is older than me and he's been out there for months."

"Conan Doyle is a doctor. You won't find him out in the field like an ordinary soldier. You'd be a common or garden infantryman, you know that, don't you, bottom of the pile?"

"Mounted Infantry, Charles. At least I wouldn't have to walk."

"There is nothing to joke about in this."

Charles sat down again. He closed his eyes, pinched the bridge of his nose. He was starting to get a headache. Neither spoke, for quite a while.

Then, Edmund said, "Doesn't it stir you up when you read

about Magersfontein and Stormberg and now Spion Kop and the terrible time our boys are having of it out there?"

"I'm not saying it doesn't 'stir me up', as you put it. But one must remember that this is essentially a dishonest war. If there was no gold in the Witwatersrand, we wouldn't be having this conversation."

"That's all very well, Charles, but right or wrong we have the war now and we must fight it. Poor 'Tommy Atkins' has gone out there in good faith – you have to acknowledge that."

"I fail to see how Edmund Jeffers joining the army is going to help 'poor Tommy Atkins'."

"It is the only thing of any value that I can do right now," Edmund said, with a huge sigh. He rubbed his stockinged feet together. "Don't you see?"

"If you wanted to please your father-in-law, you couldn't do any better than this. It will suit him very nicely having you out of the way and especially in perilous circumstances."

"Then I will please him for the first time in my life. Anyway, I probably won't see action at all. By the time I'm trained, the whole thing will be over."

"No, it won't," Charles said. He poked at what remained of last night's fire to see if it would come alive, but it wouldn't. "You'll be killed. And then what?"

"I don't like that ending at all, Charles, too tragic. I'd prefer to arrive home from South Africa trailing clouds of glory. Much better outcome. That way we have standing ovations and warm glows all round."

"We could always go away, to Rome or Verona," Charles said. "Do some research for *Coriolanus* perhaps? Get ready for when all this nonsense has died down and you're back at the helm, in your rightful place."

Edmund looked apologetic. "No, though thank you for the

offer, Charles, but I have made my decision. I hope you will stay here, look after the Colosseum for me."

"There is no point," Charles said. He gazed into the spent fire. He resolved to say no more on that topic. He could not admit aloud that for the last decade his mission in life had been to serve Edmund Jeffers, not the Colosseum. It was Edmund's prowess, Edmund's intuition, Edmund's ability to rally even the lowliest to the one cause, that inspired him daily. It was Edmund's quips and stories that amused him. Without Edmund the Colosseum was simply a theatre without heart or soul.

"I would take it as a great personal favour to me, Charles, if you would stay, keep an eye on things as only you can do. I trust you, I trust your judgement implicitly."

"But it is no longer the Colosseum."

"It will be again when I return," Edmund said. He paused, swallowed, put a forefinger to his temple, summoned the necessary conviction. "And when I do, I want this place in good shape."

Charles stroked his upper lip while he thought about it.

"Yes, of course I'll stay," he said, finally. "If that is what you want me to do."

"I suspect Violet will want to take a managerial interest in the place. Let her, Charles. Work with her. She has a sound head and she deserves to get what she wants as compensation for a miscreant husband."

"Your behaviour has always been exemplary," Charles said, not thinking of Violet at all.

Their conversation came to a close and Edmund went to get washed and changed in his dressing room.

Charles remained, staring into the fireplace at the cold white ash. He did not move for a very long time.

Chapter Thirty-one

A week later and *Julius Caesar* was performed for the last time at the Colosseum. In playing Cassius, Edmund felt almost on the verge of madness and without any sense of proportion. In the fight scene with Brutus he was too violent and in the reconciliation too sentimental. On several occasions he missed his cue and even upstaged his colleagues. The final curtain went down and, while they were all still assembled there, Edmund apologized for his repeated blunders then hurried off to his dressing room to change.

A light buffet supper had been arranged for cast and crew in the downstairs saloon to mark the ending of the run. Edmund was adamant that he did not want a farewell party. He could not have borne that. He was simply taking a break for a while, he explained.

The saloon was softly lit, the atmosphere muted. Edmund had told no one, other than Charles, that he was joining the C.I.V. and he wanted to keep it that way. He drifted from group to group, expounding on his plans. He would rest for six months, he said, then travel and after that begin the research for his next undertaking which had yet to be decided upon. He had a fancy for something dark and demonic, *Faust* perhaps. He beguiled them all into thinking that within a year everything would be back to normal; he beguiled himself into thinking it. For still there was the hope even at this late stage, that one divine intervention, one great seismic jolt would right his world in an instant.

The night wore on. Tom Harper, the head carpenter, proposed a toast to the Chief and there were three ear-splitting cheers for him. After that, Edmund chose to leave, fearing that in his fragile state he would be overcome by emotion if there were further accolades. Charles, who was standing by the door, gave an approving nod as Edmund made good his escape.

He managed to get out of the theatre into the lane beside it without being seen. Coming out onto the main thoroughfare, he glanced back at the theatre, at the billboards and the hoarding announcing the forthcoming *Our American Cousin* with Roger Yates' name emblazoned everywhere instead of his own.

He was at Trafalgar Square before he realized he had forgotten to tell Violet that he was leaving the party so he scribbled a note to her on the back of an envelope saying he was going to stretch his legs for an hour or two. Then he commandeered a youth for sixpence to take it to his wife at the Colosseum.

The midnight trains had left already from Charing Cross and the last omnibuses had long since gone but there were stragglers on the streets yet – mostly young couples too much in love to countenance separation and parties of exuberant bachelors whistling and shouting at every passing cab in the vain hope of attracting a vacant one.

He found himself drawn to the river and made his way along

Craven Street towards it. A mist was stealing down, not smut-laden but clean for a change. It blurred the edges of buildings, dimmed the light from windows and street lamps and wrapped everything in a somnolent haze. It was as though the city herself had let out a long, sweet sigh of content. As usual the sight of the river, the connective tissue of this amazing metropolis, excited him. The width and power of it, the salty, brackish smell of it, the sheer relentlessness of its onward flow made him shiver. He leaned on the wall to take in the view downstream. In the soft night sky, the dying braziers on Westminster Bridge formed a distant arc across the water, of orange stars, like Heaven come to Earth. Big Ben chimed once, a fading peal on the moist, cold air. He had abandoned himself to this city, lost his heart to her.

He tore himself away, wanting to walk, to sight-see. It wasn't the famous buildings he yearned for – they were everyone's – but his own familiar haunts, the ordinary places that he now realized meant so much to him. He headed for New Bond Street where he dawdled to look in the shop windows at the gloves and shirts and jewellery on display. Once he had been a valued customer here, once he'd had a normal life that necessitated the buying of such items. It was important to remind himself of that because, since his meteoric fall from favour, it often felt as though he had no past.

The Doré gallery announced the forthcoming Augustus Egg exhibition and on the poster outside was a reproduction in miniature of the notorious triptych that had caused such uproar a generation ago, the artist daring to show sympathy for the unfaithful wife in her final degradation. But now, in more enlightened days, Egg's work was lauded, the man himself hailed as a masterful interpreter of the human condition. Was this progress, Edmund wondered. In time, would all shades of difference be accepted and understood, including his own? Or was this just further proof of the fickleness of mankind? The pendulum swings first one way, then back the other. Likewise, our attitudes and beliefs, governed by nothing higher than fashion, with no fixed moral standard, only a constant state of flux.

He ambled down Oxford Street, stopping at the bookshops he often frequented, and in the window of Burleigh's his eye lit on a first edition of *She Stoops to Conquer*. At first the urge to return next day and purchase it was strong but before he had walked a mere hundred yards the desire had gone.

He went away from the shops after that, zig-zagging at will through the sleeping streets of Mayfair, arriving at Belgrave Square some time later to find outside his door a carriage and Violet alighting from it. He pressed himself into the darkness of the park railings where there was enough foliage to conceal him. He would allow her time to get inside and off to bed before he entered the house. In some perverse way, he found it amusing that here he was, hiding in the shadows, a fugitive from his own life.

After what seemed like a decent interval, Edmund opened the front door only to find Violet still in the hall. The servants had gone to bed. She was standing at the foot of the staircase wide-eyed, as if he was the last person she had expected to see here in his own home and at this hour.

"I have received my call-up papers for the C.I.V.," he said. "First I go to St. John's Wood Barracks and then to South Africa."

"I did not know that you were contemplating such a move."

"I have told no one except you. And Charles, of course."

She was about to make some comment about that but stopped herself. Instead, she said, "When are you going?"

"Next Monday."

"It's very drastic."

"You and your father have made it impossible for me to remain here."

"You made it impossible for yourself, remember?"

But Edmund had no fight left in him. He said, "It is the only way I can see of moving forward, of doing some good. I won't go back the road I came with my tail between my legs. No, never that."

Her body seemed to lose some of its rigidity and she gave him a faltering smile before casting her eyes down, like a penitent. Such a docile, blessed creature, once she had got what she wanted.

"I praise you for this, Edmund." She raised her eyes and already the happy release of his impending departure had worked upon her face, smoothing her forehead, easing her expression. Even her lips seemed plumper. "This is a huge sacrifice and a noble gesture. Patriotic duty aside, I know that you are doing this for my benefit as well as your own and I thank you for that, most sincerely."

With some awkwardness she hesitated before ascending the stairs. He could step forward now and offer her his arm. She would take it and they would go upstairs together, not reconciled – there was no escaping the mutual acceptance that their marriage was dead – but united nonetheless.

"I have letters to finish," Edmund said, turning towards the morning room.

"Goodnight then."

She went upstairs with so light a tread that the only sound was the rustle of her skirt.

In the morning room, Edmund wrote to Marguerite begging her to excuse his recent neglect and explaining how events had led to a situation where currently he was without theatre, work or wife. He told her that shortly he too would be going to South Africa. On the envelope he wrote Marguerite's name but had no address for her so he slipped it into another envelope and directed it to Leopold with a note for him to pass it on. Leopold was the only one who could reach her now.

Chapter Thirty-two

Throughout Britain, the Recruiting Officers were busy during the first few months of 1900. Men were needed and men they got. In London, large numbers signed up for the City Imperial Volunteers. Some were experienced with horses and could handle a gun but most, like Edmund, had exaggerated their skills in these areas. The new recruits were all types. They were MPs, journalists, property owners, magistrates, merchants, stockbrokers, teachers and, of course, actors. In the main they were sedentary, middle-class types who were prepared to serve in the force as ordinary private soldiers and for that reason they gained the nickname 'gentleman rankers'. The training was brief, their departure much publicized. They were seen off from Southampton with great ceremony and cheering throngs but once they arrived in South Africa there wasn't one among them who believed himself a proper soldier.

To complete their training and acclimatize, they were stationed at Port Elizabeth in the Cape for several weeks where they were taught to ride and shoot. The rest of their time, rather pointlessly in Edmund's opinion, was taken up with 'housekeeping duties' by which was meant the obsessive cleaning of kit and quarters and the white-washing of just about everything including walls, steps, buckets and even stones. Then there were the twice daily drills on the parade ground which raised so much dust that afterwards the whole rigmarole of polishing belts and guns and boots and buckles had to begin again, followed by the hosing down of all objects in the vicinity that were painted white. It was monotonous, futile and very tiring in the heat.

One particular afternoon, Edmund had been detailed to get rid of weeds from a path, rarely used, that ran behind the kitchen. He had spent hours bent double plucking them out of the gravel with a knife when Corporal Williams came to tell him that he had been summoned to H.Q. by Lieutenant-Colonel Pattinson. It was such a relief to be able to stop what he was doing that Edmund hardly gave a thought to what could be the reason for this interview.

He washed his hands and face in the bathroom and smartened himself up before heading off for Battalion Headquarters which was located outside the compound a quarter of a mile away in a large white villa.

Originally, the house had been built by a wealthy Dutch industrialist, but had been commandeered in later years by the British military for its own use. Many of the building's features were, individually, pleasing but when taken altogether the effect was ostentatious to the point of ugliness. There were colonnades, stained-glass windows, mosaics, a tower of sorts, and in the garden a pond with a working fountain, surely the height of extravagance in a climate such as this where it must require constant replenishing.

Edmund was brought into Lieutenant-Colonel Pattinson's

office and told to wait. On the walls were the usual regimental photographs, rolls of honour, swords, ceremonial shields and, in recognition of the fact that they were in Africa after all, a splayed lion skin and above it a pair of tribal spears crossed in the middle. The sideboard and desk were large and dark mahogany and had obviously been shipped all the way from the mother country. There was a suit of armour in one corner, over the fireplace a painting of St. George astride his horse killing the dragon, and on the hearth a tapestry fire screen with a pattern of roses on it. Being here in these surroundings it was quite possible for Edmund to imagine himself back in England except that he was sweating, and the open windows, though shuttered against the noonday heat, let in sounds that were distinctly un-British, like the chattering of vervet monkeys from the nearby trees and the pad of bare feet on the path outside. He went to the window, peeked out through the wooden slats to find his earlier suspicion confirmed. A string of kaffir servants were scurrying back and forth between house and pond, hauling cans and buckets of water which they emptied into the fountain.

At this point Lieutenant-Colonel Pattinson came in, large and round, a walrus of a man, with folds of flesh on the back of his neck and a drooping, sandy-coloured moustache that concealed his mouth.

"Sit down, Jeffers," he said, suppressing a belch.

He took his own seat behind the desk and made a bald study of Edmund.

"It seems you have a few friends in high places yet, Jeffers," he said. "Despite the foul rumours circulating about your private life. Yes, influence has been brought to bear on your behalf." He seemed reluctant to continue, fell into a stubborn attitude from which he had to rouse himself. "I am to inform you," he said, with a sigh, "that you are being offered a commission. Second

Lieutenant." He flicked the corner of a letter that was sticking out from under his ink blotter. "Do you even know what that is?"

"No, Sir."

"It's the bottom rung." Pattinson shifted his weight from one elbow to the other and back again. "Some bloody twit in the War Office is responsible for this, a jumped-up clerk who should know better than to give in to political bullies."

Edmund nearly laughed out loud. He had a notion that Charles was involved in this, somewhere along the line.

Pattinson looked at him, long and hard. "Now, why should I sanction such an appointment, Jeffers? Tell me that. I'd be very interested to hear what you have to say."

"I'm at a bit of a loss, Sir," Edmund said, knowing there could be no right answer to Pattinson's question.

"What exactly do you know about war, Jeffers?"

"I know that it is humbling, Sir," Edmund said.

Pattinson let out a guffaw. "So eloquently put," he said. "I suppose that's the kind of drivel that pleases gullible audiences at your theatre."

"Well, if you regard the likes of Lord Salisbury and Mr. Gladstone and the Prince of Wales as gullible, then –"

Pattinson held up a hand. "Save the litany of names for someone who cares." He paused, his breathing heavy. "You don't realize this, Jeffers, but you are about to learn a very important lesson and a difficult one for a man such as yourself, living as you do in a world where everyone is self-obsessed. But you're in the army now. And in the army the self is always sacrificed to the common good." He sat back in his chair, looking rather pleased with himself. "And that is why I say to you now: if you have any decency at all you will refuse this commission on the grounds that you lack experience, on the grounds that you haven't a bull's notion of what warfare is or what it requires from you, on the grounds that you could endanger the lives of those serving with you."

Evidently Pattinson, despite all his guff, had no power whatsoever to stop the appointment.

"When you put it like that, Sir, you leave me with no alternative," Edmund said, allowing a smile to surface. Here was an opportunity to distinguish himself – he could not let it pass – but the resolution he felt on the spur of the moment had more to do with a desire to best the man sitting in front of him. "You leave me with no alternative but to accept," he said. "And thank you, Sir, for doing me this honour."

Pattinson frowned. His eyes bore down like slivers of flint.

"Let's hope that none of us will come to regret that decision," he said.

The C.I.V., along with the 3rd and 10th Battalions of the Imperial Yeomanry and the 38th Battery, mobilized at last as part of Lieutenant-General Ian Hamilton's force. They left Port Elizabeth and pushed northwards into the Orange Free State. Despite the danger, Edmund preferred being out in the field like this. Life was still humdrum – they could proceed for days on end without incident – but it was less regimented than it had been back in barracks. The scenery was stunning, the skies awe-inspiring. On their marches they had sighted herds of Thomson's gazelles and zebras fleeing from the approaching army and, not so shy, flocks of carmine bee-eaters perched on the acacias like brilliant candles on a Christmas tree. The colours, the strange terrain, the wonderful wildlife had a mesmerizing effect.

There were hardships too. Poor rations and little to be found along the way to supplement them, and uncomfortable beds – simply a kit-roll on the ground at the horses' feet so that often one got trodden on by an animal in the middle of the night.

Edmund was in charge of 'stables' which meant looking after the horses with his subordinates while everyone else was resting. He liked caring for the animals but after a long day's march it was exhausting to have to make up feeds for the next day or take the horses out for a grazing which could last anything up to three hours.

It was, however, the dust that Edmund found hardest to bear. It got everywhere – in his eyes, up his nose, down the back of his throat so that when he swallowed it was like sandpaper on his tonsils. It got into the food, the water, into his blankets, into his socks. When he nodded his head, it spilled from the brim of his hat.

They saw action for the first time at a place called Boshof. A minor skirmish, they encircled the enemy early on, killed the Boer commander and claimed victory with the loss of only three lives. This success boosted the confidence of the unit to such an extent that they were ill-prepared for the next engagement which took place at Lindley, a Boer-held town to the east of Kroonstad. The C.I.V formed part of a section under Captain Peters that split temporarily from the main column. A couple of miles outside the town they fell into an ambush and, though a message for help was dispatched immediately, seventeen men were killed and fifty more were taken prisoner.

They had to bury the fallen out there on the veldt where no one would ever find them again. Piles of stones and carved wooden crosses, strings of horseshoes, even tin cans were used to mark the graves, but they knew nothing would survive this ruthless landscape with its wild animals and scorching sun and wind and rain. No one wanted to leave these lads out here, lost forever.

Edmund lived up to his promotion as Second Lieutenant. He

had commanded six hundred employees at the Colosseum and leadership came easily to him. He was a quick thinker too and well suited to the unpredictability of warfare. Near Bloemhof he had saved Corporal Williams' life by knocking him flat with his fist when the man was too dazed to take cover. On another occasion he had vehemently warned against using a particular crossing on the Valsch river because he thought he saw a glint of metal coming from there. Captain Peters was sceptical at first but further reconnaissance confirmed that the Boers had made a trench of the river bed and were indeed lying in wait for them to advance. Thus forewarned, they were able to use artillery against the enemy and with considerable success. Afterwards, Captain Peters congratulated Edmund on his keen observation though he was quite unable to conceal the fact that he was surprised his Second Lieutenant possessed it.

Captain Peters was a man who had spent more than twenty years in the army, who believed that good soldiers were the product of training and discipline. He distrusted natural ability. He was himself a strict disciplinarian. His watchword 'neatness is obedience' was passed from officer to officer like a mantra. He did, however, apply the same high standards to himself as he demanded from his men and in these arduous conditions, when not even officers had much more than a thimble full of water per day, he was always clean shaven and immaculately uniformed. Neither outgoing nor inspirational, he was not the kind of man who could ever be popular. His main attribute was thoroughness and Edmund dealt with the consequences of this every day.

The column always halted at noon for sustenance and to take sanctuary from the sun at its hottest. While the rest were eating lunch, it fell to Edmund, as Second Lieutenant, to organize Field Punishment No. 1. This involved chaining offenders – soldiers who had been court-martialled and sentenced to this – to the wheels of a gun carriage. They were left thus under the blistering sun without food or water for two hours. They were not allowed to sit or even to hang from their chains. When the order came to make ready, they were released, often in a state of near collapse, and were expected to continue for the rest of the day without any break. Many were on half rations which they ate as they walked along behind the gun carriages.

It was, to Edmund's mind, a nonsensical exercise. Surely it was counter-productive to purposely debilitate men who could be called upon to fight at any minute? He kept his opinions to himself. He had learned already that in the army the only questions that were listened to were ones that had pat answers.

Chapter Thirty-three

Captain Archibald Peters was not pleased at being attached to a unit of which at least half were volunteers. From the start, he did not have a good opinion of such men, expecting them to be unblooded, undisciplined and untidy. And so they had proved to be. It was a relief to have got this far without any major mishap befalling them.

He felt, after all his years in the army that he deserved better than this. His track record, while not sparkling, was a solid one. The greater part of his army career had been spent abroad: in India dealing with local uprisings and in South Africa during the Zulu War and the First Boer War. He had come straight from the Sudan to this current conflict. Experience had taught him that, to soldier well, you needed good men under you. And that was a commodity he did not have. The Yeomanry were middling, but the C.I.V. were soft. They were office workers, artists and shopkeepers and, though one had to suppose they were driven by some form of patriotic fervour, none of them really understood the mechanics of war and fighting. A few weeks of basic training was not enough to knock even a modicum of sense into most of them.

That was why he was sitting here now passing sentence on this buffoon in front of him, a printer by profession, who felt it was perfectly acceptable to "go for a walk" outside the camp in the middle of the night with a lantern in his hand.

"You could have brought the Boers in on top of us with your light," Captain Peters said. "Common sense should tell you that."

A flicker of something crossed the man's face. Hardly shame or regret, more like boredom.

"Or you could have been shot by our own sentries."

A little reaction to this news as it involved some personal danger.

"Twenty-eight days Field Punishment Number 1 and a cut in rations for a week. Record it in the Punishment Book, Lieutenant Hodge, and mark this man's pay book half pay for a month."

That made the defendant wince out loud.

"You said something, Private?"

"No, Sir."

"Good. I don't want to see you or hear you ever again. People like you are a danger to their comrades."

"Yes, Sir."

Afterwards, when they were finished court-martialling for the day, Lieutenant Hodge, counting up the entries in his book said, "Twenty-two today, Sir. Thirty last week."

"We're losing our touch, Lieutenant. We'll have to get stricter," Captain Peters said, compelled to make it sound like a joke.

Hodge nodded unsurely.

He was an able officer and seemed trustworthy, Captain Peters thought, though it was always difficult to tell with these fellows who had never really been tested in the field.

There was nothing much to do for the rest of the afternoon, this being a day of rest. The chaplain conducted an evening service and afterwards Captain Peters retired to the officers' mess tent.

The air was thick with tobacco smoke. A round of cards and several games of dominoes were in progress. Captain Peters sat apart from the rest, poring over his journal. It was the same small book he'd had for years and the marbled covers were worn and dirty. He recorded events in it whenever he felt moved to do so and to save space he wrote with the tiniest hand, leaving no gaps between lines and with each word clear and sharp. Mostly, he detailed the Battalion's movements and his own observations on the progress of the war. Occasionally, he put in anecdotes about army routine. It was his intention that one day his sons would read it and know something of the life he led. His five sons lived at home in Hertfordshire and he did not see them very often. Whenever he was with them on leave they swamped him with tales about prep schools and rugby and Grandpa's bees and the rowing championship and jelly and custard for tea, but rarely did he get the chance to tell them anything about his own life, bar the more sensational bits like the time a lion dragged off one of the African porters.

He and his wife, Florence, had decided to lead separate lives on separate continents for the sake of the boys' education which they felt would be superior in England. Once a year, perhaps twice, Captain Peters spent a month with his family and these interludes, while they were pleasant and relaxing were also rather aimless and he always felt somewhat relieved when the time came for him to report back for duty. Thinking of home was often easier than being there and if, in the months following his leave, he received a letter from his wife confirming that she was 'expecting' again, the rush of warmth and satisfaction, the anticipation of new life on the way was experienced with much more intensity from afar than could ever be possible in the bosom of his family.

The card players were getting rowdy. Jeffers had won the pot again – a collection of coins and cigarettes – and he was ragging the rest of them about it. Laughter and clapping . . . he knew how to entertain. An imposing fellow and physically large with a curious dancing expression about the mouth which made it look as though he could burst out laughing at any second. What he had to be amused about was a mystery. The scandal that had broken about him in London was talked about even as far away as the Sudan. Of course, here in South Africa, in a state of emergency, there were more important issues to think about and it was barely mentioned. But everyone knew the chap was ruined.

It was too late for another round of cards and so the party broke up. The dominoes were put away, the men sauntered out. Jeffers was the only one left.

"You have cleaned them out yet again, Lieutenant Jeffers," Captain Peters said.

"To the victor, his spoils, no matter how miserable," Jeffers said. He laughed as he swept the last of his winnings off the table.

"Sit down, Lieutenant."

He pulled over a canvas chair, grinning still, and sat.

"I haven't spoken to you properly since your promotion. How do you find it, being a member of the officer class?"

Jeffers pulled a face. "There are perks. The coffee is good, Sir."

"There are men who would give their right arm to –"

"I know there are, Sir. I am being facetious."

"Facetious? In the army?" Captain Peters said, trying to sound ironic and failing.

"I am, of course, grateful for the appointment but probably it means less to me than it would to a 'real' soldier, Sir."

"Well, it shouldn't." Captain Peters closed his journal, stuck his pen down the spine. He considered for a moment or two. "No, in fairness to you, I am used to stock answers when I ask that question so I wasn't expecting an honest reply. I haven't worked with a great many volunteers before . . . different mentality . . ."

"Yes, Sir."

"If I am not mistaken, you were an actor in your previous incarnation."

"That is correct, Sir."

"I do not go to plays. I mean no offence when I say that, I simply state a fact. I am never in a place where there is a play on."

"You are too busy dealing with reality," Jeffers said. "Which, on the whole, is preferable. I once heard acting described as 'the absolute misrepresentation of everything we hold dear and true'. I liked the description, I must say. It's the use of the word 'absolute' that appeals. After all, credibility is what every actor craves."

"Quite," Captain Peters said, aiming to put an end to all this talk about acting. "And what do you make of army life, Jeffers? It must be very different from what you are accustomed to."

"I find it . . . unusual."

"You do not like to be ordered about."

Jeffers grinned, entirely at his ease. "There is that to it, Sir," he said.

"There is more?"

"Let's just say that the experience so far, has been . . . disorientating."

"So, you have formed opinions about us, about the military?"

"I have, I suppose."

"Then, please, feel free to express them."

"No, I have served such a short time . . ."

"I like to know the minds of the men under me."

Jeffers stroked his chin, then suddenly leaned forward. "As one man to another, you mean?"

It was hard to tell if he was joking or not.

"Yes," Captain Peters said. "As one man to another."

"Basically, I am a civilian looking in at the army . . . and what I see," he shrugged his shoulders apologetically, "is a huge monster lying flat on its back, unable to right itself because it is bound up in chains. This creature is helpless." He narrowed his eyes the better to gauge his superior's response. "The chains are rules and regulations."

"A colourful image. But you will have to be more specific. If rules and regulations are hobbling us, give me an example."

"All right, I will. For instance, is it really necessary to keep polishing kit even when we're out campaigning? There are plenty of other chores to be done and the men are exhausted. A gun has to be kept in working order, I can understand that. But belt buckles? Compasses?"

"Perhaps," Captain Peters said. "To your untrained eye, these rituals seem superfluous. It is not the task that is important, only the values that are instilled in the breast of the man who carries them out. These values are obedience, pride, industry and efficiency. Without them the army cannot function."

"Yes, these are the very qualities I demand from my own theatre staff. And the only way to get them, I believe, is through leadership and encouragement and productivity. I do not set my people empty tasks that only bore and tire them. I would not see the point."

Captain Peters wondered if Jeffers was at all aware of his own grandiloquence. It was almost laughable.

"You would do well to remember, Lieutenant, that while you put on plays, we fight wars. Any lapse in discipline can lead to lives lost. I do not think that the stakes are quite so high for you in your line of work."

Jeffers laughed. "You are right," he said, stretching his arms behind his head, good-humoured even in defeat. But there was a guardedness about him that Captain Peters could not ignore.

"Come on, Lieutenant, there is something else, I can tell. You might as well finish what you've started."

"Enough of my waffling," Jeffers said, but with a bold stare that announced he had plenty to say.

"Continue, Lieutenant. I promise I will not hold it against you."

"Well, it's just this, Sir. There will always be slackers, I know that, but these are, the majority of them, good men. They have proved themselves already in the field and . . ." His brow was crinkled. He looked conflicted.

"Go on, Lieutenant."

Jeffers ran his hand through his hair which was thick and a little too long. "I have no appetite for it, I'm afraid, Sir," he said. "I mean, for shackling men to cartwheels like dogs or depriving them of food or stripping them of privileges for smoking in their tents when it is perishing outside. I understand the need for discipline in a force this size but –"

"You are very open, Lieutenant. I asked you to be," Captain Peters said. "And given your rank, you see more of this punishment than most, so perhaps that has coloured your judgement. But let me remind you of this. Discipline is built like a house, brick upon brick, with obedience the mortar and we, as officers, are responsible for supervising the construction. Any dilution of the mortar and the whole edifice tumbles. This is not just me talking. This is Hannibal, Clausewitz and all the best military brains going back for centuries."

Jeffers nodded his head and pursed his lips but it was obvious he was unconvinced.

"I am told that you persuade the NCOs to deal with matters of insubordination themselves so as to avoid men being court-

310

martialled," Captain Peters said. "Tell me why."

"They are good men, Sir," Jeffers said.

"That is not what I asked you."

"Then perhaps that is what you should be asking."

"I consider that last remark insolent, Jeffers."

"I am sorry, Sir. I thought we were speaking as two human beings."

"It is a fact," Captain Peters said, raising his voice to drown him out, "that where errant behaviour is not tolerated, where there is a rule of law that acts swiftly, with repercussions, the common soldier learns to respect and obey his betters."

"Or else he learns that there is no justice for the likes of him within an organization such as this one."

"There is no room for democracy in the military, even you should know that. The army is a machine. You press the button and off it goes. It is only weak-minded fools who believe there is any time for negotiation in the middle of a war."

Jeffers remained silent. He knew when to keep his thoughts to himself.

"Thank you for being so frank but we will not revisit this topic, Jeffers," Captain Peters said.

At that, Jeffers stood up and saluted. "Goodnight, Sir."

"And get a haircut, Jeffers. At least look like an officer."

When he was gone, Captain Peters moved his chair so he was sitting directly under the lantern hanging from the apex of the tent. He returned to his journal.

Because he thought it would interest his boys, he wrote: "*Disgraced actor, Edmund Jeffers, joined Battalion. Recently promoted to Second Lieutenant. Affable fellow but a little arrogant. Has unsound views re military.*"

He stopped, went back and crossed out the word 'unsound', replaced it with 'dangerous'.

311

Chapter Thirty-four

Marguerite watched with interest the changes that took place at Jordanswood. The new theatre was superb. On a small scale – three hundred seats – it was imposing nonetheless, with a plush auditorium and, backstage, multiple flies and towers and the most up-to-date scene-changing mechanisms, enough to rival any venue in the West End. It was a showpiece: beautiful to behold but underutilized. The Jordanswood Musical Society was formed in a hurry and they staged a variety show for the inaugural night. An evening of Gilbert and Sullivan was promised for some time in the near future. Marguerite had been pestered into starting up a drama club and was currently auditioning members for parts in Jerome K. Jerome's *Miss Hobbs*, which she judged would be ready by late spring. But most of the time, the little theatre was idle.

Another new project at Jordanswood was well underway. This involved the construction of a large extension to the East Wing which, when finished, would be the new Hydropathic House. Dr. Asgard spent a great deal of his time overseeing this building site, as he had done before with the theatre, and in the evenings when the labourers were gone, he was often to be seen up there, clambering over bricks and under scaffolding, examining the day's progress, dreaming his dreams. He still made a point of speaking with as many patients daily as was possible but these exchanges were becoming briefer and rarer as more of his time was swallowed up in supervising the fitting out of the new building.

A Doctor Hargreaves took an interest in Marguerite. He was a pleasant-mannered man of about forty, rather shy. When sitting, he always hunched his shoulders and dipped his head, a habit which, taken in conjunction with his hooked nose and knobbly fingers gave the impression that the man was somehow misshapen all over. Standing up, however, it was as though he unfolded himself and he proved to be remarkably straight and tall. Athletic, even. He was older than the other physicians and had recently returned from Canada where it was said he had held a post with much more responsibility than he now had.

He saw Marguerite every day and had much more time to spend with her than did Dr. Asgard. Their conversations together were so agreeable and so natural – not just therapeutic – that she felt sure Dr. Hargreaves must derive some modicum of pleasure from them just as she did. He liked to read plays, he told her, but never went to see them performed as he much preferred to engage with the written word. Marguerite countered that no drama could live until it was staged in front of an audience, that no matter how closely one studied the text reading it was still like watching another man eat your dinner – you were at a remove and therefore deprived of any real satisfaction.

They discussed playwrights too. He was, he said, a fan of Sophocles and Congreve. Marguerite suggested he read Tennyson's *The Cup*.

"I know that you will love it," she said. "I just know."

When next they met, she asked him if he had read it and his

eyes watered with emotion. He declared it "a stupendous work".

"What it must be to be able to write like that," he said.

"Do I sense a hankering?"

"Not at all. I am a man of science through and through."

"That is good to hear. Men of letters are ten a penny but good doctors, I think, are a rarity."

"Most of us are just very ordinary doctors," he said. "That is what the authorities want – they don't like to be questioned. Good doctors, unfortunately, are bursting with ideas . . . which makes them a nuisance."

"You sound disillusioned."

"Not at all. I take inspiration from my patients and they never fail me. However, I am less fond of my superiors."

"Does that account for your sudden return from Canada?"

"There is no use in my denying it, I suppose?" His lips twitched.

"No, I knew you were a troublemaker from the start," she said.

Sometimes Marguerite told him about past productions she had been in, of the great actors she knew. When he listened, he took his glasses off and then she could see that his eyes were a rich hazel colour, almost golden.

One day, he said, "Congratulations, Miss Davenport, on breaching my poor defences. I have taken your advice and bought a ticket to go and see Jones' *The Masqueraders* which is playing on Saturday next at Altbury." He paused. "In fact, I have arranged for a small party of patients and staff from Jordanswood to attend the matinée. I have permission to include you in the invitation if you would care to go. I think the outing would do you some good and I would also welcome your commentary on the night."

It was an occasion of great excitement. On the appointed

314

afternoon, a party of fifty gathered in the hallway of Jordanswood House with Dr. Asgard and Sister Barnes there to see everyone off. The public patients, who formed the majority, were transported with their attendants to Altbury in hired coaches and they left a quarter of an hour earlier than the Jordanswood carriage which took the remaining private patients, along with Dr. Hargreaves.

Marguerite found herself seated next to the doctor in the vehicle. Eliza Morely, the temperamental governess, was that day in especially good humour and she had brought with her some needlework for the journey which she resorted to whenever the road was smooth enough to allow it. Miss Brewit and Miss James, two elderly ladies and long-term inmates of Jordanswood, sat opposite each other while Mr. Roberts, the law student, occupied the seat across from the doctor and looked at no one, lost in his own thoughts. The conversation was pleasant, touching on the weather and what delights the village of Altbury had in store for them.

The day was very mild for the time of year and the hoods of the landau were down so Marguerite could see that the driver sitting on his perch was the very same man who had brought her to Jordanswood with Leopold months before. He looked even more miserable now than he was then, hunched over as though he was sick. The back of his neck was scrawny above the collar of his coat, which was blackened and shiny with grease.

About two miles out from Jordanswood, the road narrowed and ran close to the edge of a steep gorge, at the bottom of which was a fast-flowing river. The way across it was by a five-arch bridge which was just visible a quarter of a mile off and well below them in the next village.

They had already begun the descent, which was steep, when the driver, looking across the gorge, spotted a farmer with a heavily laden cart set on a parallel course towards the bridge. He cracked his whip and announced, "It's one at a time on that blasted bridge down there."

The horses trotted, broke into a canter. Mud splattered the sides of the carriage. The driver lashed out again. The grey's back legs slid in under him and he almost sat down. The bay stumbled. The two animals recovered but they were so spooked by their near fall that they took off at even greater speed, careering down the hill on uneven ground, sliding in the wet, the carriage swaying dangerously. With every lurch, the passengers could see down into the ravine. Eliza Morely squealed. Mr. Roberts began to spout gibberish. The two elderly ladies held onto the carriage door for safety.

"Slow down, or you'll turn us over!" Dr. Hargreaves shouted.

But the driver had lost control. He was without physical strength himself and the carriage's momentum was pushing the horses on. They were heading for disaster.

Dr. Hargreaves got to his feet. The rocking of the vehicle was so violent at this stage that he had to hold onto Mr. Roberts' shoulder to keep his balance. He traversed the carriage and climbed onto the seat opposite so that he was standing up behind the driver but with nothing to stop him from being tossed over the side. Mr. Roberts, in a startlingly sane move, made a dive for the doctor's legs and anchored them against the back of the seat. Dr. Hargreaves leaned out precariously and, stretching his arms either side of the driver, he managed to take hold of the reins. He pulled and the driver pulled and between them they managed to slow the horses, eventually bringing them back to a walk. The only sound was the sucking of their hooves in the muck.

Marguerite was amazed to find that she was shaking all over.

Instead of offering thanks, the old driver muttered, to no one in particular, "We'll be waiting all day now to cross that damned bridge."

"Then wait we shall," Dr. Hargreaves said, sitting down again.

They were in such a state of shock that they were all bereft of words until Eliza Morley leant over and clasped Dr. Hargreave's hand.

"Thank you, Doctor," she cried. "Thank you for saving our lives."

The other two ladies relinquished their hold on the furniture and expressed similar thanks. Mr. Roberts twitched and sniffed and re-entered his own little world.

Dr. Hargreaves gave instructions to the driver that he was to go no faster than a walk, then he turned to Marguerite.

"And you, Miss Davenport. I hope your nerves have not been shattered by that experience."

"I have always had nerves of steel, Doctor," she said. "My legs, however, have turned to jelly."

He laughed. "A little like my own."

"No, you were quite the hero," she said.

"Not a role I am accustomed to playing, I can assure you."

"And yet you took it on so naturally. Yes, you are a hero," Marguerite said, teasing him. "You just don't know it."

When they reached the village they had to wait while the farmer took what seemed like forever to cross the bridge. He walked alongside a dozy-looking horse pulling a cart with a big load of mangolds in it. The farmer gave them a cursory nod as he passed and Marguerite wondered if he knew they were from the asylum.

When the carriage moved off again, Dr. Hargreaves said in a low voice, privately, "Tell me, Miss Davenport, if you were not an actress, what would you like to do?"

"I don't think anyone has ever asked me that question

before," she said. "In fact, I'm sure of it. And I've always been too busy earning a living to think about it much myself."

"Then think about it now," he said. "Allow yourself that luxury."

She would have answered, 'Get married and have children,' except that she felt that didn't count. He was asking her about an alternative career. So, she said, "I'd quite like to be an explorer – somewhere warm because I can't stand the cold. I'd discover rivers and mountains and have them named after me or perhaps there is some particularly fascinating and attractive animal that I could lend my name to. Yes, I'd like to live on in some way."

"Yet you have not mentioned the most obvious way to live on," he said.

"Which is . . .?"

"To procreate, of course."

The carriage wheel rumbled over gravel.

"You have caught me out," she said, looking away from him at the stone cottages that lined the route. "You see, I can be nothing other than an actress."

"Perhaps therein lies your trouble."

"I am unable to have children." She spoke it in a whisper.

"I'm so sorry," he said. "But, of course, love of any kind lives on."

They left the village behind and the horses quickened their pace to a trot. Pastures opened up on either side of the road.

Eventually, Marguerite found the courage to face him again.

"Well, now that you have had your fun with me," she said, her tone buoyant once more, "let *me* play with *you*! As you seem to have a jaundiced view of the medical profession, what would you do if you were not a doctor?"

He gazed down at his hands as though pondering what other uses they could be put to. For all his physical strength, at that moment he looked frail.

"If I were not a doctor," he said, "I would die."

When they got to the town hall in Altbury, Dr. Hargreaves left her side and busied himself with organizing seats for everyone. It ended up that Marguerite sat in the row ahead of him.

The Altbury Amateur Players who put on the play had some good actors in amongst the appalling ones and the audience was forgiving, the mood convivial. Marguerite found that she enjoyed herself. On the way back in the carriage, wrapped in a rug, she listened while the others enthused about the play.

"I hope it wasn't too tedious for your West End sensibilities, Miss Davenport," Dr. Hargreaves said, turning to her.

"On the contrary," she said. "I found it most stimulating."

"Then I consider the trip a huge success," he said.

It was as though the excursion to Altbury awakened Marguerite. She could not stop thinking about that night's performance, how to improve it and what changes and cuts could be made to the play itself to render it more effective. She had not felt so invigorated for a long time.

She was sitting one day on the window seat in the front hall, looking out over the tiered lawns, when Dr. Hargreaves found her. He pulled up a chair and sat down. He said she was looking well which pleased her as she had spent some time the evening before pinning her hair in curls, a chore she had never had to do herself before, and was unsure of the results.

They spoke of what Dr. Hargreaves termed her "inner state". He frowned as he listened.

"I believe you are ready to leave Jordanswood," he said, at last. The frown did not lift. "You need to work, to engage with life once more, to make decisions about where you want to go. To remain here any longer would, I think, be detrimental to your recovery."

319

It felt like he was holding a cage door open and he was waiting for her to fly out.

"You think I should leave?" she said.

He nodded. "I do. But it would be wise for the moment to steer clear of old romantic attachments and to avoid new ones too, until you have re-established your equilibrium. Allow yourself time, you deserve that. Be good to yourself, nurture your career if that is what you choose, nourish your soul, appreciate what a wonderful woman you are." He gave a faltering smile and his eyes locked with hers just long enough to convey more than doctorly concern. He took off his glasses, put them back on again. "You will be fine," he said.

She trusted him.

"Yes," she said. "Yes, I will."

"Then I shall recommend you for a discharge. You will have to be assessed first by Dr. Asgard but I think you can count on a favourable outcome." He stood up, held out his hand to shake hers.

She had never touched him before. His grip was firm, his skin warm.

"Thank you, Doctor," she said.

Marguerite had not been in Dr. Asgard's office since the day she first arrived at Jordanswood with Leopold and was committed. She had forgotten how impressive the room was with its high ceiling and formidable portraits and all that light flooding in through the two front windows. On that occasion, she had not noticed that there was an upstairs gallery which ran around the four sides of the room with every inch of wall space up there devoted to books.

Dr. Asgard was sitting at his desk in the centre of the floor, looking completely at one with his surroundings and not dwarfed by them as one might expect a small man to be.

"Ah, Miss Davenport," he said, looking up from his work and beaming at her. "Always a pleasure." He invited her to sit. "And looking resplendent too. What a gown – what colour in your cheeks!"

"All down to you and your famous staff because I have been pampered beyond all reason here," Marguerite said. "But I believe, Doctor, that I am ready now to go home."

"So I hear."

He opened a folder in front of him, his smile fixed. His expression seemed to say, 'proceed'.

"I have been rescued and nursed back to health at Jordanswood," Marguerite said. "For which I am very grateful. But it is time to go home."

Dr. Asgard followed this with silence. He sat with his hands cupped together on the desk. Every part of him was still except for his thumbs which circled around each other slowly, first in one direction, then in reverse. He did this for quite some time before he spoke.

Then, "It gratifies me to hear you speak with such confidence, Miss Davenport. I believe – well, the evidence is here before my very eyes – that there is a marked improvement in your condition. But . . ." he compressed his lips as if holding back words, then saw fit to release them, "I need to remind you that you are suffering from a debilitating mental illness which –"

"Which, happily, I am now cured of, Doctor."

"You have responded well to the treatment here – regular habits, good food, proper sleep – well, you know my views on those subjects. But experience tells us that a structured day such as we have here is impossible to maintain once a patient resumes his or her former life. Be in no doubt, it is this ordered existence that is enabling your recovery, a recovery that is not yet complete.

Without this regime, there is no doubt in my mind that you would sink again into a melancholic state and perhaps irretrievably." He breathed in deeply, held the air in his lungs. "It is, therefore, my considered opinion that you should remain here . . . that you *need t*o remain here for quite some time to come."

"But Dr. Hargreaves thinks I am better – he has recommended that I be discharged . . ."

"No. He has recommended that you be assessed by me, regarding your suitability for discharge. There is a difference. I know this is disappointing for you but I would be failing in my duty if I released you."

Marguerite sat a little straighter. "I am well and I want to get back to my life. My audience will forget me. Dr. Hargreaves says I am ready to go back and –"

Dr. Asgard thumped the desk with his fist. "Dammit, woman, Hargreaves has no business telling you such things. I am Superintendant here. Your future is decided by me."

Silence descended. Dr. Asgard gathered himself, produced a smile that was like a scalpel – sharp, unflinching.

"Miss Davenport," he said. "You must understand this. The mind is a very fragile entity and particularly so in your case as I believe your condition to be a hereditary one. I just want to see you fully fit before you leave here, that is all. A necessary precaution for your own good."

"You once said, Dr. Asgard, and not so long ago either, that I was the best judge of my own mental health. And I appeal to you now to hear me when I say that I am certain I can go back to my old life and remain well. I am able to do it, I want to do it and I need to do it."

"Your own feelings are, of course, a valuable guide. However, we medical practitioners make judgments based on science and experience and let me tell you –"

"Then I will discharge myself," Marguerite said.

Dr. Asgard stroked his beard right down to its very tip which he curled several times over his index finger.

"We have been through this before, have we not?" he said. "You were committed into our care by your doctor, by a local magistrate and by Lord Barrie. The doctor and the magistrate act in an official capacity only. In effect you can only leave Jordanswood with Lord Barrie's consent and mine. Lord Barrie wishes you to stay here, I know that for a fact. And, as I have already said, I am against your leaving too."

"So, I am a prisoner."

"You are a patient. And we at Jordanswood take our responsibility to you very seriously."

Marguerite stood up. Her chair scraped on the marble floor.

"I have done nothing wrong, I have committed no crime and yet I am incarcerated like a felon."

"Please sit down, Miss Davenport. We can discuss this."

"There is nothing to discuss, you have told me so yourself. It is all decided. I am to be kept here, against my will, in this – this prison."

Dr. Asgard leaned forward.

"I take grave exception to that remark, madam. Kindly refrain from making fraudulent comparisons between Jordanswood and one of Her Majesty's gaols. You do not know what you are talking about."

Marguerite walked over to the window then back again.

"Leopold Barrie is not my next of kin."

"Lord Barrie took responsibility for you in the absence of anyone else when you posed a threat to your own life."

"I beg your pardon?"

"He took responsibility for you when you posed a threat to –"

"That is something I never did."

"The doctor's letter clearly states — I have it here." He extracted a page from several others in the file. "It clearly states that you had attempted suicide once already and that you had said you were going to do it again. It was on that basis you were committed."

"Then falsely so. That doctor was a friend of Leopold's. I saw him for barely five minutes. I don't remember his even asking that question."

Dr. Asgard, disconcerted, put away the letter and leant his elbows on the closed file.

Panic began to rise in Marguerite as she remembered Dr. Asgard and Leopold shaking hands with exceptional warmth. She recalled the long talks between them in the doctor's office and the two of them taking their regular tour of the building work. And what of that envelope she had spied one afternoon, being passed from Leopold to Dr. Asgard?

"Is he paying you to keep me here?" she said.

"All private patients are paid for here."

"I mean, is he paying you extra?"

"That is a scurrilous accusation," Dr. Asgard said. "I demand an apology."

"And I demand an answer. For how much longer will I be deprived of my liberty, Doctor? Have you and my lover decided that yet?"

Dr. Asgard's anger seemed to build and then suddenly melt away. He settled back in his chair with a horribly self-satisfied look.

"What a pity it would be, Miss Davenport, if delusional thoughts such as these were to spoil your hopes of an early release ... especially as you have been making such good progress all along."

"I am being detained here against my wishes, against every

medical argument that can be made, against the law, I shouldn't wonder. And all for the convenience of one and the greed of another. Where is your Hippocratic Oath now, Doctor?"

The unfairness of it all brought on a wildness in her, a feeling that she must either flee the scene, or fight, or simply destroy. She began to pace up and down, wringing her hands. There was a weight on her chest that seemed to impede her breathing.

"I am a healthy woman locked up for no proper reason – I won't put up with it – I simply won't."

"These are morbid thoughts, Miss Davenport. Deeply morbid . . ." His voice was low, stealthy. "This is a serious setback. I will call Sister Barnes. She will take care of you."

"No," Marguerite said, realizing now the danger she had put herself in. "That won't be necessary."

She composed herself, looked down at the man who had so much power over her and regretted that she had revealed so much of what she knew.

"Actually, I accept your decision, Doctor," she said, forcing a smile. "I may not agree with it but I do accept it."

The following morning the residents of Jordanswood awoke to find that Dr. Hargreaves had left in the middle of the night. The word went about that his sudden departure was caused by his having conducted himself improperly with an unidentified female patient. Dr. Asgard had caught him in the act, it was said, and fired him on the spot.

With Dr. Hargreaves gone, Marguerite had no one. She couldn't approach any of the staff with her suspicions about Dr. Asgard and Leopold. There was no proof so it was unlikely they would believe her and even if they did, and spoke out, she was sure Dr. Asgard would find a way of dealing with them as he had done so successfully with Dr. Hargreaves.

Among the patients there was none she could confide in either. She had learned since her arrival at Jordanswood that all asylum inmates believe they have been wrongfully interned and none of them are interested in any grievances but their own. Furthermore, even though they complain long and hard about their individual cases, not one of them really expects anything to change.

Who was there to help? She could not burden Lewis, a man at war, with her troubles. And so she wrote to Edmund. Though his reputation was ruined, surely he must still have a few useful connections? And even if he didn't, she knew he would do all in his power to aid her. In the letter, she described Leopold's treachery and Dr. Asgard's collusion in it. She maintained that she was fully recovered from her state of melancholia, that this was a view endorsed by a Doctor Hargreaves – now wrongfully dismissed and for whom she had no address – and she pleaded with Edmund to intervene on her behalf and get her freed from Jordanswood.

There was a basket in the front hall where staff and patients could leave letters to be collected by the postman on his rounds. It was commonly known that patients' letters were opened and read before they were allowed off the premises and so it was necessary for Marguerite to seek out an alternative route for hers. Kitty Stevens worked by day at Jordanswood as an under-housemaid and went home every evening to the village of Uppercross. She was young enough and poor enough to appreciate the few shillings Marguerite could afford to tempt her with. And so it was to Kitty Stevens that Marguerite entrusted her letter to Edmund. The girl promised to post it when next she had a day off.

Marguerite settled down to wait. In the wake of her interview with Dr. Asgard, she felt herself being watched more closely and could not go about the grounds with the same freedom as before. Always there seemed to be an attendant lurking nearby. Sister Barnes offered so many times to bring her lunch on a tray to her room that Marguerite suspected a plan was afoot to put drugs in her food and drink. And so she became extra vigilant. She made sure only to eat in the communal dining room and only when she could serve herself at table, never accepting anything already served up on plates in the kitchen. She drank nothing except water which she poured from the tap herself. She was aware that in the eyes of others her behaviour was becoming increasingly peculiar and that this would not be to her advantage when it came to trying to prove her sanity later on. But it was, she thought, the only way in which to protect herself and, hopefully, it would not be too long until Edmund rescued her. As regards Leopold, she wondered how she should receive him on his next visit to Jordanswood. Should she confront him on the issue of her incarceration? Or promise not to be an encumbrance and beg him to let her go? Or perhaps she should pretend ignorance about it altogether?

One day while she was tidying her room, a knock came on the door. She opened it to find Sister Barnes standing there bearing a little silver tray on which there was a letter. Her letter to Edmund.

Marguerite stared. It occurred to her to try denying all knowledge of it but she noticed that the envelope had been opened with a paper knife and resealed with a piece of sticky tape. Across the top of it were the words, '*Return to Sender*' and underneath was scribbled her name and the address of Jordanswood. She recognized the hand. It was Violet's.

"This, I believe, belongs to you," Sister Barnes said, pushing the tray at her.

"I don't understand," Marguerite said, picking it up. She

327

could not comprehend how Violet had got hold of the letter or why it had been dealt with in this fashion. Still, there was the slim possibility that no one at Jordanswood was aware of its contents. "How unfortunate," she said. "I was sure I had the right address. Never mind, I was simply requesting that certain of my effects be sent on. It seems I will have to wait. Such a pity."

"This letter should have gone through the normal channels, Miss Davenport, as you are well aware."

"Oh, but it did," Marguerite said.

"I think not." Sister Barnes gave a frozen smile and bowed her head. "You know, people are very much mistaken in thinking that the postal service is a lifeline, Miss Davenport. In my opinion, it never is." She was standing across the threshold of the room as though about to step in. Then, quite suddenly, she moved back into the corridor and her demeanour changed. "Let me bring you a cup of tea, Miss Davenport." The tone was polite, but her eyes were ice cold.

Chapter Thirty-five

The bulk of Lieutenant-Colonel Ian Hamilton's column continued northwards to Pretoria while the C.I.V. along with the Yorkshire Light Infantry and some Middlesex Yeomanry changed direction. They were charged with clearing the triangle of land that lay between the Orange River in the south and the two great railways east and west that dissected each other at Johannesburg.

The Boers, outnumbered, had taken to guerilla warfare. Small commandos darted out of nowhere, committed acts of sabotage, then melted away again into the landscape. The Boer leader Christian de Wet had evaded pursuing troops so many times that even the Tommies were singing about him. *'We seek him here, we seek him there . . .'*

The British Military Command decided that the only way to combat so elusive an enemy was to starve him out, to cut him off from the provisions, fresh horses and forage that were made available to him from every like-minded Boer farmstead in the vicinity. To this end, they were systematically sweeping the countryside clean, evacuating properties, slaughtering livestock, accumulating refugees along the way. As time went on the Corps slowed, weighed down by the sheer volume of civilian lives it was dragging around with it in a succession of ox wagons. Fatigue set in, the soldiers weary of destruction, the women and children sullen, pining for their homes. It was time to stop, to offload their human cargo, but they didn't.

Up ahead, a farm, no different from dozens of others they had been to before, a cluster of buildings, redder than the earth, huddled against the elements. It was such a bare, inhospitable place that the only reason for habitation in this particular spot, Edmund surmised, must be the presence of water.

A hundred yards out two clumps of wild Syringa formed a natural gateway from the veldt to the farm. The refugees were left here to avail of what shelter could be got from the trees against a penetrating north wind while the company, under Captain Peters, moved in.

As they went, Edmund's horse yanked at the reins, coughing and wheezing, his neck a lather of sweat, despite the cold. On their left they passed two walled kraals of about an acre each, one with a thick belt of trees round the perimeter for summer shade while the other had been trampled to mud by a flock of sheep who were cowering now in the far corner.

The house, when they came to it, was differentiated from the outbuildings by a dilapidated verandah attached to the front. It was early morning but already smoke was coming from the chimney. Captain Peters raised his hand and the patrol halted in the yard. The sheds were checked for snipers. Rifles were trained on the windows of the dwelling, though they knew from reconnaissance that there were no men in this place.

A woman emerged from the house. She was dressed in a dirty smock with a cardigan on top and lace-up boots. She rested her hands on her hips and a little girl hiding behind her peeked out through the crook of one elbow. A boy of about twelve came out and took his place beside them on the porch. He was holding a cudgel and stood with his legs apart, a stance he must have learned from his father. Beneath knee-length trousers he wore black stockings, all holes.

"You are Mrs. Viljoen?" Captain Peters said, from the saddle.

The woman nodded. She had the kind of broad, full face that neither time nor hardship nor sorrow would ever ravage. Old age might give her white hair or a slight stoop but her skin would always be smooth and plump.

"Where is your husband, Mrs. Viljoen? Denys, where is he?"

"Over at the Griesels' to borrow an axe – ours is broken."

"We have evidence that your husband is away on commando, Mrs. Viljoen, engaged in a guerilla war against Her Majesty's Imperial Forces. He has contravened the conditions of his amnesty under which he swore to lay down his arms permanently. Therefore, I have here written authority to confiscate all your possessions, including livestock."

The woman frowned. "My husband is away with friends," she said. "Go see for yourselves."

Captain Peters dismounted, went up the front steps.

"Denys will be back tonight," she said. "I promise you. He is helping Old Man Griesels to build a sheep crush."

"Please stand aside, madam," Captain Peters said.

The boy lurched forward, turning the cudgel in his hand threateningly but Mrs. Viljoen caught him by the shoulders and pulled him back.

"He means nothing," she said.

Captain Peters stared at her and the boy. With his riding whip he motioned to them to move away from the door, which they did, leaving the way clear for him and several other men to enter the house.

Edmund dismounted. His feet, previously numb with the cold, ached now. He tied his horse up and followed the captain. As he passed where mother and son were standing, the boy in sudden fury struck out at Edmund, kicking him on the shin bone. Edmund swore out loud. The woman, fearing retribution, bundled her son behind her and leaned back over him, her arms spread. In that position, it became obvious that she was expecting a baby.

"Please, he's only a child," she said.

There was terror in her eyes. Edmund could smell her sweat.

"What's going on out there, Lieutenant Jeffers?" Captain Peters shouted from inside.

"Nothing, Sir," Edmund said. He turned to the woman. "Gather your belongings. Take my advice – you don't have much time, save as much as you can."

He went into the tiny parlour where several men were already hacking at the piano, reducing it, in situ, to firewood.

Mrs. Viljoen followed him in.

"Please," she said. "Take what you want but leave the house standing. We can't go to a camp. We know what they're like. We'll die. Please."

She held his arm while she spoke, a firm grip that annoyed him.

"Go!" he shouted. "If you don't hurry, there'll be nothing left. Go!"

"But my children, the baby . . ."

Captain Peters spun around.

"Get that damn woman out of here at once," he said.

Privates Rogers and Hardcastle grabbed her by the arms and marched her so quickly out of the room and down the front steps to the yard that she lost her footing and ended up being dragged the last bit with the little girl clinging to her dress. The boy watched all this from the verandah. He tightened and loosened his grip on the cudgel, incensed and terrified at the same time.

Edmund went out to him.

"Put it away. It's useless to fight," he said. "Go to your mother and sister, they need you."

"Papa told me to protect them . . ."

"Don't hurt my son, don't hurt him!" the mother was crying out.

There was only one way to end this.

Edmund patted the pistol in his holster. "I will shoot you, boy, if you do not go to them."

At that, the child, relieved of whatever sense of obligation had seized him, ran down the steps to his mother and sister who were kneeling on the ground. They pulled him down with them, hugged him, held his hands. They were praying.

He went back into the house and pushed his way along a small corridor into the kitchen which was warm with the smell of baking. It was overrun with soldiers rummaging through cupboards, sweeping crockery off shelves, scattering books and clothes in their search for anything of value. Bags of flour and meal were trundled out. The floor was slippery from so many wet boots going over it. Edmund found a sack under the table that had a few onions left in the bottom. He threw in some garlic and alfalfa.

Easterby came up behind him. "You making a collection, Lieutenant?" he said, showing the tail feathers of a chicken he had hidden up his tunic. He gave a lop-sided grin, "Died of old age, poor dear," and he transferred the still-warm bird to the sack.

Edmund opened the door of the stove before anyone else might think of it and using a spoon he managed to pull out two loaves of bread and threw them, along with their tins, into the sack. He ran along the hallway that was so narrow his shoulders bumped off the walls on either side. The men were on the roof now, lighting it with burning oil rags. Into the woman's bedroom. He opened a drawer and scooped clothes out of it straight into the sack, tossed in a crucifix that was hanging on the wall. Smoke billowed down from the eaves and flames crackled. There were shouts to evacuate the building. Off to the children's room for the same blind gathering of clothes and belongings. He grabbed two pillows as he left and shoved them under his arm.

Outside, the woman and her children were sitting on the ground, watching the remains of their piano being tossed onto a wagon. More useful items were loaded onto another, along with the spoils from countless other households just like this one. There were rolls of bedding, sacks of grain, teapots, kettles, buckets and in amongst these were less practical items that had caught a soldier's eye – a fancy plate, a brass hand bell, even, wedged between a bedstead and a milking stool, a framed family photograph.

Edmund dropped the sack on the ground in front of the dumbstruck family and threw down the pillows. His form cast a shadow upon them and the little girl buried her head tighter into her mother's armpit.

"It's the best I could do," he said.

The boy was the only one crying, tears streaming down his face, dripping off the end of his chin – tortured by his failure to save the family from this.

"There's food at the bottom," Edmund said.

The mother looked up at him, her face wide and slightly stupid-looking. This was a woman who had borne children, who fed and cared for them in the harshest conditions, who slaved in the kitchen, worked on the farm, who bullied the soil into yielding up its meagre crop, a woman whose existence was so closely bound to this land it must never have occurred to her before that she could be left destitute. One might have expected her to be distraught at the prospect but a horrible calm had come over her. She started to speak but he did not want to listen. He walked away, left her behind.

Everything was changed. The muddy kraal, on his right now, was a scene of slaughter as the sheeps' throats were being slit with bayonets. The air around the field was fuggy with the smell of wool and grease and faeces and blood and the tang of fear, not a smell at all, but a taste, like gall in the mouth. The soldiers were wet to their thighs in mud and blood. Edmund watched the animals stagger, heard the terrorized bleatings of those awaiting the same fate. The men's voices were steady over the filthy sounds of death and dying – the spluttering, groaning, shivering. Edmund kept walking, the thought somewhere in his head that by retracing his steps he could undo all this destruction.

Out front, the clumps of Syringa were like two battleships in full sail on the wide, flat ocean and further off, a belt of hills against the skyline seemed like another country. He was so distracted by the view that the sound of Captain Peters' voice took him by surprise.

"Jeffers, where the ruddy hell do you think you're going?"

Edmund stopped. He was at the corner of the outermost kraal. Twenty yards up from where he stood a sheep was being butchered. The carcass, flayed already, was suspended from a marula tree by a wooden stave that had been driven through the animal's hocks. The pelt and the guts steamed underneath in a sloppy pile. Captain Peters was supervising the operation. His pale breeches and tunic had stayed miraculously unbloodied in contrast to the two native scouts who were sawing at the animal and cutting pieces off it and whose leather aprons were black with gore.

Nearby, Lieutenant Hodge squatted, sharpening an array of knives against a large stone. He laid out the instruments on a white cloth in order of size, taking care to keep their handles in a straight line.

"Do I have to repeat myself? Where in – ?"

"I volunteered to fight a war, Sir," Edmund said, turning to face him. "Not lay waste to half a continent like this."

Captain Peters tucked the riding whip under his armpit and marched over to Edmund.

"You can keep such thoughts to yourself, Jeffers. I won't have you infecting the minds of others." He looked around to see who might have heard but within earshot there was only Lieutenant Hodge, who seemed oblivious, and the two Africans who couldn't understand anyway. He turned to go back to his task then reconsidered, came back. "Look, Jeffers," he said. "This is unpleasant work, we all know that, and you're not the only one who finds it hard. But believe me, this is the only way. We must deprive the enemy of his supports, bring him to his knees."

"We have been doing this for months and I have not yet seen one Boer fighter brought to his knees," Edmund said. "Only women and children."

"Sentimental nonsense," Captain Peters said. "No one wants to move families from their homes but if it is a case that they are endangering our own men, then it has to be done. These people are supplying commandos with fresh horses and food, with guns in some cases. To kill us. Remember that."

Lieutenant Hodge ceased what he was doing. He sat back on his heels to examine the blade of one of his knives.

"This is not the way an army should be conducting itself," Edmund said. "Going around like sneaks, bullying the weak while no one is looking. We should be above all that. We only strengthen the Boer resolve with such cowardly acts."

"Do not talk to me of cowardice, Jeffers. The worst and most shameful form of cowardice is when a man shies away from carrying out a distasteful act, simply because it is distasteful, even though it is clear – crystal clear to anyone who has watched the progress of this war – that here lies the quickest and surest way to bring about an end to hostilities. A swift resolution – that is every soldier's duty. That is your duty."

They both became aware now that Lieutenant Hodge was taking an interest.

Captain Peters moved closer and lowered his voice.

"I have served in the army all over the world. I have been destined for this life since the age of fourteen and yet you, an actor, fresh from the stage, think that you know better. And not only that, you imply that my motives and the motives of the entire British Army are in some way morally reprehensible and inferior to your own. Well, I won't have it, Jeffers." Every muscle in his face was taut. "I order you to return to the house immediately to supervise the loading of the wagons."

Edmund turned away and looked out over the veldt.

"Did you hear me, Lieutenant? Remember you have taken an Oath of Allegiance to your God, your Queen, your country."

"We'd be better off swearing loyalty to the postman if it would help us understand our own humanity a little better. This, what we are doing here, is not worthy of us."

"We are fighting a war. Right is on our side. We do what has to be done."

Edmund shook his head. "To find myself pitted against women and children is abhorrent to me. As it should be to anyone. And I will not forgive the War Office for hoodwinking me into this. They have got me here under false pretences. What I thought was noble has turned out to be grotesque." He gave a bitter laugh. "Perhaps that makes my contract with them null and void."

"I have seen soldiers fall to pieces under fire or when being bombarded with shell but there is no excuse for this – this display, Jeffers. You are an officer, for God's sake – the men look to you for example."

An uprooted thorn bush driven by a gust of wind scudded off past them and away over the red, dusty plain. Edmund followed it with his eyes.

"Get back to work, Jeffers. That is an order."

Lieutenant Hodge was watching them.

"This is the last time I'll say it, Jeffers. Get back to work. Disobey and you'll be facing a court-martial."

Edmund steadied his breathing but could not bring himself to look at his commanding officer. He saluted.

"Yes, Sir," he said and walked back towards the burning house.

Chapter Thirty-six

Marguerite sat in her bedroom, gazing out of the window. A carriage drew up and Leopold got out. Even though she had been watching for him to arrive, she did not rise to go down and meet him. The sun shone through the glass and she yielded herself to its warmth, closing her eyes. She must have slept. Then, with a jolt she was awake. She stood up with sudden purpose only to find herself frustrated yet again, fixed to the spot and dithering as always happened. It was as though the instant she had a thought, even a vital one, it scuttled away before she could fully grasp it. She waited, a long time. It came back. Leopold. She was to see Leopold. She was going out for the day with Leopold.

By the time she got down to the foyer there was no sign of him so she just waited at the bottom of the stairs, clinging to the bannisters. Dr. Asgard's office door opened and Leopold and the doctor emerged together, laughing and talking. They saw her, a blankness passing over them, she thought, as if a few seconds had fallen out of the world and she was the only one who noticed it. Dr. Asgard bowed and excused himself. Leopold came to her side.

"You've been unwell, I believe," he said and his voice was loud and soft at the same time. "But you're much better now." Then, laughing, he tapped her arm. "Why, Marguerite, what is this? We're going for a ride in the carriage, my dear. Remember, I told you. Very pretty, yes, but you'll catch pneumonia in it."

She looked down and saw she was wearing a green, silk skirt and a cotton blouse with lace sleeves. She recognized neither garment.

"At least, let us get you a warm coat," Leopold said, guiding her back upstairs. "But first, look . . ." He held something out. "A little gift."

"What is it?"

"Why, it's a book, of course," he said. "Goldsmith. *The Vicar of Wakefield*." He put it into her hand.

She stroked the leather cover which was so soft that she had to look and see that her hand was really touching it.

"I haven't got a pocket," she said. Her head felt tight and the inside of it creaked like a ship's timbers on the high seas.

"We can leave it up in your room," Leopold said.

He put his arm around her shoulder but it felt so heavy that with every step she seemed to sink lower. She gasped.

"It's all right, my dear, I've got you," he whispered against her cheek.

Upstairs she lay on her bed.

"I've changed my mind, I don't want to go out," she said.

Leopold looked at her uncomprehendingly and she wondered if she had said the words she thought she did. She closed her eyes anyway, past caring.

He covered her on the bed with the coat he had taken from the wardrobe, tucking it in all around her. She could smell her own perfume on the collar – lily of the valley.

"Poor, sweet thing," Leopold said, brushing hair from her face.

She pushed his hand away. There was reason to resent Leopold, to wish him gone, but she couldn't for the life of her remember what it was.

"I've brought some letters from your apartment," he said, sitting back.

"One from Lewis?"

"Yes."

"Oh, please, let me hear Lewis's voice."

The pages rustled as he unfolded them to read and though she tried to find her brother in his voice, he kept getting lost in all those words.

When Marguerite opened her eyes next, she was all alone. Lewis's letter was on the pillow beside her. She reached for it.

Marguerite, it said,

Why do you not write, dear sister? This silence worries me. I can only surmise that a mail train somewhere has been destroyed and your letter along with it. If, however, this is not the case and you have merely been negligent, then please rectify matters now! You have no idea how much you occupy my thoughts.

Since I last wrote, the nature of this war has changed and we are no longer required to engage with the enemy head on which is a boon, I suppose. The Boers have new tactics and our side has adopted a slash and burn policy which has created thousands of refugees. At Bloemfontein, a camp has been set up to house them and our unit detailed to run it — not as appealing as it might sound. We have eighteen hundred women and children here and enough tents and food for six hundred. I won't describe the conditions to you as they would appall any right-minded individual.

At close quarters the Boers are a strange people. The men are rough-clad types who spend more time with animals than with humans. The women are stocky. The children are wild — many don't go to school at all. It is as though they are bred to take over the farms and can have no other direction in life. Nothing else seems to matter here. They live in wooden shacks, miles from each other and from any civilization and only come together once a week to pray. Such lives of hardship, it makes you wonder what they are fighting for.

As for the blacks, they have a hard time of it here. They work on the farms like slaves and often sleep outside with the dogs even when temperatures are well below freezing. They are a downtrodden lot, afraid even to meet your eye though I am told that there are tribes, the Barolongs and the Ngwato, who would put the fear of God into any white man.

How has Edmund weathered his particular storm? I'd give anything to hear one of his convoluted stories. Remember when we three sat in the drawing room together? Can we ever be the same people again?

Marguerite, you must write, let me know you are well. I could bear it all so much better if I knew that.

All my love,

Lewis

Having finished the letter, Marguerite stared at the tallboy against the wall opposite. It was made of burred walnut. The surface, pitted from age and wear, had a rich, rosy patina with dark spots and swirls running through it like ink diluting in water. Maybe, from way up in the sky, South Africa was like this with its hills and lakes and rivers and dry, cracked earth. And the people just dots.

Chapter Thirty-seven

One epidemic succeeded another at the camp outside Bloemfontein. The Boers led such solitary lives on their farms that they had no natural immunity to any of the infectious illnesses that broke out when they were corralled together like this.

It was always the children who came off worst. The measles took a slew of them, their faces so pink and swollen that Lewis thought them bonnier in death than they had been in life. Pneumonia, dysentry, typhoid took their toll too.

Some months into the camp's existence, the youngest inmates began to die from malnutrition. There was no escaping the blame then. The little corpses were laid out in torn-up petticoats with eucalyptus leaves tucked into the folds like St. Sebastian's arrows. The women came together to pray over them. Some mothers lost two and three children this way. They were the ones who didn't cry, not even when they heard the graves being dug outside the perimeter. They watched Lewis and his comrades carry out the bodies to be buried, watched them place the pathetic bundles in the ground and didn't shed a tear.

They were strange women. Was it Africa that had toughened them so, the cruel weather and terrain, the ferocious beauty of the place, the savage suddenness of life and death here? Or was it inborn, a genetic gift brought with them from the Old Country, their determination like a core of steel inside them? Perhaps this was the secret of their survival here. For they had a certainty that was both terrifying and shocking to behold. They believed this country was theirs, given to them by God and the fighting would not cease until they had it. No sacrifice was too great in the achievement of this aim. Their God was the right God, their lives were the right lives. They valued only their own history, their own traditions, their own wisdoms. When a child was sick they admitted no outsider, not even the camp doctor, but persisted with the herbal remedies of their ancestors even when it was obvious these were failing.

Perhaps the notion of Empire had instilled similar staunch feelings in the British side though Lewis had to admit that he had never felt anything like the devotion these Boer women had for their cause. It was their intransigence, their preparedness to follow their convictions to any extreme that he could not comprehend. And for what? They wanted to preserve their way of life, they said, as if it was somehow enviable. But he had seen the way they lived. They scraped an existence off a few miserable acres of dry, hungry earth with the highlight of each solitary week a ten-mile trek in an ox cart for Sunday worship; they bore sons whose fate was to lift the burden of hardship from their father's shoulders only to spend their own best years toiling beneath it themselves; they watched their daughters – eager, fresh-faced girls – diminish with the years.

Lewis, in common with some of the other soldiers, smuggled in packets of powdered milk for the infants and dry biscuit for the older children. The women sometimes talked to him then, about their homes, the food they cooked, the wild animals they had seen. They spoke but they never fully engaged. Their attention always drifted, eyes constantly scanning the horizon as if expecting, at any moment, to see their menfolk riding to the rescue.

Frieda was the only one among them who asked about England and what he did before coming to South Africa. At fifteen, on the cusp of maturity, she lacked the robustness that was typical of the Boer female. She had blonde, wispy hair that would never thicken and a slight frame with the kind of long, lean limbs that no amount of feeding can fatten.

What first drew him to her was how like Marguerite she was. Not in the obvious, physical way because in that sense they were unlike. No, what struck him was a certain similarity of expression. Frieda's face, like Marguerite's, was alive to every feeling she had, even the most transient. As a result, her features were never in repose and it was this aspect of her that reminded Lewis so strongly of his sister. That and her caring nature. Frieda was the oldest of six children, the only girl, with quite a gap between her and the next sibling and so was always to be seen with one or other and sometimes all of her younger brothers in tow. And she was kind to them, as Marguerite had been to him.

Lewis began to give her things. Usually, it was paltry bits of food spared from his own meals, sometimes corn bread bought from the kaffirs and once the half-eaten leg of a chicken stolen from a couple of soldiers too drunk to notice the theft. He told her not to share these gifts with anyone else but to keep them for herself and tell no one for fear there would be trouble.

To begin with she was suspicious, despite his assurances that there was nothing he required in return. When at last she realized he was telling the truth she made a friend of him and was very easy in his company. She taught him a game with stones and a ball that she and the other children called by an unpronounceable name. It was akin to the 'Jacks' he had known as a boy though he pretended ignorance of the rules and made all kinds of mistakes on purpose to make her cross with him.

He loved to sit on the ground and watch her playing with her brothers. Once or twice he sketched her. She was intrigued and kept rushing over every few minutes to assess his progress. The end result delighted her so much that he pulled it out of his notebook and gave it to her to keep.

She asked him if he was an artist and he laughed and said no, he knew his limitations, but he wanted to be an architect so he could create beautiful buildings.

Her mouth dropped open.

"That's wonderful," she said, in such a way that he knew she meant 'full of wonder'.

Long silences bothered neither of them. In fact, Lewis often did not notice until he went to speak that no word had passed between them for quite some time. Frieda was content to mind her little brothers and Lewis to sit and dream or watch her. When he was with Frieda he wasn't a soldier or a guard or even an Englishman. He was just Lewis.

The daily round went on. Twice a day, they filled water butts, doled out inadequate rations and disposed of the dead. These chores were interspersed with the usual army drills and inspections, the purpose of which was presumably to put the cast of normality on proceedings.

Night passes were easily got so, every weekend, contingents of men descended on Bloemfontein where they drank themselves silly in the bars there, returning to camp more exhausted and sicker than ever.

It was on one such evening that Lewis ventured to town. He

had gone early but unlike the others who crushed into the nearest pub, he had chosen to remain outside for a while. His incapacity for alcohol was well known amongst his friends and he preferred to join them later when they were intoxicated themselves and less likely to push drink on him for their own amusement. He sat down on the wooden verandah of the Bottle Store.

The atmosphere was heavy and warm, with no hope of a breeze. Lewis was gently stewing in his uniform. From where he sat, he faced out onto the main square, a drab expanse of yellowing grass which the residents, with admirable optimism, insisted on calling 'The Green'. In the middle of it was a flagpole bearing a flaccid Union Jack. Surrounding this patch of scrub were buildings that were incongruously grand. There was the English Club with its imposing stone façade and the Parliament Building and various offices several storeys high which were every bit as commanding as any institution in Threadneedle Street. In the suburbs there were immaculate, white bungalows where elderly English ladies could be seen cutting roses and chrysanthemums in their gardens. For despite being the capital city of Orange River Colony, Bloemfontein had retained much of its colonial past. The Boers had fled the city prior to its surrender, leaving behind the staunch ex-patriates along with the kaffirs and uitlanders, all of whom welcomed the British occupation of their town. Consequently, here deep in the Boer heartland, 'Tommy Atkins' felt more at home than he had anywhere else in the country and this paradox was an endless source of amusement to him. The joke ran that De Wet was now De Cold, having been forced out into it by the British.

A distant sound came, like marbles rolling around the inside of a tin and in the air there was an agitation, a shifting tension as though there was a storm on the way. Heads turned, townsfolk peered expectantly down Church Street. Lewis coughed, experiencing a sensation like pepper catching on the back of his throat. He covered his mouth and nose with a handkerchief to protect himself from the red dust that was starting to rise in clouds now, driving everyone else indoors.

But Lewis remained, not wanting to miss this spectacle, the arrival of yet another British Army Division. Watching the procession of guns, oxen, horses, wagons, mounted soldiers and poor sods on foot seemed to dispel what had become a permanent state of disillusionment in Lewis. A pride surged within his breast at the sight of them – nothing to do with patriotism or displays of strength, more inspirational than that. It was their humanity that touched him. It was written all over their faces, faces ravaged by hardship and horror and exhaustion after months out on the veldt. He admired the way they looked up at windows and into store fronts and clicked their tongues encouragingly at the wall-eyed mongrels that stood and stared at them. It was hope that was keeping them alive, the hope that this would be a better place than the last, that they would be let sleep for six hours on the trot, that they would get a boiled potato in their mess tins instead of biscuit, that they would have a chance to wash their underwear. He could take a lesson from them. Hope, humanity, courage – these can be small things, as well as large.

A rider detached himself from the main body as it went past and reined in his horse close to Lewis. Above the din of hooves and wheels grinding along the street, Lewis became aware of shouting. It was this man, an officer, his slouch hat pulled low over his face, evidently peeved at not receiving the obligatory salute. Lewis stood to rectify matters but the officer had swung his leg over the saddle and dismounted in less time than it took Lewis to stand. He was in for it now. But no, the man was grinning. He tilted back his hat to reveal his face. Eyes, bloodshot and red-rimmed from too much sun and dust, cheekbones higher and more prominent than he remembered and with shrunken V-shapes beneath them, mouth, thin and full of humour. There was no mistaking Edmund Jeffers. They clasped hands, embraced briefly, slapped each other on the back. But once the initial greeting was over and they sat side by side on the wooden step so many disparate thoughts crowded Lewis's head that he did not know what question to start with and they sat there awkwardly, watching the troops pass by.

At last, Lewis found the questions to ask. How long had Edmund been in South Africa? With what regiment? Which commander? What had been their route thus far? Where were they bound? Edmund was generous with his answers, making witty observations. He said that in his experience individual intelligence decreased in direct proportion to the numbers of men grouped together.

"The bigger the army," he said, "the stupider."

That made Lewis laugh.

Quickly, they moved on to more personal topics. Lewis enquired about Marguerite. She was well, Edmund told him. "Leopold has her ensconced in some private convalescent home out in the countryside," he said. "Somewhere in Surrey, not sure exactly where."

This came as a shock to Lewis.

"You didn't see her then before you came out here?"

Edmund held up his hands as if to ward him off. "Guilty as charged," he said. "But you must appreciate I was rather caught up at the time with that other business."

"What is the name of this home?" Lewis said.

"Jordanswood." And then, in response to Lewis's accusatory stare, "Perhaps, if you had stayed, Lewis, she wouldn't have needed to go anywhere."

An edgy silence followed that was difficult to break but Lewis tried anyway.

"I'm sorry things turned out so badly for you back in England," he said. "It was all over the newspapers before I left."

"Yes, they devoured me, didn't they?"

"I'm shocked to see you here though," Lewis said. "I never thought that you would leave the Colosseum."

"Believe me, I had no choice in the end."

"And what about the staff, the actors . . . ?"

"I didn't just turn my back on them –"

"That's not what I meant . . ."

Edmund raised his eyebrows in disbelief. He stretched his legs out in front of him, rubbed one knee as if it was giving him some grief.

"Actors and crew are still there, under contract to Leopold Barrie," he said, his attitude somewhat resentful. "So, everything goes on as usual, except without me."

An insect stung Lewis and in response he slapped the side of his neck, but too late to kill the pest. He could feel other small lumps on his skin where he had been repeatedly bitten. It was time to go indoors.

"You can see now, can't you," Edmund said, not looking at him, "why I chose to keep my private life a secret from everyone, in view of what has occurred since? You can't blame me for that."

But Lewis would not be drawn. He didn't know how to respond, was so unsure of his own feelings towards Edmund on this matter, that anger was the only one that ever came to the fore.

In front of them, the procession of men and animals and supplies began to thin. Several dogs ran in among the remnants, scrounging for scraps that might have fallen from the backs of wagons.

"You're here," Lewis said, rousing himself. "And that's surprising after all you said about this war."

"I am as patriotic as the next man when I see my countrymen in trouble," Edmund said, getting up. "Give me some credit."

He went to his horse, put his foot in the stirrup. The sudden fall of his shoulders seemed to suggest that he might return to the step, sit down again beside Lewis, let time unravel so they could begin their conversation again and this time hold on to the cordiality with which it had started. But no, he mounted up, looked down at Lewis with eyes blacker than ever, like one of those characters he played on stage who were so consumed by their own personal battles that they were unreachable to ordinary humans.

"I see you're a lieutenant now," Lewis said.

"Yes," Edmund said, with a tone so cold it turned them into strangers instantly.

Lewis stood to attention, raised his hand in a vicious salute. He spun around then and went up the steps into the Bottle Store. From inside, he watched discreetly through the window as, at first, Edmund lingered and then with sudden resolve dug his heels into his horse's sides with such vigour that the poor beast took off at a canter.

Lewis browsed amongst the tinned goods and drinks that were for sale in the shop but kept going over in his head the conversation he had just had with Edmund, wondering how it had ended so disturbingly. In time he calmed himself, tried to decide between a bottle of lemonade and a quart of bulls' eyes but his funds were so low anyway that he left with nothing.

Chapter Thirty-eight

Marguerite found out subsequently that she had been for several weeks at Jordanswood under the influence of a tranquillizing drug. She had never been able to establish how the first dose was given, without her knowledge and despite her vigilance, but once she had taken it her will was broken and she had surrendered herself to the daily medication. It affected her memory. Some days were complete blanks but she did, however, recall sitting in the hall at Jordanswood one morning and seeing two carriages pull up.

Leopold got out of the first one and her own medical practitioner, Dr. Richards, descended from the second, followed by Dr. Hargreaves. The three men came in. To her mind they moved too fast and reminded her of great birds swooping in on black wings, so much so that she put up her arms to protect herself from them. Doctor Richards sat down with her, took her hand in his and rubbed it as though it was cold. He spoke soothingly and perhaps she answered him but all she could remember now was Dr. Hargreaves standing there, looking down at her with an expression of absolute horror on his face. Leopold loitered a little way off, his back to them. After a while they went into Dr. Asgard's office, leaving her alone outside. The meeting was brief though there were raised voices. When it was over, Leopold marched straight past her without acknowledgment and got into his carriage which drove off immediately.

Dr. Richards and Dr. Hargreaves reappeared, followed by Dr. Asgard who used the bell pull in the hall to summon two attendants and give them succinct orders. It was only when Dr. Asgard turned to Marguerite, made her a tight, little bow and wished her a safe journey home that she realized what was happening.

Dr. Richards was standing beside her, shaking his head and muttering words like "disgrace" and "outrage".

Dr. Hargreaves said nothing. When her bags were brought downstairs he took them straight outside to be loaded up.

She must have fallen asleep soon after getting into the carriage because the next thing she knew she was getting off the train at Victoria Station. A cold wind whipped along the platform and she felt everyone was looking at her and knowing where she had come from. She began to tremble. Dr. Hargreaves wrapped a travel rug around her and kept his hands on her shoulders, guiding her through the crowds. They said goodbye to Dr. Richards in the darkness on the pavement outside the station. Then Dr. Hargreaves beckoned a hackney cab, helped Marguerite into it, got in with her and took her to her apartment in Knightsbridge.

The front door was opened by Betty, who gave a formal curtsey and then, succumbing to emotion, threw her arms around her mistress and drew her inside. Dr. Hargreaves brought in the luggage. He gave Betty some instructions, wrote down his telephone number on a piece of paper and, by the time Marguerite turned around to thank him, he was gone.

Marguerite fell straight into bed and, when she opened her eyes next day, she thought herself back in Jordanswood until she saw Betty leaning over her.

"I thought you'd never wake, ma'am," Betty said. "It's gone four o'clock in the afternoon. Let me get you something to eat. What could I tempt you with?"

"Was Dr. Hargreaves here today?" Marguerite said.

"Good Lord, no, ma'am. The poor man was totally done in last night."

"Yes, of course," she said. "How very selfish of me. It's just I have so much I need to ask him. Have you any idea, Betty, how he managed to whisk me away from Jordanswood like that? I hope it was legal."

"I'm sure all will become clear in good time, ma'am."

"And what of Leopold and Dr. Asgard? Will they be in trouble over this?"

"That I cannot say, ma'am, and you're not to fret about it either. You just rest and get well. Now, how are you feeling this morning?"

Marguerite sat up in the bed. "I feel a little more like myself," she said. "Which I haven't done for a long time." She began to weep.

"Oh, ma'am." Betty put a hand to her mistress's brow as if this current distress was brought on by a fever. "You're home now, safe and sound. Dr. Hargreaves is your guardian angel. When I think of what was done to you – and we all believing that Lord Barrie was looking after your best interests . . ."

Betty went away and came back with some tea and toast which Marguerite took on a tray on her lap with the pillows plumped up behind her. The little bedroom fire was burning brightly. Betty drew back the curtains to reveal a cold, drab scene outside, the sky a muted grey and laden with snow, trees skeletal and black, but this was her own view through her own window and the very sight of it made her rejoice. She only wished Lewis was there to share it with her.

Dr. Hargreaves had instructed Betty that Marguerite was to have no visitors for at least a day and so she remained in bed, dozing on and off, and only got up in the evening for a little supper, retiring early. The following morning when she woke her mind was much clearer and after she had eaten her breakfast she decided to sort through some of her mail. She sat in the armchair by the fire with her writing box on her knees and a pile of correspondence on the cushion beside her. The rest of the morning was spent like this in quiet contentment. At long last, she wrote to Lewis. She read a little. Betty came in at one with her lunch on a tray.

"Dr. Hargreaves called," she said. "He left some pills for you in case you had trouble sleeping. And said you have an appointment with Dr. Philbert tomorrow afternoon at two o'clock."

"Oh?" Marguerite said. "Did you tell him I was awake?"

"I did, ma'am, but the good gentleman seemed to be in a hurry."

In the weeks that followed Marguerite saw no more of Dr. Hargreaves. Daily, she expected him to visit but he never did. He called on the telephone and spoke only to Betty, assuring her that Marguerite's release from Jordanswood was effected in accordance with the law and promising that Leopold and Dr. Asgard were being dealt with. And while this information eased her mind in relation to her status, she was saddened beyond measure by Dr. Hargreaves' absence, in the purely physical sense. She just wanted him near.

Life returned to normal; Marguerite resumed her treatment with Dr. Philbert; friends began calling. She recovered enough of her old spirit to dress herself one day in a dazzling, sky-blue, twill suit with matching hat and feather. Thus attired and feeling unstoppable, she ventured down to Her Majesty's Theatre to meet Herbert Beerbohm Tree with a view to getting a job there.

Tree was thrilled to see her and brought her into his office. He looked at her mischievously, scratched his balding head so that the few hairs he had stood up on end.

Before she even had a chance to come to the purpose of her visit, he said, "Well, my good woman, we want you and we want you now. The world has been deprived long enough already."

A week later, rehearsals began for *Hedda Gabler* and six weeks after that it was opening night. It came too quickly for Marguerite who felt her confidence crash as the deadline neared and suffered from an unhealthy desire to be back at Jordanswood where at least there was no risk of failure. But, by curtain up on opening night, she had recovered her nerves and from the moment her first words were uttered she embraced the experience. It was visceral – her intensity matched the audience's. She was in a heightened state of emotion as was everyone else in the theatre that night. At the close of the play, when Marguerite went out to take her bow, she walked across a carpet of flowers that had been thrown onto the stage in her honour. There was a standing ovation. The applause was deafening. She bent down, scooped up some of the flowers, held them tight to her bosom, blew kisses to her admirers. Herbert came out to join her on stage. He took her hand and raised it in a gesture of triumph. The atmosphere became even wilder, with clapping and whistling and the stamping of feet.

The next morning the *Illustrated London News* carried the headline: "**She's Back!**"

★ ★ ★

One night after a performance, William brought a card to her dressing room. It was from Dr. Hargreaves, a request to come and see her backstage. She was to dine with Herbert and Maud later so she let Dr. Hargreaves wait while she got dressed in a burgundy velvet gown with fur trim and rubbed a little scent into her temples. Martha, her dresser, arranged her hair nicely, then left.

Dr. Hargreaves came in. He was wearing tails and a silk cravat and was carrying a cane, all of which were appropriate for the occasion, but which seemed out of place on him. She had half expected to see him in his white hospital coat. He held out his hand but she stood and stretched up to kiss him on the cheek. He lowered his head to accommodate her, then sat down, fumbled for his glasses and put them on. He cleared his throat.

"What a wonderful night," he said. "You were splendid, the play was splendid. And before you ask, no, I hadn't read it before I came here tonight. I simply let myself . . . float away. You were splendid, did I say that already?"

Marguerite smiled. "You look well," she said.

"That's my line, Miss Davenport. We doctors have a very limited repertoire, you know, but recognizing rude health is part of our brief."

"Please, call me Marguerite." When he did not return the compliment, she said, "Your mother and father thought it best not to give you a forename then? You were born Dr. Hargreaves, were you?"

"Cedric," he said with a frown. "Any problems regarding your sleeping patterns?"

"None whatsoever."

"Good. I am glad to see that you are not too much unsettled by your experience. Are you still going to see Dr. Philbert in his rooms?"

"Occasionally," Marguerite said. "But really I feel I have no need of him now."

"Then you are happy?"

"Yes, I suppose I am," she said, catching a glimpse of herself in the mirror and looking away.

"I called by your apartment a few times to check on your progress. Your maid Betty was very helpful."

"You should have spoken to me directly," she said, and then fearing he might have noticed the rebuke, "I just mean it would have been easier. To have it from the horse's mouth, so to speak."

"Medically speaking, very often a third party is more informative, especially when in a position to observe the patient over a long period of time."

"I see," Marguerite said. "Well, I am and always will be extremely grateful to you, Doctor Hargreaves . . . Cedric . . . for all that you did. You lost your job and your good name over me."

"You exaggerate."

"No, I don't. It would have been much better for your career to have left me rot at Jordanswood."

"No," he said, with undue force. "I could never do that." He seemed rather shocked at his own outburst and followed it up with, "Because that would be unethical."

"Of course it would."

"I was suspicious from the start, you know. Dr. Asgard was always reluctant to discuss your case in any depth. Then, when I suggested you were fit for discharge and I was expelled from Jordanswood within hours – well, obviously something was amiss."

"He spread the most horrible rumours about you."

"And threatened to report me to the authorities if he ever heard from me again. However, once I got to London, I could not resist making certain enquiries on your behalf. I spoke to Dr. Richards and Dr. Philbert about you and established that there had never been any indication that you were liable to take your own life. The magistrate who signed the Reception Order was defensive, but said he accepted a Dr. Vaughan's recommendation."

"Vaughan? Yes, Leopold took me to see a Dr. Vaughan among others . . . I barely remember it . . ." She paused. "Cedric, I truly believe that Leopold was paying Dr. Asgard to keep me at Jordanswood."

"Yes, you are probably right and certainly that scenario did occur to me but there was no way of proving it. The documentation supporting your committal appeared to be in good order and there is no one at Jordanswood who will speak out against Dr. Asgard."

"So what did you do? How am I here today?"

"I am ashamed to say I resorted to brute force. I have a friend who does some weight-lifting in his spare time and together we visited Lord Barrie at his London home. We tried gentle persuasion first and when that didn't work, we explained, very calmly, that unless you were released from Jordanswood within the week we – that is, John and I – would waylay him in the street when he least expected it and beat the living daylights out of him."

Marguerite clapped her hands. "What I wouldn't give to have seen his feathers ruffled like that!"

"Fortunately, he submitted straight away," Dr. Hargreaves said, looking quite pleased with Marguerite's response. "I was aged seven the last time I engaged in fisticuffs and that was with a classmate who demolished me within thirty seconds. I remember running home to my mother with a split lip and a seriously damaged sense of pride."

"Then this was totally out of character for you? So what impelled you to do it?"

He took some time to reply.

"I don't like to be thwarted," he said, finally.

"I have not seen Leopold since," Marguerite said. "But will there be a fuss, do you think, over what happened?"

"There is no point in pursuing the likes of Lord Barrie through the courts. He has enough money and connections to protect himself from any accusations."

"I would not want to take that route anyway," Marguerite said.

"I did take the liberty of warning him to stay well away from you, however."

"Thank Heavens."

"As for Jordanswood, we have no actual proof of any wrongdoing. Besides, Dr. Asgard does good work there. He is a good doctor who wants the best for his patients – there was no gain for himself personally. But I have alerted the Medical Council to be vigilant."

"You are a hero for the second time," Marguerite said.

"What?"

"Remember, when we went to Altbury to the theatre and the carriage nearly toppled over?"

"Oh that, yes."

He looked so uncomfortable with this that Marguerite changed the subject.

"I heard that you have found alternative employment," she said.

"I got a position almost straight away at St. Thomas's. Yes, after only days. John, the weight-lifter, is a registrar there."

"Then you are happy too?"

"I expect so," he said grimly.

The silence that followed seemed inordinately long.

To end it, Marguerite said, "Please, be my guest and join us for supper tonight. I am dining with Herbert and his wife. They would be delighted to meet you. I have told them so much —"

Dr. Hargreaves stood up, felt his breast pocket frantically then, realizing he had his glasses on, he took them off and put them away.

"No, no," he said. "I have eaten already. But thank you for the very kind offer."

"You won't escape my clutches that easily," Marguerite said. "We will dine together another evening."

"I think not," Dr. Hargreaves said.

"Gracious, is my company so awful?"

"On the contrary. That is the problem." He scratched his head as though he was thinking hard and looked down at the floor. "You must remember I am a doctor and you are a patient —"

"I am no longer *your* patient," Marguerite said.

"I understand that but still it would be unfair of me to . . . I would not want you to feel indebted because of what has . . . I take the doctor-patient bond very seriously . . ." He scratched his head even harder. "Look, sometimes patients develop strong emotions towards their doctors. It is simply gratitude masquerading as something else."

"Why, how presumptuous you are!" Marguerite said. "In the first place to assume that I harbour feelings of any kind towards you, and in the second to believe that I haven't the wit to know the difference between true regard and obligation."

"Oh, it is too complicated . . . and I have offended you."

"I think you should allow that I understand myself at least as well as you do."

361

"You are right, I am presumptuous. I will leave."

"How infuriating you are. You start the conversation and then you run away."

"Hero be damned," he said, forcing a smile. "I'm a coward really."

"Never that."

"Really, it was not necessary for me to come here tonight to see you in person — I could have put all you needed to know in a letter — but I wanted to know you were all right. I was selfish. And now, I have upset you and myself . . . I should say goodbye."

There was a shake to his voice. He took her hand in his, held it to his lips, his eyes shut tight, and kissed her fingers.

It was the briefest, tenderest brush but so intense that it felt to Marguerite as though the whole of his being, his love, was distilled into that one touch.

"Goodbye," he said.

And she knew he meant it forever.

When he was gone, Marguerite turned and looked at her reflection in the mirror which was blurred by the tears in her eyes. She pulled off her earrings and decided to cancel supper with Herbert and Maud. She was in no humour now to sit across the table from harmonious coupledom.

Chapter Thirty-nine

Violet Jeffers took well to the role of wronged wife. She had never sought pity from others and nor did she now but her delicate situation had drawn largely sympathetic support from the public. And this, she had to admit, was rather pleasing.

In the theatre, amongst those who actually knew Edmund, she was less comfortable. Here, the Chief was deified and his supporters fell into two camps. The first considered his infidelities with men the minor transgressions of a great artist, only to be expected in one so energetic and inspired. These were the ones who patted her on the arm and simpered while they talked of "creativity" and "needs" and the "rebel nature of Art". The others were less sympathetic. They deigned to commiserate with her, their eyes darting in every direction but straight at her and she knew they believed she had failed Edmund in some fundamental way to make him behave the way he did.

Privately, Violet coped very well. She could not say that she missed Edmund. In fact it was a relief to be freed from the tension that his presence caused both at home and in the theatre.

The details of Edmund's exposure, while they were extremely embarrassing did not, however, cause her to suffer from any sense of personal shame in the matter. From birth, she had been encouraged by her father to have pride in her ancestry, in her wealth, in her dark good looks, in her intelligence, in her own capabilities, and that habit of a lifetime did not desert her now. She had total belief in herself, in her own blamelessness, in her ability to transcend the current fiasco. It vexed her that Edmund had been unfaithful, that he had broken the wedding vows he had made to her before God and the world. But on a deeper level she remained relatively undisturbed. She did not torture herself – as many a wife before her had done – with torrid imaginings of her husband's adulterous acts. Even she was surprised by her own equanimity.

There were advantages to Edmund's absence, professionally speaking, too. For Violet was not, she decided, an actress. No, her true métier was as a manager and she set her sights on becoming one. As usual, her father was her greatest ally and his ninety-per-cent ownership of the Colosseum silenced any opposition. Under his guidance, she took an increasingly stronger hand in the running of the theatre and managed to weed out some of those employees she deemed "too loyal" to Edmund. For it was impossible to work amongst people who still venerated him. Thankfully, the sycophants Roger Yates and Nicholas Bland, dissatisfied with the fare now on offer at the Colosseum, had left of their own accord. Lawrence Alma-Tadema would never be asked to work for them again. Albert Considine, the stage manager, would not be having his contract renewed in September owing to concerns – mainly Violet's – about his growing dependence on alcohol. James Armstrong, musical director, she was working on.

Charles Gray was a more difficult proposition. He was astute, very good at his job and had been at the Colosseum for so long that he was regarded as an institution in much the same way as the theatre itself. It would take time to undermine him. Unlike Roger and Nicholas, there was no possibility he would just up and leave in a fit of temper for he had made a promise to Edmund to stay. And he would never go back on that. No, his devotion to Edmund was complete. Comic, at times. She remembered once seeing Charles scuttling along behind his idol with a notebook and pencil in hand, ready to scribble down whatever ideas came tumbling forth from that prodigious brain, even the most inane remark to be preserved for posterity. Sooner or later, Charles would have to go too. For it was Violet's ultimate goal to have all key personnel in the theatre replaced by people who knew Edmund only by reputation.

According to plan, Leopold gradually withdrew from the administration of the Colosseum, leaving Violet, in effect, the manager. She had learned a lot from just watching and listening over the previous months. She had watched the scene painters at work as they created new backdrops, watched the property master take care of his store ensuring everything was in its right place and labelled, the dance master rehearsing the steps of a galliard. She had watched the actors bouncing lines off one another, the boys in the towers raising and lowering the flies, the costumiers selecting the appropriate style for each character. She had discovered what each task was and how long it took, the degree of difficulty, who gave the orders, who worked the hardest.

From very early on she established that she would brook no argument on business such as the casting of roles, or the choice of plays or music. She was willing to take advice in these areas but, once the decision was made, she was not for turning. She remembered that Edmund had once said, "A play will either fail or succeed. If it fails, the trick is to ensure it does so spectacularly." And so she was never afraid to go with her instinct.

It was the smaller issues she had difficulty with, like when to give in to an actor, when to heed the carpenters' incessant whines about poor-quality timber or the pianist's tantrums over the degree of 'out-of-tuneness' of her instrument. Where was the line between tyranny and weakness? Edmund could rant on forever or listen or laugh these things off in an instant, but Violet had nothing like the same intuition or rapport with her company. These were the moments that constantly defeated her.

Violet first met Walter Penn Warren when she and her father were auditioning for the post of leading man at the theatre. It had been a long afternoon. They were weary and unimpressed by the string of candidates they had already seen. Walter Penn Warren was the last to come out. He performed a piece from *Hamlet*, hardly original, but he brought to the part a faintly swashbuckling style that was hard to resist. They asked to meet him afterwards in the office.

He was a fine-looking man, thirtyish, with black hair parted in the middle and flattened on either side with oil. His well-trimmed moustache was generously wide with upturned tips which gave the impression he was smiling even when he was not. His skin was rather sallow for an Englishman and hinted at some foreign blood in his heredity. He spoke at length on every topic they raised and was charming to boot, but was let down by an inferior body of work. He listed bit parts with a touring company in Yorkshire and two or three other slightly more substantial roles at the Pavilion in Blackpool. He was currently playing Iago in Brentwood. One had to admire his audacity in approaching the Colosseum on the basis of so little.

When Leopold suggested that he had almost no credentials to

qualify him for the post, Walter said, "You are right, I need more experience. And I will make up for that once I get the job."

He was handsome, confident and, most of all, intelligent. He avoided engaging with Leopold on a man-to-man basis and made Violet as much his focus during the meeting as her father. She suspected he did this not for altruistic reasons but because he had worked out the power structure within the Colosseum and was already exploiting it. That kind of pragmatism, Violet admired.

The interview terminated with a lot of good will on both sides and it was agreed that Violet and Leopold would go to Brentwood to watch Walter performing in *Othello* the following night.

But when he left and they were alone, Violet said, "Do you know, Papa, I think he will do."

"Yes," Leopold said. "I like his punch."

When they saw him act, they were satisfied, and so Walter Penn Warren was hired immediately and rehearsals for *The Uncommon Good* began. This was a light comedy concocted for them by Clement Evans with nothing more to it than some witty banter, a very deaf archdeacon and a young couple crossed in love. One half of the couple was played by Walter Penn Warren, the other by Dorothy Lee who had been 'borrowed' from The Lyric while that theatre was being refurbished.

There was only one set in the play, the archdeacon's sitting room, with each act taking place at a different time of day – the morning, the early evening and the dead of night – which required merely a change of lighting and a rearrangement of props to achieve. It was a simple piece, economical to stage and, with a cast of only five, an ideal play for Violet's directorial debut.

Dorothy Lee managed her part well enough. She was winsome, quite pretty, with a rosebud mouth and button nose, and even dimples in those plump cheeks of hers, the kind of person who would be a girl until she was an old lady. But there was an unnecessary crudeness about her that Violet did not like. However, they had got her at short notice and were glad of her. On stage together, Walter far outshone her.

The five actors were sitting in a semicircle on the stage reading through Act Two with Violet at the helm. This was how Edmund always approached the text except that he read out loud all the parts himself while the cast listened. Violet had no wish to do that. She did the listening instead and took notes. She felt that things were going quite well until Dorothy came to the line, "*Oh, don't, Your Worship! I can feel me eyes watering . . .*" and uttered the words with such vulgarity that the whole meaning of them was altered.

Several of the crew guffawed in the background.

Violet halted proceedings.

"It is 'my' not 'me'," she said. "Remember, you are a gentlewoman, Dorothy, not a milkmaid. And aim for a lighter touch, please."

To which Dorothy replied, "Any lighter and it'll fly away." She threw her hands up in a graceful, fluttering arc to illustrate her point.

The other actors tittered.

Violet held the script out in front of her and demonstrated exactly how she wanted the line read.

Dorothy repeated it but gave the line nothing – let it fall into silence, like a stone dropped into the middle of a deep pond.

At that point, the stage door opened and, between them, William and Thomas carried in a trestle table with tea and sandwiches and other dainties on it for the cast's refreshment. Chairs shifted. Walter rose and stretched himself. Fearing that it would be impossible to stop them anyway, Violet indicated that they should take the much yearned-for break.

Dorothy got up, ceremoniously dropping her script onto the vacant chair behind her.

"Well, that was illuminating," she said, for all to hear. Her little rosebud mouth was drawn into a tight knot as she joined the others at the table to inspect what was on offer.

Violet remained seated. The flare of a match from the wing caught her eye. It was Charles, sitting in the prompter's chair, his legs stretched to full length and crossed, the black suit so dark against his pallid skin that it made him look cadaverous. She resented his presence, his witnessing of her inadequacies, his opinionating, his smug face.

She was isolated, sitting all alone in the middle of the stage, yet she could not with dignity get up and mingle with the others. Perhaps she should demand a public apology from Dorothy for her insolent behaviour or was that making too much of it? She wanted to regain the actors' respect, to continue the rehearsal in a friendly atmosphere that would be productive. She doubted that confrontation, which could leave her looking foolish, was the best way to achieve that result, yet an alternative eluded her. She looked down at her script, skimmed through half a page, went to the next. She wished the break was over but dreaded continuing with the reading too. She glanced at the table and saw Walter giving William instructions. Within seconds, William was at her side with a cup of tea and a plate of egg-and-cress sandwiches. She took them from him, smiled, felt slightly less abandoned. Later on, when she dared to look again, she saw Walter and Dorothy in deep conversation. They were walking together out towards the wings, their heads inclined. Walter had slipped his arm around Dorothy's shoulders. They turned and came back, Dorothy holding her cup in one hand and her saucer in the other. Walter's mouth was close to her ear and he tapped softly on her forearm with his finger. She was nodding.

After the break, Violet called them all to order and they took up their scripts and began again. When they came to the contentious line, Dorothy undertook it exactly as Violet had requested, delivering it with such panache and wit that there was applause from all present.

Violet smiled her approval, raised her hands aloft to clap. Dorothy stood to receive the accolade and bowed respectfully to Violet before resuming her seat.

It was, of course, Walter who had wrought this change in her, who had manoeuvred her into complying with Violet's version of the line. How he had managed to do so was a mystery to her.

She looked at him. Tactfully, he cast his own gaze downward.

Chapter Forty

There was a public house in Church Street just off the main square that Lewis liked to frequent. Inside, it was small and rectangular in shape, with the floor, walls and ceiling all wooden. The overall effect was somewhat claustrophobic and led to the place being known to regulars as 'The Coffin' though there was nothing gloomy about it. The furnishings were spartan but the atmosphere was always merry and there were mirrors everywhere, even one or two screwed to the ceiling. They were not for the purpose of decoration but were strategically placed so that the proprietor, a Mr. Joshua A. Thrupp, could keep an eye to any trouble amongst his customers, who were mainly soldiers and a rowdy lot. Thrupp, a wiry fellow in his fifties, worked in the bar himself and was very proud of his physique and of his reputation as a tough man. His sleeves were permanently rolled up so as to show off his muscular arms and he was unnaturally keen to break up arguments and show the younger men who was boss. It was well known that he kept a three-foot-long club beneath the counter in case of fighting and he wasn't backward about using it.

This night, the place was packed, the air thick with smoke and sweat and dust. Lewis was sitting on the wooden bench against the back wall with others from his company. In the middle of the room one of the lads was attempting to sit on the floor whilst balancing a pint of beer on his head. Everyone in the place was egging him on, clapping and chanting.

He wobbled, the glass fell off his head and smashed on the floor. There were cheers. Thrupp came out from behind the bar with a wire broom. He grunted a few complaints but really he was prepared to tolerate most pranks if by doing so it guaranteed custom. He swept the glass into a corner for his kaffir boy to clear up and with the point of his boot rubbed a filthy rag over the wet area to dry it. This display of housekeeping somewhat dissipated the playful mood in the bar. There was a hiatus while some went outside to the lavatory and others decided to move on altogether.

That was when Lewis first noticed Edmund sitting with his back to the bar, looking directly at him. Perhaps he had been there all along and that thought made Lewis uncomfortable. Their eyes met briefly but they did not acknowledge each other. Edmund turned to the barman, ordered a drink and then, before Lewis could even think about escape, he approached, carrying two glasses of whiskey. He set them down on the table then slumped into the chair opposite Lewis. This seemed to be the cue for everyone Lewis had been socializing with up to then to suddenly desert him and within seconds he found himself alone with Edmund at the back of the bar.

"Was it something I said?" Edmund jerked a thumb at Lewis's departing companions.

Lewis shrugged his shoulders.

"You're out at the refugee camp, aren't you?" Edmund said.

"Yes, I am."

Edmund pushed one of the glasses of whiskey across the table towards him.

"Come on, Lewis," he said. "Keep me company." He raised his own drink for a toast. "To Thrupp's Bar, that it may never run dry. God Bless Her and all who sail in her." He took a gulp, grimaced. "Rougher than turps and twice as lethal," he said, with a shiver. "Just what the doctor ordered."

Lewis never drank whiskey but he took a sip now. The liquor seemed to evaporate on his tongue. He stared at a mirror on the wall to his right that had a picture on it of a girl with a garland of roses in her hair.

Edmund rested his elbows on his thighs, head dipping, as though he might fall asleep where he sat.

"You've been on quite a spree," Lewis said.

"Have I?"

"This isn't your first port of call at any rate."

"No, I was on a quest. Made the mistake of imbibing at every stop along the way."

"You'll never reach your destination at that rate."

Edmund looked down into his glass of whiskey as if he had just spotted a fish swimming in it, then glanced up. "I felt bad about the other day," he said, his eyes flitting away again. "The other week, whenever it was. We just seemed to get off on the wrong foot, I don't know why. I've been thinking about it ever since."

A silence followed this. Lewis was too tongue-tied to break it.

"I thought we were good friends," Edmund said. The alcohol had brought looseness to his body but there was tension in his face. "Do you feel I have neglected your sister, is that it?"

"Yes." But then Lewis shook his head. "No, that is not the truth. You have been very kind to her. I shouldn't have left her when I did. I am to blame."

"I am sure she is being well looked after. I know you turn

your nose up at money but Leopold has plenty of it and he can afford the best of everything for her."

"You have that wrong. I do not turn my nose up at money," Lewis said. "Except where it is the money that defines the man rather than the other way round."

"I envy you your piety," Edmund said, with an annoying flicker of a smile that made a mockery of Lewis's words.

"I buried a child today," Lewis said. "A little girl, ten years old. I knew she was going to die for a long time. Her eyes were sinking back in her head, a little bit further every day. She was nice." He paused. "Instead of watching her, I should have put my hands round her throat and squeezed the life out of her. That, at least, would have been honest. And kinder, to get it over with quick."

"I don't know which is more shocking," Edmund said. "The child's death or your reaction to it. It is not your fault she died. You are too hard on yourself."

"No, I'm not," Lewis said.

Across the room, Thrupp was polishing the counter top with wide, circular strokes. The carousers had moved on elsewhere, leaving just two groups of men chatting at the bar.

"You are not responsible for what is happening in that camp," Edmund said.

"Of course, I am. We are all accountable."

"You are punishing yourself unnecessarily."

"I am merely facing the truth. You think it is better to lie, to live a lie?" The words burst from him with unexpected vehemence. He was no longer talking about the camp.

Edmund realized it too. He said, "I know I should have told you and Marguerite and Charles about . . . well, about myself really. But it seemed somehow impossible then. There was so much to lose . . . my friendships, my family, all I had worked for . . ."

"We have all faced those dilemmas."

"Well, I'm out in the open now, discredited on three continents for my sins."

"You merely succumbed to the truth," Lewis said. "There is nothing courageous about that. You should be proud of who you are, instead of which you have denied it and in doing so you have denied all of us."

Edmund looked stunned by this remark.

"And what's more, you seem to carry the notion that somehow you are the sufferer, the victim in all this."

Edmund emitted a sound that was somewhere between a laugh and a roar.

"I have no home or livelihood nor even the respect of ordinary, decent people. I have lost all I hold dear. If that's not suffering, I don't know what is."

"Did you think, if I knew, that I'd start pestering you in some crude manner?"

"No, of course not!"

"Because I didn't think of you in those terms." He did not add that he had fought against such thoughts, believing them to be impossible. "And all the times when you could have told me . . . you should have given me that much."

Edmund extended his hand. "I never meant to offend you, Lewis, and I'm sorry that I have. Let us shake and be friends."

But Lewis was driven now. "One should always declare oneself," he said. "No matter what the consequences. One cannot live well otherwise."

"That's just too much moralizing for me," Edmund said. "Let's shake hands and forget all about it."

But to accept Edmund's offer of friendship seemed somehow more complicated than refusing it.

"I'm sorry but I can't forget how you lied to us," Lewis said, and with that he got up and left.

Outside, the cool quiet of the deserted street soothed him. A damp mist was falling. Heading in the direction of the main square he was surprised to find his step was unsteady as he did not think he had drunk that much. Behind him, he heard a door bang and hurried footsteps on the wooden planks. Then Edmund's voice calling on him to wait. But Lewis refused to slacken his pace.

Nevertheless, Edmund caught up with him.

"Look, I'm sorry for everything. How does that suit you?" he said, with quite an edge to his voice.

Lewis walked on with more determination.

"I'm sorry, for Christ's sake. I'm sorry for the war, I'm sorry for the weather, I'm sorry for the fact that you have ruddy holes in your socks. What more can I say?" He reached out for Lewis's arm to try and slow him down. "Come on, Lewis, surely you can –"

"You're drunk," Lewis said, shaking him off. "And too glib for someone who has caused so much hurt."

"Oh, I've caused plenty of hurt all right," Edmund said. They had reached the long side wall of the hotel where it ran up to the square. "To Violet, to Charles and . . . but what are you saying . . . that I've hurt *you*?"

"When you deceive people like that, they end up feeling used."

"But you said hurt."

"No, I didn't." Lewis walked on even faster. It was all getting too confusing for him now.

Edmund grabbed his elbow. "Wait a moment," he said. "Talk to me. Why won't you forgive me? Are you afraid?"

"Of course not," Lewis said, pulling away with such force that he lost his balance and staggered sideways against the wall of the hotel.

Edmund grabbed him by the collar to pull him up then pinned him back against the pebbledash.

"You're full of wind, Lewis," he said. "You talk of hurt . . . but you won't explain. Do you –?"

"Shut up!"

Lewis struggled fiercely to free himself but he was held so fast that he could not move effectively. The pressure of Edmund's fist on his throat caused him to gag.

At that, Edmund released him. "Jesus, I'm sorry. That was wrong of me." He backed away, bent forward, his hands resting on his knees as if he had just run a marathon. "I'm sorry, so sorry."

Lewis fought to get his breath back. He watched as Edmund straightened up and turned around with eyes so full of pain and sadness that the sight of them made him want to weep.

A moment of indecision.

Then, Edmund came right up close.

"Say nothing," he said. "But know this is the truth of it." And in one swift movement with his thumb he traced the outline of Lewis's mouth, bent down and kissed his lips so fleetingly it felt like his breath.

Just then, a gang of soldiers came around from an alley at the back of the hotel. They were singing bawdy verses, arms wrapped around each other as they went along.

Lewis broke from Edmund and joined the soldiers, who were from his own unit. He walked back to camp with them, arms linked. But he didn't listen to any of their jokes or join in with any of their songs.

Chapter Forty-one

On arrival in Bloemfontein, Edmund's unit was billeted to St. Mary's convent and junior school which had been commandeered already by the military. The classrooms were used for offices while the assembly hall, duly partitioned, served as living quarters for some of the top brass. Otherwise, from private soldier to officer, the men were housed under canvas on the playing fields at the rear. The horses were cared for at a farm half a mile away.

After so long out on the veldt it was a relief to be stationary. Captain Peters increased fatigues and drills: "An idle soldier is not a soldier at all." On top of that, the horses had to be exercised and fed and groomed but still Edmund found there was time to enjoy the more recreational side of barrack life.

A 'Soldier's Home' had been set up in a barn-like building at the furthest edge of the sports field and was a great place to socialize when off duty. Presided over by Reverend Falkner, the Anglican Chaplain attached to the 3rd Grenadier Guards, it was a hub of activity. Mineral waters could be bought at cost price as well as biscuits, tobacco and oranges. There were chess tournaments every week and sometimes 'talks' by whatever 'expert' from among themselves could be persuaded to speak. They were modest entertainments but much appreciated by men who had been out in the field for weeks on end.

Such was the peace within the school walls that one got the impression sometimes there was no war at all going on. Edmund surrendered himself to it. He was not a spiritual man but he recognized peace when he found it. Sitting all alone, in the nuns' garden, the setting sun an orange glow, he liked to convince himself that he had just landed here, that he had no past, no future, that the present was all. Because there were thoughts he wanted to suppress – that awkward encounter by the hotel wall for one where, drunkenly, he had declared himself to Lewis only to be rebuffed. He never would have been so open except that he had thought from their conversation that night that Lewis harboured similar feelings to his own. For Lewis had been very much in Edmund's thoughts of late – those precious afternoons in Marguerite's apartment when they drifted in and out of conversation had become enshrined in his memory, moments that were often revisited while undergoing hardship out on the veldt. And now that he was free of encumbrances – wife, theatre, reputation – and in a foreign country, he had finally given in to his natural urge. Perhaps that was selfish of him – no doubt that would be Lewis's view – but it had felt wholly right at the time.

He was sent one afternoon into town on a mission to locate webbing for the quartermaster when he saw Lewis sitting on the edge of a stone horse trough outside the public library. He resisted the temptation to pass behind him unnoticed as it seemed somehow dishonest to do that.

They greeted one another with restraint and Edmund

stopped. Lewis kept his eyes trained on the people passing, the wagons being loaded. It was a very hot day and evidently Lewis had doused himself with water already as his shirt was all dark patches and his hair was dripping onto his shoulders. He was perched peculiarly on the lip of the trough, his rump thrust back, his torso thrown forward over his knees. It took Edmund a second or two to understand that he was giving his rear end a good soaking in the cool water beneath him.

"You're a genius," he said, on discovering this. "You should patent it."

Lewis just closed his eyes against the sun.

They baked together in silence and Edmund was about to say goodbye and move on when Lewis spoke.

"Is your wife going to divorce you?"

"I should think so. Eventually, that is." And then, just for the sake of talking, he added, "Though I doubt she or her family would like all those sordid details bandied about a courtroom. There is the traditional route – seaside hotel, lady of doubtful reputation, photographer under the bed . . ."

Lewis still had his eyes closed, making it difficult to know if he was really listening.

"The best thing would be for me to die. To die in battle. Actually, to die in battle planting the British flag on top of some hard-won hill. Do you think that would bring me some honour at last?"

"What of your obligations to your wife?"

"I feel like I'm facing the counsel for the prosecution," Edmund said. "Why all the questions?"

"I want to know."

Edmund took a deep breath, tried not to let the exhalation sound like a sigh.

"Well, financially, Violet is very comfortable. She comes from monied people. But, in addition, I have settled the house in her name and also she has my share of the theatre and there is some money in –"

Lewis heaved himself out of the trough in one sudden, sucking movement. From waist to knee he was drenched, water pouring off him in torrents.

"I don't give a damn what you've given her," he said. "What does she require from you? What does she expect? Spouses have a right to expect, you know."

"Well, what she expects, I am prepared to give," Edmund said. "My loyalty, my support, my friendship, love. Fidelity is not part of the equation. Both of us accept that now."

Lewis was frowning. He lashed out at a fly that was buzzing around him.

Suddenly, a young man was standing with them. Edmund had not noticed him approach. He was very dark, gypsyish, and he had a wooden crate balanced on his shoulder. He introduced himself to Edmund as Georgie Carr. He swung the crate down to the ground and offered them each a ginger beer out of it.

"Old man Thrupp must be suffering from heatstroke," he said, producing an opener from his tunic pocket to take the caps off their bottles. "Passing by his place just now and I said, joking, 'Any leftovers?' and he handed me six bottles, free, gratis, and for nothing."

"And there are some who say there is no God," Edmund said. "Cheers."

The liquid was warm and yeasty. It satisfied his thirst while making him feel sick at the same time.

Georgie Carr downed his in one go and followed it with a great belch of satisfaction. "That is so good," he said, wiping his mouth with the back of his hand. His face was moist with sweat and a thin line of black hairs more suited to an adolescent than a grown man glistened across his upper lip. He and Lewis were close in age. Edmund felt old and staid beside the two of them.

"I saw you in a play once," Georgie said to Edmund. "At the Colosseum."

"Yes, that would be me all right."

"Beautiful theatre."

"It is indeed."

"Big."

"Yes, six hundred seats," Edmund said, looking at Lewis.

"No plays out here, by Jove," Georgie Carr said.

"Not so far anyway."

Lewis remained aloof throughout this exchange.

And then, Carr said, "We've been out bargain-hunting, haven't we, Lewis? Show him what you got."

At that, Lewis re-engaged with them.

"Yes," he said, grinning. And, rooting in his shirt pocket, he pulled out a gnarled piece of beef jerky that, even from where Edmund was standing, smelt high. "Three for a penny at Joyce's. I'm sure there are still some left if you —"

"I don't think my stomach would thank me for it."

Lewis smiled. He put the jerky back in his pocket, took a gulp of beer which went down the wrong way and caused him to cough violently. Carr gave him several hard blows between the shoulder blades which helped but Lewis remained doubled up, in a paroxysm of laughter now, his shoulders shaking with mirth. Carr, laughing too, continued to slap and stroke Lewis on the back.

Eventually, when he could speak again, Carr said, "Should have known you'd need burping after your bottle, Lewis."

Which comment caused the two of them to be amused all over again.

"I should go," Edmund said, sensing that he was not wanted.

He slid his empty bottle back into the crate.

Carr, recovering, reached over to get him another. "Go on," he said. "It isn't often we have it."

"No, really. I've had enough."

Lewis stood up then, panting from all that coughing and laughing, his eyes bright, a pink flush to his skin. And then suddenly, his face was devoid of any expression. With a vacant gaze, he ran a hand over his hair. Edmund, hesitating, bade him farewell and Lewis just stood there, staring.

Chapter Forty-two

At the Soldiers' Home, it was decided to hold a table-tennis tournament and Reverend Falkner looked for volunteers to help him with the organization of the event. Edmund was one of twenty who offered their services and they were kept busy over the coming week. Posters were made and put up all over the camp and in the town and a full day was set aside for the construction of the tables. The nuns had recently discarded a number of old blackboards and these, trimmed and sanded and supported on trestles, made the perfect playing surface for the game.

The competition was for doubles only and was much talked about in advance. On the day, a Sunday, it drew a large crowd. Six tables were arranged on the grass in front of the Soldiers' Home with enough room round each one for a circle of onlookers. Some of the contestants were only in it for the fun but there were enough crack players involved to lend the occasion a competitive edge.

When it came to the final, the other tables were cleared away and the audience gathered around the remaining one. Those at the front sat, while those at the back stood on stools and chairs and even stepladders to see what was going on. It was a close contest, with the C.I.V. pair pitted against the Royal Engineers and every point on either side was cheered wildly.

Edmund had positioned himself towards the back of the crowd from where, because of his height, he had a fine view of proceedings but he could not help being distracted by a huddle of men just behind him who were still placing bets even though the match was well underway. One of them, he noticed, was Lewis. He had seen him several times throughout the day and avoided him, a tactic which Lewis must also be adopting as they had not met face to face once, despite being confined to a small area. It was ten all in the fourth consecutive game when Edmund heard a voice beside him. It was Lewis.

"I hope your boys have been eating their greens," he said. "I've got a shilling riding on them at 10/1."

"A shilling?" Edmund said, taken aback by Lewis's friendliness. "By golly, a shilling!"

"That's nothing to what some of the lads are putting on," Lewis said. "A month's wages, one of them. The Reverend Falkner would be horrified if he knew."

The table tennis provided the crowd with plenty of thrills before it was all over and the C.I.V. team emerged as the victors. Lewis let out an unholy cheer and went off to collect his winnings. Edmund could see him waving the ten-shilling note above his head and, as he went along, several of his colleagues patted him on the back or ruffled his hair.

"Congratulations," Edmund said when he came back.

The tidying-up had started. All around them stools and ladders and benches were being carted away.

"Do you know Fraser's Bakery?" Lewis said, without warning.

"No," Edmund said. "Should I?"

"They sell Belgian buns."

"Well, that's good to know."

"With currants and icing. Haven't you ever had one?"

"No, I seem to be deficient in that department."

"They could still be open," Lewis said. "Fraser's. Only it's bad luck not to spend your winnings as soon as you get them."

"Is it?" Edmund said, reduced to gawping.

"We could go there, to Fraser's, you and I," Lewis said.

"Well, there's an idea," Edmund said.

Lewis went to fetch his bicycle which he had left at the foot of the statue of Our Lady in the front garden of the convent, and they headed into town.

The heat of the day and all that standing around had left Edmund's limbs feeling heavy and so they walked along slowly. Lewis's hair stood out from his collar, the day's sweat stiffening it like starch. Once or twice, as they bumped against each other, Edmund felt the pressure of Lewis's upper arm against his own.

They spoke casually of the table-tennis tournament, of life in the camp, life out on patrol, and then Edmund said, "Georgie Carr not here then? Doesn't he like table tennis?"

"Oh, he likes it well enough. He's a topnotch player himself —"

"Yes, I thought he might be," Edmund said, only half joking.

"But he's on duty 'til eight."

"How is he these days? On the receiving end of any more manna from Heaven? Handsome fellow . . . eh?"

Against the silence that followed, the crunch of their feet on the ground seemed to Edmund almost intolerable.

Eventually, Lewis, in a highly amused tone, said, "Look, he's engaged to be married, you know. To a girl from Dorchester. I've seen her picture and very pretty she is too."

"Oh," Edmund said, relieved. Then, "Am I really that transparent?"

"As glass. And you an actor," Lewis said, laughing now. "She's called Josephine, by the way. She sent him a packet of carrot seeds recently and he's sown them in a little patch he's dug. Waters them every day. Says when they come up they should taste of England."

"If it was me, I'd prefer that they tasted of carrots," Edmund said. "Factory smoke and rain are not flavours that appeal especially."

They reached the bakery just in time to buy the last half dozen buns which they took to a bench across the road from the shop and devoured.

As he finished the last one, Edmund said, "So that is a Belgian bun, is it? I'm impressed." He licked his fingers. "There must be other things this great country of Belgium has produced?"

"Anne of Cleves?"

"I'm only interested in edible items."

"Wiener Schnitzel?"

"No, thank you, sounds like a cat's sneeze. Besides, isn't that Austrian?"

"Blame the Austrians anyway," Lewis said.

Edmund stood up, shook the crumbs from his trousers. Did Lewis actually want his company or had he invited him here simply to show that he bore no resentment?

"I think I've been dossing long enough," he said. "I need to get back, help with the clearing up."

"Oh yes, of course," Lewis said, getting up too. "I forgot." He mounted his bicycle, turned it around so it faced towards St. Mary's.

"There's no need for you to ..."

"I'm only killing time," Lewis said, preparing to move. "That's all, just killing time."

He pedalled in half turns so as to stay level with Edmund as he walked. They went back through the town and out towards the school. When they got to the parish hall, the windows were open and from inside came the sounds of a brass band warming up. The two men stopped and waited for the musicians to play a tune in earnest but when it came, their rendition of the Radetzky March was so awful, so plodding and so out of tune that Edmund covered his ears.

"It's like a herd of elephants shrieking," he said. "Come on, let's get away from here."

"They're better than they were," Lewis said, following.

"You mean it is possible to sound worse than that?"

"Oh, much. They've been practising every night for the last two – Who wrote the Radetzky March anyway?"

"Practising for the last two what?"

"Was it Strauss?"

"Practising for the last two seconds, I'd say, by the sound of them."

"Weeks, actually." Lewis dragged his toes through the dust, brought his bicycle to a halt. He stared at Edmund. "Every night for the last two weeks I've suffered them playing the Radetzky March."

"But why?" Edmund said. "How? What brings you here when your camp is three miles in that direction?"

Lewis remained stock still, his feet planted on the ground either side of his bicycle, a look of such fragility on his face that it was, at first, alarming.

"Please don't make me spell it out for you," he said.

In his head, Edmund went through various scenarios, shying away from the one he favoured only to come back to it.

"No, you'd never be that daft, would you?" he said.

Lewis looked down, nodded gravely as though admitting some awful crime.

Edmund grinned. "You bloody fool," he said, as softly as he could. "Bloody, bloody fool."

After that, Edmund and Lewis met regularly in the evenings when they were both off duty. Occasionally, they went for a drink but mostly they just wandered around the town. One time, they came upon a game of horseshoes taking place on the Green and they were encouraged to join in. Edmund kept everyone entertained with complicated throws and funny posturing and quips galore but it was Lewis who won the game. The other players honoured him with a necklace of tin cans strung on a ribbon which they draped round his neck with great ceremony. It was a joy to watch Lewis, beaming throughout, as happy as if he were being crowned King of England.

Often, they just sat down somewhere to let Lewis sketch and it intrigued Edmund how, when he was drawing, Lewis always brushed his hair back off his face even though it was far too short to get in his way.

"It helps me concentrate," he said, without taking his eyes off the water pump which he was studying at the time, when Edmund remarked on this.

One Sunday afternoon, on the pretext of exercising the horses, Edmund took two from the farm, one for himself and one for Lewis. Lewis was no horseman but he had ridden enough to be able to control the quiet bay that Edmund brought for him. They went three miles out from Bloemfontein, staying well within the protected zone, to a deserted Boer farm that Edmund remembered from patrolling the area. The house was invisible to the surrounding scrub, being situated in the sunken flood plain of a vast, ancient river which was now a dribbling spruit. The outhouses had been burnt and tumbled but the dwelling itself was only partially destroyed. The roof was gone in places but the walls were still intact.

They tethered their horses and set about preparing a meal for themselves with the supplies they had brought with them. Lewis gathered some dried wood and dung and made a fire with them while Edmund opened two cans of beef in gravy, emptied them into a pot and nestled it in amongst the burning sticks to heat. Then he went to the spruit and collected water in his billycan. He put four eggs into it and, after removing the bubbling stew, set them on the fire to boil. When the food was ready, they sat together on a large, flat rock and ate the beef with forks, straight from the pot, accompanied by hunks of bread torn from a stale loaf. They were hungry and, apart from the odd comment, didn't talk very much. The eggs they wrapped up in handkerchiefs to eat. The water in the billycan continued to bubble and fizz. Edmund reached into his pocket for a twist of paper that contained some salt which he passed to Lewis.

Lewis said, "You're right. You can't eat an egg without salt." He used what he needed and returned it.

The intimacy forced on them by the remoteness of the location, the preparation of a meal together and the unspoken expectation that each held of the other seemed to have a paralyzing effect on them. Edmund felt a powerful urge to remount his horse and return to the sanctuary of Bloemfontein, the peace and solitude of the convent garden.

A multicoloured grasshopper landed on Edmund's egg and sank its legs into the soft yolk. Edmund pulled it out.

"Meat in the omelette tonight, I see." He eyed the offending insect. "Though this monster looks quite capable of consuming me." He flicked the creature clear. "Which is not exactly what a fellow expects from his supper, is it? Still, if you were to put this on the menu at the Savoy, everyone would want it."

He finished his egg, threw the shell over-arm like a fast bowler into the thicket beyond, then stretched himself and lay back on the sun-warmed rock, closing his eyes and shifting his body to find comfort in the bumps and hollows beneath him.

"And speaking of which," he said. "I wonder who's on the Savoy terrace right now."

"No one."

Edmund opened his eyes to find Lewis lying on the rock beside him. He was rolling a stalk between thumb and forefinger, glaring at the twirling seed head that was inches from his face.

"The world is here," he said, throwing the grass away and turning his face to Edmund's. "If you'd only stop talking and see it."

Edmund raised himself up and, leaning on one elbow, he looked down at Lewis. He had such a beautiful mouth: wide, the upper lip with a flowing curve to it like the line of a bird in flight, the lower one plump and round as a falling wave.

"If I stop talking," Edmund said, "there's no knowing what I might do."

"Then, for pity's sake, hush."

They went into the house, threw a bedroll onto a narrow wooden cot and undressed. They were both hard already as they felt their way into an embrace that was so slow and tender it seemed as though they were afraid of breaking one another. Edmund pulled Lewis tighter to him and the feel of Lewis's skin against his own, along his torso, down his legs was delicious. He buried his face in the crook of Lewis's neck, breathed in the scent of wood smoke and gun oil, nuzzled the golden hairs which yielded like barley before a gust of wind. Their bodies took over and they broke from gentleness to urgency, swept along by a deep, muscular, crescendoing tide.

The rush and thrill as he spilled into Lewis was like nothing Edmund had felt before. His veins were pulsing from fingertips to toes, every nerve in his body was alive and aching, his heart was leaping, his head whirling. And then supreme joy and sadness overwhelmed him, not just his own, it seemed, but the whole world's, intermingling in his breast, surging through his whole being, bringing him, finally, to tears.

Afterwards, when they lay together, Lewis's head on his shoulder, Edmund looked up through the hole in the roof above them. The sky was unclouded, so brilliant, so intense, so truly blue that it hurt his eyes to look at it.

Chapter Forty-three

The Boer farm became a haven over the next few weeks. Edmund and Lewis went there whenever they could. They tidied the inside of the house and made rough repairs to one part of the roof so that at least the kitchen was protected from bad weather. They salvaged bits of crockery and other utensils and managed to get the stove working again.

"For the winter nights," Edmund said, though they both knew his company would be long gone by then.

This attempt at housekeeping was more an act of faith than a real attempt to bring order. It was an investment in each other that had little to do with the place itself.

During the day, they walked the bank of the spruit and found deep pools full of fish which they tried to catch. First, they sharpened sticks and tried to spear them but this method failed so dismally that they bought some muslin from a draper's in town and made nets which proved very successful. To cook the fish, they wrapped them in layers of bushwillow leaves and pushed them into the white-hot ash of the fire until the leaves were scorched through and the skin underneath was crisp. Often, these fish were so full of bones that the only prudent thing to do was to chew the flesh and suck the goodness from it without swallowing, then spit out the mush that was left.

Edmund always made the same joke – "That turbot is a bit off" – and it seemed to get funnier with every telling.

As soon as they discovered there were brown trout in the spruit, scarce though they were, they threw everything else back in favour of them.

Sometimes they went into the water themselves. The pools were too small and rocky for much swimming or larking about but it was nice to sink neck-deep in the icy water to cool off.

After supper they would lie in wait to observe a mother aardvark and her baby who always emerged from the undergrowth at sundown to attack the termite mounds that were plentiful round about. Later, they played cards or sang songs, each trying to be louder than the other. Sometimes, lying on his back, Edmund recited poems and ballads, declaiming in round tones to the moon and the stars above. Lewis did his best to outwit him by requesting what he considered to be obscure passages from Shakespeare or rhymes he remembered from his own childhood. What Edmund did not know, he simply made up and Lewis did not notice.

They made love with such intensity, such unalloyed and absolute pleasure, that Edmund felt longing like this could never subside. He was happy, too happy.

When they were apart, between assignations, the days passed slowly for Edmund. In his everyday life he found himself mining every conversation, every event, every nuance in the weather or variation in routine for anecdotes he could share with Lewis when next they met. All the time he was not with Lewis was spent in anticipation of when he was.

There were, however, certain subjects they did not talk about. One was the inevitability of their separation. The other was the detrimental effect that working in the Boer camp was having on Lewis. The hardship and loss of life that he witnessed daily had worked upon his nerves. Often when they slept together, Edmund would wake to find Lewis sitting bolt upright, breathless and trembling, eyes staring. And when Edmund asked questions all Lewis would say was that it was bad enough working in the damned place without speaking of it too. All he seemed to want, to need, was Edmund's arms around him, Edmund's body curled around his. And then he would fall, almost instantly, into a peaceful sleep.

Then, it happened. Edmund received orders that his unit was on the move again. They might or might not return to Bloemfontein.

It was their last evening together at the Boer farm and while they did the usual, ordinary things like getting supper and walking along by the spruit, the fact that this could be the last time they would ever do so, overwhelmed them and they were silent for the most part.

After they had eaten, Edmund watched Lewis from a distance, the evening sun so low and piercing that he had almost to shut his eyes to see at all. Lewis was sitting cross-legged on the ground with a leather-bound sketchbook balanced on his knee. With his pencil held out at arm's length, he was gauging the angles and proportions of a teak tree on the other side of the spruit. The tree was contorted, having grown up through a gap in the rocks and it made an interesting shape. Lewis gave it all his attention, his mouth reduced to a thin, tight line, his brow furrowed.

The truth was – and Edmund felt faintly disloyal even

thinking it – that Lewis would never be an artist. He was not particularly talented in that line. He had facility but his pencil strokes were not bold enough and his drawings lacked style.. What made him exceptional – and this to Edmund was revelatory – was that he recognized his limitations, accepted them and was happy still, just to create.

Edmund had only ever known excellence all his life. The very first time he stood upon a stage he knew he had the ability to transcend the banal, knew he had the power to touch men's souls. There was never any doubt about it. Had he not possessed that gift he would not have persevered with acting; there would have been no point. And yet it was that very pointlessness he so admired in Lewis. If the drawings were pedestrian, the spirit behind the hand that produced them was anything but. Here was a man who approached life in exactly the same way he did a sketch – with a nature so honest and open, so full of hope and belief, so heedless of other people's opinions that had he, Edmund, merely been told about such a person, he would have said simplicity of that kind, where it is not due to idiocy or cunning, was impossible in a human being.

Lewis snapped shut the sketchbook and tucked the pencil behind his ear but kept looking at the spruit and the tree, assessing them, as though in his mind's eye he was sketching the scene again and this time better. After some minutes he came back to where Edmund was lying.

Edmund put out his hand for the sketchbook.

"Can I see?" he said.

The drawing had failed to capture the sinuous twist of the tree trunk which was the only reason for tackling the subject. The foliage was too scribbled and shapeless to be effective, the stream looked static. It made a pleasant study but nothing more. A speck of dust appeared on the page and Edmund blew it away.

He stroked the paper to ensure no damage done.

"It's beautiful," he said. "Really beautiful."

Lewis shrugged his shoulders, more pleased with the comment than he wanted to show.

Edmund gave it back and, as he did so, he turned his hand over and brushed it against Lewis's palm. Their fingertips hooked together, caught.

"I love it," Edmund said, a shake to his voice.

Lewis grinned, put his pencil back into his breast pocket and buttoned it up.

Chapter Forty-four

January, 1901, and Lord Roberts, now ex-Commander-in-Chief of the forces in South Africa, returned to England to a hero's welcome. The ailing Queen, confined now to a wheelchair, received him at Osborne where she honoured him with an earldom and made him a Knight of the Garter. This was to be her last official engagement. Eight days later, Queen Victoria died.

The nation was thrown into a slough of despond. To lose a monarch who had reigned for sixty-three years was cause enough for mourning but public morale was already dangerously low due to the painfully prolonged conflict with the Boers. Barely realizing it, Britain had become embroiled in a futile guerilla war, with casualties mounting, as well as costs, and no end in sight. The British people, exasperated and saddened by what was happening, put their faith in Lord Kitchener, newly appointed Commander-in-Chief, to resolve the situation. Kitchener had unusual ideas about the best way to win this war and now he was in a position to put them into practice.

From the beginning the Boers had used space to their advantage, travelling lighter and therefore faster than their opponents. Kitchener set about curtailing this freedom of movement. He instituted a scheme whereby blockhouses – concrete structures 13 foot by 13 foot – were built all across the veldt, strung together by wire fences which created a crisscross pattern of barriers over hundreds of square miles. As a result, commandos would either cease to function or else be flushed out into the open and forced to do battle. The maintenance and patrolling of this 'blockhouse' system with its lookout posts and endless stretches of wire became the main occupation of many a British regiment in certain zoned areas.

Other units, including the C.I.V., spent their time further afield, sweeping across the country in an attempt to drive the enemy back against these wire cordons where they could be easily killed or captured. Every month the 'bag' was totalled and the results relayed. The figures were encouraging.

Edmund's patrol had spent all morning scanning the landscape for signs of enemy activity. They had seen nothing of note, apart from a herd of springbok and a fresh rhino carcass with a great hole in its head where the horn had been hacked out with machetes. They were about to turn back when a distant circle of acacia trees and a thin line of vegetation indicated the presence of water ahead and they set course for that instead. They walked the horses to allow them to cool down before getting there.

Edmund dropped the reins across his horse's neck and stretched in the saddle. He wiped sweat and dust from his face with the crook of his elbow. Now that their pace had slowed, a deadening heat radiated up from the ground and threatened to overcome him. Some way off, beneath the acacias, he thought he saw scattered rags and an aasvogel, a carrion bird, hunched perfectly still among them. It was only when they got nearer that he realized the shape wasn't a bird at all. It was a boy, a young boy, seven or eight years old.

He was sitting on the ground, arms wrapped around his legs, chin resting on his knees, eyes open but listless. Behind him was a scene of such horror that Edmund could barely look at it. Captain Peters covered his nose and mouth with his kerchief. What had appeared to be rags from far away turned out now to be corpses: a kaffir woman and two young boys. The woman had met her death slowly. She was naked, her breasts slashed, her thighs torn, her face so battered that her eyes had almost disappeared. Across her stomach lay a chunk of bloody meat, which on closer inspection revealed itself to be the poor woman's tongue, presumably cut from her while she was still alive. Sergeant Pelham, examining the body, moved the victim's head and a fly came out through her parted, blood-caked lips.

Edmund's stomach heaved.

The two boys who lay on either side of the woman had cleaner deaths, each shot in the head, their legs positioned in such a way that it looked as if they were running. A bloody trail showed that the youngsters had been killed fifty yards away and then dragged here. Judging by the amount of blood along the way, this had been a long, drawn-out process which suggested that it was the boy who had hauled them, quite a feat for a child this size. It was his final act of kindness, letting them lie in the shade of the acacia trees.

"All right," Captain Peters said, putting away his kerchief. "Let's get Lieutenant Hodge up here, find out what happened."

Lieutenant Ian Hodge was a reservist, a teacher of French and Latin by profession, who with his propensity for languages had taken it upon himself to learn several since arriving on the African continent. He was young, only twenty-seven, but had the considered slowness of a much older man.

He ambled up now and crouched down beside the boy, who did not move. He spoke gently, first in Afrikaans, then Baralong but the child understood neither. He tried another few words that Edmund could not identify. Still there was no reaction. Hodge patted the boy on the shoulder and stood up to address Captain Peters.

"He appears to be in shock, Sir, and he's dehydrated," he said. "It's possible he may be Tswana. There are plenty of them in the hills around here but, in that case, I can't communicate with him. I'm afraid I've exhausted my supply of languages."

The boy was given water while the search went on for a scout who could speak Bantu. A strong fellow called Mbeke was found who, when he saw the dead bodies, was so terrified by them that his mouth dried up and his eyes flashed white. He relayed the boy's answers in Baralong to Hodge but was too afraid to show any warmth or pity for the boy in his dealings with him.

"Well?" Captain Peters said to his Lieutenant. "Does he know who's responsible for this – this atrocity?"

Hodge cast an eye over the dead.

"These are the boy's mother and his two brothers," he said. "It happened yesterday. They were going to the market at Jacobsdaal to sell some mealie cobs when they had the misfortune to run into a unit of uitlanders who questioned them about where they had got their maize. Wouldn't believe them when they said they had grown it, accused his mother of giving information to the Boers and receiving food as payment."

"He's sure, is he, that it was uitlanders?" Captain Peters said.

"Yes," Hodge said, steadily. He had deep sockets that threw his eyes into shadow. "Our comrades in arms. They beat her, cut out her tongue . . . did other unspeakable acts . . . made her sons watch, then killed the three of them. Makes you ashamed . . ."

With the toe of his boot, he kicked at a stone embedded in the earth, kept at it until it was free, then seemed to forget about it. "Left this poor wretch alive to tell the tale and to put the fear of God into the rest of the blacks to stop them collaborating with the Boers. He says he wishes they had killed him too."

"Definitely uitlanders?"

"Yes, Sir."

Captain Peters looked tired. He let out a deep sigh. "The military police at Bloemfontein will carry out the necessary investigations. Send a telegram, Lieutenant, when we get to Brandfort. In the meantime we can't leave the boy here."

Mbeke was summoned again and through him further enquiries were made.

"He's from a settlement about six miles north of here," Hodge said. "Unfortunately, the Tswana use different names for all these mountains and rivers so it's difficult to know which ones he means."

Edmund dismounted, took a map out of his saddlebag and spread it on the ground.

"No point even looking," Captain Peters said. "These kaffir villages are here one day, gone the next. Nobody even bothers recording them."

Edmund looked over towards the mountains. He said, "Ask him what he calls the highest peak over there. Maybe we could work it out from that."

"Too complicated," Captain Peters said. "And inaccurate. We don't have the time to go off on a —"

"The boy surely knows his own way home, Sir," Edmund said, folding up the map. "Let him lead us."

"We're not ruddy nursemaids, Jeffers," Captain Peters said.

"Look," Edmund said, gesturing wildly at the slain family. "Just look. Our side carried out this revolting crime. The least we can do is bear some responsibility for the boy."

"And so we shall," Captain Peters said, turning away. He stood up in his stirrups to flex his muscles. "The nearest kaffir refugee camp happens to be at Jacobsdaal only six or seven miles away. I need a volunteer to take him."

"May I do it, Sir?" Edmund said.

Captain Peters spun around. He was frowning. He would have preferred an offer from someone else, but he said, "All right, Jeffers." Then, taking out his own map, he dismounted, laid it on a rock and briefed Edmund as to the location of the camp. Edmund checked for his compass and he was given a full flask of water and a few extra rations.

"You're only half a mile from the protected zone," Captain Peters said. "And you should easily get back to Brandsfort before it's dark. If you get caught out, bunk down in one of the blockhouses – don't risk travelling by night."

Edmund saluted.

Captain Peters hesitated.

"I'm warning you, Jeffers, there are Boers behind every rock and tree in those hills. It would be madness to attempt any . . . any sort of nonsense."

"Yes, Sir."

Half an hour later, when men and horses were rested and refreshed, Captain Peters ordered the company to mount up.

"Don't delay, Jeffers," he said, before departing. "And report to me when you get to Brandsfort."

Men and horses pulled out and Edmund and the boy were left alone. The child had remained in a trance-like state throughout all this, his stare directed away from the carnage at his back. Edmund offered him a drink of water but there was no response.

The corpses should be covered, Edmund thought. It was the

decent thing to do. From the surrounding trees he cut some small branches with his knife and kept laying them across the dead woman and her sons until the bodies were completely hidden by foliage. The boy did not look around once, not even when one of the branches, in a miscalculated throw, brushed off his shoulder.

Edmund knelt down and recited the Lord's Prayer over the deceased. When he was done, he sat beside the boy and tried to find out his name by using sign language. He suspected the child understood perfectly well but would not co-operate on the basis that enough had been taken from him already without his offering more. And who could blame him for that?

"We have to go now," Edmund said, standing up.

There was panic in the boy's eyes.

Edmund had to lift him to his feet and turn him round so he could say farewell to his family but the child fought this move with a sudden and ferocious energy, squirming and burrowing his head deep into Edmund's stomach to avoid looking.

"Let's just go," Edmund said. "Get away from here."

He lifted the child onto his horse, positioning him forward in the saddle to make room for himself. Gathering up a tuft of mane, he gave it to the boy to hold then mounted up behind him.

Heat rose off the top of the boy's head along with a whiff of grease and skin. His back was dry, dusty and his shoulder blades stuck out like wing buds. They rode on for twenty minutes or more until their way forward was blocked by the ubiquitous barbed-wire fence. Edmund took out his binoculars to scan up and down the miles and miles of intersecting wire, searching for a blockhouse. The very idea of dividing and subdividing the vastness of the veldt like this took a particular suburban mentality that was at once awe-inspiring and ridiculous. A wry laugh escaped him at the sight. The boy turned around to look up at him, his eyes fixed on Edmund's mouth as though he could actually see sound emanating from there. His eyelashes were long and so black and shiny that they seemed wet.

He said, with a gesture to himself: "Moruti."

His name, Edmund supposed.

"Well, Moruti," he said. "Pleased to make your acquaintance."

The nearest blockhouse was a mile and a half away to the west so they continued in that direction, keeping the wire fence on their right. Edmund talked – about what, he hardly knew – but his talking and the child's hearing him forged a link between them that felt comfortable. The boy's body began to roll with the motion of the horse.

As they neared the blockhouse they entered a maze of barbed-wire corridors designed to protect the outpost from night-time raiding parties. A British corporal stood on the front steps awaiting them while several native guards, rifles at the ready, watched from the upper storey. After a cursory salute, the corporal bounded down the steps.

"Any chance you got some smokes on you?" he said. "I'm all out."

Edmund leaned down and gave the corporal the pack of cigarettes he'd had in his pocket for the last month.

"They're yours," he said. "Keep them."

"Cheers, mate."

"How much further to Jacobsdaal?" Edmund said.

"Four miles. You'll smell it before you see it – filthy lot, those kaffirs. And the diseases . . ."

"I best be off," Edmund said, trying to ignore the disappointed look in the corporal's eye. Who wouldn't be lonely, stuck out here in the middle of nowhere with only a handful of natives for company?

"Keep to the fence," the corporal said. "And enjoy the scenery. Barbed wire as far as the eye can see." His laugh verged on the hysterical.

After an hour of riding, they stopped for a break – some water and a strip each of biltong to chew – but there was no resting out there in the open under that relentless sun so they continued the journey. The boy was tired, the vertebrae in the back of his neck standing out as his head drooped. Edmund began to sing a song. It was one he had known forever.

"Two lovely black eyes.

Oh! What a surprise!

Only for telling a man he was wrong,

Two lovely black eyes!"

Edmund had an incredibly weak singing voice. It was a thin tremolo, more out of tune than in, but the boy seemed happy enough with it and after a while, when he became acquainted with the tune, he started to hum along so that their voices blended to produce a sound, hardly joyful, but celebratory nonetheless.

Edmund drew back. Their unison was somehow disconcerting and he stopped singing. So did the boy. The silence that followed was deeper than any before. Eventually, the boy swung round in the saddle to face him, his brow wrinkled, tears brimming over. It was as though this sudden breaking off of the song was more difficult to bear, more bewildering than the half-blocked-out bloody events of his recent past.

To comfort him, Edmund sang again.

"Better, far better, it is to let,

Lib'rals and Tories alone, you bet,

Unless you're willing and anxious to get,

Two lovely black eyes!"

They got the stench from the camp a mile out. It came like

a punch in the stomach and got stronger as they neared, like gas and rotting carcasses rolled into one. Moruti bowed his head, plunged his hands in under the horse's mane.

Close up, the camp was nothing more than a collection of makeshift shelters covering an area of about five acres. Edmund had seen the Boer camp at Bloemfontein with its overcrowded bell tents and open sewers but this was worse, much worse. Here, there were no tents at all, only mounds of animal hides, blankets and in some cases, newspapers, beneath which people were sheltering. The inmates, all kaffirs, had wasted bodies and ghost-like stares and they squatted or lay down on the ground in varying states of lethargy. Even the approach of two strangers did nothing to rouse them. Edmund and the boy passed amongst them, sick moans on all sides. Human filth was everywhere. The watery eyes and blown-up bellies, the whimpers and grunts, the ground, the grass, the flies, the sticks, the stones, the very air, reeked of contagion.

A sergeant came out of the watch house, a man of middle years who had somehow managed to remain pale in this country where the sun burnt everything. His mouth, down-turned, signified either grim forbearance or cruelty, possibly both. He saluted Edmund, nodded at Moruti.

"Come for a holiday has he, Sir? He'll have the time of his life here."

Edmund dismounted, left Moruti sitting in the saddle.

"His family was slaughtered, out on the veldt."

"Unfortunate," the sergeant said, tapping Moruti on the leg, indicating that he should come down too.

"Slaughtered horribly," Edmund said.

"Probably no other way of being slaughtered, Sir," the sergeant said, with an air of disrespect that Edmund chose to overlook.

"What will happen to him here?" Edmund surveyed the camp. There was no movement anywhere. "Will he be put with a family?"

The sergeant exhaled loudly in a way that was almost a snort. "I doubt that'll be necessary," he said.

"Why not?"

The sergeant grimaced. "You leaving him here or not?"

"He's very young," Edmund said. "Surely there is someone who can mind him?"

"If he's lucky, God Almighty," the sergeant said. "And if he's not, well . . . we're back to God Almighty again."

Why, Edmund thought, was he bothering to ask these questions? This place was certain death for the boy. He knew it, the sergeant knew it and probably Moruti knew it too. The child was still sitting astride the horse, his bony shoulders and chest rising and falling with rapid breaths.

Edmund lifted him down but one of Moruti's hands remained tangled in the horse's mane and, though his feet reached the ground, he ended up standing with his arm twisted up over his head. Edmund began unravelling the coarse hair from around the small, sweaty fingers and while he did, the child, trusting him, kept his hand outstretched.

"I'm sorry, there's been a mistake," Edmund said, pulling away the last strands of mane. "He wasn't meant to come here."

"This place not good enough for you then? Jesus, what did you expect?" the sergeant said. "It's as good as any, I'll have you know."

"No doubt it is." Edmund lifted Moruti back into the saddle and then got up himself. "But I'm taking him home," he said. "Where he should have gone in the first place."

"You're mad. This isn't Maida Vale, you know. Go into those hills and you're in bandit country. If the Boers don't get you, the

Zulus or the Matebele will be more than happy to do the job."

"I'll take my chances," Edmund said.

"Bit impulsive, aren't you, Lieutenant?"

"Yes," Edmund said. "But usually in the wrong way."

"You volunteers are all the same," the sergeant said. A remark that went some way to explaining his poor attitude from the start. "Think you know better than anyone else. Well, you wouldn't want to be disobeying orders, you know. You could be in a sight of trouble if you were doing that. Just ask yourself, is this little nigger worth it?"

"Thank you, Sergeant," Edmund said. "That'll be all."

The sergeant went back to his watch house without saluting.

Edmund turned his horse. He didn't know why he hadn't decided this before. Probably, it was the fear of being found out that had stopped him. But when he thought about it, realistically, Captain Peters wasn't likely to be checking up on the whereabouts of a native child. No one cared what happened to the kaffirs.

They rode back some of the way they had come and then, guided by the compass and Moruti's prompting, veered north-easterly. In front of them, way off on the horizon, a rash of hills rose out of the plain – purple, orange, magenta – like beacons.

Chapter Forty-five

As soon as they reached the foothills, night fell like the dropping of a curtain. The pitch black forced them to rest a while and wait for the moon to climb high in the sky. Edmund lit a candle, took out what was left of their food supplies: a little water, some dry biscuit and a tin of Maconochie. This last item fascinated Moruti so much that he dug into the congealed fat, fished out every chunk of meat and vegetable it contained, and lined them up on a rock to admire before consuming them.

When there was enough light from the moon, they resumed their journey. The route was uphill and arduous, the ground slippery with loose stones. Progress was slow.

After a couple of hours, from his own knowledge of the area, Edmund guessed that the settlement was not far off but he was relying on Moruti to find the exact way. Which he did.

At an old, gnarled, stumpy baobab tree, Moruti turned in the saddle, a look of excitement on his face, and pointed to their destination.

Soon they were at the village, a collection of dome-shaped

huts surrounded by a high, grass fence and a great ditch about twenty feet wide. The grass gates remained closed to him but Edmund could feel eyes watching through the gaps. He waited.

The gates swung open and four men marched out, holding flaming torches aloft, but they did not cross the bridge over the moat. Behind them, an inquisitive crowd was beginning to spill out through the entrance. Edmund, remaining in the saddle, helped the boy get down. There was shouting. Nobody looked friendly. Moruti did not move from Edmund's side until a robust, grey-haired woman broke through the throng and walked across the mud bridge towards them. The child ran to her, threw his arms around her waist and buried his head in her stomach. Edmund suspected this was the grandmother and already, without any words being exchanged, she was weeping, gazing up at the night sky as though pleading with the stars to spare her this misery. She thrust the boy from her, quizzed him, presumably about what had happened to his mother and brothers. Moruti was crying and his answers prompted the woman to let out a high-pitched wail. She squeezed the boy tight against her and rocked from side to side on her bare feet. Other women came forward to console the pair, patting the boy and the grandmother and howling just like them. At that moment a line of young men crossed the bridge. They had Mausers – Boer guns – at the ready and, though they stayed back from Edmund, they eyed him with suspicion. They looked like they needed someone to blame for this tragedy. Edmund did not know whether to try and explain or just leave. He did not know what Moruti had said. Perhaps they thought he was one of the murderers.

Just then, another man emerged from the village. He came across the bridge too and the crowd parted to let him through. He was well over six feet tall and bare-chested. His skin gleamed in the torchlight. He carried a spear. He stopped in front of

Edmund and stared at him. He was so tall that their faces, despite the fact that Edmund was on horseback, were almost level. The young men with the guns closed in behind him.

He said, "They are dead?"

Edmund nodded. "Yes. A woman and two boys."

The man's nostrils flared, a shiver shot through him, the life drained from his face. This must be the husband, the father of the dead boys.

"I'm sorry," Edmund said, the words, even to his own ears, empty, useless.

When Edmund arrived back to the camp at Brandfort, he went to report to Captain Peters but found him already retired for the night so he sought out Lieutenant Hodge instead.

Hodge was sitting cross-legged on a blanket outside his tent. Beside him, a candle in a jar cast a flickering light over a game of chess he was playing against himself. He looked up at Edmund's approach.

"Ah, you're back," he said. "All is well?"

"Yes," Edmund said. "Sign me in, would you?"

Hodge reached back into his tent for the register, to which a stubby pencil was attached by a string. He checked his watch for the time and recorded it.

"You look done in," Hodge said, throwing the book back inside. "Join me in a shot of rum? Might fortify you."

Food was what he really needed but the offer of alcohol was too tempting to refuse. "Yes, why not?" he said, and sat down beside the lieutenant.

Hodge drained what was left of his own drink, then reached under the blanket for the bottle. From it he filled the metal cup that he had been using himself and passed it to Edmund.

"Sorry it's secondhand," he said, and went back to poring

over the chessboard. "Do you play at all?"

"Never had the patience," Edmund said. "Anyway, I'm that class of a twit who can't abide losing, not even against himself."

"I have the answer for that, my friend," Hodge said, and Edmund noticed now that his words were blurry, his lips stained from the rum. "Cheat, cheat, cheat. I cheat. Never used to." He continued to study the game laid out in front of him but his mind seemed somewhere else.

Edmund took a gulp from the mug. The liquid was syrupy and reminded him of throat lozenges.

Hodge said, "You know, at Critchley where I teach, we tell our boys it's not the winning that counts, but the playing. To play well is everything." He moved the rook, kept his hand on it, then returned it to its original square. "All a load of bunkum, of course."

Edmund did not speak. He felt he was required to listen.

Hodge continued, "I come from a very ordered world, you know. Bells ring to tell us when to get up, when to change class, when to eat, when to exercise, when to sleep. It's all so neat and disciplined and good and fair. We convince ourselves that we are preparing our boys in the best way possible for Life. And then you come here to find that all the rules have been changed, that nothing matters, only winning, that there is no order, that concepts such as 'good' and 'fair' do not exist and that you shouldn't expect them to." He pushed the chessboard away – some of the pieces fell over – and leaned towards Edmund, his eyes filmy. "There are some who will say they were only kaffirs but what we saw today . . . what had been done to that woman and her children . . . it sickens me to think we're on the same side as the men who did that . . ."

"The Boers would have done it just as readily if they had suspected her of leaking information to us," Edmund said.

"Because she probably was an informer, you know. The kaffirs don't understand this notion of 'sides'. Why would they? Has anyone, in the whole history of the world, ever been on their side?" He finished off in one go what was left of the rum.

"After being out here, I don't think I can ever go back to Critchley," Hodge said. "We should be preparing our youth for mayhem. If we do anything else, we are only deceiving them. And I won't do that."

"Don't, for the love of us all, let the little monsters grow up without aspirations," Edmund said. "At least show them the ideal – they might even aim for it." The tortured expression on Hodge's face made it impossible not to tease him. "So, I'm afraid it's down to you and your ilk to ensure that each new generation improves upon the last. Otherwise the human race is doomed. The future of Mankind rests in your hands, Hodge, not to be too blunt about it. So you see, Critchley needs you. And besides – think about it, old boy – who else would have you?"

Hodge laughed. He righted the chess pieces that had fallen over and stared down at the board.

"The boy is safe?" he said, without looking up.

"He is," Edmund said.

Chapter Forty-six

The military police in Bloemfontein conducted an investigation into the murders of the Tswana woman and her sons. In the course of their enquiries they sought to interview the surviving child and only witness to the event who, according to the report filed by Captain Peters, had been interned at Jacobsdaal camp. The register there, however, showed no admission for that date and the M.P.'s might have left it at that – there were so many people untraceable due to the war – except that the sergeant on duty, quite unnecessarily, had noted in the Day Book that a native boy was brought to Jacobsdaal on the day in question by a Lieutenant of the C.I.V. and then taken away again.

It was this discovery that led to Edmund being summoned to account for himself in a room at the back of the town hall in Brandfort. He entered to find Captain Peters already there. He was sitting in a rickety, wooden swivel-chair with his back to the door and he did not turn around when Edmund came in but continued, with his riding whip, to tap out a funereal rhythm on his boot. In contrast, the two policemen were conversing together by the window at the far end of the room.

Edmund stood to attention. The two South Africans stopped talking.

Eventually, Captain Peters swung around. He pointed to the policemen with his whip, a slight tremor to his hand.

"Lieutenant Jeffers," he said. "Kindly explain to these gentlemen and to me, if you would be so good, what you did with the native boy we came across on patrol last Tuesday."

"I took him back to his own people, Sir."

"Address your remarks to these officers, if you please," Captain Peters said, turning away again.

"His settlement is in the hills, six miles north of where we found him. I took him there," Edmund said.

The policemen produced a map and asked him to pinpoint the exact location which he did. There were other questions too. One of them had a list and they worked their way down through it.

"The boy said it was uitlanders who did it," Edmund said.

"Yes," the man nearest him said. His white shirt was almost blinding to look at in the sunlight streaming through the window. "But there are so many units currently roaming around the countryside, it's difficult to establish which one."

"Well, I hope you find them. They should be held accountable."

"They should be." There was an unmistakable note of doubt in the man's voice that Edmund did not like.

Captain Peters had not spoken throughout the entire interview but now he said, "Thank you, gentlemen. The matter, as far as we are concerned, is settled."

The M.P.'s dutifully thanked Captain Peters for his co-operation and took their leave. They closed the door behind them when they went out and it was as though with their departure all life was sucked from the room.

Edmund was rooted to the spot.

Captain Peters, facing away, remained motionless for a long time then, very slowly, he turned around.

"I know I should have informed you, Sir, of my movements," Edmund said.

"Is it your mission in life, Jeffers, to make a total fool out of me, a laughing stock? Because you're doing a damn good job of it. I give orders and you, an officer, choose to ignore them. Now, what message do you think that sends to every last one of the great unwashed under my command?"

"I'm sorry, Sir. I disobeyed and I apologize for that but in the circumstances, I —"

"To Hell with the circumstances!" Captain Peters bellowed, his face reddening now. "The message it sends, God damn you, is that anyone, even an officer can do what he damn well pleases in this unit and get away with it!"

"Yes, Sir. But if you had seen the place in Jacobsdaal you wouldn't have . . . You have sons of your own, Sir."

"Do not dare to mention my sons in this, or any other, context. The trouble with you, Jeffers, is that you have been insolent from the outset and I won't tolerate it any longer."

"Yes, Sir. But I was sure it meant certain death for the boy and I couldn't, in all conscience, leave —"

"Damn you, Jeffers, do you suppose you are the only one here with a conscience? I have a conscience." He thumped his chest. "I have a conscience." He got up, walked to the wall, turned, walked back again with forced composure. "My decisions must be made on the basis of what is practical and what least endangers the lives of my men. I cannot depend on conscience alone. Some decisions are hard to implement, painful for all of us, Jeffers, but they are made for good reasons. In this instance, straying into open territory as you did, you could have been taken by the enemy —"

"But I wasn't, Sir."

"You could have been taken by the enemy. Information, key information could have been extracted from you or you could have been killed. It's as simple as that."

"Nothing out here is simple," Edmund said.

Captain Peters went to the window, looked out.

"You are popular with the men, Jeffers, I know that and perhaps you do these things to curry favour with them. But you are misguided. Any idiot can have their subordinates' friendship – what you need is their respect."

Edmund said, "It was within my power to save the lad, to save his life and it was the right thing to do. Surely you understand that?"

"This has nothing to do with understanding," Captain Peters said, sounding very weary. "Haven't you learned that by now? You have disobeyed an order and you will just have to take the consequences."

"Then so be it."

"Very stoic of you, Jeffers. Easy to be noble about it now that you've been discovered. If you had declared yourself at the very start, I'd have more respect for you."

"Yes," Edmund said. "I'd have more respect for myself."

Captain Peters turned around. His anger had diffused but he had withdrawn to a colder, distant, more dangerous place.

"I will not be undermined like this, Jeffers," he said, fixing him with a dead stare. "As you know, I demand absolute obedience from my officers, it is vital to give good example to the men. And you – you have failed miserably in this respect."

He stopped, breathed steadily. Edmund couldn't quite decipher the look on his face, whether it was prompted by

418

disappointment or disgust.

Quite suddenly, Captain Peters returned to the swivel-chair and sat down, turning away from Edmund.

"It grieves me to do this," he said, "but I will be referring this matter to the relevant authorities. I do not like to have my officers court-martialled – it is demeaning for the whole outfit – but I am afraid in this case you leave me no option."

Chapter Forty-seven

The crowd was large and two rooms had been made into one for the occasion by opening out the dividing doors. The resulting space was impressive for a private dwelling. At the far end from where Marguerite sat was the grand piano, raised up on a wooden platform. The intervening area was taken up with row upon row of chairs but still there was plenty of room for people to mingle before the performance began.

The house belonged to Henry and Isabella Walker who were lately come to London from Edinburgh. They were young and wealthy and eager to be known in the right circles. Certainly they had made themselves popular with the local musical fraternity by offering their sumptuous home as a venue for the monthly recitals that no one else wanted the bother of hosting.

Marguerite looked about herself and found nothing to surprise or challenge the eye. The Walkers were too careful for that. The paintings were predictable, the furnishings and décor perfectly comfortable but conventional. There was some Meissen on display in a bow-fronted cabinet and, on a low table at the fireplace, an array of snuff boxes, carefully arranged. This air of restraint ran like a theme throughout the household. So much so, that the abundance of indoor plants – on windowsills, in corners, on pedestals – was like an intrusion. There were aspidistras, rubber plants, palms, ferns of every description, enough to rival the hothouse at Kew which seemed to indicate that somewhere a secretly reckless hand was at work.

Marguerite had come to the party with Herbert and Maud. Herbert was keen to find a backer for his next production and thought this the ideal place to find one. Maud was conversing nearby while Herbert had gone off to reconnoitre the room and establish what persons of note were present. Marguerite was sitting on the chaise longue where already several admirers had buttonholed her. One young man had been bold enough to request a lock of her hair, had even produced a pair of scissors from his pocket with which to carry out the task, but Marguerite had refused.

"There'd be nothing left of me if I allowed that," she said, more indignant than she allowed him to see.

How she missed Edmund! He would have loved it here. He would have teased the Walkers about all the foliage, of course, and likened their drawing room to a jungle but it would all be done with irresistible good humour. He would have told wonderful stories to whoever cared to listen. And later on, if he had been called upon to do so, he would have given one of his famous recitations, summoning up from nowhere the most devastating passion and dumbfounding the room at a stroke. The evening would be so much more fun if he was here. As it was, Marguerite was beginning to feel a little bored.

At one end of the chaise longue was a potted palm, a plant so large and ungainly that it leaned out from the wall and appeared about to topple over. Through its fronds she saw a man approach but, feeling disinclined to engage with strangers just now, she turned her head away and hoped he would pass on. The man, however, stopped beside her.

"Miss Davenport," he said. "Marguerite. What a pleasure to find you here."

Marguerite looked up.

"Dr. Hargreaves," she said, acknowledging him with a nod but not with a smile.

"May I sit?" he asked.

"As you wish," she said.

He settled himself on the chaise longue beside her, juggled with the cushions and shifted his position until he was fully comfortable.

"I trust you are keeping well, Miss Davenport?"

"In what capacity do you ask?"

"In my capacity as your friend?" he said.

"Ah, so the doctor-patient bond has expired?"

"Six months is a long time," he said.

"You would be the best judge of that."

"Your spirit, at least, is up," he said, in such a way that it was impossible to know what he was feeling.

She herself did not know what she was feeling either except that, though he irritated her, she welcomed his presence.

"What are you doing here?" Marguerite said, turning to look at him properly.

Here in this contrived setting, he seemed somehow untamed. She knew that he was unpredictable, that his behaviour was not formulaic, that feeling not propriety governed his actions. She looked around at the gathering and saw only people who were hidebound by convention. In a moment of whimsy it seemed to her that Cedric and the luxuriant plant life all about them were the only truly natural presences in the room.

Cedric Hargreaves confused her; he was a dichotomy. Despite the astonishingly athletic body, the powerful frame, he bore himself with almost too much modesty. He was a man of the world yet, socially, he was quite awkward. His bookishness was at odds with the spontaneous bravery she had witnessed firsthand. He was an intellectual, meticulous and incisive, and yet here he sat beside her, anxious-eyed, his brow furrowed, apparently hurt by her callousness.

"No, that was rude of me," she said. "Let me rephrase. May I ask what brings you here?"

"I made the acquaintance of Mr. and Mrs. Walker when their son contracted diphtheria earlier this year. He is well again, thank God – a lovely boy and here tonight. He and I had many conversations about music while he was ill. Anyway, on foot of that, I was invited to come and hear Mr. Whitelaw play the piano and to have a few glasses of champagne and possibly to indulge in some pleasant conversation."

"I'm afraid I haven't provided you with the latter," Marguerite said, lifting her glass to her lips. "Though the champagne is good and I am sure Mr. Whitelaw will not disappoint."

"I am not disappointed thus far with any aspect of the evening," Cedric said.

She took another sip of champagne, watched the other guests and let her attention slide away. She was not ready yet to forgive him fully.

After some time, Cedric said, "I think, shortly, that I will return to Canada."

With a little choke in her throat, Marguerite swung around to face him. Her cheek flushed as she realized how the speed and force of her response had exposed her.

"Oh," she said, trying, too late, to keep her expression blank,

"I am sorry to hear that. Your patients will miss you." And then, because there was a strange, empty pause. "Indeed, I will miss you too."

He observed her closely as a scientist would study a culture. Then, having gleaned whatever information he required, he averted his gaze.

"Your reaction interests me," he said, after a while.

"I am not one of your experiments, Doctor."

"I hope I have not been the cause of any grief to you."

"As I say, I am not one of your experiments and I do not wish to be dissected, especially not here, in public."

"No."

"I find you ungallant tonight. I have only ever seen you before in a heroic light."

"I am fallible, like everyone I know."

Marguerite sighed. She considered getting up and leaving him there but she remained seated. What she really wanted to do was change the tone of their conversation but didn't know how. They both sat looking in opposite directions and, as the seconds passed, it became more and more difficult to introduce a new topic. She glanced frantically around the room for inspiration.

Dr. Hargreaves said, "I seem to have the unfortunate knack of offending you every time we meet."

She softened. "You do," she said.

"God only knows what chaos would ensue if I actually set out to be obnoxious. A diplomatic incident, I should think – gunboats in the harbour."

"Then at all costs we should do our best to be civil," Marguerite said. "And I shall start. Now, tell me, how is St. Thomas's?"

He was looking right at her, into her but did not seem to hear her question.

"I said, how is St. Thomas's?"

"Oh, St. Thomas's. Busy. Yes, very busy. But do you remember Jordanswood?"

"It is unlikely I will ever forget it."

"I mean the trip to Altbury."

"You make it sound like a holiday excursion."

"It was very enjoyable."

"And the play. The play was very good," Marguerite said.

"That too." His smile was unsure.

She wanted to touch his face, smooth away the wrinkled brow.

Just at that moment, Lady Harcourt and Mrs. Dalrymple approached to speak with her and Cedric stood up to relinquish his seat.

"I will leave you to your friends," he said. "They are kinder to you than me. I bid you good evening, Miss Davenport." And away he went.

Throughout the rest of the evening, she looked for him, but there was no sign and she took it that he had left early. Mr. Whitelaw played beautifully but somehow Marguerite's heart resisted the sway of the music and as the evening wore on she lost patience with Schumann and Liszt in a way that had never happened to her before.

The concert ended and people were gathering their belongings, fetching their shawls and coats when next she saw him. Evidently he had been outside. His hair was damp from the night mist and the shoulders of his black jacket glistened with moisture. Upon his face there was a look of such intent as he approached her, that those around her fell away.

He came and stood beside her. His golden eyes, so troubled before, seemed at peace.

"I have returned," he said. "As you can see. And perhaps I will not be going to Canada after all." He paused, seemed about to fumble for his glasses then thought better of it. "Would you do me the honour of allowing me to escort you home, Miss Davenport?"

"Gracious, what has brought about this change of heart?"

"There is no change. You see, I knew my own feelings from the start . . . I was less sure of yours."

"How very shrewd of you," she said, not unkindly.

"When I came to see you at the theatre that night I could have succumbed so easily – I think I went with that intention – but I am glad for both our sakes that I did not."

Marguerite smiled. "You are a very patient man."

He helped her into her coat and they went outside to where there was a line of cabs waiting.

"You did not reply to my earlier request," he said. "May I escort you home? I promise not to argue. In fact, I shall remain silent for the entire journey. That way, we should get along famously."

Marguerite smiled, held out her arm to him.

"I think we could risk discussing the weather, Dr. Hargreaves . . . Cedric," she said. "It shouldn't come to blows. At least not on this occasion."

Chapter Forty-eight

Britain was in uproar. The lady philanthropist, Miss Emily Hobhouse, had returned to England from visiting the concentration camps in South Africa and she had news. She reported that conditions in the camps were so appalling that, far from alleviating the sufferings of Boer women and children, these camps were actively contributing to the deaths of thousands every month. To support her claims, she brought with her photographs of skeletal children on their deathbeds and countless testimonies from the internees.

But the Conservative government was having none of it. The figures put forward by Miss Hobhouse were inaccurate, they said. The inmates of these camps were not in any way prisoners; they had selected to be thus accommodated and surely they would only do that if there was plenty of food being provided along with a comfortable living standard.

Questions, however, continued to be asked by the Pro-Boer lobby and other religious and philanthropic groups about the running of the camps and the welfare of the inmates. Finally, to calm public disquiet, the Fawcett Commission was set up to investigate the controversy.

Everything Miss Hobhouse had said was confirmed by the Commission. The Liberal leader, Sir Henry Campbell-Bannerman, asked the rhetorical question "When is a war not a war?" and answered it himself with, "When it is carried on by methods of barbarism in South Africa." David Lloyd George went further. He accused the government of operating a "policy of extermination". The British public, horrified by the misery inflicted on Boer families in their name, were doubly horrified by the deception of their own government which had willfully concealed the truth from them. A shameful truth, now known to the whole world.

Charles Gray, even at his most cynical, could not have predicted what he now read in the newspapers. The disclosures of the last few months had thrown a sombre hue over the whole city but Charles' mood today was even blacker than usual. He had long awaited a communication from Edmund in response to a detailed letter that he had sent him outlining certain unwelcome changes at the Colosseum and seeking guidance in how to deal with them. That very morning a postcard had arrived from Edmund. The picture showed a covered wagon outside a hardware store with a man loading supplies into the back. On the reverse side, Edmund had written, in his customary almost illegible hand:

Charles,

Weather, hateful! Accommodation, wretched! Night life, verminous! Food, putrid! Reminds me of Scunthorpe on a good day. Stay put, old chap, no matter what!

Edmund

It was disappointing. Charles had hoped for more than this brief note in return. For the Colosseum was, to his mind, in danger. Not in the financial sense – in fact, the theatre was currently very secure. Since taking over, Violet had staged a number of cosy, domestic dramas of no consequence, each with an ending happier than the last. People were sick of hearing bad news from the war, she maintained. What they desired when they went to the theatre was to escape from all that. They wanted plays that reinforced the notions of certainty, warmth and love.

Charles did not agree.

"Our patrons want gristle to chew," he said. "Not pap to suck on."

He informed her – how could she not know? – that the Colosseum had a well-earned reputation for presenting serious drama. Loyal audiences expected to be challenged by productions here. Indeed, they would be disappointed if they were not.

Violet ignored his protests and continued to put on the kind of sentimental rubbish she actually seemed to like. It had to be said that these offerings generated a middling return. There were no disasters.

And then came *The Miller and the Maid*. From the very start, attendance was poor and it looked as though the Colosseum audience had, at last, overdosed on saccharinity. This could be the one to cost the theatre dearly. By the end of the first week they were playing to houses only a quarter full.

In *The Miller and the Maid*, there was a scene where the heroine and her friends went swimming in the sea. To achieve an ocean-like effect, the stage was strung with lengths of blue tulle which were lifted and shaken from either side to simulate the movement of water. The actresses, wearing swimming costumes 'swam' in this. Then, during its second week, in what Charles considered to be a monumental breach of taste, Violet persuaded the ladies of the cast to discard their togs and don a type of semi-sheer body stocking which, obscured by the rise and fall of the waves, gave the impression that the wearer was naked. It was a

429

provocative move and there was endless argument about it in the Press and at dinner parties up and down the country – but the end result of it all was that the theatre was full every night for six months after that and the Colosseum coffers received a very welcome injection of cash.

Violet was much praised for her inventiveness in saving the Colosseum from ruin.

Walter had the audacity to say to Charles one day, "She's just what this tired, old place needs, you know. New blood, new ideas. No one else could have got us out of that pickle."

"No one else would have got us into that 'pickle', as you call it," Charles had said.

Walter clicked his tongue. Was he agreeing with or rebuffing him, Charles wondered. Impossible to know this man's real opinions. He was an opportunist. He revealed nothing of himself except, when it suited, his ruthless ambition. Though it was wise to be wary of him, Charles could not commit to disliking him. There was, after all, something to be admired in his single-mindedness and he was, always, thoroughly charming.

No, Charles reserved his animosity for Violet. It was her recklessness, her complete disdain for the experience and traditions upon which the Colosseum was built that angered him so. She had no right to take uncalculated risks with this venerable theatre. The Colosseum was not her creation, it was Edmund's. It was Edmund who had slaved for years, fought off bankruptcy, built an empire. And she would dare to gamble with it, on a whim. She was too young, too protected to know what failure meant or to understand its full destructive power.

But his own objections were like cries on the wind and getting fainter all the time. Leopold owned ninety per cent of the theatre; Violet controlled it; Walter manipulated everyone in it. Together they proved an irresistible force. Against them, Charles felt his ideas, his beliefs, his style of management, his business contacts, his fiscal policies, everything about him was becoming increasingly irrelevant. It felt as though he was simply fading away from his own life and he began to wonder if he was an anachronism, a creature shackled to the old century, stuck in the past, condemned to obscurity like passing time. He needed Edmund here to convince him otherwise, to reassure him. Edmund was the only one who could make a stand.

"Charles." It was Violet. She and Walter had come into the office without him even noticing it.

Walter had sat down in the fireside chair. Violet was at Edmund's desk opposite – he would never call it Violet's even though she had long ago made it her own. She did not sit down. She was excessively pale today and drawn. Her eyes looked tired, though on closer scrutiny, deep down, there was a light in them. It was as though she was keeping all her vitality on the inside.

"Charles," she said, "we have decided to put on a revue, a satirical piece with specially commissioned songs in it."

"Yes, why not?" Charles said. "You have already turned the Colosseum into a bordello with naked bodies everywhere, so indeed why not a Music Hall too?"

Violet sighed. "You know very well that there is no actual nudity on stage."

"As good as."

Violet took her time, found her smile, and said, "Let us focus here on the revue. It is something different, I grant that, but even you, Charles, must appreciate that times are changing and we need to change with them."

Charles shuffled the papers on his desk. Instinctively, he hid Edmund's postcard under a pile of advertising circulars.

"And who is to write this revue?" he said. "Who is to write the music?"

431

Violet glanced at Walter, then back to Charles.

"That has yet to be decided," she said. "But Walter would like a creative input."

Charles suppressed his natural reaction to that prospect – safer by far to do so – and simply nodded his head. This announcement, he knew, meant that the revue was going ahead no matter what he said at this stage.

"George Grossmith would be a good fellow to have on board," Charles said, maintaining a neutral tone. "He can turn his hand to anything, even satire, I'm sure. And he is very funny."

"I don't like him," Violet said. "Besides, Walter has other ideas."

Charles looked at Walter who was facing him in the armchair, that famous half smile of his firmly in place.

"Yes, I have approached Patrick De Winter," he said, nodding and widening his smile to reveal flawless, even teeth. "He says he is interested."

Charles could not help himself. He said, "Not De Winter? Not that idiot who wrote the comedy about twins separated at birth, one brought up a cockney, the other a toff?"

"Yes. He did very well by it at the Hippodrome," Walter said.

"So we are trotting along after the Hippodrome now, are we? Whatever they do is good enough for us?"

"They made a handsome profit with it," Violet said. "Which is what it's all about in the end."

Involuntarily, Charles slapped the desk. "No, it's *not*," he said. "It's about making something beautiful that lasts forever in peoples' hearts. How can you work in this theatre and not know that?"

Violet rolled her eyes. "Survival is paramount," she said. "Commerce first, art second. You should know that, Charles. You are a man of business, are you not?"

432

Walter, with the briefest dart of the eyes at Violet, intervened to prevent things getting nastier.

"It is always an advantage to have a well-trained eye like Charles'," he said. "As well as unerring nous."

Violet, as if her hand had been slapped, pulled away and began rummaging through the pile of correspondence on Edmund's desk.

Walter continued, "If Patrick de Winter is not available, then certainly we should consider approaching George Grossmith."

Violet returned to the discussion. "You will like it, Charles. I truly believe you will. It will be topical." All of a sudden, she was carefree. "We can change some of the lines week to week depending on what is in the news. It will be fun."

"Perhaps, Charles, you could use a few of your contacts at the *London Times* to get us some attention," Walter said. "Along the lines of . . . 'attractive female manager, groundbreaking revue' . . . you know the kind of thing. There has to be an article in it somewhere."

So they had a use for him after all.

"I'll see what I can do," Charles said, because that was his job and because it was in Edmund's interest to keep the Colosseum afloat in whatever shape or form. "But I should think Edmund would disapprove," he said.

"Edmund is not here," Walter said, leaning forward in his chair suddenly, as though he had been waiting for this topic of conversation to arise so he could pounce on it.

"But he soon will be," Charles said.

"He may never return," Walter said.

"Perhaps you should prepare yourself, Charles, for that eventuality," Violet said, with some satisfaction. "How would you cope, I wonder?"

Charles chose to ignore this comment. He considered it

433

offensive that Violet should refer with such sardonic ease to the possibility of her own widowhood.

"Join us for lunch?" Walter said, as though all that had gone before was just friendly banter. He got up, clapped his hands together. "We could discuss other publicity ideas for the upcoming revue." Then, "We're going to Romano's. Doesn't even that tempt you?"

"Thank you, but no," Charles said. "I have work to do and I should like to take a little stroll before two."

When they left, Violet did not say goodbye.

Chapter Forty-nine

It was the dreadful routine of the camp as much as the horrors within it that wore Lewis down, the daily round of supplying too little rations and too little water to too many people. There was no respite from it. Certain thoughts hounded him. He hated himself for continuing to work in a place that was causing the deaths of so many, though he was unsure what other choices were open to him. When not on duty he suffered a kind of mental collapse so that even rituals like washing and dressing became monumental acts of will. He was enough in his senses to recognize that this was how Marguerite's illness began and he put up a fight. He started every morning with renewed hope and vigour but as the day's events unfolded this confidence waned. He came to believe optimism was just another form of self-delusion.

If he had been able to see Edmund he might have managed better. Edmund, by his very presence, would have convinced him that the world was intrinsically good. But he was away on manoeuvres, had been for eight long weeks, on a fruitless mission to root out what remained of the fighting Boers. It was becoming clear to Lewis that this war was so disparate, so immense, that it would never end.

Lewis was sitting in the tent, on his bedroll. In honour of King Edward VII's coronation, every soldier in his service had been issued with a special celebratory bar of chocolate. Lewis could only stare at his. The wrapper was royal blue and pristine, with a picture on it of the portly regent in profile. The other lads in the tent had eaten theirs already.

A ball of scrunched-up paper hit Lewis on the side of his head. He didn't look up.

"Davenport's expecting his to multiply," Stevens said. "Now, this might come as a shock, dear boy, but it takes two for that lark to work. Let me explain . . ."

Out of the corner of his eye, Lewis could see Stevens making lewd gestures with his hands.

Lewis began to rock back and forth. He didn't feel like speaking.

"Bloody idiot," Stevens said.

"That's enough." It was Georgie Carr from several beds away. "Let him alone, can't you?"

"Listen, Lewis, I'll trade you for that chocolate." This from Edgar who had rolled to the edge of his bed on Lewis's other side. "One pair of socks, guaranteed no holes."

"You can't bargain with him," Stevens said. "You know he won't answer you, thinks he's several cuts above the rest of us."

"I told you, shut it, Stevens," Georgie said.

"I'm offering two pairs of socks." This from Byrnes. "Two, and my cleanest long johns."

A round of laughter.

Lewis took up the chocolate and buttoned it into his breast pocket.

"Crack your face to smile, would it?" Stevens said. "Moody fucker!"

There was a sudden, violent movement as Georgie Carr made a lunge for Stevens, grabbed him by the neck and whacked him across the head.

"I told you already, leave him be!" Georgie said. "What does it take to get through to you? You know he's not himself."

Lewis, though he watched all this, felt oddly removed from the action. It was as though he was separated from it all by a pane of glass that rendered him untouchable, unreachable. He got up, opened the tent flap and stepped outside. The air was humid, almost a physical weight.

Georgie followed him out. He had a quizzical look on his face.

Stevens, from the safety of the tent, shrieked out after them, "Pair of arseholes!" in such a high-pitched, hysterical voice that the insult was instantly rendered harmless.

"Will we ever put manners on him?" Georgie said, grinning.

They walked away together through the maze of bell tents that housed the soldiers. The evening sun was low and there was still plenty of activity about with men sitting around brewing coffee or whittling away on sticks. Georgie, hands in pockets, stubbornly sauntered, so that Lewis was forced to hold back in order to keep pace with him.

"That fellow Stevens is a major nuisance," Georgie said, his relaxed tone undermined rather by his close observation of Lewis. "Mean-spirited." They walked on past a group of men who were doing press-ups together. "One wouldn't want to take him too seriously."

"No," Lewis said.

"Everyone hates him – you know that, don't you?"

Lewis nodded. He hadn't the energy or will to talk about Stevens.

After some time, Georgie said, "You're all right, Lewis, aren't you? Only you seem a bit . . ."

"What? Yes, I'm fine. Just need some time to myself . . . a bit of peace and quiet."

"That your way of telling me to get lost?" Georgie said.

"No offence meant," Lewis said, knowing that none would be taken.

"You're sure you couldn't use some company?"

"Sure," Lewis said. "I've got a job to do."

But still Georgie waited.

"Go on," Lewis said, breaking into a grin. "Scat."

"Then it's back to the lion's den, I suppose," Georgie said. "And if you hear screaming, that'll be Stevens getting castrated. Long overdue, in my opinion." He turned around, headed back the way they had come, lifting one arm above his head in a farewell salute.

Lewis watched him go, then made his way from the British cordon across the parade ground and into the Boer section. There were no fences to negotiate, no guards even, except the ones around the quartermaster's store and on lookout.

Lewis passed along the wide path that cut through this seething heap of humanity. Where the soldiers' tents were orderly and uniform, here it was chaotic. So many people washing, eating, cooking, crying, having babies, vomiting, defecating. From the latrines, channels of filth leaked out, making the ground soft and oily and putrid. Each tent was surrounded by stacks of miscellaneous items – no room to store them inside – pots and pans, chairs, trunks, candlesticks, washboards and tubs, a dog kennel, piles of clothes, books of music, a hobby horse, anything that it had been possible to salvage in that last, mad rush before their homesteads were destroyed. There was no space between tents, only clutter, though each family knew the boundaries of their own belongings. An object moved two feet to the right or left could spark a vicious argument and often did.

But even in the midst of this degradation there was to be found normality of a kind. The women were standing in groups, chatting to one another like ordinary housewives, their day's work done. The children were playing out in the path – amazing that they played, even on the brink of starvation. And now that the weather was warmer, they would keep going until nightfall.

Lewis was searching for Frieda but a quick look into her family's tent just off the main sweep told him she was not there. Probably she was out and about with one of her brothers. There had been of late an air of gentle distraction about her that seemed to suggest her mind was at a remove from the urgencies and grind of the purely physical world. And perhaps this mental absence accounted for the marked deterioration in her condition, for she was getting thinner by the day, it seemed, and he wondered if she was managing to get her rightful share of the family rations or if she was losing out to her five boisterous brothers.

He found her eventually out on the perimeter of the camp where someone had once attempted to cultivate a patch of ground then given up, leaving behind a square of mashed-up earth. She was crouched down here with her baby brother, Jan, showing him what fun could be had from a spoon and an enamel basin and plenty of loose soil. She picked up a handful of fine, dry dirt and let it pour out through the bottom of her fist. The little boy reached for it and laughed as it spilled over his hands.

"He thinks he's at the seaside," Lewis said.

She looked up, smiled at him. "We have never seen the sea," she said.

"Oh, the sea is marvellous – so wide and open and carefree."

"It's making you smile, thinking of it," she said. "You have a girl back in England, a girl you take to the seaside?"

"No," he said.

"My mother thinks you are . . . I don't know the word . . . '*soet*' for me.

He frowned. "Sweet on you? No, you're much too young for me."

"I am glad," she said. "Because some of the soldiers here, they don't care about that."

"I know." He looked away.

She stood up, leaving the baby to play on his own. He patted the earth with his spoon, gurgled away to himself.

"It would be good . . . to go to the seaside," she said.

"When the sun is shining you can't beat an English beach," Lewis said. "Brass bands, candy floss, buckets and spades, donkey rides." Even as he spoke he doubted ever having been in a place the like of which he was describing.

Frieda's eyes opened wide. "What is candy floss?" she said.

He laughed at her innocence. "Spun sugar. And not very nice either."

"I would eat it," Frieda said.

"I wish I could take you to Brighton. We'd have fun there." He was shocked to find himself using the word 'fun' in this hellhole. Surely that was some kind of blasphemy? His brain was fevered obviously. He fought against such thoughts, sobered himself. He reached out for Frieda's hand and slipped her the bar of chocolate. "Here, hide it before anyone sees," he said.

She gave a little gasp when she saw what he was giving her.

"Promise me you'll keep it all for yourself," he said.

She fumbled in the folds of her skirt for a pocket in which to hide it.

"Promise me," he said. "I want you to promise."

And then, Frieda's mother was suddenly standing between them.

"Promise nothing," she said, snatching the bar of chocolate from her daughter. She shoved it back at Lewis, prodding him in the chest with it. "We don't want your filthy currency," she said.

Her voice and accent were much harsher than Frieda's. Her mouth was small, ungenerous and above her upper lip there were deep, dark furrows. She had an indelible frown.

"No, I want you to have it," Lewis said.

"Do you think I am stupid?" the woman said, becoming wild-eyed. "So stupid that I don't know what this means?" She dropped the chocolate on the ground at his feet when he wouldn't take it back.

"No, you don't understand," Lewis said, in a low voice. "I'm giving you the chocolate. I want nothing in return. It is for you and your family."

"Then why you give it to my daughter and not to me?"

Their raised voices had drawn the attention of a few onlookers, women who drifted closer to watch, arms folded, passing judgement.

"Because I wanted to. Because I like Frieda. Because she is thin."

"He meant nothing bad, Mother," Frieda said, laying a hand on her arm. "He was telling me about his country and the sea."

"*Gaan weg!*" the mother said, rolling her shoulders as though ridding herself of a burden. "*Gaan weg!* You cheapen yourself with this type of man."

Frieda hunched and started to cry.

"The blame is all mine," Lewis said. "She has done nothing wrong, believe me, and neither have I. It's not like that."

He reached down, picked up the chocolate, offered it again. "It would please me if you would take this – enjoy it with your family."

The woman sneered at him. She bent down, scooped Jan up

out of the dirt, held the child so fiercely to her body that he seemed momentarily bereft of air.

"You have taken from us our country, our men, our homes," she said, ignoring the baby's whimpers. "You are killing our children in this stinking camp and you offer me sweets?" Her lips were wet with spit. "We hate you. Yes, hate you. All of us hate you, even the pretty, young ones who make eyes at you."

He hated her too, hated her pinched face, her narrow outlook, hated her for subverting his kindness, for not allowing him to prove his own decency.

He was trembling. He had the chocolate in his hand and he tossed it at her. It hit her in the chest.

"It's yours," he said, leaning right in over her, wanting to frighten her. "And know this. If I really wanted your daughter, I would take her for nothing."

The woman's eyes looking up at him were black, shining. She gave him a long, slow smile to show that the victory was hers.

The incident haunted Lewis for the rest of the evening. He was upset by what Frieda's mother had said but, more than that, he was appalled by the way he had reacted to it. There was no excuse for threatening a woman. The force of his anger and frustration had taken him by surprise, as had his lack of self-control. He would have said that this outburst was uncharacteristic but, the more he thought about what happened, the more he realized that it confirmed a suspicion already growing in his mind: that he was losing the battle to be himself. For surely the smallest cog in the machinery of torture was as necessary and as culpable as the largest. Therefore he, as much as anyone, was responsible for the contaminated water supply, for the inadequate rations, the lack of blankets and medicine. Every child that died, he killed.

That night he dreamt that he and Edmund were travelling together upstairs on a London omnibus. There was no roof and the weather was windy and cold. Because all the passengers, including themselves, were wrapped up in coats and scarves, it took a while before anyone recognized Edmund. But then, in a discreet way, one or two began to steal glimpses of him. A lady, very well dressed, smiled at him. Suddenly, a grey-haired gentleman took it upon himself to get up and make a speech in Edmund's honour. He stood at the front of the vehicle and bowed when he had finished. In response, Edmund raised his arms and on cue, to the delight of all, rose petals drifted down on top of them out of the sky.

The scene was so beautiful and unexpected that Lewis reached out for Edmund's hand but Edmund recoiled from him. The passengers now noticed Lewis for the first time and regarded him with loathing. He was sweating profusely, exuding a thin brown substance that was slippery and foul-smelling. The more he tried to suppress it, the more it seemed to flow. Human excrement was coming out through his pores. Stains were spreading on his trousers and his jacket. A puddle was forming on the floor beneath him.

Lewis woke then, breathing hard and in a lather of sweat. Naked to the waist, he had kicked off his blanket and was cold now. His body was like marble to the touch. He pulled up the cover but still could not get warm and lay there, huddled, unable to go back to sleep. He became acutely aware of every snort and scratch and sigh of his companions and a terrible restlessness of mind and body afflicted him. Eventually, without disturbing the others, he got up, put on his tunic, took his rifle and left the tent.

Outside, the air was crisp, the stars high and bright in the sky, which made him feel like his own mind was clear too. He went to the guardroom, a wooden shed raised on stilts, used his own key to unlock it. Ammunition and supplies were piled high around the sides but there was plenty of floor space in the middle.

He stood, staring at a box that contained a dozen spools of thin wire and was gripped by another bout of inertia. As the minutes ticked by his stomach heaved and he vomited, thin stuff that left a poisonous taste in his mouth. He thought about Edmund and the last time they had been together, how they had cooked their meal over an open fire and he had done the sketch of the spruit that Edmund said he loved. There seemed no way back to that now.

He lowered himself to the floor with his legs splayed out before him, positioned the weapon, released the catch. He pressed the barrel hard into the bone so it would not rebound. His finger shook on the trigger.

Chapter Fifty

The court-martial took place at Brandsfort. Edmund was dismayed to find that the trial was presided over by Lieutenant-Colonel Pattinson from Battalion HQ in Port Elizabeth, the very man who had, begrudgingly, given Edmund his commission. He was joined by two other men, a Captain Prescott from the Royal Engineers and a Captain Wainwright from the Somerset Light Infantry. The three officers sat side by side at a table that was too small for them, Pattinson in the middle, dwarfing the other two. At another table, set apart and angled to the first, sat Captain Peters and Lieutenant Hodge. Edmund was sitting alone on a chair facing them all. They were sworn in. The rain hammered on the roof above them and, despite there being windows all along one side, the deluge robbed the sky of light and plunged the room and its occupants into a deadening grey.

Edmund was told to stand.

"We meet again, Lieutenant Jeffers. I knew somehow that we would," Pattinson said. "This is a very serious charge. Disobeying a lawful command given by your Superior Officer."

He stopped short of following this statement with a 'tut, tut' but Edmund could read it in his eyes. If anything, Pattinson was even fatter than the last time they had met. The man's shoulders and chest heaved with every breath, his lungs labouring valiantly against the mass of flesh pressing down on them.

"You understand the penalty," Pattinson said. "If you are found guilty. It ranges from imprisonment to death, as this court sees fit."

"I do, Sir." Before entering the courtroom Edmund had been assured that the risk to his life was small yet the mention of the death penalty here caused him some discomfort.

"What is your plea?" Pattinson said.

"Not guilty."

"Captain Peters, what order did you issue to Lieutenant Jeffers on twenty-seventh of February last in relation to the native boy that you and your patrol discovered destitute on the veldt?"

Captain Peters stood up. "I told him to take the child to Jacobsdaal where there is a refugee camp for blacks, Sir."

"Lieutentant Jeffers, where did you take him?"

"I took him to his home, Sir."

"On what authority, may I ask?"

"My own conscience, Sir. The boy belonged with his people in the hills and, after what he had been through, he deserved that chance. At least, I thought so."

Pattinson leaned back in his chair as though no further proof of the defendant's guilt was necessary. His stomach was very tight and round and it looked like a ball stuffed up his tunic.

"Your own conscience, eh?" He glanced at his trusted colleagues either side of him. "This is what comes of letting civilians – actors – into the army." One captain grinned at this remark, the other frowned. "Well, let me remind you, Lieutenant

446

Jeffers, that in the army, not conscience, no, not even God Almighty himself, can override orders given by your superior."

"I did not regard Captain Peters' command as lawful, Sir."

"What?"

"I did not consider it lawful at the time and I do not now, Sir."

"Explain yourself, Lieutenant."

"Let me quote," Edmund said, and read from the piece of paper he had been holding throughout. "From the *British Army Officers' Field Manual*: '*An officer shall do all in his power to ensure the safety and wellbeing of any civilians he or his men come into contact with.*'"

These words were greeted with blank looks from the three adjudicators.

Pattinson sighed his impatience.

"In this case," Edmund went on, "I do not feel that Captain Peters did all within his power to uphold the boy's rights as outlined in the Manual. We all know that Jacobsdaal is a squalid place and full of disease. His chances of surviving it were slim. It was, in my opinion, wrong to send him there when we didn't have to."

Pattinson threw a questioning look at Captain Peters.

"I would not risk my men's lives, Sir, taking him up into the hills. Jacobsdaal was the only safe option."

"Quite right." From Pattinson.

"And I am not in the habit, Sir," Captain Peters said, a quiver to his voice, "of sending children to their deaths. I had my men to consider as well as the boy and I made the best decision I could under the circumstances."

"We could have brought him with us to Brandsfort," Edmund said.

"And do what with him, for God's sake?" Pattinson said,

447

getting red in the face. "Set him up in business, buy him a farm?"

"The nuns would have looked after him in the convent."

"Jacobsdaal was the right place for him," Pattinson said. "His mother was passing information to the enemy."

"There is nothing to suggest that she was and anyway, '*Let not the sins of the fathers be visited on the son*'," Edmund said.

"I'll thank you not to preach at us, Jeffers."

"That was the Bible, Sir," Edmund said.

"I am well aware of that."

There was a long silence while they all listened to Pattinson breathing. The two captains, neither of whom had said a word so far, looked more uneasy than ever, thinking that they were expected to fill the void.

But Pattinson resumed at last.

"Captain Peters, what is this man's record like?" he said.

Captain Peters began to speak but the weather had worsened outside and the thunder of the rain on the roof drowned out his words.

"Louder," Pattinson said.

Captain Peters coughed. Edmund noticed for the first time that his forehead was shiny with sweat.

"Lieutenant Jeffers has been under my command for twelve months," he said. "From the start his behaviour has been challenging, to say the least, and I have had to speak to him on a number of occasions."

"You had to 'speak' to him?" Pattinson said. "That's a bit limp, isn't it? Perhaps if you had taken the appropriate action earlier, Captain, we wouldn't be here today."

"Yes, Sir."

"In general, what is discipline like in this unit, Captain? I see from your records that field punishments are well above average."

"I do not tolerate any laxity, Sir."

"Either you are over-zealous or you have a bunch of ruffians under you. Which is it?"

"I would say neither, Sir."

"What proportion of your men are volunteers, Captain?"

Captain Peters seemed reluctant to answer. He shifted his weight from one foot to the other but there was no evading it.

"Approximately fifty-five per cent, Sir."

Pattinson's expression showed that he had got what he wanted to hear.

"Not soldiers at all then," he said. "Only playing at it."

"Hardly," Captain Peters said, with more than a trace of exasperation in his voice. "These men are now well-trained, they have seen action, they —"

"They are undisciplined. As your own punishment log shows."

"I am strict," Captain Peters said.

But Pattinson was not listening. He had turned his attention back to Edmund.

"So, not only have you disobeyed orders, not only have you undermined the integrity and authority of Captain Peters, but you as an officer have given the worst example to men who badly needed to be shown the best. Do you have any idea how serious that is?"

"Yes, Sir," Edmund said, aware now that proceedings were taking a dangerous turn.

There was another lull. The captains' pens scratched as they caught up with their note-taking. Pattinson kept up a steady tapping with his finger on the desk.

"Have you anything else to say, Captain Peters, regarding Lieutenant Jeffers' conduct?"

"Only that . . ." Captain Peters, his hands joined in front of him like a supplicant, had the anxious look of a man who knows he has lost control of the narrative, "I would like to put it on record, Sir, that Lieutenant Jeffers has many fine qualities. He is popular with the men and has displayed, on occasion, good leadership. In fact, he is one of the hardest-working soldiers in my unit."

Pattinson and his two cohorts sat immobile, evidently stunned by this declaration. As indeed, was Edmund.

Eventually, Pattinson nudged the man on his right. "You better make a note of that, Captain," he said.

According to protocol, Lieutenant Hodge was called upon as 'Soldier's Friend' to bear witness for the defendant. He spoke well but with an urgency that alarmed Edmund and hinted at the possibility that he and others foresaw a very unfavourable outcome. Hodge told the court that Edmund was one of those who had enlisted to join the war effort in the wake of 'Black Week', prompted to do so by the catastrophes that had befallen his fellow countrymen. In relation to the substantive issue, he maintained that it was not Lieutenant Jeffers' intention to disobey Captain Peters' orders from the first but it was more that as they travelled together, the boy's plight affected him and when the crux came there was no superior officer present to consult. That was when he took the matter into his own hands. Any soldier in the same situation would have been similarly moved.

When Hodge was finished, Pattinson cast his eye around the room. There were no questions.

"We are concluded, gentlemen," he said, getting up and leaving.

The two captains followed him out to discuss their verdict.

Chapter Fifty-one

Lewis woke up, a searing pain in his right leg. He was in a bed with white sheets and blankets. The walls were white, even the light was white and piercing. He closed his eyes for a minute to rest them. When he opened them again Sergeant Ridley was looming over him with his bulbous nose and skin the texture and hue of a pickled gherkin gone past its best. Lewis pulled back. Sergeant Ridley showed some mercy by sitting down on the chair beside his bed.

"You're in the hospital," the sergeant said. "And you've made a right pig's ear of that knee, shattered the joint. Christ, what were you thinking, a young man like you? You'll be lucky if you ever walk again."

"I had to get out of there, Sergeant," Lewis said. "I couldn't take any more −"

"Shut it," Sergeant Ridley said, leaning in much too close again. "Now listen to me, don't you go spouting that claptrap to anyone, you hear?" His voice was hushed though there was nobody in any of the neighbouring beds. "Now that you're back

451

in the land of the living those boys from H.Q. will be sniffing around and they'd be only too delighted to hear you ranting on like that. Before you know it they'll have you court-martialled and sent off to the military prison at Port Elizabeth."

"At least I'd be away from that camp," Lewis said.

"That's just daft talk. You could get a year in jail for what you've done, if you're lucky. They could decide you were on active service and send you to the firing squad, you know."

Lewis had not anticipated that eventuality. "Oh," was all he could muster.

"Listen, lad, I'm on your side. I'm here to tell you that if you play your cards right you'll be going home instead of jail." Sergeant Ridley pressed closer still. Hairs sprouted from his nostrils.

Lewis turned slightly away. The sergeant's proximity was more alarming than the prospect of any court-martial. He could feel the man's breath tickling his ear.

"This is what happened, right?" the sergeant said. "You were restless during the night, couldn't sleep, felt sick. You went to the guardroom to occupy yourself constructively, that is, in cleaning your gun. You were taken ill, threw up – the evidence was all over the floor – the gun fell out of your hands and went off. Shouldn't have been loaded, of course, and take one severe rap on the knuckles for that, but . . ." Here his voice changed to a comic falsetto. "'*It was all one terrible accident, Sir, and when can I go back to my unit?*'"

"I'm never going back," Lewis said.

"Not bloody likely, is it, the job you done on that leg? But you've got to play the game. Save that namby-pamby talk for your Great-aunt Ruby when you see her. You say the right things now to the right people and, I promise you, they'll be shipping you home in no time. You listening?"

Sergeant Ridley sat upright again and Lewis took the

opportunity to try and pull himself up in the bed in order to gain some height and perhaps enable himself to take control of this conversation but he found even the slightest movement was agony so he sank back.

"You know, that's not why I did this – to try and get home. And I'm not ashamed," he said, wincing from his attempt to move but trying to sound forceful at the same time. "I shall tell them the truth. I'm perfectly willing to pay the price for my actions."

The sergeant gave a hopeless laugh. "Look, sonny," he said. He had the air of a man who was summoning up every ounce of his very scant supply of patience. "You, along with all the rest of us well-intentioned idiots – they like to call us soldiers – well, we've been paying the price since first setting foot in this open cesspit of a country. In case you haven't noticed it, the top brass in this prehistoric circus that is the British Army are all either incompetent or mad, usually both. Poor 'Tommy Atkins', of course, is the fool in all this. Whatever he's asked to do, he just does it, including putting his life on the line for a bunch of power-crazed lunatics. There's not one of them gives a tosser for you or me. It don't matter to them if we live or die in the torments of Hell. All they want is tiffin at sundown. Think about it, lad, and you'll see that you've paid enough already without looking to pay more."

"I did this so I could stop torturing those people," Lewis said. "And the military authorities should know about what's going on –"

"They do, son, they do."

Lewis gulped. He stared at Sergeant Ridley's world-weary face and felt ashamed of his own naivety. He said, "I couldn't lie under oath."

"Why not?"

"Because a man's word is his word and it would be dishonourable to –"

"Look, these are the people who sent you up Spion Kop," Sergeant Ridley said, shaking his head so his cheeks wobbled. "They left you in a trench up to your oxters in the blood of your friends though they were too far away to see that. And now they have you starving women and children in the name of Charity. You think you owe them the truth? You think these people have any idea of what the truth is or what is just or right? I can't believe you would be so careless as to put yourself at their mercy. Because I can assure you they have precious little of it."

Lewis felt very hot. He lifted the blanket and waved some air over his legs.

"One cannot lie before one's God," he said, into the space beneath the bed covers.

"You are right, one cannot," the sergeant said. "Only God can look into the human soul and know the truth of it. Speak to your God all you like but don't sacrifice yourself on this other, man-made altar. Do you hear me?"

The heat, the sergeant's words, the pain, made Lewis fretful. He pushed the blanket down as far as he could but still didn't feel comfortable.

Sergeant Ridley watched him squirm. "We're the poor mugs, you and I," he said, at last. "And even we have to draw the line somewhere, this far and no more. You've a good record, Davenport, and I'm going to vouch for you, which believe it or not should help. With any luck you'll get away with this but you've got to watch that mouth of yours. Lie through your teeth, son. Lie and live to tell the tale. And this much I'll guarantee: when you get to my age, you'll look back and know I was right."

He stood up, groaning as he straightened and Lewis realized for the first time that he was old, in his fifties. He should be at home, fishing or going to the theatre, collecting coins, whatever his favourite hobby might be. He knew nothing of the man, knew nothing of most of his fellow soldiers beyond how they held their nerve in battle and whether they could cope with boredom well.

"Whereabouts are you from, Sergeant?" Lewis said.

"Staffordshire. Tiny place nestled between hills with nothing to mark it out but a pottery and a slaughterhouse and a lot of nosy neighbours." He sniffed, his eyes took on a vacant stare as if he had passed into some other realm. "You know, I often dream I'm on the cart-track that brings you up into the village from Penkridge. It goes uphill for miles and I'm sweating. As I get nearer I can hear dogs barking – everyone has dogs round there, great hunting country. Even nearer and I can smell bread baking in someone's kitchen. Maybe it's mine . . . That's when I wake up." He looked down at Lewis, back in the here and now. "Take my advice, lad. Go home, do what we'd all do if we had the chance."

Just as the sergeant said, two lieutenants came to see Lewis the next day. One was a large-limbed man with a loose gait, a long neck and a stoop that reminded Lewis of a giraffe. The other was smaller, compact, had very neat, thick hair and a well-trimmed moustache. He had the look of a man who kept himself always in check. He was the one carrying the notebook.

They stood at the foot of Lewis's bed and continued to exchange anecdotes about various horses they had known over their lifetimes, all of them great 'characters'. Only when this conversation reached its natural end did they turn to take stock of Lewis. The smaller of the two introduced himself. He was Lieutenant Masterson and his colleague was Lieutenant Smythe. They explained they were conducting an investigation into what they termed his 'disablement'.

They found chairs, sat down, and produced a pocket Bible. As requested, Lewis took the oath. Lieutenant Smythe, the one like a giraffe, rested his ankle across one thigh and looked about for something to take his interest. Lieutenant Masterson settled down to the business in hand. In a flat tone he took Lewis's personal details and wrote them down in the notebook.

Lieutenant Smythe swapped his legs around. He took hold of his shin and pulled it in towards him with the same action as an oarsman.

He said, "Forgot to tell you, Harry. Old Corkie came a cropper last night while out hunting. Won't be fit for the match on Saturday."

"That's a stroke of luck, eh? He's a cracking fast bowler. What happened exactly?"

"Ruddy impala took a sharp turn and Corkie tried to do the same but took a crash from his horse instead. Arm broken in three places."

"Ha, so even the beasts of the field have it in for him."

Smythe chuckled. "Nothing now between us and the Perpetual Cup."

Lewis could tell these were men who had not been long in South Africa. They were still, in their heads, living in England. He found himself resenting their cut-glass accents, the luxury of their upper-class world. He hated their graceless confidence, their affinity with horses, their ability to ignore human suffering, their willingness to concentrate all thoughts, all efforts, on the winning of a regimental cricket match.

They asked him questions about how he had received the injury to his leg and he lied with ease. He lied with a conviction he didn't know he had. He used the story that Sergeant Ridley had fed him.

Lieutenant Masterson took his time writing it all down. He handed the notebook to Lewis to read and got him to sign it. There was the faintest whiff of cologne off him.

"The Second Royal Fusiliers were at Spion Kop, weren't they?" he said. "Were you there, Davenport?"

"I was, Sir."

"I hear some of our chaps lost their sense of direction that day, ended up taking tea and scons with the Boers. Hope you weren't one of them."

Lieutenant Smythe snorted at this, anticipating sport of some kind.

"No tea and 'scons' for us," Lewis said, making much of this alien pronunciation of the word 'scones'. "We were hemmed in by the dead – the stinking, leaking, disintegrating dead."

Lieutenant Masterson gave a twisted smile. "Because you look the type of man, Davenport, whose first thought is for his own skin."

This from someone who probably had not yet seen any action.

"I enlisted before the war even began," Lewis said, leaving it to Masterson to work out the corollary to that.

"Now, listen here –"

"I say, Harry –" It was Smythe who had allowed his attention to be taken by a couple of nurses at the other end of the ward. "I say, we're finished here, aren't we? How about interviewing those two lovelies instead?"

Masterson craned his neck to get a good look at the two women.

"Not bad," he said, standing up. "In the circumstances." Then, to Lewis, viciously, "We have plenty more enquiries to make, Private. You needn't think this is the end of it. Men like you deserve –"

But Smythe had sprung into action already and was at the top of the room conversing with the two nurses. One of them gave a soft, high-pitched laugh like tiny bells being shaken, the sound of which seemed to distract Masterson completely.

"I won't waste my breath further," he said to Lewis. "Suffice it to say, we'll be seeing you again soon."

With that, he licked his hand, used it to smooth down his hair then went forward to impress the ladies.

Sergeant Ridley, in his sworn statement, said that Private Lewis Davenport was an excellent soldier who had been mentioned twice in dispatches and had never shown any sign of a wavering nerve. He had an exemplary record. The self-harming was, in Sergeant Ridley's opinion, an unfortunate accident.

Georgie Carr corroborated Lewis's claim that he had been unwell when the shooting occurred. He said his friend had a sick stomach all day, that he was feverish and that, after they had gone to bed that night, he was delirious.

In the end, the army authorities decided against taking the matter further. There was no case to answer, they said.

Given the severity of his injury, it was decided to transfer Lewis first to the hospital in Port Elizabeth and from there back to England where he would have to undergo further surgery to his knee.

The news that he was soon to be home brought no relief to Lewis. His mind was in turmoil. Why had he inflicted so serious a wound on himself? And why had he lied when he should have owned up to the fact? He hadn't thought it through properly at all. For what had he done, only engineered it so that he was going to be thousands of miles away from the one person in the world who could make sense of all this – Edmund.

And as if that personal loss wasn't enough he was, in addition, burdened with the feeling that he was living in a sort of moral vacuum. He had lied under oath. He had sworn on the Bible that he would tell the truth and then had not done so. What did that say about him? How could he justify perjury – his own and others', for Sergeant Ridley and Georgie Carr were involved in this too. They, it seemed, had no qualms and though they tried to persuade him to their view, they could not. For he was convinced that he had discredited himself. He had found out that he was the type of man who used Honour as some sort of yardstick against which to measure out daily rations – a little today, none tomorrow, the day after, plenty – and he was disappointed in himself.

It was arranged for Lewis to travel with an army supply unit as far as Fauresmith, from where he would be transported by train to Port Elizabeth. Nurse Reynolds, she of the sulky mouth and skin like milk, put his leg in splints and got him dressed early next morning. He was then taken by stretcher to an open wagon that was waiting outside the hospital. Nurse Reynolds, tougher than her soft looks implied, had quite a tantrum when she saw where he was to be put.

"It won't do," she said, to the sergeant in charge. "This man is sick."

The sergeant put on a face as if to say he doubted that but he relented all the same. More blankets were found and an old sheet was stretched over the metal hoops of the wagon to make a sun shield, albeit a flimsy one.

Lewis was laid into the wagon. His head was pressed up against a row of water butts, and even with several layers of blanket beneath him, the wooden boards made a hard bed. He was sweating so much that his trousers and shirt were stuck to him. The bandage on his leg felt too tight.

The wagon began to move. He'd had a shot of morphine prior to leaving the ward so the journey was painless but he was agitated and uncomfortable. The constant swaying of the wagon made him nauseous. Hours went by and eventually he fell asleep.

When he woke, they were stationary. He propped himself up on his elbows and looked over the buckboard at his feet. He could see lines of men waiting for food. Others were sitting or standing in groups, smoking cigarettes. It seemed they were situated on the bank of a wide river and he noticed the air was fresher than it had been earlier.

A sergeant, his face the colour and texture of crumpled brown paper, brought Lewis his lunch – a cup of Bovril and some dry biscuit, neither of which he could stomach. All he wanted was water, he said. He was burning up.

The sergeant handed him a canteen and Lewis gulped hard on it until it was snatched away from him.

"Have a care, mate," the sergeant said, wiping the rim and screwing back the lid. "There's others here besides you, you know."

Perhaps he meant there were others more worthy? Lewis's knee started to pound – the painkiller was wearing off – and his leg felt so hot that he asked the sergeant to take him down to the river's edge and let him sit in the water there.

"You sure you want to do that? There are Boers encamped a couple miles upriver so there's probably a ton of their shit in that pretty little oasis."

"Please," Lewis said.

The sergeant shrugged. "Your funeral."

He summoned a young private to help. They put down the buckboard and reaching over the sides, hooked Lewis beneath the armpits, slid him to the edge of the wagon and lowered him down to the ground on his good foot. The pain shot down through the bone of his other leg like an axe splitting timber. Although the sergeant and his helper supported him, the twenty yards down to the river were a torture. They took him some way out into the water, helped him to sit down in it, then left him alone.

Lewis, with his hands under him and the water taking his

weight was able to move out deeper until the ice-cold numbed his wound and the water came up first to his waist, then to his chest. Behind him he could hear the sergeant and the private talking together. About him?

"Well, it's no picnic for anyone, is it?" one said.

"Certainly not, but you've got to keep on, haven't you?"

Lewis tried not to listen. He was reminded as he sat there of the time they were crossing the Tugela what seemed like a hundred years ago. A bold soldier, full of high spirits, had dived in. This place was very similar, the same golden water, the same rainbow-coloured pebbles on the bottom. But the atmosphere was very different. He didn't know and didn't care what the name of this river was and it was unlikely there would be any rogue swimmer or any whoops of joy or cheering or spontaneous communal disobedience or affable officers looking on.

The current tugged at his trousers and sleeves and he felt insubstantial enough to be swept away by it. He contemplated his own insignificance then relieved himself where he sat in the river. He washed his face in the water to hide his tears.

The order came down that they were to move off. With his hands under him once more, Lewis reversed himself to the shore where he was helped up by the sergeant and the private who were waiting. By the time they got back to the wagon, his leg was burning up and the splints felt so tight he thought they might burst. He was helped back onto his blankets and chose to remain sitting with his back against the water butts. He pulled up his trouser and asked the sergeant to slit the bandages on his leg.

"Is that wise?" the sergeant said.

"I can't stand it any longer," Lewis said, almost pleading with him.

"You know best," the sergeant said.

"I'll leave you two lovebirds alone then," the private said, and ambled off to have a last smoke.

The sergeant's blade jerked as it cut through the crêpe binding his leg but, once it was done, the splints fell away and the pain became a dull ache.

Lewis pulled the wet bandages off. His knee was swollen and angry-looking with red, purple and yellow mottling around it. A piece of gauze clung to the actual wound, a pinkish, green substance seeping through it.

"Oh, Christ!" The sergeant turned away, rubbed his nose. Then, still with a look of disgust, he gathered up what was left of the bandage and draped it over Lewis's leg. "Let's do the bluebottles out of their supper, eh?" he said. For the first time, he spoke kindly.

He urged Lewis to lie down and patted him on the shoulder. His eyes were screwed up tight as though he was focusing hard on him now for the first time.

"You need to rest yourself," he said.

The rest of the journey was hellish. Lewis slept and woke and could not tell the difference. Edmund was there bending over him, his hair fallen forwards over his brow, his scent everywhere, soap and snuff intermingled.

He was put on the train at Fauresmith and taken off at Port Elizabeth without his even knowing it.

He regained his senses outside the hospital in Port Elizabeth in time to note the arched windows, the balcony railings around the roof, the quaint clock tower. It was like entering a fairytale palace. The interior was almost entirely marble, the coolness of which had a calming effect on him. He shivered. He lay on his stretcher looking up at the dazzling chandeliers. Boots squeaked on the floor, voices were hushed.

He was taken upstairs to a long ward where the windows

were catching the last glimmer of the evening sun. A nurse helped him out of his clothes and into bed. She hardly spoke but she smiled all the time and he liked her touch. The pain in his leg was different. It was deeper, more penetrating, as though the bone was being gnawed by a demented wild animal.

The doctor sighed when he examined Lewis's leg.

"This infection will have to be cleared," he said, as though Lewis was in some way to blame for it. "Only then can we decide how to proceed."

He wrote on Lewis's chart and showed it to the nurse who held his gaze for a second or two, then nodded.

"Nurse will get you tidied up," he said, making a circular motion with his pen over Lewis's injury. "And give you some medication."

Once the nurse had cleaned and dressed his leg and he had taken his tablets, Lewis requested a pen and some paper. He must write to Edmund, tell him where he was and what had happened. The nurse fussed around him while he tried to write but, yet again, he couldn't find the proper words with which to explain his own stupidity and selfishness and in the end he threw the pen and paper aside. He was gripped with a sudden fear that he might die here amongst people he didn't know. He felt he couldn't breathe properly.

The nurse soothed him, settled the bedclothes over him. Her skin had a freckled, rosy glow, like it had been buffed by a bracing English wind. That and her totally carefree smile somehow put Lewis in mind of a holiday he had once, cycling across the fens. He closed his eyes.

She patted his hand.

"You leave that love letter 'til the morning," she said. "You'll feel much better then."

Chapter Fifty-two

They had ridden twenty-five miles since sun-up and were tired. Thankfully, the wind and the rain that had whipped them mercilessly all day long had now ceased and the evening, though it was cold and damp, was at least tranquil. Edmund, sitting on a square of Macintosh, leant back against the trunk of a marula. He took out a notepad and pencil that he had borrowed from Hodge and set about writing the letter he had been mulling over for days.

15th September, 1901

Dear Lewis,

I have just spent the last two weeks in solitary confinement at Brandsfort. Not a pleasant experience! I shall regale you with the details when next we meet but I am happy to say that for once – in my own opinion, though not in the military's – I come out of it all pretty well.

But that is not important now – I merely mention it to

explain my absence. Imagine my horror, when on returning to Bloemfontein I found out about your accident which occurred while I was locked up. My enquiries established that you had been transferred to Port Elizabeth and when I telegraphed the hospital there they assured me that you were comfortable — though I will not be wholly satisfied until I see you with my own eyes.

There are the usual rumours circulating regarding the cause of your injury, that it was self-inflicted. I only tell you this because I know you will be worrying about it and I want to reassure you that while there are some who would damn you for it, most don't care one way or the other. For myself, I have come to the conclusion, belatedly, that to live with dignity one must first honour oneself. I suspect that this is your way of doing just that and therefore I regard it as a brave act.

I hope and pray that you are not in too much pain and that you will soon be on the boat back to England. With any luck this war will be over shortly and I can go home too and be with you there. It sounds so simple, doesn't it? And why shouldn't it be? When you get this letter — and I will post it as soon as I can, otherwise you will have left the hospital — please write to me. I am thinking of you always and won't be able to relax until I know that you are fully recovered and ensconced in Marguerite's apartment awaiting my return.

Now that I am back with Captain Peters et al, it is business as usual. We have left Bloemfontein for good. The troops with us are some Buffs Militia, Yorkshire Light Infantry, Australian Light Infantry and some Middlesex Yeomanry. We are like the Israelites wandering in the wilderness but without the benefit of a Moses to lead us. No one seems to know what we are doing or where we are going but one presumes we are part of a pincer movement to entrap De Wet.

The one thing we do know is that we are all miserable. Last night was the third in a row that it has rained and we lay under Mackintoshes, the ground turning to mud beneath us. All night long my hand rested on a little sketch you did of the pump in Bloemfontein — I keep it buttoned up in my chest — and I felt so close to you I began to worry that perhaps you were dead and that your spirit had somehow homed in on my heart. Stupid imaginings! I dismissed them at once. The thought of a world without you in it is just unbearable.

By the time we struck camp tonight, we were all starved. I was sharing supper with Ian Hodge. While he lit a fire in an old anthill, I took a string of horses out onto the veldt to graze them. I lay down on the scrub, even though it was wet, closed my eyes, listened to their tongues tearing at the grass, the chink of their harness, the rustle of their feet and I forgot where I was. I felt almost happy.

When I rejoined Hodge after an hour he had put together a meal of fried eggs, jam chupatties and cocoa. In all my days dining in the best restaurants in London, I never had a finer supper!! My turn to forage for food tomorrow but he has set a very high standard indeed. We think about food all the time. Amazing how the world shrinks to the size of one's stomach when one is famished.

He's a sound chap, this Hodge. From Scarborough originally, he teaches at Critchley where I am sure he is loved by the boys for his patience and kindness. He has what I call 'weight' by which I mean a concern and wisdom beyond his years. Even here, right in the middle of a war, you cannot forget that he is a teacher. And it is most encouraging to find a teacher who still finds so much to respect and wonder at in the world. He is always picking up stones to examine them and taking notes. Yesterday we were suddenly besieged by locusts which made us all curse to blazes and lash out murderously at the beggars. But there was Hodge standing still in the midst of them – trying to catch one, if you don't mind! He did and took great delight later in studying its hideous, red body and khaki wings. In your absence, he is good company. But enough of him. He is not you.

Over the last few weeks, I have had plenty of time to think and I have come to some very important conclusions. I miss you, Lewis. You are the best, the truest, the most beautiful human being I have ever met and to say that I love you – there, I have thought it long enough! – goes nowhere near describing the depth of my feelings. (Dear Censor, before you get to work with your blue pencil please be aware that the words I am about to write are ones that probably I will never utter aloud. I should, but as an Englishman I am genetically prevented from doing so! By all means strike out whatever poses a threat to the safety of our troops etc but an expression of love – even if you deem it inappropriately directed – is but 'a blossom passing fair, playing in the wanton air' and of no harm to anyone. So please be kind to us.)

I love you, Lewis. I admire you, I lust for you – oh the torture of it! – there is no remission, no sea of calm for this pitiable body. I want to get drunk with you, I want to lie beside you under the night sky, listening to the snuffle of nocturnal creatures. I want to watch you do the ordinary things – open a can of meat, shade your eyes from the sun, whistle in that way you do through your teeth that is more like pitched breaths and is criminally untuneful. I want to do other things too that would just look crude written down.

The moment we re-encountered each other in Marguerite's dressing room after 'Julius Caesar', I knew. One sentence from you and I was hooked, my spirit soared. If it happened so suddenly in a play I'd toss it back to the author and say 'Don't be so ridiculous!'.

Of course I would not admit my own feelings then but I could not ignore the pure joy I experienced on those afternoons we spent in Marguerite's front room, watching the street, talking, remaining silent. My God, even playing backgammon was fun with you! I suspect Marguerite knew the truth long before we did.

And as for those few — oh, how few! — times we spent together at the Boer farm, they were for me glorious. I felt so whole, so fiercely happy there that parting from you was like losing myself in a fog.

We will meet again soon, back in Ol' Blighty, with any luck and I will stand before you like a tongue-tied youth, I know I will, without any words to express the way I feel. Take me in your arms then, Lewis, put your ear to my breast and listen, just listen, to what my heart tells you.

Your ever loving,

Edmund

He folded the letter, put it into his breast pocket with Lewis's sketch. He would look over it again tomorrow night and see if he could improve on it but he felt so much better for having committed his thoughts and feelings to paper.

Chapter Fifty-three

A large plateau rose out of the plain like a miraculous eruption. Nestled into the base, almost flat against the rock was a Boer farmstead, a two-roomed shack with nothing to mark it out except the great white flag spread across its roof announcing the inhabitants' surrender.

Captain Peters called the company to a halt. Most dismounted to stretch their aching legs but Edmund remained in the saddle. He took his feet out of the stirrups and rotated them first this way then that to get the blood circulating again. He surveyed the scene.

On one side of the sorry little house a thicket of mimosa and bushwillow threatened to engulf it. On the other, trailing away, was a line of dilapidated buildings with doors hanging off their hinges. In front, a tiny pond served a handful of listless ducks and was clogged with droppings and moulted feathers. This was the only sign so far of any livestock about the place. The pens attached to the farm buildings were empty as were the kraals further out. The ground was strewn with discarded buckets and farm implements and a cart was upended. But just as it seemed the place was deserted, a dog started to bark from inside the house.

Edmund dismounted, feeling very sore. The trough seemed to have a fresh supply of water and he let his horse drink from it but stopped her before she had too much. The poor beast stamped her foot and shook her head in protest at being denied so he led her away from temptation and sat on the ground away from the rest, his back against a wooden fence post. He looked out across the veldt. A clutch of greenery miles off could have been a settlement of some kind but otherwise there was nothing human in that landscape. As he sat there, the vastness of their task – the army's task – seemed to press down upon him. Every day was spent like this, pursuing an invisible enemy. It was stalemate.

Ian Hodge came and sat beside him. He offered Edmund water from his canteen.

"I'm told it's nearly over," he said. "Even De Wet realizes there's nothing to be gained from stringing us along like this. They've lost. They should focus now on trying to win the peace settlement."

"There are plenty 'Bitter-enders' out there," Edmund said, "who might have other ideas." He reached into the pocket of his tunic for some dry biscuit which he broke in half, giving one piece to Hodge. He stared off into oblivion. "You know, sometimes I wonder if I'm better off out here, wandering around aimlessly," he said. "At least I'm doing no particular harm to anyone."

Hodge laughed. "You'll go back to the theatre when this is all over. That's where you belong."

"Do you think so?"

"Well, of course."

"Realistically though, do you think the British public will

have me after all that salacious reporting in the newspapers?"

"I don't see why not," Hodge said. "The British public, it seems to me, is remarkably resilient. They don't mind being aware of certain facts about a person as long as they are not constantly bombarded with them." He paused, summoning his thoughts. "You won't be returning as a war hero, not with your record, but you have done your duty by your country, and voluntarily too. I think they will respect you for that." He raised his eyebrows playfully. "Probably better that there are no more courts-martial however . . . But before you know it, you'll be back where you were, at the top of your game."

"Yes, at the top of my game," Edmund said. Then, "And you'll be back at Critchley. I always picture the place in full sunshine with sports days and regattas and smiling parents – ludicrously rich ones, of course, which are the best sort. Am I fooling myself? Perhaps damp walls and ink stains and boys falling asleep on their desks would be nearer the mark."

"It's all of those things," Hodge said, grinning. "And yes, I am looking forward to going back. I have things to tell the boys, important things."

Edmund got up and tightened his horse's girth.

"I was never any good at school," he said. "Failed at everything, even English. A four-year-old could spell better than me. Pitiful really." He patted the horse's neck. The crack of a rifle. Then another. Everyone dived for cover. Shots were fired back indiscriminately. The ducks scooted off the pond. Edmund found himself crouched behind the upended cart along with Hodge and Captain Peters.

Captain Peters peered over the wheel.

"I think we're only dealing with one," he said.

He signalled to Sergeant Harris who was fifty yards behind them to take two men and skirt around the back of the house.

Another shot rang out, followed by a cry of pain, and some kerfuffle behind the water trough.

A few seconds later someone shouted out, "One in the arse! Just a graze!"

"Sounded like the gunfire came from the Mimosa," Captain Peters said.

Meanwhile, the dispatched soldiers had entered the house and Sergeant Harris yelled out that it was empty.

"Let out the dog!" Captain Peters shouted back and he ordered the men around him to keep their sights trained on the animal.

A scruffy-looking creature like a miniature coyote came trotting out, nose to the ground. He went round in circles until he picked up the scent he wanted and with tail wagging he bounded into the Mimosa. They had the gunman's position now.

"Come out with your hands up," Captain Peters shouted to whoever was hiding. The Mimosa rustled. They all expected a figure to emerge but instead there came a frenzied bout of shooting. Several bullets buried themselves in the cart behind which Edmund and Hodge and Captain Peters were crouching. Another hit a metal blade on the windmill which was in motion so it ricocheted down along the rest of the blades like a stone caught in the spokes of a bicycle wheel.

Captain Peters ordered the entire unit to target the clump of Mimosa then gave the order to fire.

Nothing could survive that onslaught. They listened. Silence. The smell of cordite stung their nostrils. Then, there was a cry. It came from further to the right where the foliage was even denser and they had not expected a presence.

"*Piet? Piet?*"

The voice was light and Edmund's blood ran cold at the sound of it.

"It's a child," he said. "I swear it's a child."

Captain Peters looked over the top of the cart.

"Come on out now, boy, and you'll be all right, you hear?" he shouted. "Be sensible. You must come out."

But again the plaintive call, "*Piet? Piet?*"

"He's looking for his brother – or whoever it is we've just killed. Couldn't we let him be, Sir?" Edmund said, in a low voice. "The war is nearly over. What does it matter at this stage?"

Captain Peters frowned his annoyance. He shouted over the top of the cart, "Come on out. We'll give you one minute."

"Sir, we could just go on about our business, leave this boy alone. No one need know." Edmund sensed in the men around him an eagerness for this suggestion and several expectant heads turned to Captain Peters.

"That's enough, Jeffers." Captain Peters took out his watch, held it in his hand. "The minute starts now."

"The war is nearly over and we've won it. There is nothing to be gained from killing this child," Edmund said.

"Then let him surrender. And we do not know that this is a child. Or that he is on his own."

"Then surely with all our might we can disarm him, or them – take them with us as prisoners," Edmund said.

At this, Hodge sat back on his haunches and withdrew his gun which seemed to be the cue for several others to do the same.

"You're unsettling the men, Jeffers. Hodge, all of you, take your positions."

"Please, Sir, think again," Edmund said.

"By dishonouring the white flag, this person or persons has contravened the Geneva Convention. We have one man down already, goddammit. He could kill the next." Captain Peters was ashen-faced. "Ten seconds to go."

Hodge rested his rifle butt on the ground.

"We could try and get behind him, Sir," he said.

"The minute is up." Then, louder, as though to drown out any further objections, "I said, the minute is up."

"Sir?" Edmund said, placing a hand on Captain Peters' forearm. "Sir, I think you will regret this."

Captain Peters shook him off. He looked left and right but without seeing either Edmund or Hodge.

"Company, take aim!" he shouted.

Hodge, a look of terror on his face, reluctantly leant forward, one knee on the ground.

It was grotesque, an entire unit of British soldiers ranged against a single farmer's son.

"One last call. Come out with your hands up," Captain Peters said in a voice barely raised. A stillness had descended on him as though he was reserving all his energies for what must follow.

"Let me try and speak with him, Sir," Edmund said. "Please."

"Don't be ridiculous, Jeffers." Then, to the men, "Get ready —"

There was only one way to stop the slaughter. Edmund threw down his weapon, raised his hands above his head and walked out into the open.

"Hold your fire, men," Hodge said, at once.

"Jeffers, get back here now!" Captain Peters roared.

Edmund kept walking, wanting only to rescue this boy. He hadn't a thought for anything else. And what a glorious state it was to be in, his actions and motives unadulterated. Never before had life seemed so simple. Through the branches, he could make out a grey, felt hat sticking up behind a rock. What a wonderful notion, he thought, to go to war and keep a tally of lives saved.

Behind him, some of the men were clapping. A cry, "Good on you!" went up, and one or two cheers, followed by more.

"Stop, stop now, Jeffers, and we'll forget about it." Almost a plea from Captain Peters. "Stop, or I will fire."

There was hush. A click.

"Edmund, for Christ's sake, do what he says!" Hodge.

A sound like a crack and then it was as though his legs had been taken from under him. He was lying on the ground. Bullets whistled over his head, ripping up foliage. Leaves and twigs rained down. Beneath him the ground felt wet and he knew he had either urinated or else it was blood, a lot of it. He felt the kind of fear that told him he had never really been afraid all his life. A distant ringing came into his ears. Hands were laid on him. Someone was slapping his face, another was pulling at his thigh. He could get his own, warm, meaty smell. And looking down, spreading out from him, there was a deep red blossoming.

Captain Peters had shot him, actually shot him. In the leg, as was intended. But Jeffers fell, blood spouting in an arc over him, his leg shaking like it was trying to rid itself of an itch and Hodge knew straight away the bullet had hit an artery.

The sniper chose that moment to make a dash for the house. In a barrage of gunfire he was brought down within seconds. Captain Peters sent three men in to search the tangle of bushes and only when he got confirmation that there was no further danger did he allow the medics to go out to Jeffers.

One of them tied up his thigh with a tourniquet, the other pressed down with all his weight on the wound.

Hodge knelt down in the tide of blood and lifted Jeffers' head onto his knees for a pillow. The man was losing consciousness fast. He slapped him hard around the face to keep him awake.

The medics worked fast, hands quick and nimble, voices confident. The tourniquet was fastened, the talking ceased, a pulse was sought.

The man with his fingers on Jeffers' neck shook his head. He felt for his wrist. Nothing. Then he closed Edmund's eyes.

Hodge removed the dead man's head from his lap, replaced it gently on the ground. He stood up, walked away, turned to be sure of what he had just witnessed. A trail of bloody footprints led from the corpse. A man's life, he had a man's life on the soles of his boots. It made the very act of walking obscene.

The body of the first sniper was dragged out from the thicket, a fresh-faced lad of nineteen or twenty. The dead dog was thrown down by his side. The other one, sprawled out near the house was young, very young. There was no sign of a gun on him. Two brothers, so alike. What a morning's work.

Captain Peters was just standing there with pallid skin and staring eyes. He was like a man awakened from a bad dream to find reality was even worse. He knew, just like everyone else, that Jeffers' killing changed everything. That one act defined him now forever as an outcast. A knot of soldiers had gathered around him and he did nothing to disperse them.

"Fucking murder," Cartwright said.

The crowd swelled around Captain Peters. He was shoved in the chest and he stumbled back a step or two then he was pushed forward. The men were tightly packed around him and looking to vent their anger. Hodge dived into them, pulled and pushed them apart.

"Break it up, break it up," he yelled. "Now, before it's too late." He grabbed Cartwright, knowing he was at the heart of it, and shook him hard by the shoulder. "Call them off," he said. "Call them off and get the shovels, or you'll be facing the firing squad, you hear?"

"You saw what he did. You taking sides with him?"

"I'm taking the side of law and order and so will you if you want to get out of this alive."

Cartwright stared at him.

"This is your last chance," Hodge said, his hand feeling for his gun. "Get the shovels."

Cartwright slouched off, gesturing to his buddies to leave Captain Peters alone. By then, Sergeant Harris had joined Hodge and between the two of them they restored order and got the digging started.

Hodge went over to Captain Peters who was still straightening his tunic as if a smart appearance was his only concern.

"You all right, Sir?"

"Yes, thank you, Lieutenant."

"Fetch the captain's horse," Hodge ordered.

He helped Captain Peters to mount up. Once back in the saddle, the Captain managed to regain some of his stature. He rode up and down barking out instructions, supported now by Hodge and Sergeant Harris.

They buried the three corpses. The only grave to be marked was Jeffers'. They erected a rough, wooden cross with his name scratched onto it, as if anyone would ever find this place again.

Their work done, the company moved on. A silent, sour mood prevailed, each man lost in his own thoughts.

Chapter Fifty-four

When they got to Kroonstad there was an inquiry. It was headed by Lieutenant-Colonel Pattinson, who had come up from Port Elizabeth for the hearing. He was assisted by Surgeon-Major White of the Royal Army Medical Corps.

To open proceedings, Corporal Whittaker, who was one of the medics present at the scene gave evidence that Second Lieutenant Edmund Jeffers was shot from behind, that the bullet entered his body slightly below the left ilium in the pelvis and exited through the front of the thigh thereby severing the femoral artery. This resulted in a massive haemorrhage and the subsequent death of Lieutenant Jeffers within minutes.

Captain Peters was called upon to provide information concerning Lieutenant Jeffers' record. He told the Inquiry that Lieutenant Jeffers had received one official reprimand and had been convicted by court-martial for disobedience only a month prior to his death. Lieutenant-Colonel Pattinson himself gave the details relating to that case and added that he had found Lieutenant Jeffers on that day and on a prior occasion to be opinionated and recalcitrant, a difficult man to govern. When questioned further about the events that led to the shooting, Captain Peters said that Lieutenant Jeffers had chosen blatantly to disobey orders in full view of the rest of the unit and, in doing so, had undermined his authority as Commanding Officer. Also, he had endangered his own life and possibly the lives of others by his conduct. For these reasons, Captain Peters had considered it necessary to take drastic action. He gave fair warning of his intention to shoot and aimed for the Lieutenant's leg, just below the knee but with the target moving away from him, his aim was unreliable and he regretted deeply the tragic consequences of this error.

Lieutenant Hodge and Sergeant Harris confirmed the truth of Captain Peters' account. They were also commended for their prompt action in maintaining discipline immediately after the event and in averting a situation which could have become very ugly indeed.

It was decreed that Captain Peters had acted in accordance with various subsections of the Army Discipline Act of 1880.

In summing up, Lieutenant-Colonel Pattinson said that despite Lieutenant Jeffers' ignominious army career, this was a very sad case. A man's life had been cut short. But it should be remembered, he said, that Lieutenant Jeffers' death was brought about by misadventure. Captain Peters had acted with honour and done his duty and it was to be hoped he could put this unfortunate episode behind him and continue to soldier well as part of His Majesty's Fighting Forces.

"Hear, hear," Surgeon-Major White said.

Violet was notified of Edmund's death and the circumstances surrounding it.

There were plenty of English journalists in Kroonstad in

anticipation of the war's end and they relayed information to the newspapers back home. Thus it was reported in Britain that Edmund Jeffers, the renowned actor, had died while on active service in South Africa, shot by his own commanding officer in order to prevent him, in an act of gross disobedience, from endangering the lives of his comrades.

They were billeted to a school for the duration of their stay in Kroonstad and Lieutenant Hodge had formed the habit every evening of spending time in the sewing room which was largely unfrequented and where he could sit alone and write his letters home.

He had never been in the room at this particular hour when shafts of sunlight sliced through the window obliquely, casting one half of the room in shade while the other was radiant. He had positioned himself on the darker side of the room, in the cool, and was observing the shifting patterns of light across the floor and furniture, a sight which afforded him some strange comfort.

It came as a surprise when he looked up to find Captain Peters standing in the doorway. There was a heaviness in his stance that suggested he had been there for a while.

Hodge stood up and saluted.

Captain Peters motioned to him to sit down again and remain at his ease.

"We'll be pulling out on the seventeenth," he said, coming into the room. "Going to Klerksdorp, to protect the railway there." He dithered, then sat down awkwardly on the opposite side of the workbench from Hodge.

In the expanse between them lay a heap of fabric scraps, some scissors and spools of thread that were all tangled up together. Unfamiliar things.

Captain Peters coughed to clear his throat. "I never said thank you properly for that day – you know the one I mean," he said. "I have recommended you for a decoration."

"Thank you, Sir."

"But I wanted to express my gratitude personally too."

Hodge capped his pen, put it down.

"There is no need," he said.

"I was glad to have you there. You acted swiftly and bravely in a very difficult situation. I know you were quite friendly with him."

"It was . . . well, it was a terrible thing to happen."

Captain Peters nodded. The skin around his jaw line seemed to have loosened of late and when he looked down it bunched over the collar of his shirt. He got up and walked to the open window, leant with his knuckles on the sill and looked out, but you could tell from the set of his shoulders that all his thoughts were here, inside this room.

"No," he said, as though Hodge had asked him a question. "No, I was never a man for the theatre. But I was in London in '97 for the late Queen's Jubilee. Brought us all the way over from Lahore to join in the celebrations. We were assigned to Chelsea Barracks." There was a longish pause while Captain Peters looked up at the sky. "You remember what it was like, Hodge? Pure joy. People singing, people dancing. We marched through the streets and crowds lined the way, cheering and waving flags. We marched to the Colosseum – that was his theatre – to see a play that I can't remember the name of. He was in it, Jeffers was, played a doddering old man. Talented, really talented. When he came out at the end to take his bow, wig in hand, I couldn't believe he and the old codger were one and the same. I was shocked. He was such a tall, handsome, imposing fellow. I remember I was quite shaken about that."

481

The silence that fell seemed incomplete.

"I suppose that's what actors do," Hodge said, to fill the gap. "They convince you that what you see is the truth, only to have it all come tumbling down in the end."

"All very well in a play," Captain Peters said.

"You never mentioned that you had seen him on the stage, Sir."

Captain Peters' gaze fell from the sky and plummeted to somewhere below the window. "I had to do it, you know, Hodge, he had to be stopped . . ." He leant forward, further out of the window. "I know I did the right thing but sometimes I wonder if I did it for the right reason . . . He was very popular – he was all the things I am not and perhaps –"

"No, Sir, that is not what happened."

Captain Peters breathed out through his nose, long and hard, as though expelling unclean air.

"I did the right thing," he said. "Trouble is, now I have to live with it."

He turned back into the room again and looked shaken as if he had come face to face with a ghost out there.

"I was just thinking the other day," he said. "I haven't seen my wife or my children for two years . . ."

Chapter Fifty-five

Leopold Barrie awoke on the morning of his fifty-fifth birthday in fine form. He bathed at leisure, dressed and came downstairs for breakfast. Constance was waiting for him at the table and as soon as he was seated she handed him his gift, a gold cigarette case encrusted with emeralds.

"From Garrard's," she said.

"How thoughtful," he said, kissing her. The object was so slim and smooth it felt nice in his hand. He slipped it into his inside pocket.

Later on that morning, Violet called in with a present for him too. She was all talk about some project that she and Walter were working on and Leopold was not displeased to hear Walter's name mentioned so often. He was the kind of young man who did not spurn advice and who understood the world as he, Leopold, understood it.

"Is he good to you?" Leopold said.

"I beg your pardon?" Violet flushed. She put her gloves back on as if she was about to leave but then she said, "Yes, he is," with a slight toss of the head.

"I'm glad." He took the ribbon off the tiny package Violet had given him. "Just guard against the gossips. Remember you are a widow and still in mourning. Even if your husband has disgraced himself in more ways than one, it is beneficial to show grief. You are in a strong position, Violet. Don't waste it."

"As if I would," Violet said, allowing him the briefest of smiles.

He opened the box she had given him. Inside was a signet ring with the initials L.B. entwined around each other. He put the ring on his little finger. "Perfect, just perfect."

Violet bent down to kiss him. Her skin was cool.

"You are happy," he said. "I can smell it off you."

When the postman came, there was even more cause for celebration. Leopold received a letter from his broker informing him that now the war had ended his investment in Rhodes' company, the Gold Fields of South Africa, had doubled since the previous year. Should he want to sell, there were several buyers lined up who were willing to oblige.

He lunched out at the Ritz with Frederick Portman and Albert Mason, both of Baring's Bank and when it was discovered in the course of conversation that it was his birthday, the hotel took the liberty of presenting his party with a flaming Baked Alaska, along with strawberries in Armagnac and a bottle of champagne, all on the house.

At three o'clock in the afternoon, Leopold was due in Islington to officiate at the opening of a new library there.

He was met at the front door of the library by the librarian, a short, thin man, as deferential as an undertaker, who escorted Leopold into the library where quite a crowd had gathered in the main hall. He was introduced to the other guests at the top table – a councillor, Mahon Walsh, with whom he was already acquainted and a lady activist, Ada Lawless, with whom he was not. She was by far the more interesting of the two. Her features – a long, pointed nose and very high cheekbones – were sharp but stopped short of being severe and instead brought a wonderful delicacy to her face that was very pleasing to behold. Not beautiful by any means but she had the confident bearing of a woman who believed herself so. Indeed, he was quite willing to be convinced himself. She was wearing a close-fitting, burgundy coat with a velvet panel down the front of the bodice. Her waist was very slim. She took off her gloves and laid them on the table in front of her.

"What a marvellous enterprise this has turned out to be," Leopold said, looking around.

"He would have been delighted if he could see it. And so proud that it bears his name," Ada Lawless said.

"Did you know him then?"

Her cheeks coloured. "Well, not personally," she said. "I did not mean to give that impression."

"No, I did not know him either," Leopold said, to alleviate her embarrassment. "Fine man though, fine man."

The room was filling up with corporation officials and politicians and newspaper men. The last two rows seemed to contain ordinary people from the area. Leopold scanned the room, as he always did now. It was a constant fear of his that Marguerite Davenport and he might one day turn up at the same function – he had not seen her since that last day at Jordanswood.

The Librarian, sitting on Leopold's right, stood up to begin proceedings but no one took any notice of him. The chatter in the room went on unabated.

Leopold rapped his knuckles on the table.

"Order, order," he called out. A hush descended.

Taking this opportunity, the Librarian said, "I would like to

485

welcome you all . . ." His voice cracked. He cleared his throat, began again. "I would like to welcome you all to the newly erected Clive Potter Memorial Library."

There was a round of applause for this. The Librarian went on to introduce the guest speakers and gave a potted biography of each. He called upon Leopold to address the audience, describing him as a "most honourable gentleman, generous benefactor and devoted friend to the people of Islington". In fact, Leopold's contribution to this whole enterprise had been minimal. He had given a small gratuity, attended only one meeting and been selected, in his absence, by the building committee to represent them at the opening ceremony.

Leopold stood up. He blessed the audience with his most benign smile.

"Thank you for your kind words, Mr. Chairman," he said. He adjusted his cuffs before starting his speech. "Clive Potter, as we all know, was a great journalist and a vigorous upholder of children's rights. Through his devastating series of articles on child prostitution, he took us by the scruff of the neck and showed us close up the miserable lives of the innocents caught up in that most evil trade. Since his death in 1899, which I regret to say remains unsolved, a grand total of twenty-six brothels, all of them dealing in children, have been closed down in the Greater London area. That is twice the figure for the previous five years." Spontaneous clapping. "Clive Potter lived not half a mile from this very spot. He was loved and respected by all his friends and neighbours here in Islington and, therefore, it is only natural that his name should grace the front door of this most worthy venture. In these parts, Clive Potter is an institution. And that is true, quite literally now." A murmur of amusement went round the room. "Every time that door opens . . ." he pointed over the heads of the audience, "Clive Potter's memory is kept alive." After this, there was a huge round of applause, with some of the pressmen whistling and stamping their feet.

Councillor Mahon Walsh was next to speak. He described in painful detail how the building work was undertaken from the laying of the first brick to the choosing of the paintings on the walls.

Ada Lawless spoke about the benefits of books and reading for all children but especially for those who were deprived in other areas of their lives. She had great poise and was very sure of her subject, demonstrating each point she made with carefully chosen statistics. On the side of her neck, there was a tantalizing little mole which was either covered up entirely by the collar of her coat or else just visible, depending upon which way she moved her head. For the duration of her speech, Leopold could not take his eyes off it.

Afterwards, tea was served, the guest speakers remaining at the top table to have theirs.

"That was a very fine talk you gave," Leopold said to Ada.

"We women have voices too," she said.

"Believe me, I know it," Leopold said. "And mostly of the scolding variety. I am a martyr to the women in my house."

Ada raised an eyebrow. She was older than he had at first thought. Thirtyish.

"Perhaps you deserve it," she said.

"I hope so," he said.

She smiled ever so faintly but he could see she was amused.

"You know a lot about children and the way they learn," he said.

"I used to teach."

"Did you indeed?" He eyed her fine coat, let his eyes wander over her bust-line. She had diamond rings on her fingers, an antique gold bracelet on her wrist. She was old stock. "You would never pass for a schoolteacher," he said.

She took this as it was meant, a compliment, and gave him a broad smile.

"When I was growing up in Cambridgeshire," she said, "we had a school on our estate for the tenants' children and I taught there."

Her eyes were turquoise, very light in colour as though they didn't have their full quota of pigment.

"What fortunate children they were," he said. "To have you as their teacher."

"Oh, I only taught when I felt like it," she said. "I'm a great believer in being free to do as one feels."

"Then I hope for your sake you will always be rich and beautiful," he said. "Because, take it from me, we are the only people who can get away with it."

She laughed out loud at that, then was whisked away from his company by the Librarian who had a delegation from a local school waiting to meet her. He watched as she moved smoothly through the crowd, followed her with his eyes until he became aware of another presence at his shoulder.

He turned around to find a woman standing there. He had noticed her earlier because she was striking, despite her unkempt appearance. She was holding by the hand a child of about three, presumably her daughter. Both of them had the same shock of wild red hair, made all the more startling by the drabness of their attire. There the resemblance between the two of them ended, because the child was exceedingly plain.

"Didn't recognize 'oo you were talking about," the woman said.

"I beg your pardon?"

"Potter," she said. "Clive Potter. That wasn't 'im at all. Only thing 'e ever did that was any good, was create 'er." She indicated the child. "And that was by accident."

Leopold looked at the little girl. Her eyebrows joined across the nose.

"When you are older, you will come and use this library," he said to her, trying to sound as though he liked her. "And you'll grow up to be very proud of your father."

"Not if I have aught to do with it," the woman said.

"What is your name?" Leopold said, straightening up and addressing the woman full on.

"Rosalind Doyle."

"And why are you here, Rosalind, if only to scoff?"

"To see what kind of 'ero you made of 'im."

"So you do not approve?"

"It's what I thought. No one in this room knew 'im but me. That Clive Potter you were talking about is like someone out of a story."

"A fiction created as much by himself, I am sure, as by anyone else," Leopold said. "But what do you want me to do? Stand up and announce to the world that he wasn't like that at all, undo whatever good has come of his life?"

"No," she said. "Wouldn't be no point to that. It just 'as to be said, is all. The truth gets lost much too easily and then we can't find it when we need it."

"The truth about any of us is only what we allow others to see of ourselves," Leopold said. He did not know why he was being so frank with her except that he found it useful sometimes to clarify his own thinking on such matters. "Which means that, for the most part, we spend our lives engaging in a lethal juggling act. Very important not to have greasy fingers."

"And what do you do, Lord Barrie, when you're juggling and you drop a ball, as you must sometimes?" Rosalind said. "Hide it?"

Leopold froze. "You overstep your mark," he said.

489

"That's the beauty of being a woman in my position. There ain't no marks."

Leopold reached into his pocket thinking, at this juncture, that money was required to get rid of her.

"Don't you dare," she said. "I'm well provided for. Got me own 'ouse, if you can believe that. My poor old aunt looked after me in 'er will. Which is more than 'e, Potter, did. I may not 'ave status, but I do 'ave means." She patted the child's hand. "Come on, sweet'eart, let's leave them to their game."

Leopold was oddly shaken by this exchange but he hid it well and mingled with the guests anyhow. He was much in demand, was guided from one group to the next and introduced all round.

One lady clutched at his arm.

"Lord Leopold," she said. "Thank you for creating such a splendid monument to Mr. Potter – this library is magnificent."

Politicians shook his hand and congratulated him on a job well done. They said the people of Islington, the people of London in general, owed him a very great debt.

He looked around for Ada Lawless in order to say goodbye to her and saw that she was shaking hands and bidding farewell to various officials outside the front door.

By the time he got there, she was already sitting in a hansom cab but Leopold raised his arm to stop the driver from pulling out.

"Miss Lawless," he said, approaching the cab and speaking to her through the lowered window, "are you, by any chance, going to King's Cross Station? Perhaps we could share."

"No, Lord Barrie." Her smile was teasing. "Going in the opposite direction actually. Hampstead."

"Hampstead, eh? Then give me a moment . . . let me think of an excuse for going to Hampstead . . ."

"Do you need an excuse?" she said.

"Not if you don't."

Ada pushed open the door of the hansom. "Then you are very welcome to join me," she said, moving over.

Leopold was barely settled in the seat when he reached for her hand. His forearm rested on her thigh, which was full and firm. He looked at her. Her lips were parted as she waited for him, on the brink. Never before had he been so bold with a woman on first meeting her.

Chapter Fifty-six

It was unseasonably cold and damp for May and the pavement was gritty beneath Charles Gray's shoes as he walked over Westminster Bridge. He headed down onto the Albert Embankment where he found an empty bench to sit on, the hospital at his back. He watched the passers-by — a few elderly gentlemen out for their morning strolls and a large party of German tourists, all of them dressed in knickerbockers and brogues and carrying alpenstocks, looking more suited to climbing mountains than sightseeing in the city.

He didn't have long to wait. After a few minutes, he spotted Lewis Davenport coming towards him from the Lambeth side but was surprised to see he had a limp and was proceeding slowly. As he came nearer, it became evident from the look of grim determination on his face that walking was quite difficult for him. He carried no crutch or stick to support himself but took his time, stopping for breath whenever necessary.

They exchanged greetings. Charles thanked him for coming. Lewis was panting slightly. He sat down awkwardly with his bad leg, rigid, stuck out in front of him.

"I didn't know you were injured out there," Charles said.

Lewis leaned forward and tapped his shin which produced a sound like wood.

"Oh good God," Charles said, "I'm so sorry, never realized . . ."

"Much more practical than flesh and blood, I can assure you," Lewis said, laughing at Charles' discomfiture. "I can hop across streams without getting my good foot wet. And stir hot coals with it, though there is a danger of charring, as you can see." He pulled up his trouser leg to reveal some blackening around the ankle.

Charles fought back a desire to laugh.

"But what . . . how . . .? Really, Lewis, you do know how to astound. Will you be permanently . . .?"

"Well, unless I sprout another limb . . ."

"Yes, of course, silly of me. But how did it happen?"

"Self-inflicted, I'm afraid. I was working in the concentration camp at Bloemfontein which was a hell-hole. Couldn't watch those people any more so I invalided myself out of it. With hindsight, I should have done something braver than that."

"You're very open about it," Charles said.

"Unfortunately, the wound got infected and the doctors had to take the leg off. Just here . . ." He made a sawing motion across his thigh.

"That's terrible."

Lewis shrugged his shoulders.

Charles said, "Thanks to Miss Hobhouse, every jack rabbit in the country knows about the horrors in those camps, the terrible death rates, our own government's cover-up . . ." He considered for a moment before going on. "But perhaps it would be wiser, Lewis, not to be so candid about the cause of your injury . . . for your own sake . . . you know how people view these things."

Lewis laughed. "Yes, but I'm rather enjoying my disgrace," he said. "I take great satisfaction in reminding anyone who criticizes me that the British Government and the military have come out of this war a lot more damaged than me. At least I'm still walking – just about – but they've been hanged, drawn and quartered over the affair. And now that it's all over just wait 'til the British public is presented with the bill for all this folly." He scratched his head violently. "I'm afraid I'm rather disillusioned."

"You have reason to be. I'm sorry about your –" Charles nodded at the artificial leg.

"Don't be," Lewis said. "I'm rather proud of it."

A nurse came along, pushing a perambulator with an infant inside roaring its lungs out. Both men's eyes rested on the woman as she stopped near them and tried to soothe the baby by smiling and saying pretty things to it and jiggling the pram. In the end she gave up and continued on her way with the child wailing.

Charles, not ready quite just yet to get to the crux of their meeting, said, "Marguerite is splendid as Hedda Gabler. I saw her last night. It looks set to run and run."

Lewis stiffened. "Yes. She has recovered remarkably well, considering the ordeal she was subjected to." There was no mistaking the admonishment in his voice. "Thank God for Cedric, is all I can say."

"I should make it perfectly clear to you, Lewis, that none of us was aware what the true nature of Jordanswood was. We were all under the misapprehension that it was a convalescent home of some sort. We trusted Leopold to act honourably and fairly by your sister. One would expect no less from a man of his stature."

"Rank and money are nothing more than rank and money," Lewis said. "Besides, any poor half-wit should be able to see that Leopold Barrie hasn't an ounce of integrity in him."

"Well, these poor half-wits didn't."

They lapsed into a prickly silence. Charles looked down at his feet. Stretching his toes, he could trace their movement beneath the glossy patent leather of his shoes.

"I know you wouldn't have trusted Leopold," he said, at last. "But then you are not like the rest of us, Lewis. You are unfettered by . . . well, you are simply unfettered."

"They are married now," Lewis said. "Marguerite and Cedric. And I'm glad about it. He is good for her. She is very much herself in his company."

"I'm pleased too," Charles said.

They shifted the conversation onto safer ground. Lewis told him that he had found a position in an architect's office since returning home thanks to a friend of his from the army, Georgie Carr. His father was in business and had connections everywhere.

"I'm glad because I know you love drawing," Charles said.

"How do you know that?"

"I expect Edmund mentioned it at some stage. He was always speaking of you, praising you." There was bitterness in his tone and he knew it.

At length, Lewis said, "I often have the feeling that you dislike me, Charles, though you're not really sure why and that makes you grumpy."

Charles looked down at his hands and rubbed at a sandy-coloured freckle on the back of one. The time had come to tell the truth.

"Yes, you are right. I believe I disliked you from the very first time I met you," he said. "To my shame. You see, you were so very dear to Edmund. I could tell that straight off."

Lewis was staring at him with absolute clarity. He understood.

"You mean . . . ?"

"Yes," Charles said and with that one word he cast himself

495

adrift from all that was familiar. He could perhaps still scramble back to safety even at this late stage but he felt that somehow his whole life had been spent waiting for this moment – he was now forty-four – and if he missed his opportunity he would lose the very kernel of his being forever.

"I never knew," Lewis said softly.

"I asked you to meet me here today because one afternoon while I was in the theatre a military man came by. He brought with him two letters, one for Violet and one for you. I undertook to ensure that both letters were passed on to their rightful owners. The envelopes were sealed." He breathed deeply. "The one for you was from Edmund. I did not recognize the writing on the other but I knew it related to him too. I opened both of them. I make no excuses for my indiscretion. In my defence, I can only say that for quite some time before that my equilibrium had been . . . disturbed." He leaned forward, rested his elbows on his knees "As I say, I acted out of character. I should apologize except that I find I am not sorry for what I did." His mouth was drying up. He clasped his hands together to steady them. "The letter Edmund wrote to you . . . well, it was beautiful," he said. "And as I read it, I thought, here I am, nearly old. I have dealt with kings and princes, with politicians, actors, impresarios, newspaper men, tradesmen, Joe Soaps from every walk of life and done so with impeccable good manners, if I may say so. But I have never – can you believe this? – never professed love to another human being, never told another living person in pure and simple terms that I loved them." He stopped. They were both so still, so silent, it seemed Time was suspended. "Edmund was my life. I wished every word in that letter had been written by him, to me."

He paused. Lewis sat with his head bowed.

"I never even guessed," he said.

"No. Well, I made sure that you wouldn't. I have spent the greater part of my adult life in a wrangle over what is decent and what isn't. Tormenting myself with rights and wrongs, busily ignoring what Nature herself was telling me. That letter made me ask – is it possible that Love can ever be wrong? And when I thought about it, long enough and hard enough, if I kept all the dark-suited men and their lists of rules at bay and concentrated just on the beauty and purpose, the humanity, the joy that Love brings into our lives, then I had to say no, it cannot ever be wrong. It is, and always will be, the very pulse of our existence."

Lewis remained quiet for a long time.

"In that case, I am truly glad you read the letter," he said, finally. Then, "You know, I thought I would die too when I first heard Edmund was dead. I went to bed for a week and wouldn't get up. Until one morning, I thought, is more misery needed? And I decided to make it my job to remember all the good things about Edmund, broadcast them. In that way, counteract all the negatives that have been said . . ."

He turned to Charles but Charles could not speak, could not let Lewis into that place of suffering that was part now of his existence. He broke the deadlock by reaching into his inside pocket and bringing out two envelopes. He handed the first one, the one from Edmund, to Lewis. Lewis held it, studied it but made no attempt to look inside. Eventually, he tucked it into his breast pocket, stroked the fabric of his jacket over it.

Charles waited. When he judged Lewis to be ready, he showed him the other letter in his possession.

"This one," he said, "was meant for Violet. I took the liberty of copying it before I gave it to her as I suspected she might destroy it, on which count I have been proved right. Please read it."

Lewis removed the letter from its envelope, threw his eye over the contents to acquaint himself with the gist and then began to read it.

20th December, 1901

Dear Mrs. Jeffers

You do not know me. My name is Ian Hodge and I have been serving as a lieutenant with the C.I.V. in the same unit as your late husband, Edmund Jeffers. The War Office communication to you will have been very brief and, though it tells no lies, it does not tell all the truth either. As you have been made aware, your husband was shot down by his commanding officer as a direct result of his disobeying orders. The intention was not to kill him but to prevent him from pursuing the destructive course on which he was set. As a result of his injury, he bled to death.

I am sure you and your family were very shocked by the news of Lieutenant Jeffers' death and distressed by the circumstances in which it occurred. It is a terrible stigma to bear and therefore I would like to explain what happened as I believe, when you are apprised of the details, it will help you to think more kindly of your husband.

Our unit was somewhere just south of the Vaal river, when we came upon a surrendered Boer farmstead. At first, we thought the place was unoccupied but we soon came under fire from a sniper or snipers. One was killed by us directly, the other — it turned out there were two — was afforded the opportunity to give himself up but did not avail of it. Lieutenant Jeffers was of the view that he was a young boy and he volunteered to go and speak with him. There was some conflict between himself and Captain Peters on this matter, the end result being that your husband decided to act unilaterally, threw down his weapon and set off

498

towards the boy. It was then that he was shot by the captain. He died quickly and without pain.

The second sniper was killed afterwards and Lieutenant Jeffers' suspicions were borne out – he was indeed a youngster, barely an adolescent and not armed. You should know that Captain Peters, while he acted in accordance with British Army regulations and was exonerated of all blame at the Inquiry, has suffered terribly under the strain of having done what he did. Lieutenant Jeffers was very popular and the entire unit was shocked and dismayed by his death. Lieutenant Jeffers was buried at a place somewhere between Batheville and Vredefort. Prayers were said over his grave.

Despite what might be said in the popular press, now that you know the context, you may be proud that your husband's life ended with a selfless and deeply compassionate act. I hope in some way that this information can ease the pain of your loss.

It remains only for me to sympathize with you and hope that, given time, your wounds will heal.

Sincerely yours,

Lieutenant Ian Hodge,

2nd Company Mounted Infantry.

Lewis sat there staring at the letter, rereading the words.

After a time, Charles said, "I have thought of going to the newspapers with this in an attempt to clear Edmund's name – you know what they are saying about him – but this man, Lieutenant Hodge, died of enteric fever not three weeks after he wrote and somehow I don't think Captain Peters would be eager to talk about the incident. Anyway, the letter no longer exists in the original hand. Violet destroyed it. 'It is not relevant,' she said, which is true as far as she is concerned. As you know, she has just wed Walter Penn Warren. The whole of London wishes her well even though this second marriage comes recklessly soon after her first husband's death. But after all she has had to put up with, people say, she deserves happiness, no one could begrudge it to her. Now, if it came to light that her dead husband, far from being the degenerate that he has been painted, was in fact a decent human being who committed a brave act, the public might not be quite so enthusiastic about Mrs. Jeffers' new love. And Violet needs her public to like her. Business is business. She is not interested in clearing Edmund's name, she would rather it was never mentioned again. What does she care for the name of Jeffers? She is Violet Penn Warren now."

"So, Edmund will be either forgotten or vilified, is that it?" Lewis said.

"There are witnesses to what happened who could be traced, I'm sure."

"Yes, perhaps we should do that," Lewis said, distractedly.

"Of course, the other scandal will always remain," Charles said. "Though the force of it will fade with the years." He glanced at Lewis then away again. "Had you . . . the two of you . . . had you plans? How were you to live without drawing attention?"

"There is no point, I suppose, in living if you do not draw attention," Lewis said. "By attention, I mean recognition." He sat very still, swallowed hard.

They sat for a while together, looking out over the water, watching a flock of gulls as they swirled and swooped over a fishing smack.

Eventually, Lewis said, "You know there's a certain symmetry, a purity to the way things have turned out, as though in some quiet way Edmund grew into himself. No fanfare, no applause – would the real Edmund Jeffers please take a bow?" He laughed. "I expect that sounds silly," he said.

"No, not at all."

He flashed Charles a wonderful, clear, sunny smile, though his eyes were filmy and wretched-looking.

Neither of them felt inclined for further conversation. Charles sensed in the younger man the same need for solitude that he had felt on first acquiring the letters.

They both stood up, Lewis using the bench to balance himself. They shook hands.

"Thank you for giving me these," Lewis said, patting his pocket with the letters in it. "Good of you." He turned to go, then swung back. "I always knew he had behaved well at the end. I just knew, in my gut. And you did too, Charles. You and I, we are men of Faith. There are plenty more like us, I know there are."

"I hope so."

"Thank you again." He was paler, much paler than when he had first arrived.

"I trust we will meet again, Lewis," Charles said.

"Yes, we are brothers now," Lewis said, with a tremulous smile.

He walked away at a leisurely pace, managing the artificial leg with amazing deftness, a man with a slight limp, no crutch. He had more sureness of step than most others who had returned from that foreign war, their dreams shattered along with their bodies and souls.

Somewhere downriver the greyness was lifting, perhaps over Shadwell or Greenwich or even further off towards the sea. It was just a thinning of cloud really with a suggestion of light breaking through. Charles sat for a long time on the bench in pensive mood, though not really thinking at all. It felt like he had been hollowed out by this interview with Lewis, as though all his innards had been scooped out, pored over, and then just stuffed back in, any old how.

He decided not to return to the Colosseum – not today, or tomorrow either.

He got up, turned easterly and let the great river guide him towards the sea. He walked and walked for hours until at last he caught up with that opening patch of sky.

Acknowledgements

I would like to thank the following people:

· My husband George and my daughters Julie and Tess for their continued patience. This book was a long time coming!

· Margaret O'Reilly, friend and librarian who sourced anything I asked for and gave me *Baedeker's Guide to London 1900* which proved indispensable.

· The staff in the library at Mary Immaculate Training College who took such an interest in helping me.

· To Paula Campbell and Gaye Shortland of Poolbeg Press for their unstinting help, support and encouragement.

· Donal Ryan, for steering me in the right direction when all seemed, very nearly, lost.

Interview with the Author

Where did the original idea for the novel come from?

I first started thinking about writing a story about an actor when I saw Danny La Rue in drag on television. My actor was to be a music-hall star. Then I began reading about Henry Irving who was actor-manager at the Lyceum theatre in London and a very important personage in his day. I was inspired by him to create Edmund Jeffers. Bram Stoker was Henry Irving's business manager and they were very close friends and he gave me the idea for Charles Gray.

How long did it take to write the book?

A long time! I was mulling it over in my mind for ages before I put pen to paper. Then the research took forever ... and the writing was slow. A number of years, is all I can say.

Is this your first novel?

I did write another some years back but I scrapped it in the end. I have had short stories and articles published over the years. More recently, I have written several serials for *Woman's Weekly Magazine*.

What are you writing now?

At the moment I am writing another novel, this time set in Ireland during the Emergency.

Why did you choose to set the novel in the Victorian age?

Victorian society was pre-occupied with the notions of chivalry and respectability and, though standards were high, many people fell short of them. Very often improper behaviour was tolerated as long as it was not public. This seemed like the perfect backdrop for Edmund Jeffers, a highly respected actor who has a secret other life.

Also, the end of the nineteenth century was a time of uncertainty and change. The industrial revolution, Darwin, the rise of Trade Unionism and the Women's Rights movement challenged the old ways of thinking. The Boer War, which was to have been a glorious victory for the British, ended in political and military disgrace when it became known how many Boer women and children (20,000) died in the concentration camps there. About 12,000 blacks died in them too but that figure didn't make quite the same impact! I thought this setting had a particular resonance for the characters in *The Curtain Falls* as it shows how respectability and honour are not at all the same thing.

Is the Colosseum in *The Curtain Falls* based on a real theatre?

Yes, the Colosseum is based on the Lyceum theatre in London where Henry Irving and Ellen Terry reigned for many years. They had very lavish parties there and went to great lengths to be historically accurate in whatever they staged. Huge numbers of people were employed there – carpenters, gas and limelight men, extras, artists and artisans, choreographers, musicians etc. The end of the nineteenth century was a very exciting time for the theatre. Acting had finally become respectable. Productions were huge and full of spectacle and audiences wanted to be educated as well as entertained.

Did you enjoy the research for the book?

Yes, hugely. It is very exciting to immerse yourself in another time and often new ideas come with the reading. Sometimes it is difficult to know when to stop – I have four lever arch files full of notes and pictures – but there comes a time when you must let imagination take over.

What writers do you most admire?

I like Thomas Hardy, Flaubert, Wilkie Collins, E.M. Forster, L.P. Hartley. Of those currently writing, I admire Ian McEwan, Jim Crace, Rose Tremain, Justin Cartwright, Donal Ryan, Damon Galgut.

Discussion Points for Book Clubs

1. Is Edmund Jeffers an honourable man? Or can anyone be truly honourable when society dictates what standards must be adhered to? Are any of the characters wholly honourable?

2. Do we sometimes confuse honour with respectability?

3. Would you agree with the opinion that all of the characters in the novel are morally flawed in some way? And could it be said that even the most flawed has redeeming qualities and virtues?

4. In the course of the novel, the characters undergo change. What about the British nation? By the end of the book, how have attitudes changed amongst the British people in relation to Empire, war and national pride?

5. Which aspects of this novel are relevant to our own times?

6. Does *The Curtain Falls* work as a love story? Not just in

relation to Edmund and Lewis, Marguerite and Cedric, but for Charles Gray too? Does he finally open himself to love?

7. Which one of the main characters in the book interested you most and why? Which one of the minor characters?

8. Each of the women characters in the novel is trapped in a situation she finds intolerable. To what extent are they fettered by the demands and expectations of Victorian society?

9. Discuss the significance of Clive Potter and the girl Mary in the novel.

10. Do you see the death of Edmund as a triumph or a tragedy?